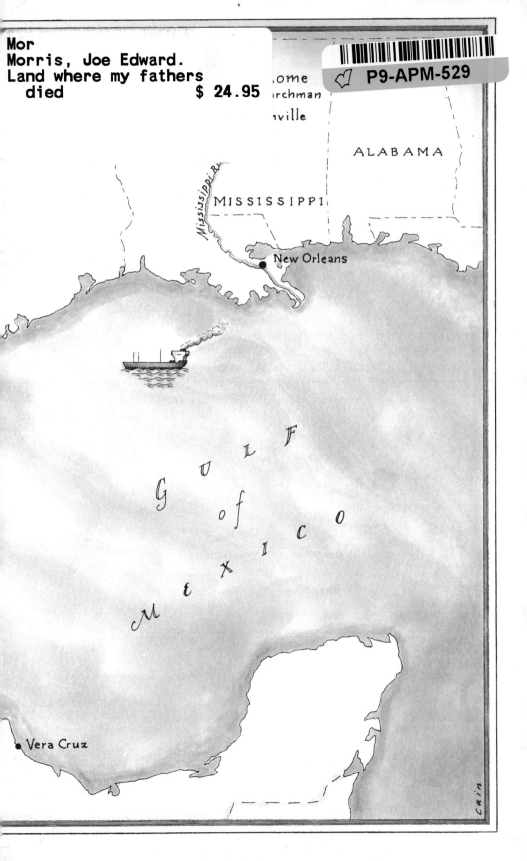

ome
rchman

ville

ALABAMA

MISSISSIPPI

● New Orleans

G U L F

of

M E X I C O

● Vera Cruz

CRin

LAND WHERE

MY FATHERS DIED

LAND WHERE MY FATHERS DIED

Joe Edd Morris

CONTEXT BOOKS   NEW YORK 2002

www.contextbooks.com

Designer: Cassandra J. Pappas

Jacket design: Charles Kreloff
Typeface: Adobe Caslon

Context Books
368 Broadway
Suite 314
New York, NY 10013

Library of Congress Cataloging-in-Publication Data

Morris, Joe Edd.
Land where my fathers died : a novel / Joe Edd Morris.
p. cm.
ISBN 1-893956-27-x (hardcover : alk. paper)
1. Americans—Mexico—Fiction. 2. Judicial error—Fiction.
3. Ex-convicts—Fiction. 4. Young men—Fiction.
5. Mexico—Fiction.
I. Title.
PS3613.²⁄₃6697 L36 2002
813'.6—dc21
2001008606

9 8 7 6 5 4 3 2 1

Manufactured in the United States of America

To my wife, Sandi

And in special memory of Evans Harrington

LAND WHERE
MY FATHERS DIED

Geneology

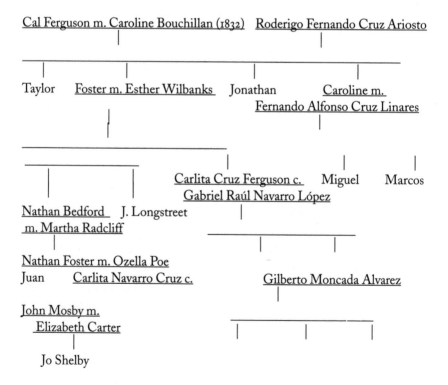

Cal Ferguson m. Caroline Bouchillan (1832)   Roderigo Fernando Cruz Ariosto

Taylor   Foster m. Esther Wilbanks   Jonathan   Caroline m.
                                                 Fernando Alfonso Cruz Linares

Carlita Cruz Ferguson c.   Miguel   Marcos
Gabriel Raúl Navarro López

Nathan Bedford   J. Longstreet
 m. Martha Radcliff

Nathan Foster m. Ozella Poe
Juan   Carlita Navarro Cruz c.   Gilberto Moncada Alvarez

John Mosby m.
 Elizabeth Carter

Jo Shelby

ONE

H E WAS ALREADY DRESSED when the sun rose, and light substantive as wind came through the window and cast shadowed bars on the wall opposite him. He flexed his feet in his boots that had been returned to him, along with the clothes he came there in six years before. He rolled his hands between his knees, stood up, and walked to the window. The sun was bright as though reflected and he cupped his hand over his eyes to see the land once more, flat and prostrate beneath the glare. Stands of cotton stretched endlessly into distant trees so far away they appeared as scratches along the undersurface of the sky. He stood awhile, let his thoughts stretch, too, then sat back down on the bunk in a supplicant posture, waiting as the shadowed bars slid slowly down the wall.

At seven o'clock, two guards came and unlocked the cell and walked him the cold steely length of the cellblock and into the sunlight. The morning air was cool for early August, dew shimmered in patches of grass, but his clothes stuck to him. He knew it would not

3

be long before the day's lid came down and head-splitting heat set in. All three strode solemnly, step for step, like soldiers preparing to present colors, across the compound grounds and into the administration building where he guessed he would be given the rest of his things and the warden would speak to him.

They entered the drab foyer and one of the guards motioned for him to sit in a folding chair beneath a wall calendar. A leggy blonde atop a red Coca-Cola ball caught his eye. She was wearing a Santa hat and her hand was raised in a flourish. The calendar page beneath read December, 1953. Almost a year behind. He turned and sat and thought about that and how the people who run prisons don't know time, or don't care, that only the people who are serving it know and care.

One of the guards sat in a chair across the room from him and slumped into a napping position and the other walked down a long corridor. There was a typewriter clicking in a nearby office, traffic droned along the highway outside. He looked at the door through which he would soon walk and wondered where he would go, what he would do? He was having to think for the first time in a while. In prison a man doesn't think, he just does what he's told. He thought about that, being arrested on the brink of manhood before he could even think like a man, before he'd ever even kissed a woman much less lost his virginity, before he could ever earn a week's wage on his own because the only work he'd ever known was on the plantation working for his daddy, who worked for somebody else.

The other guard returned carrying a brown bag. The top was folded over and it was wrapped several times with string. A white tag dangled from the side.

Believe this uns yourn, the guard said. Jo Shelby Ferguson?

Yessir.

The guard handed him the package and stood before him watching as he unwound the string and opened the sack and looked in.

It's all there, the guard said. Cept the clothes we give you yestiddy. Everthing's been in the lockbox.

He looked up and nodded and began pulling items from the sack.

Dark blue jacket. Leather belt. Cigarette lighter. Billfold. He flipped it open and saw the two twenties which were there the day they took it. They had told him at the time he could have them but he declined. Then I might not have anything when I get out, he told them. He smiled faintly at how the wisdom had caught up with him and continued his inventory, balancing objects on his thighs and knees when his lap overflowed. Pocketknife. Three quarters. Key ring holding three keys. He thumbed each separately, prayerfully, as though they might be talismans of luck or fetishes with some ancient power.

It's all there, the guard said, caustically, impatiently.

He didn't look up this time and removed the last items. Classring and wristwatch and sunglasses, the John Deere cap his daddy gave him. He tried it on. It still fit. His head surely hadn't grown, but it sure to goodness hadn't shrunk either which was the most likely of possibilities. He adjusted the bill and punched in the top so the front rose like a crown. He strapped on his wristwatch and set it by a wall clock and wrestled the ring over a knuckle that had become warped and swollen from fighting the six years he had been there. He leaned forward and slipped his billfold into his hippocket, then backwards and pushed the knife in a front jeans pocket. He hung the sunglasses from his shirtpocket, then rolled up the sack and handed it to the guard.

Yessir, it's all here.

Just need you to sign right here, the guard said and handed him a ballpoint pen with Bank of Drew written on it and a small form with a checkmark where he was supposed to sign. He signed his name and the guard took the form and the sack and said nothing. The smug face was enough.

You can have these keys, too, Jo Shelby said, jingling them on a finger in front of him. Don't reckon I'll be needin em.

The guard reached to take them and he closed his fist over them.

On second thought, I just might.

The guard grunted, turned and walked back down the corridor. Across the room the other guard snored softly, his hat pushed forward so the brim rested across the slant of his nose.

The centerpiece of the warden's office was a massive walnut desk. The surrounding walls, like some truncated menagerie, held the heads of deer and elk and antelope and bear and wild boar, punctuated by a wide-mouth bass curled in its last throes and a red-leg mallard in flight as it must have been before the warden blew it into eternity. Behind the desk were gunracks filled with assorted rifles, shotguns and automatics. Bullet-loaded gun belts with holstered pistols hung from a row of wall pegs, their butts glistening in the lone overhead light, the wattage dimmed by dead insects lying in its globe. On a small table beneath the pistols lay handcuffs and blackjacks and a bullhead flashlight. The room smelled of old leather and tobacco and something else mixed in he couldn't place.

Jo Shelby Ferguson, I believe, the warden said, looking up from a sheet of paper he held in his hand. He was a large thick-necked man with broad shoulders and receding hairline gray-touched at the temples. He wore a brown khaki shirt that stretched tight at the shoulders and buttons as though it had been grown into with some resistance.

Yessir. He removed his cap.

Well, have a seat, Jo Shelby, he said, rising ponderously from behind the desk, motioning with a large outstretched hand.

Jo Shelby sat in a leather wingback that took him further into its upholstery than he imagined a man could sit.

The warden lowered himself into his chair and looked again at the paper, scanning it over the tops of his glasses. Says here you were serving time for first degree murder.

Yessir. But I didn't do it.

The warden leveled serious eyes over the glasses' rims at him. I know, he said. All of us know that now. And the State of Mississippi is deeply sorry for what has happened and the inconvenience this has caused you and your family.

Inconvenience? He came up out of the depths of the chair, sat on its cushiony edge, and let the blood return to his heart from where it had just been blown.

Maybe that's not a good word. Maybe tragedy's a better word.

Yessir. Tragedy's the word. Wasted's a better one. He sat with his cap in his hand, turning it slowly between his knees.

Nonetheless, we are sorry. With heavy eyes he looked upon the paper, his palms turned up as though it were something broken he couldn't fix. He stayed in that attitude of passive apology for a few moments, then looked back up with the same heavy eyes that dragged the brokenness with them. Six years is a long time, for anybody, he said. One day is a long time behind bars for a crime you didn't commit. Sorry's not the right word. I don't know the right word. Maybe there ain't one for this, but I'll help you any way I can. That's the best me and the State of Mississippi can do right now.

Yessir. I'm much obliged. With the artifacts of the room in his periphery and the history of power behind them, he looked straight at the big man and nodded, but he would never ask for the warden's help. There were the scars from the one lashing he received and others around his body from the beatings and the loneliness he still carried, the isolations, the mutilated mail and ravaged Christmas packages. He would never ask for help that had another name.

I'm sure your attorney has informed you of the circumstances and why you are being released.

No sir. Don't have no attorney. State appointed one for me when I was tried and I ain't heard from him since. The guard told me yesterday. When he gave me my clothes and boots.

I see. His hand holding the paper trembled and he removed his glasses with his other hand and looked gravely upon him. The real killer confessed two days ago, he said. A nigger over in Drew. Seems he was arrested on a drunk and disorderly charge and started blabbing and never stopped. Sheriff didn't believe him at first, then checked out a few things and it all fit. After he sobered up he was so rattled he confessed to that killin and one other that had been on the unsolved list.

Do I get my rights back?

Yessir. You're fully reinstated. The Board of Corrections is taking care of everything. Your driver's license is probably expired and you'll need to get another one.

It don't matter.

Why's that?

Don't have no vehicle.

Well, you'll be able to get a job now and you can buy one. Your papers of reinstatement are being worked up and will be mailed to you. At what address?

Don't know.

You don't have a home?

Don't know. Don't think so. But you could send the papers to Mr. Jack Patrick in Rome, just up the road.

Jack Hurley Patrick, the planter?

Yessir.

Know him well. He's one of the gov'ners colonels. May be one of the reasons I've got this job, he said in an offhanded fashion that was something short of bragging. I'll see he gets them. He laid the paper on the desk, folded his glasses, put them in his shirtpocket and buttoned it, then looked back up at him. Jo Shelby, is that what you go by?

Yessir.

Do you mind if I ask you a personal question?

No sir.

You came here surely from a home. You were eighteen at the time, just out of high school.

Yessir.

Why is it you aren't sure if you have one now?

Folks are dead. Killed in a car wreck two years ago. My granddaddy was with em.

And you have no other family?

No sir, none's I know of.

What'll you do?

Don't rightly know. Guess I'll go see Mr. Pat and see if he's got work for me. Then again, might just move on. Somewhere. I'm studin it.

That where you lived, the Patrick place?

Yessir. Folks were tenants. Lived in a small house on the place. But he's probably give it to somebody else by now.

Cottonpickin's not far off. I'm sure he could use you.

Yessir. If he don't already have his crew in place. Most do by now.

You'll need a ride won't you? One of the guards can drive you up there. It's not far.

No sir. Thanks just the same. I can use my thumb.

The warden studied him awhile with a look of concern he might have for the needy on Christmas Eve, then pushed some papers together on his desk, squared them with his fingertips, clapped them once on the blotter, then put them in an envelope he licked and sealed. He pushed himself up from his chair and handed the envelope to him across the desk. Take these. You'll need them.

He stood and leaned over the desk and took the envelope that quivered in the warden's hand.

What are they?

Papers. One's a letter from me stating your clearance and release. You might need it before you get the official papers from the Corrections Board, which should be soon but you know red tape. There's a copy of your birth certificate which you'll need to get your driver's license and other things, too, I'm sure. Since what you told me bout your parents and all, you better hang on to it. There's also a letter from the prison doctor stating you were in good health when we released you. Oh. And one more thing.

Yessir.

The news folks are aware of all this, but I didn't tell em when you'd be released. I figured you'd want it that way, the privacy and all.

You figured right, Warden, and he thanked him and they stood there in the musty gloom that defined the place and eyed each other and said nothing in seconds that had no value in time.

He was facing the sun as he left the building, it was above the bill-line of his cap but the glare from the land promised a hot one. He pulled the bill down further over his eyes and draped the coat he would not need for another season over his arm. Traffic sped by and in the distance a train whistled on the tracks he would cross to get to the highway, the whistle he had heard a thousand times and dreamed of riding because there was nothing else he had heard in six years that had the sound it was going anywhere.

He walked past the guardhouse and waved to the trusty inside who waved back to him and leaned out the window and shouted good luck. He acknowledged with a doff of his cap and a final backwards wave of his hand and kept walking, his eyes following the graveled drive that sloped upward to the track where he stopped and waited. The whistle came again, out of the north, like a harmonica blown by a giant, and he stepped on the blackened tracks that ran silver along their spines and looked where the silver ran out and saw the light brighter than daylight swiveling there. The crossties rippled above the ground-shudder and into his boots as he stepped across to the other side and waited for the power which had awed him since he was a child when he laid pennies on the tracks and marveled that something could look so beautiful after such terrible transformation. He stood as close as he could and removed his cap and held it lest it too be sucked up by the roaring mass of machinery that drew anything that wasn't nailed down into its wake of noise and smoke. He watched it sail past in a clacking thunder of steel on steel till the caboose clicked by and the ground grew still once more. He put his cap back on, turned and walked to the road.

He watched the traffic awhile and tried to gather his thoughts. He looked at his watch. Almost nine. His stomach growled. He hadn't eaten breakfast. They didn't even feed him breakfast. They at least could have given him breakfast. He had paid that much. How many bales of cotton had he picked? How many bushels of soybeans? Corn? He'd spent six months in the license plate factory. How many of those had he fashioned for law-abiding citizens to pay the highest road tax in the country? They at least could have given him breakfast. Damn shame to give a man his freedom and not his breakfast with it. He ground his anger between his teeth as though there might be some nurturance in it and thought about what he should do, for he had no plans. His thinking struggled from a dark hole from which any semblance of plans had been blown a long time ago. One doesn't plan in a prison when he's been sentenced to forty years for murder, at least not in a place called Parchman. One just endures.

Cars and pickups slowed and the people in them gawked at him and the prison compound behind him. He gawked back at them until he realized he was making more of a spectacle of himself. He looked both ways, then crossed to the other side where a black trusty leaned against a stall filled with crafts made by the prisoners for the curious to stop and buy.

The trusty called his name and he called his and they communed. The trusty asked and he told him the story and they both stood silent looking at the ground in common disbelief. He saw the Indian head letter opener he had carved from a cypress stump and asked how much it was and the trusty told him five dollars. It had taken him two months to carve it. He argued it should be worth more than that but the trusty said he was following orders, that it had been there over two months and nobody had bought it. He said he'd buy it for that just as a keepesake but the trusty didn't have change for a twenty. Jo Shelby told him he could run across the road and get it, but the trusty told him he couldn't cross the road till his replacement came which wasn't till noon and that he might get his ass blowed off because the guard might not could tell a vertical stripe from a horizontal one. He chuckled with him and agreed and the trusty told him to just take it.

But you're a trusty. You might get more than your ass blowed off for doing that.

Naw suh. I'll put it in fo you.

But you'll need it.

Naw suh. Ain't goin' nowheres noway. 'Sides, I'll git it back in a crap game.

He grinned at the trusty. Now I guess that makes you a trusty trusty, don't it?

Somethin like that, the trusty grinned back with a mouth of white teeth that made his face gleam blacker.

Tell you what.

Yessuh.

I got seventy-five cents change. I'll give you that for two of them apples over there and you keep the rest for the balance on the letter opener.

Deal, the trusty said and picked the two largest apples and gave them to him along with the letter opener.

He thanked him and slipped the letter opener in his other back pocket and tipped his hat and headed north, holding an apple in each hand, biting from both in an even alternating rhythm. He walked along the graveled edge of the highway and tried thinking again, thinking that might work better, eating and thinking at the same time. Nobody would pick up a man in front of a prison and they wouldn't do it a mile from the prison where they could still see the guardhouses and turrets. And this was the Delta where he might have to walk five miles before he was away from all that the eye could see in land flatter than from wherever the word came, so he kept walking until he had finished the apples then decided to stick out his thumb and take his chances. Any ride was better than no ride, he told himself, any place better than no place.

THE PICKUP TURNED LEFT at Rome onto a narrow macadam road that doglegged through a cluttered collection of weatherbeaten clapboard stores and houses then straightened westward through short stands of young cotton that swept by in a radial symmetry so near perfect they might have been laid by a transit. The old man driving the truck was going to Tutwiler, several miles north of Rome, but said he didn't mind taking him to the Patrick place because he didn't mind helping a feller out. He was pencil-necked thin and wore a wide-brimmed straw hat the width of which was half that of the cab and added to the man a touch of caricature.

It'll be up here a short ways on the right, Jo Shelby said.

Yessir. I know where the Patrick place is at. Everbody knows where the Patrick place is at.

Hadn't always been the Patrick place.

That so, the old man said, eyeing the road seriously. Been the

Patrick place long's I been livin. Who's was it if it wadn't?

Don't make no never mind. That was long ago.

The old man spit out the window and looked over at him then back at the road. You live there?

Did. He kept looking to his right for the white fence and the pecan grove and the whitewashed mansion behind it.

Silence for a while.

Guess it's kind of a homecomin feeling, going back to a place where you once lived, the old man said.

Yessir, he said. Guess so.

Guess yore folks'll be glad to see you.

The anger was gone from earlier and he ground something else between his teeth and looked further to his right to hide his face and what might be showing there. He said nothing because to say anything meant having to tell a story again he was already woreout telling.

The truck rattled on past shotgun shacks and pine-board cabins and shanties with drunken porches and windows with no screens, women and children black as the Delta soil sitting in the doorways looking like they were waiting for something that was not coming their way, waiting being better than not waiting, a pastime to which they had adjusted. He thought he knew how they felt and how some prisons with walls were better than those without them. At least there was no false hope. A man didn't have to think and plan and he learned when the beatings were coming and when they weren't. Then he rethought what he had thought and decided he didn't know much about prisons after all.

They passed a small house on the left where Jake Patrick, the oldest son, kept the books and paid everybody on the porch on Saturdays. Next came the fence on his right and he told the old man to slow down that they were almost there. The old man, whose name he never got because he said it into the wind whipping through the windows, went through an exaggerated motion of clutching and shifting and braking, as though the truck were a living thing that might turn on him if he didn't. The truck came to a stop at the brick-pillared gate with the name P A T R I C K arched in wrought iron above it.

Much obliged Mr.—

Bonee. Name's Bonee. Like this right here. He leaned over and tapped his knee with two fingers and cast a brown-toothed grin.

Yessir. Like I said, I'm much obliged for your kindness. He opened the door and slid out and was closing it when the old man leaned over and drew his attention.

Don't believe I caught yours, young feller.

Ferguson. Jo Shelby Ferguson.

Ferguson. Ferguson. Ferguson. The old man mumbled the words under his breath like some sombreroed mystic reciting a spell, then looked up, his glaucous eyes wide with revelation. Ferguson. He said it one more time, louder, as if to mark his place while he thought next what to say. There was some Fergusons a while back. Awful thing. Say, I don't guess you . . .

But Jo Shelby was already turned and walking toward the gate and through it and up the pecan-lined drive with the belching of the idling truck still in his ears and above it a faint, You take care yo'self Jo Shelby Ferguson. Then once more. You take care yo'self. Then he heard the gears mesh and the clutch let out and the clattered lurch and the ricking of the engine fade and blend with the hum of the other machines nearby that made the Delta tick.

T H E   F I R S T   H O U S E   W A S   B U I L T over a century ago by his great-grandfather Calvin Ferguson, so removed in generations he'd lost count of how great he was. He had come to Georgia from Scotland and had no sooner hit Savannah than he heard about a treaty with the Indians in territory to the west called Mississippi where land could be bought for as little as a dollar and a half an acre and headed there with a thousand dollars rolled up in his boots and saddlehorn and longjohns and bought seven hundred acres of swamp and woodland that made him a seven hundred acre Scottish nobleman all over again, because he had lost all his in Scotland by being on the wrong side.

That was eighteen thirty and the treaty was Dancing Rabbit Creek where Chief Greenwood Leflore sold out his own people to live like the white man. Within a short time great-granddaddy Cal and his wife Caroline had three sons and a daughter and outgrew the two-room log cabin so he built another house beside it that was a spectacle for all to behold, which he could easily do because he had doubled his land holdings and owned enough slaves to buy and work twice that, and would have except for the war coming. The Yankees came and overran the land and freed the slaves and would have torched the house except the colonel calvary man who had given the order took it back when he saw the woman on the porch holding the baby and the other children clinging around her, so the story had come down. When the war was over great-granddaddy Cal took his family and their belongings and left the country and went to Mexico because he was a colonel and would be hanged for sure by the Yankees, or starve, neither of which were acceptable alternatives. All except one. Foster Ferguson, the youngest, stayed on the place with his wife Esther be-cause she had a two-month-old baby, the one that stopped the torch, who they named Nathan Bedford for the great general, and because he said leaving one's land was as big a sin as the Israelites leaving the promised land for Egypt. Two years later Esther had another son who grew up a renegade and never took any interest in the land and ended up killed in eighteen ninety-eight, a bullet through his eye on San Juan Hill in Cuba with Teddy Roosevelt and the Rough Riders. In eighteen seventy-five, for reasons and under circumstances no one ever clearly understood, though rumors had it scalawags and carpet-baggers were behind it, the mansion burned and in that same year Foster lost the plantation, when it was not uncommon for properties to change hands between sundown and sunup and named and re-named between dice throws and card hands. A wealthy Yankee named Marshall bought the place and rebuilt the mansion and when he died in nineteen thirteen, a man named Patrick bought it and remodeled it and nothing had been the same since. Except the original boundaries of the property and mule paths which were now dirt roads over which

In the sheds and hangars around the barn he saw equipment he had never seen before, glistening and lined up in a file, like machines of war awaiting a battle and fifty-gallon drums he had never seen either, too far away to read the labels. Beside the barrels and stretching out across the open field were empty cotton wagons, row upon row, eight or ten across and five or six deep, ragged with the leftover shreds from previous seasons. He let his eyes rove and tag other familiar sights. The commissary and the gin and pieces of oxidized equipment in the weeds around them. The clapboard outbuildings and the silos and somewhere behind them and the honeysuckle hedge grown high along the fence was the house he had known as home. The only one he'd ever had. He wanted to see it, but could wait. He rounded the drive that brought him in front of the house and he saw the two Cadillacs parked in front, each gleaming from fender to fender. Some things had not changed.

He stepped upon the low brick porch that ran the breadth of the house, rang the bell and listened as the chimes donged through three octaves. He waited.

The door opened and the surprised black face looking at him was one he knew, one of the few he could say he had known since birth. Her name was Cassie Mae but to him it was Sissy because that was how he learned to say it as a child and it didn't seem right to change it when he could say it right, and no one else thought so either. She was the Patrick maid and had been since most could remember. She came with the land, like his parents had, which meant her folks and his and those before them were there way before the Patricks which meant she may be the next to closest of kin he had left, even if she was colored.

Why mistuh Jo Shelby.

Sissy. He removed his cap and presented the smile she drew from him.

You done come back.

Yessum. Mr. Pat in?

Yessuh. He's in the den with Miss Pat. I'll git him for you. But lawd ain't it good to see you.

Thank you.

She left the door open and scurried beneath a crystal chandelier and down a polished hallway that ran beneath the spiral staircase he had played on as a child. Everybody called them Mr. Pat and Miss Pat, much for the same reasons he called Cassie Mae Sissy. They were probably in their sixties by now though he remembered them as young even when they were in their fifties. They were that much on the go. Tennis and swimming and horseback riding, always getup in clothes and gear that made them look like they belonged in a Sears catalogue. From various places he watched them. The treehouse his father built for him. Behind the crepe myrtles that surrounded the mesh fence that surrounded the tennis court and swimming pool. From the roof of the tool shed he learned to climb upon, so no one would see him. They took trips to Europe and the islands, as they called them, and South America and Mexico and always brought back trinkets and souvenirs for everyone. He wondered who had his and where they might be for he had treasured them more than the things Santa brought and kept them all in a shoe box under his bed and looked at them each night before he went to sleep, in light refracted through his window from the big house lights that never seemed to go out, as though there was an endless party beneath the canted roof that sat above it all like a huge dark tent pitched over a carnival. He saw it that way as a child and still later as a growing boy and even now little seemed to have changed, because all of it was like Sissy's name. But that was the Delta, he thought, as he heard the boot-steps clomping to meet him and saw the big man's shadow materialize in the light and saw he hadn't changed either.

Mr. Pat.

My, my, boy. Didn't expect to see you so soon, he said. He extended his hand and Jo Shelby shook it but there was something missing in the feel that matched up, too, in the way he was looking, like there might be more bad news than what he already knew.

They let me out.

I know. We heard it on the news. But we thought it might be another day or so before we saw you.

Didn't know it was important enough to be news.

Any time a man goes free, it's news. But if he goes free for something he didn't do, that's headline news. Makes the whole system squirm, from the D.A.'s office all the way to the gov'ner's mansion. We knew you didn't do it. Knew it all along. Come on in. Miss Pat'll surely want to see you.

He stood and eyed the man and thought about that awhile, the whole system squirming. Mr. Pat was the one who took him in because that was the way it was done. The big planters elected the sheriffs and the sheriffs wouldn't go on a man's place without talking to him first and getting him to bring the suspect in. The Penitentiary Board and Parole Board was controlled by Delta planters so it was all just one big plantation. If they knew he didn't do it, then why'd they let him sit in a cell not five miles away and let him rot like he was some diseased thing. Why did the man who was one of the richest planters in the state and one of the governor's colonels and a friend of the warden, why did he not stir a finger to make the phone calls that would have set the wheels of justice turning. After all it was a white man that had been killed and he got stuck because he was in the wrong place at the wrong time without an alibi and there were plenty of niggers roaming the countryside that night who wouldn't have had an alibi much less reasons for being even close to the wrong place at the wrong time. To make matters worse, the D.A. prosecuting the case was up for reelection and fired up for all the wrong reasons and one of the lowest on the chain of political animals who could have been yanked up and brought into line with the least little tug. He'd had a long time to think about it and thought he knew the reason, but that didn't help any either. What bothered him the most now was he knew where he was standing and where he ought to be standing and all the history crowded into the space separating him from the man looking down at him.

No sir. Thanks just the same. I been walking in the dust. Don't wanna mess up anything.

Mess up anything? Like I don't come in and out of here everyday tracking everything from horseshit to gumbo mud. Nonsense. Come on in.

No sir. If it's all the same, I just came to get mine and my folks' things then I'll be moseying on.

Moseying on? Listen to that. You can stay right here. You belong here. You can't stay in the house because we . . .

His hands were trembling about like the warden's and his eyes slid off center for a few seconds then came back, drawing the rest of his face into a sympathetic mold that seemed too readily shaped.

I'm sure you understand, he said. We needed another foreman and we've hired another man to take your dad's place. Of course, no one can really do that. Your dad was the best. The new man is trying and he and his family are living there now. He's got a wife and two small kids. But you can stay in the apartment over the garage. Miss Pat and I have already decided on that. We were going to have it fixed up for you.

We. He didn't catch the word at first from when the talking began, but it was being stamped in now and he couldn't miss it, the watered-down responsibility and loyalty and devotion his daddy had warned him about. These people were loyal and devoted to only one thing. The land. More so than even their own families. But they were wrong, his daddy told him over and over. Never forget, he said, family was first and foremost above everything except God. His daddy also told him if you spread all the money out equally, dollar for dollar, the same people would end up with it because the same people owned the land or were kin to those who did. He said nothing about people who once owned the land and lost it and what they would end up with. He guessed he didn't have to, that that was the other side of the same equation and spoke for itself.

I'm really much obliged, Mr. Pat. But all I came for was our things, me and my family's.

The man stood with arms outstretched, palms upturned, as though one struck suddenly by a paralysis, transfixed in that frozen manner for a moment, then his arms came down against his sides with a limp slap.

There's not much left of your folks' things, son, he said. His eyes were nervous, like two little beads of Jell-O he was trying to hold still. Most of the furniture went with the house, he said. What was theirs was sold to help pay for the funerals, your granddaddy's too. Which was only a drop in the bucket. I covered the rest.

I'm much obliged, he said and turned his head and spat off the porch. Not because he needed to but because it was a way of not looking up.

All the clothes were donated to the prison down the road or given away to niggers here on the place who needed them.

You just gave em away? Without asking nobody?

There wasn't anybody to ask, Jo Shelby. You were in the state pen and wouldn't be out till God only knew when. We did the best we could, the best we knew how to do. His voice fell on the last phrase and his chin dropped and Jo Shelby could detect a quaver of sincerity in the voice and the face, a tremor passing through both.

They didn't leave nothing? No inheritance? No savings? Nothing?

We checked all of that. They had no will. Bill Bogan at the bank in Drew said all they had was a checking account and it was overdrawn. I paid the balance, which was about twenty dollars.

Jo Shelby reached in his backpocket and pulled out his billfold and opened it and thumbed out a twenty. Here, this'll cover that, he said.

No way. I was glad to do it.

I insist, he said and shoved the bill at him.

No sir. If it'll make you feel any better, I owed him for two weeks work which was a couple of hundred so you got a hundred and eighty coming to you. I believe in being fair with my people.

He put the twenty back into his billfold and pressed it back into place in his hip pocket. Can't take nothing I didn't earn, he said.

Well, you were asking about inheritance and savings. You didn't earn that.

Them's different.

They stood.

What about my things?

The man scratched his head and rolled his palsied eyes around.

Well sir, he said. Now don't take offense, Jo Shelby, but you were in for forty years, twenty at the most with good behavior and we didn't think about your needing them so they went like the rest. All to people who needed them. Your mama even gave some of them away before her passing. You know your mama. I'm sure you understand.

He did. Then he didn't. He looked down at his boots and scuffed them around on the brick porch and made imaginary curlicues with his toe then looked up. There ain't nothing left? he said.

Yessir. There's a trunk. Miss Pat and I have kept it in a safe place in the garage. We were careful to put all the personal things in it, things we knew you would want someday. Miss Pat did most of it. Women have a way of knowing about those things, you know. He forced a smile and it came across like one tried on.

I cain't take no trunk with me.

Then how'd you expect to take anything else?

Don't know. I'd 've figured something.

They eyed each other in the silence of the porch shade, like two men waiting for the other to blink. Finally, Mr. Pat spoke.

Then stay here with it. I'll start you at a decent wage and you can work your way up. Who knows, the other man might decide to up and move on and you'd be the foreman someday.

I'll think about it. But I don't think I can stay now, if you know what I mean, he said. He looked at the man through squinted eyes he hoped would carry the message home.

No sir. Can't say that I do. You were born here and lived here all your life, except for the time in Parchman. We consider you one of ours and we take care of our own.

He heard the words that came out of the man's mouth and noted what they said, and again what they meant, and how some people confuse care with bondage. I'd like to look in the trunk, he said.

Mighty fine. It's in the garage.

They walked toward the south end of the long porch and stepped off and turned and crossed the side patio where the new ferns waved beneath the crepe myrtles. Wrought-iron chairs painted white sat beneath tilted umbrellas big as tents. They walked on toward the garage, Mr. Pat leading, Jo Shelby following, watching the movement of the big man. The shoulders square set, back straight, hips swaggering from side to side. The arrogance of ownership he remembered when he and his father followed him down the streets of Drew and Clarksdale, occasionally Memphis, or down field rows where a hundred years before owners by another name had walked.

The trunk was under a low hanging shelf upon which were stacked the assorted castoff playthings of the rich. Mr. Pat gripped it by a leather handle on the side and pulled it recklessly from beneath the tiered storage and over the concrete floor to where the sunlight drew a shadowed line across the opening and stopped there. You may remember it, he said. It was in the house.

Yessir. It was my granddaddy's.

Well, I'll leave you be. You won't be disturbed here. Take your time. Miss Pat and I'll be inside if you need us. Cassie Mae can bring you something to drink if you wish.

No sir. I'm all right.

The man nodded and walked through the garage towards the main house.

It was an old wooden trunk and looked as he remembered it from where it sat next to the footboard of his parents' bed. The leather straps were worn or gnawed along the edges, the top fit unevenly and the brass lock clasp dangled from its single hinge like a Vaudevillian tongue. He gazed at it a few moments with reverence then looked around to see if anyone was watching, but he was alone. A tractor sputtered in the distance. Birds fluttered playfully in and out from under the eaves. Wind chimes hanging from a corner tinkled in the breeze. There was a dampened pounding in the air, like someone hammering in the barn across the way. Then again it might have been his heart up in his ears. He felt a rush within him like that of a man standing before some sacred casket that when opened could hurt him or heal him, or both, which would be the worse because he would not know the difference and he needed to know something, even if it hurt.

First one, then the other, he pulled the straps through their tarnished buckles and unhooked the clasps then stood and waited. The sun was hot across his shoulders. Sweat collected around the edges of his cap. He took it off and slid his fingers across his temples, down the back of his head then put it back on, and squatted to lift the huge lid. He half-raised it and saw neatly folded linens, then raised it all the way up and over until it hung from its hinges. He rubbed his palms on his jeans, then touched gently the soft material that shimmered shades of silver in the slanted sunlight. Tablecloth or bed linen he had thought at first but the texture was too rich and smooth and it slid through his fingers like silk which he knew it had to be. His hands traveled over it and made out a cuff, then another, then a collar above a softer mesh of fine netting. He held the piece up in front of him, then stood and lifted it higher to see the total garment but a good part of it still lay folded in the trunk. He knew by then what it was and where he had seen it and draped it carefully in folds over his arm and laid it in the lid-shell.

He stood and pondered awhile what he saw next, their arrangement on a deep purple cloth, how neatly and carefully they had been placed, as if patterned on a wall. The framed photographs of his family. The black-and-whites of recent years and daguerreotypes of forebears he knew only through stories told to him. He remembered each and their place in the house and his eyes' memory put them there, on mantel, chifferobe, bedstand and wall. He knelt and beheld them, as one might those on the wall of a gallery, moving his eyes from frame to frame, slowly, taking each in, remembering.

He removed the pictures and laid them on the concrete then lifted the purple cloth and shook it gently. He saw the tassels and recognized the shawl and folded it and laid it with the wedding dress and looked back at an array of bric-a-brac that glittered on a bed of black cloth. Brass buttons and coins of varying denominations and a large brass buckle bearing the emblem of an eagle. There was a watch chain without the watch, a ring of skeleton keys, a fountain pen and inkwell, some folding money in a silver clip. He pulled the bills free and un folded them in his hand and palmed them carefully and saw they were Confederate but counted them anyway. Three hundred dollars worth. Of nothing, he thought.

He continued rummaging and the discoveries kept coming. One by one, he removed the items and laid them aside, thinking to himself the deeper he went the older everything got. Then his hand touched the Barlow knife. Beside it, was a revolver in a flap-holster. The knife he knew to be his grandfather's but the gun he had never seen. He unhooked the flap from the finnel and wrapped his hand round the wooden grips encased in brass and pulled the pistol out and brandished it in the light where it gleamed like new, the long barrel and the revolving cylinder, the brass frame and the name engraved beneath the cylinder, COLT. He had never shot a revolver but the grip fit comfortably in his hand, as though he could fire it right away and hit whatever he aimed at. He lobbed it from hand to hand, spun it forward on his finger, then backwards, as he had seen the cowboys do in the Saturday picture shows his father took him in Clarksdale. He half-cocked the hammer and spun the cylinder to see if there were any shells in the chambers, but there were none. With the trigger still half-cocked he worked the loading lever which came down faultless on the chamber holes then uncocked the hammer and returned the gun to its holster. He looked at the letters, CSA burned into the leather, and thought about who it might have belonged to and where it might have been and the men it probably killed. Perhaps his great-granddaddy Cal or one of his sons or his great-granddaddy Nathan Bedford or Jefferson Longstreet who died in Cuba with the Rough Riders. He had heard the stories, about how the war didn't really end when it ended and how men kept it going long after Appomatox and Lincoln and Grant, and longer still after that. Some wars don't never end his daddy told him, they just start the next one.

He retrieved the remaining articles, examining each carefully, and laid them in rows in the sunlight with the rest of the collection that was beginning to resemble street vendor merchandise on a Saturday downtown sidewalk.

A door slammed and he jumped and looked up and recognized the lady walking toward him from the shadows of the garage. She had not changed either. Her short hair had the same frozen look, little curls licking around the painted face that reminded him of something stenciled or stamped-on. Red lipstick and pink rouge and eyebrows the color of bootblack, thin as thread. She was smiling as she passed through the wide doorway and he heard the voice his mother had said belonged inside a calliope.

Why, Jo Shelby, Mr. Pat said you were here. What a nice surprise.

Howdy Miss Pat, he said and removed his cap and watched her face move through its familiar expressions of habitual courtesy.

You can put your cap back on. The sun's heating up today to burn anything human not covered up, including your arms. You better get over here in the shade.

She extended a pale hand over the trunk and he shook it once and gently in the manner he had seen others do from the hidden vantage points of his youth.

No'me. I kinda like the heat, kinda grown used to it.

Well, I've lived here most of my grown life and I'm not used to it. You suit yourself, but it's certainly cooler over here.

Yessum, he said, still holding his hat in his hand and looking at her. I'm much obliged for the packing you did.

Why, thank you. And just how did you know I did it?

Mr. Pat told me.

I tried to pack everything carefully, so nothing would break.

You done good, he said and put his cap back on. Mighty good, in fact. Nothin's broke as I can tell.

I didn't disturb what was on the bottom, she said. Somebody had already packed them in pretty good. Guess your mama did that, or your grandmama. I just put the Bible in there with them.

He knelt down and moved a hand over the black cloth that remained, felt the shape of the Bible and other objects around it.

Anyway, I came out to invite you to have lunch with us, she said. Nothing fancy. Just ham sandwiches and soup. Iced tea or milk, whichever you prefer.

He regarded her from under the bill of his cap, his thoughts traveling further than the distance between them. In eighteen years on the place he had never eaten a meal in the big house, as his family referred to it, nor had his parents or theirs as best he knew. But he was hungry and had not eaten breakfast and a sandwich and a cold glass of milk would taste good. He thought again about why he was invited now and not then and others before him to whom the invitation had never been extended.

No'me. Reckon not. But thanks anyway.

Of course, you could just eat out here.

There was a concern in her voice he could not mistake, a caring he had never before heard. He stood up and removed his cap again.

Yessum. That'd be mighty nice.

Good. I'll just send Cassie out with it, she said and turned and disappeared back into the shadows with the same quiet saunter of ownership.

He reached a hand into the near-empty trunk and massaged once more, lightly, the black cloth, probing here and there with his fingertips, guessing at the soft clumps beneath it, if they might be precious crystal or china or some other priceless commodity wrapped many times over in paper for there was that feel and touch about it, of something tucked away for the world to see at the right moment. He lifted the cloth, as one might a sheet over a sleeping child, and saw paper bundles of different sizes bound in ribbons and string and garter belts, packed around a large Bible.

The Bible belonged to the family and had been passed down through the generations. How many he was not sure. It had lain on the coffee table in the living room and was read from each evening by his mother. The bundles had the appearance of old papers, or envelopes, and were arranged horizontally from one end of the trunk to the other, as if there might be some order to them. One was thicker than the rest and tied with a wide band of red ribbon and he chose it first.

He thought about using the Indian head letter opener then decided it would be better to use his granddaddy's Barlow knife, which he slipped under the ribbon. It snapped at first touch and the sheaves of paper came apart in his hands letting off a puff of dust. He reassembled the papers into the odd-shaped deck of cards they resembled before they fell apart. He could tell from the grainy discoloration and the musty smell of decay they gave off that they were letters from a long time back. He had never seen paper that old before. Rough-textured and stiff as butcher paper and browned around the edges like it had been rescued from a fire. The envelopes bore strange stamps, pictures of men unknown to him and inscriptions in a language foreign as well. He lifted one from the top of the small stack and drew it close to his eyes. The postmark was smudged and faded and almost illegible but from the letters he could see, he made out MEXICO. The writing on the front was lean and delicate and graceful, like that from a woman's hand, and only took a little getting used to. The address was as clear as if it had been printed:

> Master Foster Ferguson
> Ferguson Plantation
> Rome, Mississippi
> United States of America.

He balanced the pack on his knee and flipped through several others. Same name. Same address. He laid the bundle aside and cupped the first heavy envelope he still held in his hand and blew into it, pulling out several thick pages that crackled as he unfolded them. He slowed down his fingers and proceeded with great care lest the paper crumble like a dead leaf. He saw the salutation on the first page then shuffled through four pages to the last and read the closing then the large flowing style of the signature which stretched across the bottom of the page in a flawless flourish of twists and curls and loops.

He looked up through the boughs of an oak across from him and thought. The only sounds were the soft tinkles of the windchimes overhead and chittering of birds in nearby bushes. He looked at the

letter again, the signature, then back up into the towering limbs of the
tree. No one had ever drawn him a picture. All he had heard were the
stories and the names with the stories. Your great-grandpa this and
your great-great grandma that and the names of children and not-
children, intermingled and spread out over time, all of it piled up in
his mind like some grotesque structure a small child might assemble in
the madness of play and destroy and reassemble in the same mad and
wild imagination. So he had to figure it out for himself. There were his
parents and before them his grandparents Nathan Foster and Ozella
and before them his great-grandparents Nathan Bedford and Martha
and his great-uncle Jefferson Longstreet. He stopped and retraced the
path again, to make sure he was sure. He'd almost run out of names.
Two were left. One was Foster, who the letter was addressed to, whose
wife was Esther, and they were the parents of Nathan Foster which
would have made them his great-great-grandparents. His thinking
reached further. Foster's father had to have been Calvin which would
have been his great-great-great-granddaddy Cal which was the one
name he had left. His wife's name was Caroline, which was the signature on the letter. He shuffled back to the first page and saw the date
in the upper-right-hand corner. *17 July 1865.*

He began reading the letter, his eyes leaning with the slanting
script, following the words across the page with the evenness in which
they were written.

My Dearest Foster,

   *Some time has lapsed since I last wrote to you on July 4 when we
crossed the Rio Grande. My sincerest apologies but we have been traveling day and night and are only fifty miles into Mexico, though it seems it
should be ten times that. We are now at a village called Pedrosney and
may remain here for a day or two. General Shelby sold some of our
weapons to the Juaristas who are a ragtag lot, barefoot and all. Their
leader is Benito Juarez, The Great Little Indian his people call him. But
to us he might as well be Grant or some other northern general bent on
taking us for all we're worth. General Shelby was low on money and de-*

cided, I guess, the heavy cannons and munitions had to go. They were slowing us down considerably. We have been traveling over sandy rough roads which has also been especially hard on the horses. For the cannon and munitions he received about $16,000 in silver and the rest in paper money which is probably worthless. General Shelby was most gracious and fair and distributed the money among us, each receiving about $85. The Mexicans are seriously divided but the good general still has hope, however dim, the French will help us. He cares for us as a good shepherd cares for his sheep.

We will stop next in Monterrey on our way to Mexico City but how long until we arrive at either place is conjecture. The land is rough and there is little water. Each night around the campfire General Shelby and his subordinates (your father is among them) decide the route for the next day. We march from water hole to water hole and often find them polluted with the carcasses of dead animals. The men's canteens are empty much of the time and when we do find a well in a village we cannot drink the water for fear of typhoid and dysentery. If we make 15 miles a day, we consider that good. From time to time we are able to trade tinned foods, coffee, and smoked bacon for fresh meat, beans, and mantequilla which is Mexican butter, but sometimes the butter is as foul as the bacon of which we have grown tired. At times the supplies run low and the men volunteer to go on half-rations every other day to save food and money. The men also stand watch for six hours at a time every other night. The fires burn until dawn which keeps away the coyotes and lobos, or Mexican gray wolves, not to mention thieves which might otherwise come in the night. We camp outside of the towns in order to avoid contact with the locals which could cause unnecessary trouble. General Shelby has taken on more a role of guide than general and tries to keep us all instilled with hope as he tries to lead us toward our new homes and only God knows where that might be. You might take some consolation in your decision to stay and your admonition of the Israelites for having left their homeland once in difficult times. Your father and I have remarked several times how we feel like the children of Israel in their sojourn through the wilderness of Sinai, for it is certainly a dry and barren wilderness through which we

*travel. General Shelby is proving to be a good Moses and we cling to the
belief he will deliver us to a place where we can start our lives anew.*

*He has tried to lead us in peace but that has proven to be quite diffi-
cult. The very Juaristas he sold the guns to almost immediately gave us
trouble. They stopped our caravan and accused some of us, including General Shelby, of stealing horses. He had trouble holding his men back and it
looked as though a fight would erupt. But as luck would have it for us the
Juaristas practically vanished when our men brandished their arms and
aimed them point blank. We talked among ourselves that the Mexicans
had heard of how trigger happy Confederate Rebels can be and how fortunate our reputations preceded us.*

He stopped to rest his eyes and take in all he had read so far along
with the amazement of what it was he was reading and how old it was
and who wrote it. Some of the names he did not understand and
words as well which he would skip and come back to, filling in with
smaller ones of his own until the sentence made sense. In this way he
grasped the story being told, the plight of the people and their struggles. And the story not being told: Their heartbreak and homesickness
and longing for the land they'd left behind, this he discerned more
clearly perhaps than all else. One other thing, too, kept stamping itself
upon his thinking as he read. The name of the general who led them.
He read on.

*Along the way we have encountered many other travelers. Men leading
their families and heavily laden burros and children barely old enough to
walk trodding beside them. We have seen long lines of pack mules trotting
and jingling along, carrying wares to sell at a local market, we surmised,
though some said their destinations were much farther and for different
reasons. Delapidated hay carts and ox drivers who whipped sickly looking animals and people walking in shabby clothing accompanied by ema-
ciated dogs. Some greet us with friendly holas and others pass us with
their sad eyes on the ground pretending not to see us.*

I will close for now, dear Foster, with hopes my next letter will be more cheerful, but it may not be so. For we are told the worst is yet to be, a vast expansive wasteland much like a desert that lies between here and Mexico City. Please know your father and I and your sister and brothers miss you and Esther and little Nathan Bedford terribly and pray for you daily. We trust the place is in goodstead and has not been burned or confiscated by the Yankees. The Confederacy may no longer be as we once knew it, but our family ties and loyalties remain as steady and strong as ever and that is what is most important.

Lovingly,
Your mother

Then her name written in full. Caroline Bouchillan Ferguson. And beneath that a postscript in smaller, finer writing:

Should it happen, God forbid, this letter never finds you, hopefully it will fall into friendly hands who will read it and preserve the story of our fight.

The sun had moved past noon for his feet were completely in shadow. A breeze came now and then. He heard the swishing of slippers crossing the breezeway and knew the sleepy cadence and soon Sissy was standing over him holding a plate and glass of milk.

Mr. Jo Shelby, you goin to eat something now. Not cause Miss Pat say so but cause I say so, she said.

It was the same tough talk of his growing-up years when she would scold him in ways his own mother never did and he would mind her in ways he would not his mother and beneath it all a restrained softness that seemed to push around the edges of her face but glistened through her eyes as clear and sure as lights.

He thumbed back the bill of his cap and looked up at her from where he sat half-reclined against the garage wall and grinned. Now if that don't beat all, he said. I get out of one prison where folks told me what to do every minute and land right smack in another where they're doing the same thing.

She stood still. He could tell she was struggling not to smile.

But I must say, this warden looks a far sight better than the last one, he said.

Her strained composure broke and she laughed heartily and bent down and handed him the plate on which lay a ham sandwich fully dressed with lettuce and tomatoes beside a generous pile of potato chips and a boiled egg that had been halved and sprinkled with salt and pepper.

I declare, Mr. Jo Shelby, you ain't changed none. You as much a sight as you ever was. I'll just set the milk right here beside you and you holler if you want more.

All right, he said, and nodded.

She placed the milk carefully beside him and turned to leave but he called her name and she turned back.

Much obliged for all you done.

Wadn't nothing. I been bringing you sandwiches since you was old enough to hold em with both hands.

No'me. Not that.

She cocked her head to one side and looked at him quizzically.

I mean *all* that you've done.

You don't have to thank me for nothin, Mr. Jo Shelby. I done got my thanks a lawng time ago and I'll git em again someday. You will, too, and she turned and he heard the measured whisper of the slippers take her back into the house.

He ate the sandwich and egg and potato chips and drank the glass of milk. In the timely fashion for which she was known, Sissy returned to retrieve the empty plate and glass just as he had finished and swapped them for a dish of peach cobbler. She told him she remembered it was his favorite. He stood and thanked her and told her she had to have worked hard and fast through the morning to get it ready but she downplayed the effort, flipping a nevermind hand back at him as she disappeared once more into the house.

The cobbler was as good as his mother's and maybe better. The crust was deep brown and flaked at the slightest touch of the fork which meant it just might melt in the peaches' syrup before reaching his tongue. He savored each bite, took in the tastes and smells, the memories they brought back. Hot summer days helping his parents pick the peaches from the orchard behind the house, climbing among the higher limbs and shaking them, the sweet aroma that filled the air. Sitting on the kitchen stool and watching his mother process and can them, his daddy helping, too, pressurizing the lids. His daddy would always hug his mother and pat her on the fanny and tell her she done good, mighty good, then look at him and tell him that when he grew up he needed to find a woman just like his mama. Memories that lingered a long time, as if there was a nourishment from them he needed far more than the food he had just eaten.

He wiped his hands on his jeans and opened the next letter in the bundle.

25 July 1865

Dearest Foster,

A day and a week has gone by since I last wrote but so much has happened. First, I hasten with the tidings that we are all in good health though tired and somewhat weary. Good news has come from Senator Guin of California. He brings a promise from Napoleon III that the French army will seize the northern Mexican states from Juarez and make of them a single state for our Confederates. We are told Senator Guin has already been made a duke by Napoleon and given him permission to colonize the province of Sonora. Of course, Sonora is south of California and a long way from us, but the news is encouraging for it bolsters our confidence in the support of the French court. We are all quite elated and see our dreams once again nearing reality. We receive word daily of other Confederates flocking south to Mexico and not a day goes by but that a few join our growing company. Senator Guin left us and headed north against General Shelby's pleading, but he said he had no place else to go. He will surely be arrested for, as you know, the Union government has officially condemned the occupation of Mexico by the French.

26 July 1865

Alas, Dear Foster,

Just as I was preparing to mail your letter General Shelby reported dismal news. Emperor Maximilian has rejected Senator Guin's plans to colonize northern Mexico with our people and convert it into a special state. It seems Senator Guin is a man of genuine interests but also one of illusory dreams and perhaps himself imbued with a touch of grandiosity. Though he is from our own beloved Mississippi I fear he has led us astray. You can imagine our disappointment but we press on toward Mexico City across this stony and grassless terrain. Winds gust fiercely and continually and carry sharp grains of sand that blister our faces. The children's skin in places looks as though it has been burned. The tumbleweeds blow around the worn legs of the horses and cause them much discomfort. We endure the heat of the day, the sun's fierce blaze causing headaches and a feverish feeling that racks our bodies. With each evening our thoughts turn to the next days trek and our spirits wane. We have ample food, but it takes more than food to survive this God-forsaken land. At night we all think of loved ones left behind and the men find some comfort in their special supply of liquor. I must confess, we women have imbibed a time or two ourselves which does help us sleep more soundly.

I must close for now and have this ready to post tomorrow. Our prayers are with you and Martha and little Nathan Bedford. You can certainly try to write but it is doubtful any mail will reach us until we arrive in Mexico City.

With much love,
Your mother,
Caroline Bouchillan Ferguson

From where the shadow ended halfway to the road he watched the heat rise from the pavement like vaporous snakes being released to roam the air.

He thought of those people long ago from whom he had descended and wondered aloud if it would have made any difference, their staying or leaving, and hoped he would read further and find it had. But the letters that followed told of troubles more horrible than the land and weather. One dated July 30 described an attack at the Salinas River by a band of Kickapoos and half-blood Mexican guerilla bandits and another told of a second attempt to massacre the party several days later at a place called Lampazos. With vivid detail his grandmother told how General Shelby galloped away from such ambushes and how the thunder of his horse's hoofs gave everyone courage and how his men voted whose side they would be on and not a man raised a hand for the Mexicans but all declared for Maximilian and the French.

He was not sure what all of this meant, but figured Maximilian was in charge of Mexico and the French had put him there and the Juaristas were rebels wanting to overthrow both him and the French. He figured the Indians had somehow got caught in between and maybe didn't know themselves which side to be on which is where General Shelby and his followers had been until they got bushwhacked by the Mexicans and Indians and knew which way the wind was blowing.

He had to pause from his reading from time to time and put everything together because it was bad enough not knowing many of the words much less the names and places which were as foreign to him as his freedom, which he was also getting used to.

He read on, the letters by this time reading like a carefully arranged journal, pulling him deeper into an enchanting past that unfolded as though he were seeing it on a movie screen for the first time: An encirclement at Monterrey by a French general and several thousand French Legionnaires and Mexican troops, their movement stirring dust that darkened the skies. General Shelby's ultimatum to the general, "Shall it be peace or war between us?" that led to a banquet and freedom to pass. The march from Monterrey to Saltillo. Encampment near a place called Buena Vista where General Zachary Taylor defeated the Mexicans. Their arrival at the city of San Luis Potosí and yet another confrontation by another French general and another temporary halt in their advance.

The next bundle went quickly for they all read much the same. Six weeks of hard journey over the rocky bush land of northern Mexico, some days making only eight miles. The words cactus and sagebrush and heat and thirst came up a lot. Hungry, rationing, water was day to day. He felt with them in their plight and at times spoke into the sultry air, offering suggestions and words of consolation, cursing the unforgiving land and the Juaristas who peopled it.

Sissy brought him a tall glass of iced tea, which he readily accepted without getting up. The garage's shadow was now well into the pecan grove. He looked at his wristwatch for the first time since leaving the trusty by the prison. It was ten past three.

He drank the iced tea as he read of their relief when they reached the highlands where the breezes were cooler and the vegetation greener and the air thin.

The climb has left us short of breath since so many of us are used to our flat homeland. The people in the villages are friendly and offer us water (which we have to boil) and allow our horses to drink from their wells. Mexico City, or La Ciudad, as the Mexicans call it, (I am learning Spanish from one in our group who speaks the language fluently but please forgive my spelling, as I am a novice) is over these mountains and we should be there within the next few days.

He felt like cheering when she told of their arrival in La Ciudad, of its glamour and church bells and the people cheering them along the tree-lined avenues that late-summer Sunday morning. So vividly did she write he could see the snow-topped volcanoes of Popocatépetl and another one called the "Sleeping Lady" and the purple aprons of land that spread downward from them. The people who strolled the broad avenue along which they rode with their half-shod sagging mules and horses toward the government offices of Maximilian. People who craned their necks and grinned at them as they passed.

Most of them wore no shoes. The rags they wore fit them so loosely it looked as though they would fall from them at any moment. Most wore no covering over their shoulders and some wore soiled woolen blankets, or se-

rapes as they call them, and many appeared to totter on the very edge of malnutrition and disease. Though many of them probably look as we do, these people are at home and we are not. Not all looked so poor. Some were dressed in all the finery of wealth and are called la gran sociedad. They made their way beside us down the cobblestone streets in carriages that rattled and clanked along. Riding along beside us on groomed horses from time to time were men wearing silk top hats, embroidered velvet jackets, pantaloons lined with silver buttons and leather boots stamped with exquisite designs. The women were dressed in gowns with mantillas and wore earrings and brooches that glittered in the sunlight. Though both seemed so proud of their beautiful city, it was difficult for me, seeing such contrasts, la gran sociedad and the ragged poor. It reminded me of home and the cause of our war and, I fear, does not bode well for this country.

The center of the city is absolutely magnifico (please forgive me as I try out my Spanish). It is a large plaza called the Zocalo and surrounding it are beautiful buildings including the National Palace and not far away the castle called Chapultepec that dominates everything. Its beauty is unequaled by anything I have ever seen, either in person or in pictures. Emperor Maximilian and his wife Carlota modeled it after their European castle "Miramar," or so we are told. We are also told inside are, chandeliers, Persian rugs and French tapestries lining the walls. Of course, we are hopeful for an invitation which should come soon for General Shelby, your father and our other leaders, met with the Emperor today. He is considering setting aside land for us not far from Mexico City where we might establish agriculture colonies and has expressed hope that we become farmers and not soldiers. All of this really seems quite logical, your father says, because the Emperor would never have sanctioned an armed force in his country. General Shelby is deeply saddened as are we all for this means he must disband the Iron Brigade as our group has become known. Some have already left us. Upon hearing the Emperor did not want them as soldiers some slipped out of their quarters for Sonora where they hoped to join various Juarista chieftains in the north and some have actually enlisted with the French. Some, your father was told, have gone to hunt gold northwest of San Luis Potosi.

Meanwhile we wait in a hotel not far from the palace. The services are poor but the facilities are adequate and the food less than appetizing. I am getting used to all of the spices the ladies use and learning the many ways chicken can be cooked. Needless to say, we are surviving as we await word on our future. I believe you can write to us now. We are told to tell loved ones to address any letters to General J. O. Shelby . . .

At first his eyes almost slid past the words, so familiar were they to him. He held the page close to his face and squinted, followed the handwriting with his finger to make sure. General J. O. Shelby. There was no mistaking the name and his heart, that seemed to have grown, was beating faster and a chill traveled the length of his spine. He knew then who had read the letters before him and probably arranged them in the ordered chronology in which he was reading them. Why he was never told of their existence, he did not know, unless they were that valuable and the world should not know and he was the little pitcher with the big ears his mother always talked about and never laughed when she said it. He looked at the name again as it was written on the page and thought for the first time in his life how good it looked and whispered it to himself, then his name afterward. His mother had said it was a good name and now he knew how good and looked over at her picture not far from him on the drive and thought a thank you to her. He contemplated once more each of the other frames in the order of their genealogy until there were no more, then understood, too, why there were no pictures of his great-granddaddy Cal or Foster because they were the ones who had abandoned the land and lost it. Maybe that was another reason he had never been told about the letters. They revealed too much for him to know back then. He held the paper once more to his eyes that were growing more tired in the hot shade and picked up where he left off.

. . . any letters to General J. O. Shelby in care of Emperor Maximilian, Mexico City, Mexico. He has welcomed us here and will surely see we receive any correspondence. Or you could write to us at the Hotel de Itur-

bide which is quite elegant (it was once the residence of a former self-pro-claimed Emperor of Mexico) with huge brass double doors and very ele-gant, velvet-covered chairs in its spacious ornate lobby. But our bills are mounting and we hope to leave soon for our colony. Besides, the place is overrun with Confederates who arrive daily from the north by stagecoach and horseback and fill the huge lobby with their cigar smoke and wild tales of war and their experiences in getting here. Your sister and I go for walks just to get away from it all. So you might do well after all to just send any correspondence (as soon as possible) under the care of the Em-peror or the Empress Carlota who would take special pains to see that our mail is delivered. The Empress speaks English and has acted as his spokesman, has expressed sympathy with our misfortunes and assured us our protection was in the best of European traditions. Chere Grand Mamam the people refer to her here and it is understandably so. She is the perfect lady.

He read her usual closing remarks and folded the fragile letter and replaced it carefully in its envelope and put his head against the wall, crossed his boots, and closed his eyes.

The next he knew someone was tapping him on the shoulder. He opened his eyes and saw Mr. Pat standing over him.

I don't know what your plans are, he said, but Miss Pat and I would like for you to feel free to spend the night in the garage apartment and stay as long as you'd like.

He looked at everything laying about him and the unfinished busi-ness still awaiting him in the trunk and thought a moment then tipped his cap bill back with his finger. Seein's I got more to do here than I thought I would, he said, that comes as a mighty welcome offer.

Good. You can have supper with us too.

He thought again then stood up and readjusted his cap. No of-fense, Mr. Pat, but I just don't feel right sittin at a table my folks never sat at.

Mr. Pat regarded him with puzzled eyes. Your folks were invited many times, boy, he said.

But they never went.

All right. That may be true. But that's no reason for you not to accept our hospitality.

May be. It just don't feel right.

Miss Pat will be awfully disappointed.

I believe you. I'm not questioning your sincerity. I just gotta do what I gotta do.

Very well. Sissy can bring you a plate.

That's good. I'd like that.

He continued reading and at six o'clock Sissy came with his dinner. She told him the side door to the garage was open and that she had prepared his bed and laid out fresh towels. He put the utensils she'd given him in his shirt pocket and took the plate and glass and found the door ajar as she had said. He climbed the steps to the small apartment which was larger than he had remembered. The furnishings were spare and simple as though hastily prepared but more than adequate, certainly more than he had been used to. There were windows on both sides, a pair looking out over the driveway and another over the back where all he could see was the land dark and flat. He placed the plate and glass of tea on a small nightstand and went back down the stairs to retrieve the letters he had yet to read. He came back up cradling them in his arms and laid them on the cot-size bed.

The bathroom was tiny but had the basic necessities. He used the john and washed up and pulled a slat-back chair up to the nightstand. Fried chicken and black-eyed peas and sweet potatoes and several sliced tomatoes and two homebaked rolls. He ate like a hunger-struck man, saving the sweet potatoes for dessert. When the tea ran out he filled the glass at the tap in the bathroom, consumed that on the spot and filled it again and returned to the chair where he sat and studied the bundles of letters. There was no headboard so he adjusted himself on the bed with his back to the wall and examined the letters as to their dates so he would begin where he left off, amazed still at their tidy order and finally concluded that his great-great-grandmother Esther had kept them in that fashion and as such they were passed down through the generations. He located the last letter he had read which concluded one bundle and he began with the next.

Several he scanned quickly. They told of the delay in Mexico City and spoke with repetition of the boring existence there and of the fears for their men, many of whom took to the fleshpots along the wide boulevards or gambling by the light of smoke-filled bistros filled with señoritas available at a price. One passage in the otherwise quiet pages did catch his eye. He looked back at the date on the front, *6 September 1865*, then back to the place he had marked with his finger.

We received word yesterday that we have finally been provided new land for our colonies. The Emperor at last issued the decree. Sadly, it was land that once belonged to the church but perhaps it is God's will that it now become ours. Your father and other leaders are working on the regulations. We are told it is about a half-million acres located a few miles off the imperial highway from Mexico City to Veracruz which has been completed as far as Paso del Macho. We have already a name for our new little South, "Carlota," for the Empress who has become our best champion. She, too, is an exile which is perhaps one of the reasons for her special warmth and sympathy for our cause. She invited several of us ladies for tea the other day at the castle and it was a grand occasion. We sat on a balustraded patio overlooking the city and Paseo. She was quite lovely and gracious, most hospitable. Like us, she is secluded and lonely and at times I think craves our affection as she does those of her subjects. She will nod with a smile at our Confederates from the window of her wooden carriage with its leather side curtains as it jogs along the cobblestone streets of this bustling city. Some of our group has been told she has a diseased mind and speak of her affectionately as "Our Carlota." Our sorrow for her is also compounded by rumors that her marriage with the Emperor is not all well for it is said he sees a secret love at his retreat in Cuernavaca, a beautiful city we are told, not far from Mexico City.

If plans go as we expect, we should depart in a few days for Carlota and face the task of carving a new homeland from these tropical environs. We read of lush vegetation beyond and the blue waters of the Gulf of

Mexico. We hope to build a cluster of towns much unlike the crude Mexican settlements nearby and modeled after the gracious elegance we left behind. Do pray for us for the task seems one comparable to the war we have been fighting these long five years.

The tempo picked up and he read faster, his eyes pulled along it seemed by some invisible thread that knitted him to the story. They traveled east to Carlota on a road that dropped downward ten thousand feet through oaks and pines and took them out of the cool mountains into a world of palms and ferns and banana trees and the blue Gulf as far as the eye could see. Heavy rains beat upon them and their animals had trouble pulling the carts along the winding switchbacks. The air was filled with mosquitoes and thick with humidity which made their breathing labored. Yet his grandmother's spirits were not throttled and she spoke of a new South that would rise, and of new plantations where tobacco and cotton and sugar and coffee would flourish in the well-watered acreage. Many joined them along the route. Old friends and people they had never met, generals and former governors and others of high repute. She met General Isham Harris of Memphis whom the family had known well before the war.

Carlota is a perfect place with breathtaking scenery and fertile soil and a climate very much like our own. We seem to be in a new Eden prepared especially for us by the Lord between the beautiful blue Gulf of Mexico to the east and the white-capped volcanic peaks of Orizaba and Popocatepetl to the west. I found myself as though cast in a spell upon seeing it for the first time. In a few months we will have shops and hotels along with hotelkeepers, druggists, carpenters, blacksmiths and bakers. People will flock to build our beautiful city and you and Esther and Nathan Bedford can visit us. You can come by ship from New Orleans to Veracruz and we can meet you there.

Large gaps in time, as much as two and three months, separated the next series. He thought a mistake had been made and checked the others. She had been unable to write as often because of the labors of settlement, he learned as he read with disappointment of efforts that fell far short of their dreams. Blocks laid out but only half-filled with buildings. Clapboard rooming houses where rent was excessively high. Crumbling adobe buildings and tumble down shops and an ongoing battle against the slime and vine-infested surroundings. Heavy clouds that hung constantly over them with the threat of rain that never came, only humidity and trapped heat that soaked them with sweat. Land prices gouged by their own Confederates and the impossible rising cost of clearing the muddy jungle. They planted cotton and sugarcane and coffee and field crops but the jungle of bamboo and banana trees and coffee bushes were everywhere and difficult to tame. Some gathered pineapples and papayas and mangoes they found growing wild among the ruined haciendas. The people before them also left groves of oranges and figs and bananas which were picked and sold. Rice, meat, beans, and flour were hard to come by as was farming equipment because of General Sheridan's successful border patrol, which included all Texas ports and New Orleans. They were often attacked by local bandits, the crops stolen or burned. In one letter she told of further discontent, of dysentery and tropical fevers such as malaria, typhoid and pellagra and primitive sanitary conditions. Ladies dressed in silken finery had to find their way through mud puddles to an outside privy. There were food shortages (good red meat was scarce) which opened the door to exhaustion and weakened health and ultimately, for some, death. Page after page the setbacks kept erupting. Infections. Unemployment. Banditry. Warfare. An earthquake.

He drew from the strength the words carried and the courage they memorialized. Not once did she hint of giving up or coming home. Despite the hardships they tried to cling to their Southern way of life. Picnics and square dances and hay rides for the young were organized as were sewing bees and reading circles for the older women. She wrote of a few imported pianos and group singings, of church gatherings and dinners-on-the-ground.

In the dim golden lamplight his eyes grew tired and sleepy, the brown ink on the brittle pages at times almost fading completely from the years of dormancy. He thought of stopping but had only a few more to go.

The last were strange and disjointed and almost impossible to read in places because of the shifting thoughts and run-on sentences. Absent was her mention of the many troubles and problems of the settlement. Instead she wrote of the trivialities of day to day living and the children and their games and new drinks she was concocting from papaya and pineapple. The writing seemed to change and take on a childlike quality and he caught himself time and again shuffling to the last page to check the name, which was hers, though blocked in large print and not in her usual cursive style. She had fallen to one of the many illnesses she had mentioned or her mind had finally broken, as he had seen happen to men in the penitentiary. Loneliness and confinement and isolation can do that, he knew all too well, and pondered her predicament in that jungle wasteland. He wondered, too, of the others and their state of mind and why his grandfather Cal never wrote or any of his sons and daughters and only she. An owl hooted from distant trees, or was it something else he heard coming from the moaning land? A moth looped from the ceiling and danced around the light, batting inside the shade, until it grew tired he guessed and disappeared into a corner of the room. She could not leave him like this and conjectured his great-great-grandfather Foster must have felt the same frustration when he read to the same point. He looked at the two remaining letters beside him on the bed and prayed they would be different.

20 May 1866

Dearest Foster,

Please forgive my previous epistles and their lack of reason for I have been quite ill with very high fevers and, I am afraid, somewhat delirious at times. But I am recovering and my strength is returning. And do not be alarmed at what follows, for we are safe and managing to survive, but our dreams are breaking and falling apart in big pieces almost daily. Today we received word that a sister colony, Omealco, was openly at-

tacked by liberales, mostly Indians under the command of the Juarista
General Figueroa. The Juaristas are closing in on the French and its bay-
oneted empire and General Shelby has passed the word to all to make
plans for escape. Your father has learned of a hacienda called Michopa
which is near Cuernavaca, a place I have mentioned in previous corre-
spondence which is about fifty miles south of Mexico City. He has been
given the name of a wealthy Mexican who has remained neutral in the
internal strife of this country and may be in a position to provide us
refuge, perhaps sell us some land. I tell you this because it seems our days
may be numbered in Carlota since the very name of our town makes us a
prime target for the Juaristas and we may no longer be able to post mail
from here. Your father reasons we can travel under cloak of darkness back
through Mexico City and then to Cuernavaca taking only our essential
belongings. Our small band could travel light and arrive in Cuernavaca
in several days. We would not be so conspicuous as the others who will no
doubt take the coastal route to Veracruz which is raided almost daily by
the Juaristas according to the reports we receive.

Forgive this short letter, but I must close. My hand is tired and my
mind drained. I will write again as soon as I can but time is running out.
Pray for us as we need all of the help we can acquire, most assuredly, the
Lord's.

> *Your loving mother,*
> *Caroline Bouchillan Ferguson*

Then, the last, postmarked not from Veracruz as had been the others, but from Mexico City.

2 June 1866

My Dearest Foster,
You must know. I cannot keep it from you. The worst has surely fallen
upon us. Yesterday our colony of Carlota was overrun by Juaristas. We
were not there to witness what happened for your father's wisdom once
again has saved us and we are on our way to Mexico City. But the reports
we have heard from the few fleeing in our direction are most dreadful. A

thousand Mexicans raided the village. They torched our houses and shops, the hard and sacrificial work of a year gone up in flames. We were told people were spilling into the streets carrying their possessions, pushing and pulling among each other trying to find wagons or carriages, anything to get them safely to Veracruz, another of your father's predictions come true. It does indeed seem ironic that the Empress Carlota, for whom our city of dreams was named, set sail from Veracruz for France.

Despite all this, we do not despair. Mexico City is well protected for now and we should pass through there soon (where I will post this letter) on our way to Cuernavaca and the Hacienda Michopa where the hacendado we are told is one to be trusted and will give us shelter. By separating ourselves from the masses we stand a much better chance of survival. Your father is staunch about not returning home. He is still much embittered that the South gave up and equally fearful for his life. We are told Sheridan's men patrol the borders and ports relentlessly. He sends his love and asks that you discontinue wiring money until the situation in Mexico has settled. He still has a large sum of money with which he can buy land. The hacendado at Michopa is aware of our holdings and worth which is one of the reasons, I am sure, we are being offered asylum on his huge estate.

This may be my last communication with you for some time but rest assured we are all safe and consider ourselves most fortunate for so many of our group are either dead, wounded or imprisoned. As soon as it is possible, I will write again. Please do not write to us as your letters could fall in hostile hands and they would search us out. Wait for word. We pray to God it will be soon I can write to you again and tell you we are safe and in good hands.

With deepest affection,
Your loving mother
Caroline Bouchillan Ferguson

He checked the bundles again to make sure there were no others then rechecked. He walked down the stairs to the garage and searched the trunk. There were none. He climbed the steps back to the apartment and scanned the room, looked under the bed. Perhaps there were others that were not packed, kept somewhere in another place by Miss Pat. He would ask first thing in the morning. He yearned for a map of Mexico to see the places about which he had been reading, to put his finger on them, know they were still there. His mind had not yet fully returned to where he was, nor did he wish it to. He went back down the stairs and got the pictures of Nathan Bedford and Martha and Jefferson Longstreet and brought them back up to the room and held them under the light and viewed them as though they were visiting him in the moment of his frustration and could answer all that was unanswered. Then he sat on the bed and thought about taking a bath but thought again that he would do it in the morning so he could start out fresh. It might be a long time before he got to take another one. He took off his boots and unbuttoned and unzipped his jeans and was about to pull them off when he heard what sounded like a knock on the downstairs door. He sat still and waited and it came again, two soft raps. He looked at the clock on the bedstand and saw it was almost nine. Sissy would have walked home by now and Mr. and Miss Pat had no reason to come. He zipped his jeans back up and snapped them, flipped on the outside light, and crept quietly down the stairs in his sock feet. The taps came once more, louder and closer together, as though the impatient hand attached to them knew he was there. He opened the door.

At first he did not recognize her. She was taller than when he had last seen her, and slimmer, but her hair was still dark and long and flowing over her shoulders. Her lips were fuller and red and glistened under the light and from where they smiled, the rest of her rouged face swept upward with a maturity beneath which he could still detect the still-innocent clean beauty that had been the only fantasy he had had in prison, for he had known no other.

Athen?

Jo Shelby Ferguson. My, my. Her arms were folded and her head cocked to one side, a wide grin holding steady. Just had to come and see for myself, she said, then reshaped her mouth into the arrogant half-smiling smirk she used when they were growing up together on the plantation, when she needed to erase the three years that separated them in age. She shook her head to toss her hair away from her eyes. He watched its silken movement in the bulb-light and remembered how it shined as fine in the sunlight on those unruffled days, flowing out behind her when they rode horses through the fields and raced bicycles down the dirt paths and ran for home when the dinner bells rang, back when one of them would have died for the other.

How'd you know?

Mother called and told me and I came on after a sorority do, she said. I didn't bother changing clothes.

Sorority? Where were you?

Ole Miss. I'm a senior there.

He contemplated the place a moment, and the money his father had put back for him to go there that was used instead to pay extra attorney's fees in the losingest of all losing causes. In seconds there swept through his mind the might-have-been's that could-have-been had he not been in downtown Drew on a Saturday night in the wrong place at the wrong time. He'd had a long six years to think about it, why her father so conveniently and readily turned him over to the authorities. He'd decided it was because he was the son of a hired hand come of age and she a Delta debutant fast arriving and they had become near inseparable and that was simply unthinkable in that highfalutin part of the world.

You okay? she said.

Yeah. My mind just wondered a minute.

Well, aren't you going to invite me in?

Yeah. Well, sure. Come on in.

And give me a hug?

Yeah, that, too, he said and he pulled her into him and held her and buried his face in her perfumed hair and whispered, God, Athen, it's good to see you, and she whispered the same back to him and added something else he did not hear and he raised his head and held her away from him so he could look at her.

What'd you say?

I said, It's good to see you and I've missed you terribly.

Her eyes teared and she tossed her hair again and lowered her head onto his chest and he placed his hand on the back of her head and stroked it slowly. She gave a tight squeeze and pushed back from him.

I'm sorry, she said.

Sorry? What for?

What daddy did.

Guess he did what he had to do.

She wiped an eye with a finger and turned her head and wiped the other then turned back to face him. I know, but it's all so stupid, the way they do things here, the decisions they make for you that they think are right. Makes you feel like somehow we're living in the stone ages. I hear it all the time. We in the Delta do it this way. Folks in the Delta don't behave like that. The Delta this, the Delta that. Sometimes I wish I'd never even been born in the Delta. He wouldn't let me come visit you. Said it wasn't the place for a lady and he was always too busy to come with me. So all I could do was write.

He said nothing and they looked at one another in the shadowed silence while the moths and night bugs buzzed and whirred in the slanted light of the half-open door until he finally reached over and shut it and invited her to come up to the room.

She walked ahead of him up the stairs and he noticed the shape her body gave to the dress and the graceful legs and how it all moved, so differently from the straight and bony tomboy he'd helped onto horses and down from trees, once pulled from the creek that ran through the property. She removed her shoes and sat with her legs crossed on the floor so her dress made a pouch between her knees and he sat opposite her with his back against the bed, his legs outstretched and feet ankle-crossed beside her. He noted the necklace, the pendant hanging from it, strange letters of some foreign language, but said nothing. She asked if he had received all of her letters and he said he guessed he had and had she received his and she said likewise, that she had. He thanked her once then several times afterward and kept telling her how much they had meant until she placed a hand on his knee and told him she knew and he needn't say another word and he felt the blush in his face above the heat of the room. They talked about growing up and laughed at exploits privy to no one but them and God. She told him about his parents and how they had struggled since his imprisonment and her last time to see them before they were killed, how brave and strong they were trying to be about it all. He sat and listened, a tear rolling off his cheek. She leaned over and wiped it with her hand as she spoke and the sounds of the night drifting through the open window carried with them a timeless monotony and for a moment he felt as though nothing had changed and he would leave when they finished talking and walk to the house and climb into his bed and hear his folks there, too.

She spoke of college and her classes and the degree in elementary education she would get in spring and that she planned to leave the Delta and Mississippi and go to Atlanta and teach, that the pay was better and Atlanta was an exciting city coming into its own. She saw the brooding cloud cross his face, placed her hand on his knee and asked if she had said something that upset him.

Naw. Not really. Just cain't see you leavin.

You make it sound like I'm going to the moon. Atlanta's not that far. Martha Faye Tate teaches there and comes home every other weekend. What about you? What will you do? Daddy wants you to stay here. Mama fixed this room up for you. The foreman he's got now is okay and all, but he really needs someone who knows the place, if you know what I mean.

Just sounds kinda different. I mean, he turned me over to the law and wouldn't let you visit me and now he wants me here working, like maybe what you said a while ago was right and he's got ever thing goin the way he wants it. He said nothing of the pendant but his eyes were on it. She noticed and covered it briefly with her hand then tried to recover the move by pretending to play with it, swinging the letters back and forth in her fingers.

You sell me short, Jo Shelby Ferguson. It just might be he wants you back here because I asked him to and told him it was the least he could do. He's felt real badly about it. None of us believed you were guilty. But daddy's big into Delta politics. He played the game.

May be. Just seems like there was another game he was playing. He said nothing more and sat looking at her, his eyes weighed down by feelings that had traveled a long way to get there and wondered if being in prison wasn't better than this.

So? she said.

Yeah?

You are, aren't you?

He averted her gaze and looked at the ceiling and thought a moment then looked back at her. Don't know. Got something I gotta do before I can think about settlin down.

Not anything that would keep you from taking something as good as daddy's offer I hope.

He reached behind him and grabbed a handful of letters from where he had left them on the bed and handed them to her.

What are these?

Just read em. You'll see. But handle em careful. There're old.

She scooted in closer where the light pooled from the bedstand lamp and opened the flap of one envelope and held it up with one hand so the letter slid out. With the care she might give to something as fragile as a fallen butterfly she unfolded the pages, smoothed them out in her lap, lifted the first page up to the light and began reading.

He watched.

Some of it's kind of hard to make out, she said and glanced up.

He nodded and kept watching. Her eyes widened and her pupils dilated in the yellow lamplight and her mouth opened and shut and opened and shut like one reading for the first time the secrets of a great mystery. She finished the letter and shuffled the pages back to the first. He knew she was checking the date as he had done when he first encountered the writings.

Jo Shelby, this is amazing. These letters are almost a hundred years old.

Yep.

Yep? I mean these are worth something.

They won't make a man rich, but they are worth something.

Where did you get them?

Your mama said she found them packed away in the bottom of an old trunk where they stored all my family's other things. Guess she didn't know what they were either, said she never looked at em.

She must not have. She never told me. What are you going to do with them?

Follow em.

Follow them. I don't understand.

That name there, he said, taking the last page from her and pointing to it. You see it?

Yes.

That's my great-great-great grandmama.

She leaned backwards out of the circle of light and anchored her hands behind her so her arms propped up her back and tilted her face to one side in the half-light. No, you don't mean it, she said.

True as truth itself. All of em are by her. She wrote em from Mexico. She and my great-great-great granddaddy Cal and all of his family cept my great-great granddaddy Foster hightailed it to Mexico when the South lost. They was gonna set up another South down there. I'd heard about it a time or two, when my folks would spin yarns on the porch at night. Thought that's what it was, just another yarn. Like grownups'll tell when they got nothin better to do.

I don't think I want to hear the rest. Surely, you're not—

So, I figure I got folks down there. I got a family down there. And I aim to find em.

She pushed herself forward and dropped her head into her hands and whispered into her palms words he could not hear. He said nothing. She remained in that posture for a while then finally raised her head and he saw the tears.

What's the matter, he said. I say somethin wrong?

She shook her head in that melodramatic fashion he remembered all too well, when she had skinned a knee or pinched a finger and the blood would be streaming but she would tell him no, nothing was wrong. Only this time he knew she was covering for something else, something too deep for either of them to touch and talk about so he left it alone and waited out the silence for her to speak again.

When are you going? she said.

T'morrow morning.

But what about clothes, and money? You don't have enough to get to the State line.

Done thought of that. I got forty dollars. Got enough clothes. Got a pistol that was in the trunk. Got me a good thumb here.

She flopped her hands in her lap and rolled her eyes.

Got all I need, he said.

She looked back at him, her eyes narrowing from their furthermost reaches of shock and amazement. All? she said.

No. Maybe not all. Just the things that'll git me there.

Somebody must have hit you on the head in that prison because you got snakes up there. You're crazy, you hear me, crazy.

Maybe so. But I done had enough time to go crazy. One thing I learned in that prison, if I didn't learn nothin else. A body'll go crazy faster out here fancy free than locked up in prison where there ain't nothin to go crazy for. And I'll sure nough go crazy if I don't do what I gotta do with the wherewithal to do it. It's what my mama and daddy would want me to do. Least I can do is make em proud.

She rolled her eyes again. Your mama and daddy wouldn't want you leaving home. They wouldn't want you leaving a good job, working and living here where they worked, where they're buried. They wouldn't want you leaving your friends, like me, in case you have forgotten. And your hunting buddies. Some of them are still around. Bo Corlew works in the gin and Billy Bryson's in Tutwiler selling cars. Saw Vince Wilkins just today at school and he was excited about your getting out. And your mama and daddy sure to God wouldn't want you striking out to some strange country where you don't even know the language, hitchhiking at that. They'd say you were crazy, too, dimwitted. You belong here, Jo Shelby Ferguson.

You just read one of them letters. Maybe if you read em all you'd understand. My mama didn't put em in that trunk for no reason. My name's not Jo Shelby Ferguson for nothing. Just read em.

She eased back into the lamplight through which moths and beetle bugs darted and read another and put it aside, then another. He fed them to her one by one, as he might morsels to something hungry and she took them and devoured each with quiet curiosity. When she was through and had laid the last aside she moved closer and reached and held his hands in hers and looked at him with eyes that seemed suddenly aged with pain and told him she would go, too, if it was her family, but she still hoped he would stay.

He walked her to the door and down the steps. He moved his hand to open the door and she grabbed his wrist and shook her head. He pulled her close and felt the difference time can make in a girl's body. She looked up and moved her face close to his and kissed him on the lips, the first he'd ever received there from a woman, a moist softness that lingered only slightly then went away, and he took it as some strange but welcome sign that he was still loved, by somebody, even if she didn't say so. And she didn't. She released her arms and he did his and he opened the door.

I'll see you in the morning, she said. You are having breakfast before you leave?

Yessum. Believe I will, he said and smiled.

She smiled back thinly in the gloom and turned and walked toward the house.

He removed his clothes down to his underwear, slipped between the sheets and turned out the light.

He watched the latticed window-shadow on the opposite wall slide downward with the rising moon.

THE SHOTS WERE LOUD and fired at point blank and the people crumpled to the ground but the man kept shooting and he hollered for him to stop and was still hollering when he opened his eyes and sat up in bed and heard the loud knocking on the door below. He threw back the sheet, pulled on his jeans, ran down the stairs and opened the door.

Mornin, boy. Mr. Pat was standing there in a white suit and white shirt and Western-style string tie.

What is it?

Sorry to have awakened you. Didn't want you to miss breakfast. Miss Pat and I and Athen are eating on the patio. Believe ya'll visited last night. His eyes were steady but behind them moved questions a man of his design and contrivance would never ask.

Yessir. He said nothing more and the two stood looking at one another until Mr. Pat spoke again.

Well, won't you join us? Buttermilk waffles and smoke-cured sausage. Sissy's best.

He rubbed his eyes and blinked. Over his shoulders he could see Sissy setting a table on the patio and Miss Pat reading the paper, sipping coffee. He guessed Athen was probably still sleeping or getting dressed.

Yessir. Maybe I will.

Good. I've got a Delta Council meeting in Clarksdale afterward. You're welcome to ride along. We can talk about the place and what needs to be done, man to man talk.

Let me think about it.

Fine. We'll eat in about half an hour.

He nodded and closed the door and returned to the room where he took a hot bath that he wished could last all day and shaved using the bar of soap to lather his face and the straight razor he decided he had inherited. He put back on his same clothes which felt different on him. Even the socks felt different and the boots coming on over them. It was because he was clean he decided and tried to remember the last time he had taken a bath and worn normal clothes.

Looks like you had a good night's sleep, Miss Pat said, as he approached the patio and pulled out a wrought-iron chair from the table. She was made up the same as ever, as though she had never gone to bed, just changed clothes to indicate she knew she had moved from one day into the next.

Yessum. For the most part.

Mr. Pat joined them and Sissy brought stacks of waffles and a platter of sausages then went back inside the house and returned with a jar of molasses and a plate of toast and large pitcher of orange juice. Mr. Pat said a blessing and they ate quietly in early morning air disturbed only by sparrows and chickadees darting in and out of the crepe myrtles surrounding them. He kept his eyes on his plate and ate sparingly, trying to remember the manners his mother had taught him that had completely unraveled in the state pen, and thinking about the blessing she always said, and wondering where Athen was but daring not to ask.

Mr. Pat studied him over the rim of his coffee cup. Decided what to do? he said, then took a sip.

Maybe, he said, and chilled a bite of hot sausage with a swallow of orange juice that burned the back of his throat as it went down.

He'd love to have your company this morning, Miss Pat said. It sure would be nice if you'd stay here on the place. You could live in the garage apartment. There's plenty to do here.

He chewed on another sausage and looked at her, trying to sort out sincerity from the pity and guilt that hung heavy as humidity in the air around them. Then he thought again and figured they'd rather have him after all than some beer-guzzling frat rat which was what the necklace was all about.

She looked back and said nothing more.

Them all the letters in that trunk? he said.

Yes, she said. Like I told you, I didn't disturb them except to put the Bible with them.

There wadn't no others nowhere else?

No. That was all we found when we cleaned out the house.

They ate.

Sissy brought more coffee and filled their cups.

Why did you ask about the letters? she said.

Just did, he said, regarding her coolly over the top of his cup.

They drank coffee and ate toast and jelly.

Ya'll know how to get to Mexico from here?

Mexico? they both said looking at him with astonishment.

Yep. Mexico.

Why the hell do you need to know how to get to Mexico? Mr. Pat said.

Just do. Which way is it?

The two looked at each other again then back at him.

A long way from here, Mr. Pat said. Too far for any of us to think about going.

How far?

More than a thousand miles, Mr. Pat said and put down his coffee cup and leaned his head over the table toward him. Depending on which part of Mexico you're talking about, he said.

Mexico City. He spooned jelly from a bowl and spread it on another piece of toast and awaited their next reaction.

Mr. Pat got a toothpick from the toothpick bowl and stuck it in the side of his mouth then leaned back and looked up through the crepe myrtle branches. In that case I'd say it's more than a thousand miles, maybe closer to two thousand.

How do you get there? He forked the last of his sausage into his mouth.

Mr. Pat studied him a moment. You could take a bus to Jackson, he said, then take one from there across Louisiana to Dallas then go south to Brownsville, then cross the border and take a Mexican bus to Mexico City.

That cost more than forty dollars?

Forty dollars might get you to Dallas. Just might, Mr. Pat said.

That's all I got, forty dollars.

Miss Pat gave a sympathetic look.

Or you could catch a ride on a barge at Greenville or Memphis and go down to New Orleans and catch a ship to Brownsville, Mr. Pat said. That way you could work and it might not cost you anything.

He stopped chewing. Go on, he said.

That's it.

You don't know the name of any of them barges, do you?

A couple. River Transport is one I know of because we've shipped some of our cotton with them. They're headquartered in Memphis. Another is Delta Barge and Towing. They operate out of Greenville.

He had quit eating and was listening.

You're not actually planning on going there are you? Miss Pat said.

No'me. Not planning. Goin.

Her mouth fell open. But why? she said. What is there in Mexico that could possibly be better than what you could have here?

I agree with her, Mr. Pat said. None of this makes any sense. You didn't come out of that pen with any drugs did you?

He looked first at her, then at him.

Nope. Come out of that prison with a whole lot less than I went into it with and I'm not talking about the clothes I'm wearing and the forty dollars I done told you about.

It was obvious Athen had not spoken to them, or she had at least kept his plan a secret. He told them about the letters he had read and who wrote them and condensed the story as best he could remember it with the brevity of his own half-grown grammar and syntax and concluded with the lack of finality of it all.

They had been sitting bent forward over the table, listening wide-eyed and open-mouthed and when he finished they turned to each other in that same spellbound focus then back at him without so much as moving a muscle except what the turning of their heads required.

So that's why you were asking about the other letters? Miss Pat said.

Yessum.

How about that, Mr. Pat said. Those letters are probably worth a fortune.

The ones that ain't there are worth more, he said.

What will you do with them? she said.

I done thought about that. I want you to keep em for me. Put em in a vault somewheres.

Of course, he said. We can put them in the vault here or take them to the safe deposit at the bank.

All but the last two. I'm taking them with me. All the other stuff in the trunk, too. I'd like to leave it here, except a few of the pictures and one or two other things.

We'll take good care of it, she said.

Yessum. Believe you will. You done proved that.

Surely, there is more we can do, she said. You don't even have a suitcase and I'll bet you don't have underwear. You'll need another set of clothes. She began sounding like his mother, rattling off all the necessary items he would need, speaking to him with emotion that broke through the frozen gaudiness which was all he had ever known so that he saw for the first time a presence of concern and lack of pretense, like she understood, as a mother would.

Don't need no suitcase, but a pouch or satchel of some kind might be handy.

I've already thought of that, said Athen, appearing from behind a crepe myrtle.

Athen, hon, where'd you come from? Miss Pat said as if she might have dropped in from the sky.

I've been standing there. She pointed behind the crepe myrtle. I didn't want to interrupt. But I thought about Jake's old Army surplus knapsack and I found it in the garage.

She walked to the table and placed the knapsack in the empty chair reserved for her. The letters u. s. army were faded but legible on the flap and the straps were gnawed along the edges. The contours along the bottom said it was not empty.

I put some toilet articles and aspirin and Band-Aids in it, she said. There's also a small lunch wrapped in tinfoil. Sissy is ready to wash whatever dirty clothes he has. That's why I haven't been down for breakfast.

Each looked at the others, wondering who would speak next and the glances bounced around the table until Jo Shelby stood up and spoke.

I'm mighty grateful. I know my clothes need washing but I'm leaving this morning and there won't be time.

He politely dismissed himself from the table and left them looking after him speechless. He went first to the garage where he retrieved the gun and holster from the trunk along with his grandfather's Barlow knife and pocketwatch with the picture of his great-grandmother Martha. He slipped the hooks back on the picture frames and removed the pictures, except some of the older ones that looked too fragile to live by themselves. All these he put into the knapsack and went up the stairs and made the bed and tidied the room as he had found it, packing what few remaining belongings he had.

They were standing there waiting for him. Mr. Pat on the driver's side of a Cadillac he had backed out from the garage and Miss Pat beside him. Athen was on the passenger side. She held a pair of blue jeans, a white long-sleeved shirt and underwear. On top of them were a pair of white socks, a tube of Colgate toothpaste, a bar of soap and a safety razor.

You'll need all of these, she said, and thrust them at him in that manner of forced care wives use to send their husbands off to war. They were Jake's and ya'll are about the same size.

I'm much obliged, he said and laid the knapsack on the hood of the Cadillac and slid the neat package into it, except the safety razor which he said he wouldn't be needing.

This might come in handy, too, Athen said, and handed him a large piece of paper that had been folded several times over. It's a map of Mexico. I found it in a pile of old National Geographics I'd been saving.

He thanked her and took it from her without looking at it and slipped it into the side pouch on the front of the knapsack.

I can take you to Clarksdale with me, Mr. Pat said, and you can catch a bus from there to Memphis straight up 61. That's your best bet to get on a barge. There are more of them there.

I'm mighty grateful, he said, but that's a tad out of my way. I would kindly take a ride back to the highway. Think I'll just hitchhike south to Indianola then across to Greenville.

Mr. Pat shook his head and looked down then back up at him. I'll be glad to do that, he said, but I think you'd be better off going to Clarksdale.

Thanks just the same, but I'm going south.

I can drive you to Greenville in my car, Athen said. It's just an hour or so's drive.

He looked at her and thought a moment.

I think it's just best I go on from the highway. But I'm mighty grateful.

She shook her head, rolling her eyes in disgust, as she walked away. She turned back.

Mama, you and daddy don't mind do you?

No, hon, course not. Come on, Pat. I forgot to give you something to take with you, and she motioned with her head and they both walked to the backdoor and entered the house.

I'll declare, Jo Shelby, if you don't beat all. You weren't even this stubborn when your mama told you you were going to take piano lessons and you faked a broken arm. She shoved a piece of paper into his hand. Here, put this in your pocket. It's got my address on it and my telephone number at school. Write to me, will you? And call if you get into trouble or if you need help.

He took the piece of paper and slid it into his jeans pocket and accepted a hug from her. Remember, she said, looking at him with eyes inches from his, there's a place for you here when you come back, and somebody who's never stopped caring.

He looked. The pendant was gone from around her neck and the necklace with it. He nodded that he understood and hugged her again, holding her close.

How long do you expect to be gone? she said, standing back and looking up at him.

Don't know. As long as it takes. Maybe the rest of my life.

TWO

T HE MISSISSIPPI DELTA IS an oval-shaped alluvial plain bounded on the east by the Yalobusha and Yazoo Rivers and on the west by the Mississippi. It begins, some of old have said, in the lobby of the Peabody Hotel in Memphis and ends on Bourbon Street in New Orleans. As a matter of fact, it begins somewhere south of Memphis and ends at Vicksburg where the Yazoo joins the Mississippi. The terrain within those boundaries is without any semblance of elevation besides the Indian mounds, which rise from it in the most out-of-the-way and surprising of places, and the levee along the Mississippi, which is the closest to a ridge most Deltans have seen in a lifetime. The major cities are Clarksdale in the north and Vicksburg in the south and Greenville midway on the river. The major highways connecting them are Federal 61 and State 82 which intersect at Indianola.

He knew all of this because he was a child of the Delta, born and bred in that part of the world that was apart from all others and virtually a foreign country in its own right and he had never set foot out of it. He knew not only those major thoroughfares but the gravel and dirt crop roads in the plantations of his county and those in the surrounding counties because more often than not they kept on going regardless of whose cotton or soybeans or corn was growing on either side and would sometimes run on for several more counties and end suddenly at a row fence or peter out in a wash. He could have been in prison thirty years and still known all of this because things just don't change in the Delta, least of all the roads. He knew, too, the people traveling them would pick him up and take him as far as they were going because he was one of them and they could tell it just by looking at him because folks in the Delta knew each other that well.

By noon he'd made nearly forty miles through small towns called Ruleville and Pentecost and Sunflower and was still in familiar surroundings when a man in a pickup let him out at the major intersection in Indianola. He walked to a nearby gas station and went inside, gave the attendant a twenty dollar bill and asked for change. The attendant was not much older than Jo Shelby. He wore a T-shirt and blue jeans covered with oil and grease marks. He took the twenty with grime-streaked hands and palmed out a ten and a five and four ones along with assorted change. Jo Shelby slipped the soiled bills into his billfold and pocketed the change except for a nickel, which he placed in the slot of a Coca-Cola machine and pulled a metal lever. A bottle rattled into the hole below. He uncapped the Coke on the opener, took a swallow, walked to the edge of the building and sat on the raised curb. He let the knapsack slip from his shoulders, opened the flap and pulled out the tinfoil package Sissie and Athen had put together. Inside was a ham sandwich wrapped in cellophane and two boiled eggs, three chocolate-chip cookies and a Baby Ruth candy bar. In the midday sun he sat and ate and thought again about where he was going. He pulled out the map from the pouch where he had tucked it and unfolded it between his legs on the concrete, anchoring it on each side with his bootheels. He shook out a cigarette and lit it and smoked as he looked at the shape of the land where he was going.

Parts of Texas and Louisiana and Mississippi appeared at the top and he saw New Orleans and traced his finger along the coastline of the Gulf of Mexico until he came to Brownsville. He stopped there and smoked and looked a while longer. Northwest of Brownsville he saw the name Laredo and further up the Texas boundary, Eagle Pass. He stopped again and remembered that was where they crossed, then started again, moving his finger slowly southward, weaving it back and forth, until he saw Monterrey and further south of there San Luis Potosí. Mexico City was harder to find because of all the writing around it but there it was in the center of the southern part of the country and the name Cuernavaca due south of it, just like his great-great-great-grandmama had written. All he needed to do was get to Greenville, then New Orleans, then Brownsville. That was all.

He clamped his cigarette in his teeth, folded up the map and put it back in the front pouch of the knapsack then took a last drag from the cigarette and ground it out with the heel of his boot.

A man in an old Studebaker picked him up and took him as far as Leland and let him off there because he was going on south to Rolling Fork. He leaned on a highway marker for nearly an hour before a car-load of teenage boys stopped for him. They were going to the juke joints in Greenville, they bragged. All of them wore letter jackets and were under age and he knew their parents didn't know where they were. They asked him where he was going but he just said Greenville, the river. The one driving said, all right, he would take him to the levee though they weren't going there. Jo Shelby thanked him and got in.

You work on the river? one said.

Hope to, he said.

They said little else to him and he listened to them the next few miles, their bantering and yaw-jawing about life on the river and river barges and whose daddy had done this and who's that, gleaning what fragments he could that would be helpful to him, until the Greenville city limits sign flashed by.

They drove down a wide oak-lined street behind which rested white-columned mansions and other large homes of different design with gables and turrets and long rambling porches. Then the houses stopped and the stores and buildings began and continued on until he could see the sodded wall that was the levee in the distance. The street stopped at the levee which rose above them. The car turned right and followed a street which ran parallel to the levee for a short distance.

When the car came to a stop, Jo Shelby asked where he might catch a barge, and the kid told him Warfield Point, a few miles away. He told them he'd pay them to take him there and they argued among themselves until the driver told them to shut up that they'd do it for free.

The car veered back northeast then cut back east then due north for a couple of miles then the driver turned left and they drove on a potholed macadam that turned into a sand road and ran straight up and over the levee onto the river bottomlands where the timber thinned out to scrub oak and a scattering of willow and cottonwood.

At the end of the road was a square-columned building with a flat top and corrugated sides that looked like an oversized utility shed. A sign across the front said BOAT HOUSE.

This is it, the driver said.

Mighty fine, Jo Shelby said and got out.

Hope you make it to wherever you're goin the driver said. Say, didn't catch your name.

It's Ferguson. Jo Shelby Ferguson.

Well, good luck, Jo Shelby Ferguson, one from the backseat shouted.

I'm much obliged, he said, and turned and walked toward the boat store and turned back to look before he entered to see the car rolling up a red cloud of dust.

He smiled to himself and hoped they would make it and considered the prospects, that between him and them he was the one more likely to get to where he was going.

He walked through the wide door of the metal building and saw a lean sickly man whose face looked like it had been sucked in from the back of his head. He was wearing coveralls and standing behind a chest-high counter. There was radio static coming from somewhere behind the counter and on either side of it all the way to the ceiling were shelves jam-stocked with cigarettes and candy bars and work gloves and soap and wash detergent and everything else it seemed you might find in a small grocery store. Further back behind the man was a door, wider than the front one, through which he could see fifty-gallon drums and five-gallon cans and large carton boxes and coils of rope stacked one on top of the other. He surveyed the area more closely and saw the radio, or what looked like a radio, on a raised table just behind the far end of the counter. He asked the man behind the counter where the head man was.

I'm it, he said. What can I do for you?

I'm looking for work.

Ain't got none here.

No, I mean work on a boat.

The man spat into something out of sight behind the counter and looked around at a chart on the wall then out the window like that was the direction his thinking had taken him. Where you wanna go? he said.

New Orleans.

Not any tows stoppin here soon, but sometimes they need a hand, the man said. Just a minute. He turned and walked to the end of the counter where the radio-looking apparatus was and spread his legs over a tall stool and sat down. He turned a knob which caused the static to crackle louder then picked up a large microphone and pushed the wide button with his thumb.

This is Greenville Boat Store, Greenville Boat Store to Baxter Southern. If you can hear me, come in on channel twelve. Come in on channel twelve if you can hear me, he said into the microphone in a coarse rumbling mutter and released the button and waited.

The static faded and a voice came over the speaker. Baxter Southern, Baxter Southern, which was about all Jo Shelby could make out because the rest was a strange mixture of static and voice that ran together. He listened along with the boat store man who seemed to have some magical talent for separating the voice from the static and heard him ask the man on the other end what the weather was like there and if he needed an extra hand and when his ETA was. Then the man said over and out and walked back to mid-counter and turned and faced him. He moved his lower jaw around like a cow does chewing cud, then spat.

Luck's the word, he said. Tow's a comin down the river now. Be here in bout a hour or so. Closer to hour and a half. Just so happens they're short a deckhand. One got sick in Memphis and had to get off. The tow won't stop here. But it's gotta fuel up, so you'll ride out on the tug and fuel-flat down the hill yonder at the dock and get on while they're refueling. But you know all that already.

Yep, he said, the word coming out weak on confidence, then asked the man for half a dozen packs of nabs and potato chips and several Baby Ruth bars and the man gathered them and put them on the counter. Jo Shelby paid for them and stuffed them into his knapsack.

That oughtta tie you over, the man said.

Yessir. Oughtta. You got any ammunition?

The man pointed toward a back wall. We got some but depends on what you want.

He opened the flap of the knapsack again and felt around all the items he had just crammed into it and pulled out the holstered revolver and laid it onto the counter beside the knapsack.

Damn. Looks old. What kind is it? the man said.

Not sure. Just got it, he said and unhooked the hammer strap and pulled the gun out and held it palm up for the man to see. He then extended it to him.

The man gripped the butt carefully, as though it were a piece of priceless porcelain or a precious religious relic, and drew it close to his eyes and ran his other hand down the barrel and over the brass frame then handed it back.

Hot-to-mighty, boy, he said. You know what you got here?

I know it's old. Been in the family a long time. Belonged to a granddaddy of mine.

Old? Hell, this thing's a lever-action Navy Colt. It's over a hunderd years old. Unless you can find some mini-balls and powder, you ain't gonna find no ammunition for this. He took the gun from Jo Shelby and showed him how it worked, where the ball went and the powder and how the lever packed the loads in. He pointed down the cylinder hole. It'd look like a little white doughnut in there after you packed it, he said. My granddaddy had one until he got old and needed money and sold it. Got a pretty penny for it.

How much?

Bout a hunderd dollars. At least that.

Jo Shelby slipped the revolver back into the holster and snapped the flap shut. Guess that's that, ain't it? he said.

For bullets it is. But you got yourself one fine artifact there. Say you're going to New Orleans?

Yessir.

If I was you, I'd go to some of them antique shops in the French Quarter and see what it's worth. Then I'd go to a bank and get me a lock box and put it where nobody could get it. Something like that earns interest, if you know what I mean.

No sir.

It appreciates. The longer you keep it, the more it's worth.

Much obliged, Jo Shelby said and put the gun back into the knapsack and buckled the flap.

Don't guess you got any beer?

Nope, the man said. You can walk down to the little store a piece yonder. The Chinaman sells it. They won't let us sell no alcohol. Not supposed to drink on the boats but it goes on.

Thought I'd ask, he said, deciding that was too much effort for a beer, even if he hadn't had one in six years. Guess I'll have a Coke then.

The man pulled him a Coke and he took it outside, sat on a thin wooden step and lit a cigarette. Below him the river stretched like a motionless brown flood. A thin treeline on the distant shore separated it from the sky and that was all he saw. The river. Father of Waters his grandfather had said the Indians called it. His grandfather had seen it and so had his father but he had not, only concocted visions of it based on what they had said they saw and the only rivers he had seen, the Yalobusha and Tallahatchie and Yazoo, and what he looked upon now was ten times all three of them laid out side by side, if not more. He took another swallow of Coke and continued to gaze upon the river and its immensity, which he'd have never believed had someone told him it was so.

He studied the small tug pulled up at the dock down the hill just in front of him which looked nothing like any boat he had ever seen, not even in picture books. It was short and had a small cabin in the middle, a boxlike tower on top of it where he guessed the captain sat and on top of the tower were spotlights and an American flag. It sat swayback in the water, like something that had borne too much for too long and its bow curved upward like a sharp nose stuck in the air and on it a sign said TROUBLE TR20. Why would anybody want to name a boat that? It couldn't be worse than where he had been and whoever named it couldn't possibly have known trouble worse than he had but maybe they wanted people to think so. Attached to it was a longer flat boat on which sat several fifty gallon drums and he figured that was the fuel they somehow got into the towboat while all three of them were going downriver at the same time and the thought of that spectacle stirred his curiosity.

He pulled out the map of Mexico again and looked at it, scanned its entirety and wondered what kind of folk lived there and how they lived and had they changed much in a hundred years. He thought of his life, how much it had changed in just six years, what was not left and what was, what he might be leaving behind, maybe forever. He thought of Athen, her eyes bright with care and the way she had kissed him, some of the things she had said, especially about his friends. He remembered them and all the great times they'd had together. Hunting and fishing year round, Sunday afternoon football in the fall, shooting pool in Drew on Saturday nights, a party or two crashed, all the pranks they'd played. Surely, they hadn't forgotten him. Surely, they were still his friends. He thought of others, too, who were still around, had to be, who would help him even if he didn't work for her daddy. Was he doing the right thing? A breeze in the otherwise still air carried the smell of something old and damp and rich, like moist leaves newly stirred in virgin timber. A crow high above cawed and swooped and lit on a utility wire then cawed again and took off. He watched where it had lit and the blue beyond and wondered if there was a life somewhere out there for him. He sat there in that pensive state for a while and nodded off to sleep.

A horn in the distance sounded once, then twice, then gave another short burst followed by a prolonged note of announcement.

Tow's a comin, the man leaned his head out the doorway and said. Better git on down to the dock.

Yessir, he said, and grabbed his knapsack and headed down the sloping spit of land which led to the water and the dock, which was something simple, warped planking laid down over fifty-gallon drums.

Hey you, a man yelled from the boat. You the deckhand going out to the tow?

Yessir.

Well git the lead out. We gotta fuel it and we ain't got much time.

He looped the knapsack straps through an arm and began running.

Hop on in, the man said when he reached the dock. He was a large man with a fat face that almost took over his eyes and reminded him of someone he'd seen in a movie with his dad in Clarksdale about Louisiana politicians.

He stepped over the side of the boat and onto its deck and the man shouted at him again.

Make yourself useful. Unhook that bow line and push us off.

He set his knapsack down on a coil of rope next to the cabin and walked to the front of the boat and wrestled a large rope from around the cavil where it was looped and threw it onto the dock then stood in place at the boat's bow waiting for another order, but the big man was busy with the other lines and hollering something at a boy on the fuel flat. Jo Shelby wondered how just the two of them managed as they did without a third and decided that maybe times were tough and they were cutting overhead.

The boat's motor revved and water churned at a full boil around its transom. As it pulled away from the bank, he realized the biggest boat he'd ever been on was his daddy's wooden fishing boat. He stood watching the shoreline drift away as though it, too, were moving. As they gained speed, everything seemed to part before him. Only the sky held steady. He wondered again if this was what he should do. A man can be brave in his dreams, traveling unafraid to places unknown until those dreams come alive. His heart quickened as the boat moved further into the river. A strange numbness spread over him, like when he hugged Athen good-bye without looking back, because he was afraid he might have stayed if he had. He felt the soft rocking of the boat and turned with it as it pointed itself toward the wide muddy stretches of river that lay before him like another world.

They entered the river's main channel and turned sharply north, moving against the current, the boat's tilted bow plowing the water and he heard the sudden strain in the whine of the motor and saw the swiftness and power of the waters pushing around them, roots and limbs and timbers and castaway pink from God only knew where sailing by at a velocity he never imagined water could have.

He propped a foot on a timberhead, shook out a cigarette, his hands around the lighter and exhaled, watching how quickly the smoke was whipped away, as though the river carried its own wind with it. He stood with his foot propped and smoked and studied the scene, watched the distance between boat and tug narrow, the caramel-colored water that swirled and curled beneath him like the muscles of a monstrous snake splitting open the land. He knew little enough about what he was supposed to do but but if he could get acquainted with where he would be working and could think ahead and act like he knew what he was doing, whether he did or not, they wouldn't tell him to get back on the boat he was on and go back to shore.

The tow grew larger and he counted six barges altogether. Two across and three deep. The sign on the towboat said BAXTER SOUTH-ERN. The craft itself was rectangular and looked nothing like a boat but more like a white frame house set adrift. He counted the decks. There were four of them, one on top of the other, each smaller than the one below with the uppermost and tiniest encased in glass behind which he could see a solitary figure. He remembered stories read in school and envisioned a river pilot behind a large wheel and thought about life on the river and how it probably hadn't changed that much.

The boats came closer.

He watched.

Men on the towboat scrambled along its deck waving hands and holding ropes and he recalled scenes from the pictures about sailors and the sea.

Be ready to catch a line, the big man yelled at him, as though he sensed inexperience, then he yelled at the kid on the fuel boat to do the same, as he began a turn with the tug that brought it near parallel with the towboat and cut his engine back to an idle and let the boat's slip-slide momentum do the rest.

He watched as the sides of the vessels came together in a soft thud of fenders and a rope was flung to him by a man on the towboat and he caught it and looped it around the timberhead beside him. He didn't have to be told what to do next and ran down the side-deck to the rear of the boat and caught another rope and snubbed it around a timberhead then looped it around a cavil.

Good work, the big man shouted from the pilothouse and gave him a thumbs up.

He smiled to himself at what he had done and the distance of lore he had covered in such a short time all the while thinking about what he should do next. But there was nothing else to do the big man said to him after he had climbed down from his pilot's perch and approached him matter-of-factly.

Just hold tight and I'll introduce you to the captain. What'd you say your name was?

I didn't. But it's Ferguson. Jo Shelby Ferguson.

Just you wait right there Jo Shelby while I hep my boy git the fuel line over to that tow, he said then turned and pushed himself up over the rear gunnel of the boat and jumped down onto the fuel flat and began yelling orders at the kid.

From his vantage at the rear of the boat he watched and marveled at the smoothness of the operation, both boats rocking against each other, moving downstream together, the tow carrying the tug alongside it like some animal might its young and the men mute in their movement of hands and muscles, as if it was all some memorized dance, or a play they had acted in a hundred times so that what they did no longer required any thought. So he just stood and watched until the fuel line was connected and the men were shaking hands and laughing and talking loud to one another like it was the first time they had ever done it, marveling at themselves that they did it right.

The big man pulled himself back up into the tug from the fuel flat and walked over to him.

Come on. Let's meet the cap'n.

He followed the man over the gunnels of the two vessels where they lay cabled, snugly against each others' fenders, and onto the wooden deck of the towboat. The big man walked toward a group of men and stopped in front of one who was shorter and leaner than the rest and looked nothing like a captain. He wore a plaid shortsleeve shirt and store-bought trousers and leather lace shoes. His thinning gray hair was cropped to crewcut length. His deep-set eyes had a faded but gentle quality about them and they studied him over half-circles that looked like welts after a licking or perhaps some pain of another source, he thought. The big man shook his hand and the others' and they all howdyed each other. He turned back to Jo Shelby and motioned him closer.

Cap'n this here is Jo Shelby . . . what's your last name again?

Ferguson.

Ferguson. Your new deckhand. Jo Shelby meet Cap'n Priddy.

Please to meet you, Jo Shelby said to the man who looked nothing like a captain as he shook a hand that felt like a piece of old leather. He looked up at the captain's sharp-featured face, the long nose jutting out like a faucet and saw a pinkish wisp of scar that curved from his ear to his mouth.

This is the crew, Ferguson, the captain said, or part of it. The rest are at their stations. He spoke with a raised emotionless voice over a roar of diesels that was louder than a hundred Mack truck engines all revving at the same time. He introduced each by name and their position. Mate. Deckhand. Engineer. He said the pilot's name, too, and pointed at the pilothouse and said he would meet him later, along with the others he would probably see at supper.

The names came fast at him and passed him, but he remembered one. Catchings, the deckhand.

Each in turn extended their hands and he shook them and said hiddy and they said hiddy back. He said nothing else because he knew nothing else to say next and the captain looked at him and broke the silence.

How long you been a deckhand?

Not long he said, but I can do the job.

That's good. We wouldn't need you if you couldn't. He grinned at the one he'd introduced as the mate. What tows you worked on? he said.

Jo Shelby looked at the light bouncing off the river as though the tremors he felt came from there. He thought a moment, trying to remember the names Mr. Pat had called out but none came to mind. He took off his cap and rubbed his fingers through his hair then put it back on again. Might not be names you'd know, he said. Most of em gone out of business. He regarded the other men's heads cocked back and their eyes squinting on him.

I see, the captain said and cocked his head back and folded his arms and raised a brow.

Uncle owned one, called the Ferguson, Jo Shelby said. A small one out of Helena. Then I worked on one called the Memphis and one called the John Mosby. Those were the only names that came to him and he was lucky to think of those with his nerves driving the shakes all the way down into his boots so he felt his toes quiver.

The Memphis, said the captain. That must be the Memphis Transport Company you worked for. But they're not out of business. Passed one of their tows the other day, just out of St. Louis. Talked to em on the radio.

Guess it went back in. It was out for a while though cause we all got laid off.

The captain's head was still tilted back and his arms folded, then he dropped his arms and spoke looking at the big man who had brought him there. Well, that happens ever now and then, don't it, Cavanaugh?

The big man named Cavanaugh grinned. Yep, ever now and then, he said and they kept grinning at each other like one or both of them could tell the other's story.

Well, you know the routine, Ferguson, the captain said. Six hours on, six off. Your shift starts at midnight. Pay's a dollar and a half an hour for newcomers. We'll dock in New Orleans and you'll get paid there and we can decide where we go from there, if you want to go back as far as Memphis with us. My other deckhand should be well by then. How the hell he caught the flu I don't know but that's what they radioed and said he had. Catchings, show Ferguson here his bunk and give him a quick once-over the boat. Catchings is mighty proud you came along, Ferguson. He's been having to work his ass off.

Catchings was short and broad-shouldered and looked to be not much older than he was. His head sat on his shoulders as though he had no neck and he had a crewcut shaved up the back so it showed the rolling and dimpling of the muscles that ran up into his skull. Jo Shelby followed him through the engine room where the noise was that of a prolonged explosion and through two sets of doors that had PLEASE KEEP CLOSED painted on them and into a narrow hallway where the roar of the engines was muted but the vibrations continued through the floor up the frame of his body and into his teeth. Catchings said nothing as they continued down the dimly-lit corridor of half-size doors, then he stopped and opened one.

This is it, Ferguson, he said. Yore home away from home. The deckhand's quarters. You get the top. I already got the bottom.

All right, he said. He stood for a minute and peered in and looked around and said nothing. The room was not much wider than the hallway. The bunks were on the right pushed up against a wall and next to them was a double-compartment chifferobe. On the left was a garbage basket and caneback chair and a small plywood desk attached to the wall. On the desk was a table lamp with a plain vanilla shade that had burn marks around the top where it had been toasted by the bulb and beside it was a small oscillating fan, the only relief from the heat. There was a window at the end with yellow print plastic drapes and beneath it was a wall furnace. Playboy pin-ups covered what wall was left over the chair and garbage basket and desk.

One man's freedom is another man's prison, or was it the other way around, he thought. Maybe the whole world was just one big prison and each man had to find the place in it he felt the freest.

Best we got, said Catchings. It's either here or up on the deck, and believe it or not, sometimes folks sleep up there. Had an engineer once who did. Said he wanted to git as far away from them diesels as he could.

Jo Shelby said nothing but wondered if you could get away from them anywhere on the boat. He brought his knapsack down from where he had it slung over his shoulder and threw it up on the top bunk. He put his hands on his hips and reviewed the cramped quarters once more, then looked back at Catchings. That's fine. It's fine, he said.

That's good, said Catchings. For a minute there I thought you was gonna say something else.

For a minute, he said, and grinned.

Catchings grinned back and said nothing but Jo Shelby had already read the man's mind, that he might still be the only deckhand on board and would still have to mop and sweep and clean toiletbowls and make up beds and check barges all the way to New Orleans by himself.

Guess we better start with the barges, Catchings said. That's what pays the bills and we're pushing some pretty fussy chemicals.

What's that?

Pure ammonia. Have to keep it at twenty-eight degrees below freezing.

Yeah?

Yeah, Catchings said and turned and headed up the hallway.

They exited through a small side door and continued down the side of the boat. I wanna walk you across the barges, Catchings said, show you the temp gauges and the lines. Watch your step going up the knees. They git pretty slippery sometimes.

They climbed the steps inside huge steel uprights and made the short jump onto the barges where they came together pressed flush against what Catchings had called the knees and he saw the loops and reloops of wires around timberheads and buttons and spools. He saw wenches and ratchet connections and large hooks.

Catchings pointed at the geometry of steel cables. If you hear them lines grunting and groaning its time to step back, he said. One of them snaps it'll slice a man in two just like he was a stick of sausage.

Jo Shelby put a foot on one of the wires to test its torque that did not give.

You ever had one of these barges get loose on you? he said.

Catchings turned around as though he'd been stung from behind. Damn, man. Don't say that.

Just asking.

Shit. Don't even think it. That's voodoo talk out here. Might jinx us.

Sorry.

But to answer your question, no, if one of these things got away, all hell'd break loose, not to mention lawsuits and fines.

Catchings led him down the length of the first two barges which Jo Shelby guessed was about as long as three football fields. They walked carefully, stepping around cavils and cables, ropes and catwalks, hopping back and forth between barges wired so tightly together they seemed as one. They reached the front of the barges and Catchings stopped and turned, swung his arm in a gesture of display.

This is it, Ferguson. All ninety thousand square foot of em.

Jo Shelby turned and looked back over the rounded gray hulls of the barges and at the white-towered towboat which seemed a half-mile back. They stood at the very edge of a rake barge where the river splashed loud beneath its upward curvature. River-spray misted them and the wind blew clean and fresh across his face and the only other sounds were the creaking of the barges shifting against each other and the diesels a faint drone almost lost in the wind.

That engineer slept in the wrong place, Jo Shelby said.

You're telling me. That's why we don't like anybody else coming out here. They might learn the secret. This here's bout as peaceful as you can get, even in summer when its bout the hottest place you can be and winter when its the coldest. Cain't nobody git to you out here. Don't have to deal with everday life. Flat tires and tore up roof and refrigerator generator gone out and electric bills and politics and what the Dollar Store got on sale cause you cain't afford it noways. Don't have to deal with none of that shit out here. We're in a bubble. Only time you git a pin stuck in it is when you call home and the wife says she's got to have cavities filled or we need two new tires or there's been a break in the plumbing or my mama's gitting married for the fifth time. But then you wouldn't know bout none of that shit, would you?

Why wouldn't I?

Cause you ain't never worked a day in your life on a boat.

There was no smile when he said it. His face was grim and his eyes tiny slits with only a hint of something looking out behind them and Jo Shelby conjectured quickly that somebody's bubble had just been popped and the real world was suddenly about to rush in.

And what if I hadn't?

Catchings turned his back and looked downriver, rotated his arms like he was winding up for something then hunched his back and ground his hands together like he was popping his knuckles. Jo Shelby waited, thinking he needed to position himself because they were getting ready to have it out right there on the front of the barge where room was scarce and the river pounding underneath and the wind strong enough to blow a man off guard if he was not flat-footed. Then Catchings turned back around grinning from ear to ear. If you ain't never been on a boat then I guess I get the privilege of living part of my life all over again and taking you on as a silent partner in apprenticeship.

I'm not sure I git your drift. You oughtta be mad enough to throw me over.

Oughtta be. But the captain liked somethin about you.

You think he knows?

Has to.

How'd you?

Them towboat names you gave. He spit to the side. Bogus as hell. Captain knew it, too. He just played along.

How'd you know?

Don't. That's just how I read it.

Why'd he let me stay?

He spit again and studied the river then looked back at him. Reckon cause he's a crusty old fart and likes folks that got gumption. Besides, he needed a deckhand something bad. Shit. We git to New Orleans a deckhand shy and the inspectors take note of that, we might lose our contract. Now that would be some kind of bad news. For everbody.

Guess that makes me a trainee, huh?

Yep. We're going to do a little OJT out here and whether the captain knows or not he won't care by tomorrow morning. Have a seat and let me go over some things with you.

Jo Shelby squatted on a button and Catchings sat on a timberhead and splayed his legs and proceeded to tell him about the fine mechanics of towboating, about the pop-off valve and temperature gauges, what unloading would be like at New Orleans and the reloading and how the inspection would proceed. He pointed with his hand to the pieces of machinery and equipment and lines involved, all the way down to the size of the lines and the ropes and which ones went where. He briefed him on what to check and clean first and the priorities on down from that. He told him about the crewmembers and their temperaments and how to handle them as if he were some amateur psychologist of river folk suddenly elevated to professorship. He told his own story, about beginnings on the river and how somebody had to teach him and his goal was to become a towboat captain no matter how long it took, that everybody had to start somewhere and shared the philosophy handed down to him by his father that it's not how long you've been here on this earth but what you accomplish while you're here and quoted a proverb from the Bible about people perishing if they didn't have a vision. When he finished, he asked if there were any questions.

Naw. Guess you bout covered it.

They returned to the towboat and Catchings showed him the rest of the layout then left to return to his duties.

Jo Shelby leaned against the side railing of the boat and studied once more the river and its muddy beauty and tried to break down in his mind where all the water came from and how it kept coming without ever ending and that it had probably been like that since the first sunrise and wouldn't stop until the last sunset. He figured that might be the closest to eternity he ever got, riding the Mississippi.

He looked at his watch. A little after five. Time for a smoke. He climbed up to the third deck just beneath the pilothouse where he could see out over the water and the land beyond the river and walked to the starboard side where he could see the sun going down. He thumped out another cigarette and noted he only had four left. Leaning on his forearms, he watched the sun become one color then another beneath a shingling of clouds that glowed orange and pink and yellow then climbed in purple heaps like the ghost mountains of a far-away land. In the rose twilight he noted, too, new colors the river took on, gun-metal blue in the quieter slackwaters along the shore and sparkling bluish silver in the main channel and he studied the rippling path of gold the sun laid down across the water and the dark composite shadow of land and saw-toothed trees overtaking the river and held all of that in his vision and smoked until the last cusp of light was driven down behind the levee and he thought of the home and family that was no more and the Athen who was and others, too, in that land strange in every way but its name.

A bell sounded below and the captain hollered at him on his way down from the pilothouse and told him it was time to eat. He flipped the spent cigarette over the rail and lost sight of it in the shadows.

After supper Jo Shelby went out onto the deck and walked around the boat, looking for a place to sit and smoke. He found one toward the stern and settled into a coil of rope at the base of one of the cranes and leaned back against its steel-bolted upright, ankle-crossing his boots on a five gallon can. He rooted his lighter from his jeans pocket and pulled one of his last cigarettes from the flattened pack, lit it and watched the smoke trail out behind the boat on the cool breeze. He had rationed out his remaining cigarettes, giving each a time—one after supper, one at his first shift break, one after breakfast, and one midmorning. By then they'd be in Natchez and he could buy more. A boat wouldn't go by Natchez and not stop.

He couldn't see his watch but guessed it was close to seven. It was near dark where he was except for the rear lights of the boat reflecting dimly off the water. The sun's pink afterglow was directly in front of him and not to his left where he thought west was then he remembered something Catchings had said earlier, that the river didn't run north and south like most folks thought but east and west. He watched the passing lights along the levee and their quivering reflections in the dark luster of the river that whispered and unscrolled beneath him like a mighty energy continually rebirthing itself. The only sound was the muffled rumble of the diesels and the soft lapping of water against the sides of the boat and the barges and the occasional horn burst of an approaching tow. He tilted his head back and saw the cloudless night sky aswarm with stars. He tried to remember the last time he had seen them like that and the gleam of their diamond-brightness touched him with memories of camp-outs in his backyard and camporees the one year he was in scouts. He spotted a few of the constellations his scoutmaster had taught him to identify. The Big Dipper. The Lady in the Chair. The Hunter. He wondered to what end they rose and set, never going anywhere. He held the gaze a little longer and saw the blinking lights of an airplane and watched its course, as though it were threading its way through the firmament. Low on the sky an evening star shone bright as a small moon and cast a single silver streak across the river and he looked around for the moon but it had not yet risen.

The breezes were cool coming off the water and billowed his shirt from time to time. He took off his cap to feel the wind in his hair. He smoked. There were flashes of heat lightning in the distance and faint glows along the horizon from city lights far removed. Nearby lights from the shore bled across the water and rippled in its current like silver fish. Occasionally they moved north and south and he guessed those were headlights from vehicles traveling the levee. He remembered a story his grandfather told, about driving from Memphis to New Orleans on the levee, that it took three days but they could have made it in two if they hadn't stopped in every dirt hole bar and spent most of the afternoons drinking. Twice there came blasts from other tows, like beasts bellowing in the night, and he watched them as they slid past, long and black and nameless. He cocked his ears from side to side and listened for the river's own sound for he knew it had to have one, something that big and moving that fast, and he heard in the river the murmur of the land, how it would sound if it could talk, and he gave to it that power . . . and listened . . . and the story of his family unspooled once more, raveled about him, and the message was one of pain and uncertainty and dim hopes, that he might find them and he might not, but that he was doing the right thing and that was what he needed to hear one more time.

His cigarette had burned down to his fingers and glowed faintly in the gusts of air. He pinched it between his thumb and forefinger and took a final drag then dropped it and crushed the stub under his heel. He looked back up at the anonymous dark and contemplated again its vastness, that it canvassed another place far away where his bloodkin sat on the long porch of a house of many rooms and spoke of the day's work and crops tended and movement of cattle on the spread and their children's future and glanced up from time to time and gazed upon the same configuration of eternity as he. He saw it like that in his mind's eye, in those fragments of Zorro and The Cisco Kid, in that memory of Saturday matinees which was as far as he ever got from his anchored world. The Hacienda Michopa. A huge house of lavish furnishings and fineries within a walled enclosure of archways and courtyards and patios and fountains. Where dark-headed señoritas with mysterious eyes sat with bright flowers in their hair and spoke of their true-loves and their dream days of marriage and children and prosperity. Fields of cotton and corn and soybeans and rice, and whatever else a Southerner might grow that he could have taken with him and thousands of acres of cattle and horses, stretching from one side of the horizon to the other, the magnificent life of a landed gentry preserved in its own selfish history, and all he had to do was get there.

He was thinking of what was ahead of him when he glimpsed the sight in the east, a full-blooded moon rising over the levee. He watched its slow climb and thought how everything seems to move in slow motion on a river or maybe that was just God's normal time and everything and everybody else was out of step in their own rush to get somewhere in life. He watched it clear the palisaded trees and hover in a darkness where its brilliance blew away the stars and any other light that wanted to shine that evening and reminded him the tricks time can play on a person. It seemed like yesteryear he had seen it through the garage doorway with her and it was only yestereve. She would have driven back to the university, back to a world he knew only through her eyes. Classes and homework and term papers like nothing in high school. Sororities and fraternities that made you feel like somebody and Saturday football games where you got to be the somebody you'd always wanted to be. Something new to eat called pizza and liquor at a place called the "tin shack" back off in the woods in the next county and dancing past midnight at The Peabody in Memphis. He never asked who with. Knowing she had changed as much as she had was enough. Six years is a long time not to see a person's face, then to see it and wonder if it was the same one you saw last. And to see it for such a short while then not again. To remember her tall and slim with a near featureless body, her hair in a ponytail and wearing nothing but blue jeans and cowboy boots, then see her in a dress and high heels, beautiful as an angel given up by the night with a face as lovely as any he'd seen at the picture show, a body as grown, a voice and kiss that said she had forgotten the worst and remembered all that was the best and would he please stay where he belonged and forget this foolish notion. And he almost did and still could. It was not too late to turn back. He turned sideways and fixed his vision more firmly on the illumined spectacle that fired the river with its changing color as it slowly ascended and wondered if he should and if he shouldn't till wondering became one with the dull throbbing of the engines and the gurgle and whisper of the river and his eyes grew weary of watching and his ears of listening. He went to his room, lay on his bunk and read the two letters once more, forcing his thinking in the direction of an enchanted land beyond, and slept.

TIME PASSES SLOWLY on a river when all one has to do is walk barges three football fields long and check lines and temperature gauges. He looked for things to do. He mopped decks he had mopped hours before and polished brass fixtures and cleaned spotlights and uncoiled and recoiled ropes and chains into neater piles. He visited with Louise, the cook, and Mr. Chiz, an older man who was the engineer, and climbed a time or two into the pilothouse and chatted with the captain. He read all of the magazines in the lounge that included a National Geographic and a two-year-old copy of Reader's Digest and found a dog-earred copy of Pilgrim's Progress. Mr. Chiz said it had been there ever since he'd started work on the boat and no one seemed to know who it belonged to. He read it, too, in his waking off hours.

He ran out of cigarettes as predicted and learned the tow would not stop in Natchez or anywhere else unless there was an emergency or equipment failure. Mr Chiz gave him a pack of Chesterfields and said he could pay him back when they got to New Orleans.

He worked his rotation, caught a nap in the morning after breakfast and one after an evening smoke on deck. He ate his meals in silence with the others, who spoke among themselves but rarely to him. Once one asked him where he came from. He said he was from Rome which raised a brow or two then told them Rome, Mississippi, that he just kind of fell into working on the river. Catchings looked at him when he said it and winked. He always told Louise the food was good and she always thanked him and seemed surprised.

Once he pulled a chair from his room and sat on deck and watched the river and its moving world, looking to see something other than willows and cottonwoods and sandbars matted with twisted debris.

He pondered the slackwaters where the river rolled around a point and the water eddied back upriver and he observed people pole-fishing for gar and bass and crappie under the points in the lake-like mirror smoothness. He remembered ponds he and his father had fished that were of equal calm and stillness and the catch they pulled from them, the way his mother padded them back and forth in her palms with flour and fried them in an iron skillet over an open fire, right there on the spot with their lines still in the water. He remembered the time the hook caught in his nose and how she teased it out with steady and gentle fingers, as though it might have been an errant stitching on a shirt she was sewing for him, murmuring all the time, it's going to be all right, it's going to be all right. And it was. He saw a man atop a mule pulling a wagon, a family picnicking under a tree, some old folks sitting on a porch and recalled hayrides through the fields on chilled autumn nights, homemade ice cream beneath the big oak on Sunday afternoons, and long summer evenings on their porch, the endless stream of stories. The images flashed before him as though they came straight from the shattered light reflecting off the river. Other fragments got caught up in the stream as well. A laugh. A look. The smell of his mother's fragrance when she tucked him in and the words she said each night: Good night, sleep tight, pleasant dreams till the morning light. Pleasant dreams till the morning light. Pleasant dreams till . . . *When you grow up, boy, you need to find you a woman just like your mama . . . just like your mama.* All that once was and never would be again. A knot rose in his throat and a film of moisture slid over his eyes and he wiped away the gathering tears before they fell or anyone saw.

He looked for a paddle wheel riverboat like the kind he'd read about in books but one never passed. Catchings said they'd quit running the year before. Not enough money. There was always a tow passing by and he counted the barges, remembering what the captain said about the river being the life artery of the country, if not its heart.

He did not see the towns and cities he had expected nor did they stop at any and there were no people on the banks at Vicksburg and Natchez waving and shouting when they passed. Whatever tales and stories he had read and heard about the river were just that and he soon learned the river did what the man in the song said, it just kept rolling along.

By breakfast the second day he began seeing dry docks and gravel piles and tow fleets along the banks, then streams of smoke smudging the sky and not long afterward the smokestacks they came from. The scene was that of a forest of steel afire and beyond it tall concrete buildings rising through the dirty gray as if they were all part of a smoking inferno.

They passed freighters and large ships at anchor in the river waiting to dock and others moored to docks that stretched end on end the length of the city. Mr. Chiz told him that Baton Rouge was about as busy a port as New Orleans, that huge oceangoing ships could navigate there with no problem at all and pointed them out and the flags they flew, the countries the flags represented. From here on the river was one busy street.

The river came alive as they passed one small town after another, each with its own jungle of stacks and fury of smoke, names many of which he could not pronounce and had never before heard, Plaquemine, Geismar, Vacherie, Welcome Covenant, Darrow, Burnside, Reserve, La Place.

By midafternoon New Orleans came into sight, its tall buildings gray and ghostlike through the heat-haze of the land, rising just beyond the shore's greenery it seemed, on land flat as the Delta, like a smoky cluster of blocks put down by a child. He watched awhile then walked the barges one more time and checked the temp gauges and stood on the top step of the knees and watched as the city neared.

Catchings climbed up the steps and joined him and together they watched the outlying sprawl of steel and smokestacks materialize and the afternoon sun bathed them with a light that somehow beautified even them. There were old warehouses with low-canted tin roofs and boat sheds leaning like dog-trot farm shacks sunk in water and behind them three and four-storied homes with balconies of iron grillwork where laundry hung and beyond all that, bunched together in one place, the tall buildings he had seen from far away, their tops just be-

neath scudding tufts of clouds. Along the boardwalk in front of the
wharves he glimpsed people strolling in fine clothes and women carrying parasols pushing small children in strollers. He looked back at
Catchings. What day is it? he said.

Sunday.

Sunday?

Yeah. That's what I said. Don't you keep up with time?

I know time all right. Just can't keep up with it.

How's that?

Another long story.

Damn, Jo Shelby. You ain't lived that long.

Might not seem like it to nobody else. He looked back at the people mingling and ambling along the street that curved with the river
and mumbled to himself.

Sunday. Well I'll be damn.

Something special about Sunday with you?

Nope. Just didn't know it was Sunday. He didn't tell him he'd not
known one day from the next for six years and never thought to ask or
check when he got out and had never given any thought to the time,
much less the day, because his head was too full of other thoughts that
had little to do with ordinary time. He glanced down at his wristwatch
then up at the sun. It seemed too hot for four o'clock.

The tow entered a wide turn in the river and glided beneath a long
trestle bridge. He watched the city sweep past then looked downriver
at the endless files of wharves, anchored barges, tankers and ships of
all sizes and shapes. He saw tall cranes with booms and long rectilinear shafts extending from buildings behind the wharves and guessed
they were part of the loading and unloading process. Sea gulls
squeaked and swooped overhead and horns from vessels both near and
far away blew, tugboats crisscrossed the river in front of them and all
of it seemed so scrambled he thought it would take as many days to
dock as it did to get there.

A tug met them midriver and guided them alongside a dock. He
caught ropes thrown to him and looped them around timberheads and

cavils and helped fit fuel hoses for the chemicals to be pressured off into big pillbox tanks ashore. He said good-bye to Catchings and Mr. Chiz and found the captain and asked if he could be paid, that he wouldn't be staying for the trip back upriver. The captain took it with an even temper and said he had to go to petty cash to pay him.

He sat on a timberhead and waited.

The captain returned with his pay. Fifty dollars in cash. He said he paid him a little extra because he'd worked some overtime. Jo Shelby asked about boats going to Mexico. He said it wouldn't be easy since he had so little experience on the river much less the Gulf or the waterway, but told him where to go to put his name in for a freighter or tanker to Brownsville or Matamoros adding that he'd be better off going to Matamoros since he could pass through customs easier there. He thanked the captain, shook his hand and got his knapsack from his cabin.

From the port side near the galley he stepped up onto the dock amid thick-muscled men in sleeveless T-shirts scurrying to and fro shouting at one another, swinging cranes and driving cargo-loaded vehicles around like it was the last day on Earth. He weaved his way through their rough and scattered energy and headed in the direction he thought he was supposed to go.

He read the names across the warehouses as he walked and came finally to the one that said Gulf Transport and climbed a set of side stairs to a door labeled OFFICE. There was a middle-age woman of stylish appearance behind the counter. He removed his hat. He told her why he was there and who sent him. She nodded politely and gave him a sheet of paper and pencil and asked him to fill out the application. He sat in a small chair behind him against a colorless wall and wrote down his name and address and other personal information the words requested. He came to the part that said references and he paused and scratched his head with the end of the pencil. He wrote down Captain James Priddy, Baxter Towing then stopped and thought again, then wrote Captain John Mosby Ferguson, Ferguson Towing, then Memphis Transport without a captain. He gave the paper back to her and she took it and smiled and looked over it. She told him there was a job for him if he wanted it, leaving first thing in the morning, a tanker headed for Brownsville. He asked if it was already docked and she said it would dock later and load and he asked if he could stay on board the night that he didn't have a place to stay. She asked him to sit and wait.

He could hear the static of a two-way radio somewhere in another room and her voice mumbling through the walls. She returned to the counter and told him there should be no problem, but he would have to wait an hour or two until the boat docked. He thanked her and filled out more papers she said were necessary and asked if he had a passport. He asked what a passport was and she said nevermind, that he probably wouldn't need it anyway, but that sometimes they had to dock at Matamoros in Mexico.

You mean I gotta have a passport to git into Mexico?

If you're going to be there awhile, you do. Otherwise you just get a visa.

How do I git a visa?

They can give you one at the border. It's called a tourist visa. You'll need your driver's license, some form of indentification for it. But you will be coming back, won't you? I mean, the captain's expecting you to make the roundtrip.

Yessum. I'm coming back.

After he had thanked her and closed the door, he told himself that he really hadn't lied. He was coming back. Some day.

THREE

THE FIRST TIME he saw the roundness of the world he was standing in a Delta cotton field far from buildings or trees or lightwires and the second time was not much different. Surrounding him now was nothing but wind-plowed water flecked with foam and above him a sky that changed only at sunrise and at sunset and at night wheeled its mythical patterns in the self-same sequence he had known since childhood, as though that was all there was and ever would be, as though movement was an illusion and the vessel on which he sailed yet one more prison he had somehow managed to fall into.

The sun blistered his skin during the day and the wind chilled it at night and it seemed there was no escaping either. If he stayed in his small room, his stomach yawed and pitched with the ship and everything that had gone into it came out until there was just air and not much of that left either. Stay on deck and look at what's causin it and it'll go away, somebody told him. So he did and the sickness left him for a while. But it was always there, waiting for him.

When he boarded and handed his papers to the first mate, he was informed of his routine and duties and directed to his room and assigned his bunk. That was all and every bit of it was accomplished in less than ten minutes and without a kind word. The rest of the large boat he discovered for himself in his off hours. He paced it off from bow to stern and guessed its length at five hundred feet. He learned what the forecastle was and the house amidships which contained the pilothouse and quarters for a few of the crew, and the "poop" which was a topside deck at the stern. He explored all of these as well as the main machinery spaces and pump room, the higher levels of deckhouses and dining room and crew's lounge and the maze of cargo areas that were divided into individual tanks and the watertight compartments kept empty to keep the tanker afloat should something happen. He asked few questions and learned mostly by watching and listening.

His chores were fewer and simpler than on the tow and he quickly learned the worlds of tows and tankers were as different as the Delta and the hills. On a tanker a deckhand was a deckhand and nothing else, someone who swept and mopped decks and hallways and rooms, made up beds, emptied trashcans, cleaned putrid toilets, and polished brass fixtures if there was time left over. In the hierarchy of men at sea, he was low man on the totem pole.

He drew a day shift which made the transition easier but sleep at night was a dream hard to come by. There was the groaning and grinding of the rocking ship, the nausea and vomiting, pain when his sunburned skin moved against the starched sheets. What sleep did come moved in and out of him, through him, like wind through a tunnel. He caught naps when he could and sat on deck wherever he could find shade and browsed through year-old magazines he found in the crew's lounge.

His roommate was a small, older man from Venezuela who spoke little English but between them they knitted a language of utility and camaraderie and found a trust in the silences in between. His name was Edgardo and he had been at sea since he was nineteen, he told him, flashing the number on his fingers. He had no family and knew no other home. Jo Shelby pointed a finger at himself and nodded and the man grinned and said somos hermanos, we brothers, and pulled a bottle from beneath his bunk so they could drink a toast. The liquid was clear as water and went through him like a string of hot barbed wire. Edgardo told him it was tequila and would take away the sickness of the sea but Jo Shelby told him with a pantomime of hands he'd rather keep the sickness than be cut up and burned alive and they laughed together and drank again.

He told Edgardo his story and why he had to go to Mexico and Edgardo listened with steady eyes and showed no emotion. Then he reached into his knapsack and pulled out the gun and the little man's eyes widened and he took another drink and said he was loco, that he could not get into Mexico with a gun. He told him the gun was worth many dollars and Edgardo only shook his head and said it was worth nothing if he was in jail and he would be in jail a long time, that in Mexico no one cared about gringos and he would have to pay many more dollars than the gun was worth to get out of jail. He commenced pacing around the small room, gibbering Spanish, gesturing wildly with his hands. Jo Shelby let him finish the fandango then said it didn't matter, that he was going to Mexico anyway and Edgardo threw up his hands and went to bed.

He read and reread the letters and studied the map, charting the course he must take. He found a pencil and drew lines from place to place, between names he remembered from the letters and some he did not—Matamoros, Monterrey, Saltillo, Matehuala, San Luis Potosí, Querétaro. He wondered how he would travel and how he would eat and sleep, not knowing the language of the people. He showed the map to his new friend, but Edgardo only shook his head and twirled a finger at his temple. Did they have buses and trains, could he hitchhike, he asked, holding out his thumb. Edgardo stood up, looked through the small portal and said again he was crazy, gesturing that he should stay on the ship. Jo Shelby tried to explain that he could not stay, that he had to find his people, that he had no one else in all the world. Edgardo narrowed his eyes and thumped his thumb against his chest.

Yo sólo me tengo a mí. No necesito a nadie más.

The words he did not know, but the message brimming from the man's eyes was clear and he nodded he understood and nothing more was said. But he wondered long afterwards about that kind of loneliness, a person having only himself and nothing more and no need of nothing more. *Family is first and foremost above everything else in life, boy, except God, and don't you never forget it.* He had not forgotten. But a family that's dead and gone couldn't love him, couldn't hug him and tell him everything's going to be all right, and watch him make something of himself and he was glad more than ever he was going to Mexico.

The ship sailed for three days and on the third day they passed more ships than usual and at midmorning he saw land off the starboard and further in the distance on the horizon a lighthouse. He asked a deck mate and the deck mate told him they had just passed South Padre Island and the lighthouse ahead was Port Isabel but the ship would go further inland to the Port of Brownsville and dock there.

He performed his morning chores and when there was nothing more to do collected his belongings and packed his knapsack and climbed the steps to the pilothouse. He knocked on the door and the captain came out. He told him he was going ashore and would not be returning and explained his reasons. The captain, a square-shouldered and square-faced man that reminded him of an older Catchings, listened, then grunted and muttered something about deckhands being a dime a dozen, then turned and entered the pilothouse. He did not tell him to wait but Jo Shelby waited. He returned in the same huff in which he had left and shelled out six twenty-dollar bills and a ten which he said was out of petty cash, that he wasn't paying him for his total three twelve-hour shifts because he was jumping ship then turned and entered again the pilothouse before Jo Shelby could tell him the money didn't matter, that all he wanted to do was to get to Brownsville and he had done that and was much obliged.

He found Edgardo in the aft section assisting with the pumps and told him good-bye and Edgardo wiped his brow with his hand and told him once more that he was loco, that he should stay on the ship. He asked him how to get to Mexico and Edgardo told him to get a taxi and tell the driver he wanted to go to the bridge and to have his passport ready.

But I don't have a passport.

You no have pasaporte?

Nope.

No pasaporte. No pasaporte, he muttered to himself and shook his head in bewilderment. No pasaporte y una pistola. I take back. You no loco.

Much obliged. I didn't think I was.

You muchísimo loco, he said. No pasaporte, no México. No pasaporte y una pistola, the caboosa. Comprende?

Yeah. All right. But the lady said I could get something called a visa, you know, for visiting.

Cómo?

Visa. I can get a visa.

Oh, sí. Visa. Visa, yes. But that for only short time. Not long time.

And she said my driver's license would do.

Driver's license, he said and shook his head wistfully. I do not know about driver's license. Maybe. I do not know.

All right. I'll just do the best I can, and they shook hands and wished each other well and he left.

He made his way down the metal gangway and onto the wharf and asked a dockworker where he could catch a taxi. The man pointed toward a passageway between two warehouses and said he might get one at the street on the other side but good luck, that Brownsville wasn't New Orleans and there weren't many taxis.

The street was crowded and lined with cars but he saw none that looked like a taxi. He thumped out a cigarette, lit it and waited. The sun was hot but the air was crisp and the heat had a clean, uplifting feeling about it. For the first time he noted the palm trees up and down the street and thought that strange, palm trees in Texas. Texas was supposed to be sagebrush and desert. He finished the cigarette and lit another. Cars came and went but still no taxi. There was a small store across the street that looked like it had been blown down and propped back up several times. A large Grapette sign hung from the awning. He remembered how good they tasted.

He was to go get one when a white Ford with a green light on top approached. He stepped onto the street and waved his arm. The driver leaned his head through the open window and asked where he was going.

Mexico.

The driver nodded, and Jo Shelby got in and the car lurched forward.

How much is it to the border? Jo Shelby said.

Five bucks to the bridge.

That where I cross over?

Yep. At one of em.

There's more than one.

Yep. Two. The new and the old.

Which one'll git me into Mexico the fastest?

The driver turned and regarded him momentarily with casual scrutiny, then turned back around and placed his hands on the steering wheel. I think the old one might be best for you, he said.

That's where I wanna go.

They crossed a stretch of highway where the land on either side was parched and lifeless. Weather-beaten shacks that looked unlived-in and stores with unpainted siding and signs tilted over doorways. Dust-coated cars parked in small yards where children played and no grass grew. Now and then a palm tree rose out of the ground and lay against the sky like a stemmed star pasted on blue canvas.

This place looks like a desert, he said.

Been in a drought for some time. You ain't seen nothing yet. Wait'll you get into Mexico.

They rode on. He thought about the gun and what Edgardo had said. He patted its hard shape in the knapsack and thought.

They crossed what had to be the Rio Grande and he commented but the driver said it was the Resaca de la Guerra, an old tributary of the Rio Grande that went nowhere. They continued on, entered the outskirts of the town, passed through the downtown, buildings that looked the same as any town he'd ever been through. He leaned his head slightly out the open window to see a theater marquee, as if he might stop a spell and see something he hadn't seen in six years. A STAR IS BORN the bright red letters said, the "N" dangling where it had slipped off its rails. There were names beneath the title but the only one he recognized was Judy Garland's. The first time his parents took him to the picture show was in Clarksdale and The Wizard of Oz was playing. He wanted to go again but it was there only a short time and moved on like all movies do. But he never forgot the song, the one his mother would hum singing him to sleep. He hadn't seen many rainbows in his time, but the song made you believe they were there, and he began humming it softly to himself.

The taxi turned a corner and in the distance he saw a bridge.

That it up ahead?

Nope, the driver said. That's the new bridge.

He drove almost to the new bridge then made a right turn, then a left, then another left and drove for a block or two. Jo Shelby saw the second bridge, a steel framework of vertical and slanting uprights and crosspieces, trusses and plates on concrete pilings that looked like four bridges built separately then hooked together. In the center there were upright girders and pivot wheels on a track so the bridge could separate and turn to let boats on the Rio Grande pass.

The car stopped and he paid the driver five dollars and fifty cents, which was what the meter said. The man took the money but his left hand remained there, open-palmed holding the bills and change.

That's all ain't it, he said.

What about the tip?

Tip?

Yeah. Something a little extra for the info I give ya.

I ain't got much. Didn't know I was gonna have to pay for anything you said.

The man made a fist around the money. Never mind buddy. Good luck, and he geared the car into low and scratched off.

He stood for a minute and studied the situation. A median divided the street leading up to the bridge and on the median sat a small booth and in the booth a man in a brown uniform seemed to be collecting money from people entering and leaving the bridge. Past the booth the street merged again and crossed the bridge and along the left side of the trestle ran a narrow catwalk where people strolled. Some coming, some going. He turned and looked behind him. There was a row of buildings that housed commercial stores and midblock an alley that ran between them. What he had to do he could do there. He crossed the street between two slow-moving cars and stepped up onto the curbed sidewalk. Cars were parked in front of the stores and a few people were window shopping. A shopkeeper spoke with two customers looking at a window display of shoes. They looked up and stopped talking, regarding Jo Shelby with detached suspicion, then resumed their discussion.

He looked both ways before entering the alley. He walked past garbage cans and empty boxes, the refuse of several days. A cat came out and scurried underfoot and he stepped in an oil-slick puddle to avoid it. Halfway down he stopped and looked both ways again and saw no one. He removed his knapsack from his back and swung it atop a garbage can. He unbuckled the top flap and flipped it back and looked left and right once more before retrieving the holstered pistol. He unsnapped the holster flap and removed the gun and hiked his pants leg and slid the gun barrel into his boot, then lowered his pants leg and smoothed and straightened it around the boot. He took a few steps to see how it felt and it slid a few inches further between the bootleather and his shin. It moved no further. He took a few more steps. The barrel rubbed against his ankle but he wasn't going far and figured he could get along with a blister or two which he figured was the worst that could happen.

He walked back, thinking about the empty holster and how he would explain it. He stopped short of the small booth in front of the bridge and thought some more. The gun was stolen in Brownsville, he was keeping the holster because it was a gift from his grandfather and he needed it to remember him by. He thought a while longer to let the story sink in until it felt right then approached the booth. The man inside looked at him and extended a cupped hand.

It costs to cross? Jo Shelby said.

Yessir. Five cents.

He rummaged in his pocket and came up with a nickel and gave it to the man and passed on. He stepped up onto the metal walkway and made his way slowly across the catwalk, the gun barrel and cylinder rubbing against his anklebone and shin. The walkway shook and jarred with the passing traffic and the gun in his boot shook and jarred with it. The air was hot and the sky cloudless and the sun's rays bounced off the steel girders. He looked down and saw a riverbed that might have been a Rio Grande but now was home to a small stream that trickled around its rocks. Halfway across he leaned his head over the railing and looked down and studied the rotating mechanisms he had seen at a distance but still could not put it together in his mind how it worked. He remembered something his granddaddy had said about swing bridges on the Mississippi and decided that was what it was but wondered if it had ever swung considering the anemic condition of the river below.

He grew nearer the opposite side and saw men in military dress leaning from glass-enclosed booths, stopping cars and peering into them and waving them on. Above them a large sign said BIEN-VENIDOS A MEXICO. The red letters and the green border around them were weather-faded and badly in need of a paint job. He remembered the word from Edgardo who had taught him a handful of Spanish and he stood and smiled and wondered how long he'd feel welcome, then passed beneath the metal canopy of the checkpoint and was headed down the street when an accented voice cried out to him.

Alto!

He stopped and looked to his right. A border guard was chopping the air with his arm and waving a pointed finger toward a small concrete-block building to his right. He turned and walked toward the building as though that had been his intention all along and entered the open doorway. There was a row of counters and narrow passageways between the counters, like checkout counters at a store, and people in brown uniforms milling behind the counters talking and smoking as though they had nothing better to do. The tan-plastered walls were chipped and peeling and bare except for a few posters about Mexico. Inside the air was hot and still and unmoved by the small floor fan at the back of the room. A young couple stood at one of the counters and he went and stood behind them but a short heavyset woman of deep-brown complexion motioned him to the next one.

Pasaporte, she said.

I ain't got none.

Visa?

I ain't got that neither.

You need visa. How long you be in Mexico?

Don't know.

You tourist? You going to Matamoros to shop?

He thought a moment. Yeah. I'm going there. Need to do a little shopping.

She handed him a pencil and some papers to fill out and said she would need to see some identification, driver's license or birth certificate or anything official that would identify him. She pointed to a row of classroom-looking chairs along the wall behind him and told him to fill out the papers and come back with his identification ready.

He took a seat and mindful of the gun kept his left leg slightly outstretched to keep the pantsleg from crawling upward above the boot top where the heel of the butt rested. He studied the foreign forms before him. He decided the word Declare meant he didn't have much and checked No and checked No in all the other blocks thinking that would get him through faster, that checking a Yes might bring more attention. He opened his billfold and took out his driver's license which had long since expired and hoped the woman wouldn't notice the faded dates. He eased himself out of the deskchair and walked back to the counter, and handing the papers to the woman along with his driver's license. She studied the papers in the habit one might routine mail then looked at the driver's license. She motioned to two men of equal official dress leaning with their legs half-cocked against a nearby wall smoking and talking. They walked over and she showed them the license.

He waited.

The men took the driver's license and examined it, each in turn, and nodded in unison, and one handed it back to her.

No good, she said. You driver's license it no good. Too old.

Something quick, he said to himself. He had to think of something quick. That's right, he said. It's out of date cause the new one they sent me got lost in the mail. But it shows I'm an American. Ain't that all you need to know, that I'm a American from the United States?

She looked at him with vacant eyes and looked at the two men standing beside her. One of them jibbered something in Spanish to her then shrugged and turned and walked away and the other followed. She looked around the room as if to see if there were others watching then looked back at him and leaned over the counter and spoke to him in a tone above a whisper.

It is small mistake, she said. For small fee we correct.

What?

You license, it no is good. But for twenty dollar we make good and you get visa. You understand?

He looked around the room to see, too, if anyone was watching and no one was then turned his eyes back on the woman. You mean, if I pay you twenty dollars, I get a visa?

Sí. Claro.

But I no have much money.

She shrugged.

He pulled out his billfold once more and opened it and fingered out a twenty dollar bill and gave it to the woman. She pulled out a small piece of pink paper from a drawer and laid it on the counter in a meticulous fashion and wrote on it, then stamped it and handed it to him.

You visa. Pase, she said and motioned with her hand for him to move through the narrow aisle.

He walked carefully and slowly, not knowing where he was supposed to go. The door at the rear beside the fan said SALIDA and below it EXIT and he moved in that direction.

Alto! someone shouted from behind.

He turned and one of the men who had examined his license was pointing toward a long narrow platform no higher than a riser. The man walked quickly toward him.

Aquí, he said and pointed toward his knapsack.

He laid the knapsack on the platform and stood back.

Qué hay en su maleta?

What?

Su maleta. Abrala, por favor, the man said pointing and gesturing with his hands for him to open it.

He unhooked the straps and flipped back the flap.

The man motioned for him to take everything out.

He pulled out the clothes he had left plus toiletries he'd purchased from a mate on the tanker, then the map and letters and other items and last the leather holster. The man went through each, sorting and unfolding, folding back, then came to the holster.

Qué es esto?

I don't understand.

No tiene pistola?

No. I don't have it no more.

Ya no la tiene?

Jo Shelby turned and looked at the woman at the counter who was watching and spoke to her. Tell him I don't have the gun, he said. It got stole in Brownsville. My granddaddy who's dead gave it to me. I kept the holster cause it was his. Comprende? He had heard Edgardo use the word and it just popped out as though it had been primed.

She shook her head and spoke to the guard and he spoke back and she spoke back and they went on like that in Spanish for a few minutes, like two people arguing with nothing to argue over. Her voice was louder and her hands moving more and he got the opinion she was winning then she turned back toward him.

He want to know why you bring to Mexico if no have gun, she

said.

He'd already thought ahead. Wanted to buy me a genuine Mexican pistol to put in it, he said. A antique one. You know. Old. Mucho old. Heard ya'll had the best.

She turned to the guard again and repeated what he had said but must have added a lot of her own. It seemed it took them forever to say the little that needed to be said. The guard didn't know she had twenty dollars from him and he braced himself to get hit up for more when finally the guard slapped his pants legs with his hands and motioned for him to put everything back in the knapsack. He repacked the items and buckled the flap and stood and waited.

Pase, the man said and pointed toward the back door above which the words SALIDA and EXIT were written.

Outside the street curved sharply left from the bridge then took a long right arc. He followed it until it straightened and broadened into a wider cobbled boulevard with small trees down a narrow median, their slender trunks painted white. There were small shops and cafés on either side of the street and along the cracked and crumbling sidewalks people moved in the methodical slowness of window-shoppers. By their dress and cameras the American tourists sorted out easily from the Mexicans and he was thankful he wore cowboy boots and blue jeans and a T-shirt, then remembered his cap and decided that marked him, that what a person wears on his head and the way he wears it can nail him pretty good. Few vehicles traveled the street and the ones he saw were old American cars and trucks, discards he guessed from used car lots across the border, purchased at a discount, or stolen and smuggled across.

He walked on, passing a collection of low-slung adobe and concrete-block buildings of varying pastel colors with pane-less windows and red-tiled and corrugated tin roofs and rebar projecting upward from some, like the steel knitting of something unfinished, something yet to be. Mothers stood in doorways holding babies and men young and old sat on doorsteps and along curbs smoking and spitting. Others he saw sat in slat-back chairs around wooden tables at open air cafés where faded signs overhead said Cantina and Bar and jackel-eared curs commaed up under carwheels and against tree trunks and all of them, the dogs too, stared at him from dark faces, with the cold silence befitting a stranger come to town. It was like that for several blocks and his ankle was in pain from the friction of metal on bone and stung, he knew, from a blister already formed and burst but he kept on. The air smelled of rotting garbage thrown in the streets and backyard sewage. The dogs he passed were the scrawniest most disease-infested he had ever seen, and alone were enough to bring a quarantine down on the town. All he saw and smelled and heard brought new meaning to the term "another country" and he wondered if General Shelby and his men had encountered the same at Eagle Pass then remembered his grandmother's comments about disease and mosquitoes and all the other hardships that came much later and thought this might be the best it was going to get and he should count his blessings now so he could remember them later.

He thought the place surely had a downtown or square, like most small towns he had known, where there was the bustle of commerce and trade and cafés and stores, where he could stock up on food, cigarettes and other essentials he would need for the long trip south. He walked a few blocks further and the street dead-ended. He could only turn left and he took it, then another right and walked a few more blocks further, noting the continuing decay and deterioration of dwellings and people alike and decided he had gone far enough. He stopped and asked a man of uncertain mind sitting on a stoop where the downtown was and the man just cocked an ear and shook his head.

Matamoros! Where is Matamoros?

The old man rubbed his beard stubble with a purple-veined hand and knocked a fly away from his eyes and shrugged and pointed down at the ground. Aqui estamos en Matamoros.

He looked around. He remembered a small dress shop behind him and walked back to it. A young lady was hanging what looked to be shawls on a long wire in front of the shop and he stopped and tipped his cap to her.

Buenos días.

Buenas tardes, she said back to him and averted her eyes away from the sunlight.

He asked her if she spoke English. She pinched a thumb and finger together and said poco and he asked her where the downtown was. Cómo?

Downtown. Where everybody is. Stores, he said, and sculpted the air with his hands in an effort to draw her a picture of buildings, then looped his hand in a circle for the street in front of them and her eyes lit up and she giggled.

La plaza, she said and grinned and repeated the words and put her hands to her cheeks in a delicate touch of self-congratulation.

Yes. Sí. Yes. The plaza.

She giggled again and turned so the sun brought out the finer details of her face and pointed behind him, in the direction from which he had already walked and counted with her fingers. Uno, dos, tres, cuatro, cinco, seis, and gestured a right turn with her hand, entonces a la derecha, then straightened the hand and arm, entonces siga derecho. Comprende?

Go back six blocks and turn right, he said, mimicking the movement of her directions with his hand, turn right, then go straight.

Sí.

He tipped his cap again and thanked her and was walking away from her when she called out to him.

Calle Seis.

He turned and saw her standing in the middle of the sidewalk holding up six fingers and he flashed six back to her and she grinned and he turned and continued on, thinking of her beauty and how so undiscovered she was on the back streets of a place so unworthy of discovery.

He counted off the six blocks and turned right at the sixth. The sign said CALLE 6 and the one opposite CALLE ITURBIDE, a name that rang faintly in his memory, and he marked the spot in his mind, just in case he arrived at the same conclusion as others, that he was crazy and needed to high-tail it back across the border and back to the Delta where his future was as flat as the land, but where there was at least a job, and at least one person who cared for him.

There was heavier traffic on the street and more people and stores. He could tell he was getting close. He felt his stomach rumble and he stopped and looked at his watch. Half-past twelve. He had eaten a banana and a grapefruit on the tanker for breakfast but nothing more. He walked on with the thought of a hot vegetable lunch and hot biscuits and a glass of cold sweet milk.

In the distance twin bell-tower steeples rose above cluttered one-story rooftops, their bronze plating ablaze in the unchallenged sun. The cathedral rose above the square with an aura and coloration of endless antiquity. The plaza looked like a scene cut from a picture book. Tall palms fanning high over rounded shrubs and white-trunked trees. In the center, awash in a pool of sunlight, like the miniature temple of some long-forgotten religion, a blue-domed gazebo with pink-trim arches and pink pillars. Radiating from it were narrow sidewalks bordered by low-cut green hedges before which old men sat on wooden benches and looked at nothing, lovers young and old embraced or kissed or whispered to each other, drunks slept off the night before, and children chased pigeons, mindless of the hard life slumbering ahead of them. Across the plaza opposite the cathedral was a modern official-looking building with red and green and white streamers and flags of the same color flying from its windows as though it was dressed for an event of great importance. Around the square people gathered in front of small cafés and restaurants and drank and smoked. Ragged men with two-wheel pushcarts sold ice cream and cold drinks and steaming food in bread flatter than pancakes.

He saw an empty bench and walked over to it, removed his knapsack and sat down. He was in shade, and there was a slight breeze. He removed his cap for his head to cool. Overhead birds chirped and palm branches rustled stiffly and the aroma of cooked food came with the breezes and everything that passed raised a powdery white dust. The air was warm but crisp, like rare late days of spring in the Delta, when winds from the north blew away the heaviness in the air and old people walked once more in the afternoons. He looked around for a place that was private but there was none. A policeman in a brown uniform directed traffic at a far corner, but he saw no others. If he could find a restroom, he could put the gun back into the knapsack. He narrowed his focus on the establishments that ringed the area.

Edgardo had told him to beware of food sold on the street by vendors or water not bottled and ice cream because the Mexicans used water to make their ice cream, that Montezuma lurked within these things and Montezuma would give him a sickness worse than any the sea could give him, a sickness beyond the help of tequila. He asked who Montezuma was but Edgardo just flipped his hand and said that was of no importance, to just trust that Montezuma was real and to follow his advice. He swung his eyes full circle around the plaza's festive perimeter, eliminating places that looked unclean, marking those of promise until his eyes settled on one. The sign above said CAFE EL SARAPE. The people gathered around its sidewalk tables were well dressed and the single waiter attending them wore a white apron. The place looked immaculate compared to all else he had seen.

He crossed the square, then the street, and passed the occupied tables on the sidewalk. The waiter was short and portly with a thin mustache and wavy hair brushed back uniformly from his dark forehead towards the top of his neck where it flipped up in tiny curls. He spoke first in Spanish then switched to English before Jo Shelby could get a word out, as if American were branded somewhere on him like a label on a case of goods. He remembered his cap and politely tucked it under his arm.

May I help you, señor?

Yessir. I'd like something to eat.

Just one?

Yessir. I'd like to eat outside, if that's all right.

I understand, señor, but we no have tables available on the sidewalk at this time. There is one inside. It is near the window which is almost like being outside.

All right. That'll do.

The waiter led him inside through a large dimly lit room where ceiling fans wheeled slowly overhead and the sounds of an out-of-sight kitchen rattled and clinked above the jibberish of patrons who observed him with sidelong glances affording an interruption, and leaned close to each other as though there might be a secret somewhere in their chatter. He discounted the brief and scattered attention and followed the waiter to a table where there was indeed a wide view, taking in the plaza. The open air arrangement meant whatever was on the outside could come inside and vice versa. He removed his knapsack and placed it on the floor beside a small chair and carefully eased himself into the chair and adjusted his right leg beneath the table so it stretched outward and tilted the chair to one side, moving a shoulderstrap of the knapsack under the leg as he did, as Edgardo had advised him to do to prevent theft of his only possessions, then looked up and accepted the menu handed to him by the waiter.

Señor, you wish something to drink?

Yessir. A beer. Pabst Blue Ribbon.

Sorry, señor, but we have only Mexican beer.

All right. Then a Mexican beer.

Tecate?

Whatever you say. I'll drink whatever you bring. Beer cain't change that much in a few blocks.

Sí, señor. Un momento.

Say?

Sí? the waiter said, backstepping.

Ya'll got a restroom?

Oh, señor, very sorry. Our toilet is broken. There is one across the plaza in the government building, he said. He pointed through the open air window to the long palatial-looking structure decorated in the Christmas-like trappings of celebration.

Looks like somebody's gittin ready for a party, or done had one.

It is our celebration of independence, the waiter said, standing with the erectness of pride one might give to the passing of their country's flag. In two days, September sixteen, there will be many people in the plaza. You were right to say a party, señor. A very big party. Maybe you will be here, no?

Don't know. I'm on my way to Mexico City.

Ah, México. Fantástico. Very beautiful. You will like it.

Mexico City. I'm already in Mexico, ain't I?

With the same erectness of decorum the waiter tilted his head back and laughed. Yes. Yes, indeed. No problem. We in Mexico call Mexico City Mexico because it *is* Mexico.

I see. Well, that's where I'm goin.

But there you will see even bigger party. The whole city will be a party. Anywhere you are in Mexico will be a party, for several days. You will see. I get your beer for you, he said and pivoted and went away.

A government building meant government people which meant police, probably crawling all over the place. Better to wait than to risk, so he settled with some discomfort into his vantage point on the new world he had entered and shook out one of his few remaining Camels and lit it and smoked and watched the people mill around the plaza. The families. The lovers. People going it alone. And the dogs and drunks who seemed not to know the difference.

The waiter brought his beer and set it on the table and placed a slice of lime beside it and told him the lime would improve the taste. He squeezed the lime into the beer then sucked on it and downed half the beer while the waiter stood at attention looking on.

Not bad.

Now, señor. What would you like to order?

Don't know. Hadn't looked yet.

No problem. I will come back. You take your time.

He opened the thin white menu and his eyes scanned the strange listings, down one side then the other and he saw nothing he could decipher until the word TAMAL rose from the printed mumbo jumbo. His father had taken the family once to Greenville on a Saturday night for dinner, to a place named Doe's. They ate so many tamales before their steaks arrived they had to ask for bags to take the thick T-bones home. His mother warmed them for Sunday dinner but they were not the same. He would never forget the tamales, but his father never took him back. He was in prison a month later. The price to the right said $6. He looked again to make sure. Beneath it was another price. $20. He guessed that was for several. He looked again for anything cheaper and saw a few other items but none that read like they might be good. He ran his finger to the bottom of the second page where the beverages on American menus were normally listed and checked the label on the bottle of beer before him and looked back at the menu and found it. TECATE. And beside it, $6.

Shita'mighty, he whispered to himself. A feller could go broke in a place like this just drinking. He looked around for the waiter and the waiter saw him and walked snappily to his table.

Yes, señor. You are ready to order.

Naw, I ain't. I'd like to unorder.

There is a problem, señor?

Big problem.

What is the problem? Something wrong with your beer? You need help with the menu?

I need a Wells Fargo to come in here and help me pay, that's what's wrong. He spoke quietly so others wouldn't hear but heads were already turned, ears cocked.

The waiter laughed. Oh, señor. This your first trip to Mexico?

Either one, city or country.

He laughed again, heartily. You think you pay six dollars for one beer?

That's what it says there, don't it?

That is six pesos, señor, not dollars. Six pesos about fifty cents in American money.

He looked into the waiter's wide grin and back at the menu and felt the heat flood his cheeks and the eyes of everyone in the restaurant upon him. Guess I got a education about Mexican money comin to me, he said.

No problem, señor. You no have pesos, we take dollars.

How do I git pesos?

Across the plaza is a bank, he said and pointed. Banco it says. You see?

He strained his eyes past the gazebo, through the waving branches of the trees on the plaza, and made out the word above an arched doorway and nodded.

You go there after you eat and they change your dollars for you. It better to change at a bank. They give you best rate. But for your meal, we give good rate, too. No problem.

He ordered three tacos along with a plate of sopes, recommended by the waiter because he said three tacos would not be enough for one traveling all the way to Mexico, and finished his beer and ordered another.

The waiter returned with the beer and a basket of triangular chips and small bowls of red and green concoctions that looked like thick soups. He set everything before him in a neat pattern and instructed him as to the identity and composition of each, as though he were some infant eating for the first time. Moments later his meal was brought and placed before him in decorative arrangement.

The food was good and he experimented from bite to bite with the salsas and washed everything down with another beer and had almost forgotten the gun when he moved his leg and tucked it under the chair and felt the heel of the handle ride up his shin and hook over the top of his boot. He made like he was scratching his leg and reached down and pushed it back and repositioned his leg to its former outstretched position and decided it was time to take care of the matter and get the gun back where it belonged.

He looked around again and the waiter came quickly.

Sí, señor.

Guess I'm bout ready to pay.

Sí. Un momentito. He wrote something on a small yellow pad and ripped it off and placed it on the table and waited.

Jo Shelby took the sheet and looked at it. That a seven? he said.

Sí, señor. Your total is thirty-seven pesos. In American money that is about three dollars and ten cents.

He pulled out his billfold and thumbed out three ones and pulled a quarter from his pocket and gave the money to the waiter and told him to keep the change.

Muchas gracias, señor. I wish you well on your trip to Mexico.

Thanks. Now all I gotta do is figure out how to git there.

You do not have a car?

Naw. Ain't got nothing cept my feet and this thumb here.

That is not good idea, señor, hitchhiking as you call it. Very bad idea. Many bad people between here and Mexico. Besides, it would take you a long time. Mexico many, many miles from here. Even if you have car, it take you fifteen, maybe twenty hours, a whole day, maybe longer. He rubbed a hand through his hair and shifted his feet as if to think better.

That don't leave much. A train. Maybe a bus.

I think you do better with a bus. The station is not far from here. Fifteen blocks maybe. I show you.

Jo Shelby eased up carefully from the table and reached for his cap on top of his knapsack then unhooked the knapsack from the leg of the chair and swung it over his shoulder and stood for a minute for the gun to settle into his boot.

The waiter stood watching, thoughtfully.

Then he rummaged in his pocket and singled out another quarter and put it on the table.

Muchas gracias, the waiter said and bowed slightly.

Don't mention it. Wish I could give you more, but I ain't got much.

No problem, señor. Now, you go to the bank and change your money and come back and I show you how to arrive at the bus station.

He crossed street and square then street again and entered the bank which was not unlike the one in Drew. Tellers on one side. Desks and offices on the other. He walked up to one of the windows. The lady on the other side was young. Her hair was pulled back into a ponytail and she wore long earrings that dangled around her cheeks. Her mouth was dark red and with her dark skin she was a rare beauty that didn't belong in a bank. She spoke to him in the language that was beginning more and more to make him feel stupid.

I got these American dollars here, he pulled three twenty dollar bills from his billfold, and I need to get em changed. He laid them upon the marbled ledge.

Sí, señor. Un momento.

He watched her. She scratched figures on a small pad with a pencil. Her fingers had a refined look and moved gracefully, as though they knew they were being looked at. Her head was bent downward, her features sharply defined even at that angle. She reached into a drawer and pulled out some other bills, smaller than dollars, and counted them, flicked them crisply between her fingers like she was shelling them. He kept watching, her hands, fingers, how slender, tapered, and wondered why she was working in a bank and not in pictures, then she was finished and looked up at him.

She counted the bills again, this time out loud, in Spanish, dealing them out to him like she might a handful of cards. She added several pieces of change, then said something in Spanish again which sounded like how much she was giving back to him, and smiled at him.

He tipped his cap. I'm much obliged, ma'am.

De nada.

The smile was still on her face and he didn't want to leave it. He stood for a minute and examined the thick wad of strange bills doled out to him and counted them, which amounted to something over seven hundred pesos, and suddenly entertained feelings of wealth and prestige. She was still looking at him. Her hands were on the ledge and he saw no ring on her finger and decided the next and most important thing he had to do in his life was to learn Spanish, just for insurance, in case he got stuck in Mexico. He tipped his cap again and left. He stopped and looked back at the door, but she was busy at work.

The waiter was looking for him and met him in front of the restaurant.

Señor, the terminal is not difficult to find. At the corner there you take a right and follow Calle 6. You go for many blocks. Maybe ten or eleven, to Calle Mina. Then you go left, for maybe five, six blocks. There you see the bus terminal.

Calle is street, that right?

Sí, señor. You are learning Spanish.

Yeah. Just not fast enough.

You stay in Mexico awhile, you learn Spanish very well. It is the best way.

I oughtta know it pretty damn good then fore its over.

The waiter smiled. You follow my directions. No problem.

No problem.

No problem.

I need to buy some food and clothes and cigarettes. Any stores between here and there?

The waiter looked at the small size of his satchel on his back. Sí, señor, but I think you wait until you arrive in Mexico. In Mexico are many shops and you will not have to carry more on the bus. The bus, it is very crowded.

Muchas gracias.

De nada, señor. Buena suerte. Good luck.

He thanked him again as he backpedaled away, waving, then turned and walked to the corner and turned right onto Calle 6.

His ankle was hurting more but there was no where to make the switch. There would be a restroom at the bus depot and he could do it there. He walked on.

The depot was brimming with Mexicans, all sizes and shapes and stations in life. He stood inside the doorway a moment and looked for anything resembling a restroom. He asked a man standing next to him but he knew no English and only shrugged. Then he pointed at his fly and mimicked urinating and the man smiled and pointed toward a corner at the rear of the large waiting room. He moved slowly because the place was crowded and the gun was feeling loose in his boot. He was afraid to bend and adjust it, draw attention to himself. He saw a policeman near the ticket windows and another at the door which led to the buses which he could see parked in rows outside through tall side windows. He kept walking, moving left and right to avoid bumping others who were laden with packages and luggage, cartons carelessly tied with rope, children.

The woman was upon him before he saw her coming. An old wide-bodied woman toting large shopping bags that bulged at the seams, one in each hand, so heavy she tottered with them. He stepped quickly to the side to avoid her then felt the thud of a bag against his leg and heard next the loud metallic clatter on the concrete floor and looked and saw the gun spinning in broad daylight. He reached quickly to recover it but the noise may as well have been a small bomb going off the way people scattered from around him. Before he could get the revolver back into his boot a policeman was standing over him shouting loudly in Spanish and waving to the other officer to join the discovery.

They spoke no English and would listen to nothing he had to say. He looked around for somebody who might speak English, someone who might be sympathetic, but no one came close in the gathered crowd of brown curious faces.

The station they took him to was several blocks away. The officers walked one on each side of him, their shoulders bumping his, his hands cuffed in front of him like a felon. They said nothing and he said nothing. One carried his knapsack and the other the revolver, holding it up in the sunlight, turning it in his hands, eyeing it as though it was some terrible beauty, a prize.

The exterior of the building was rough-textured, as though the concrete had been thrown on with a trowel and never layered, much less worked to a smooth finish. There were iron bars over the two front windows as well as the door they pushed him through. He stood in a small room. Several doors led off in different directions. There was nothing else in the room except metal folding chairs along one wall and a bulletin board covered with wanted posters and other announcements he could not read, not unlike the Sunflower County jail, except there he could read. He was motioned to sit which he did and the two officers left through one of the doors. They were gone awhile. He guessed they figured he wouldn't run with his hands cuffed then saw the bolt on the door he'd just entered.

He sat and thought.

They never took his billfold and he quickly moved his hands around to his left side and removed it from his hip pocket, brought it back around and cradled it in his lap and took out the money. He hoped against hope he had time to do what he needed to do. He could tell them his ankle was hurting, show them the blister to prove it. He pulled off the boot and placed it upright on the floor in front of him and slid his cuffed hands down the bootleather, one inside and one out, and pried up the insole with a fingernail. He pushed what pesos and American bills he had flat along the bottom of the boot, withholding three twenty-peso bills to keep it honest, then pushed the insole back flat. He pulled his boot back on and stretched the pants leg back over it, stood on it to see how it felt, and sat back down. He put the sixty pesos back into his billfold, because they were going to ask for that next, and returned it to his hip pocket. He had heard horror stories about Mexican jails at Parchman, from men who'd been in them and survived to tell about it, which was how they put it. Many had dirt floors and some no roofs and most just enough food and water to make a man shit and pee and keep his heart ticking. But if a person had enough money, he could get just about anything he wanted. It was not what you knew that got you out, but who you knew or who your family knew, which sometimes got you in as well. He was where he knew no one except a waiter and money might be all he could rely on. He would be damned if he was going to give his life's savings up without a fight.

One of the officers came back and motioned him to stand and come forward and made some guttural comment about a captain and he figured he was about to meet the head knocker who was in charge. The officer ushered him down a narrow dark corridor and through a door on the right which closed behind him.

A thick-faced man with acne scars and a bushy mustache sat behind a metal desk shuffling papers. He did not look up.

Jo Shelby stood.

The man wore a light brown shirt. Bars across one pocket and chevrons on the sleeves announced his authority. The room was colorless, bare concrete-block walls and barred windows high up. A single shadeless bulb hung from the ceiling.

He kept standing.

A few moments passed, then the captain spoke but still did not look up. You passport please.

He was surprised the man spoke English but tried not to show it. I ain't got none, he said. But I got a visa if you'll let me git it. It's in my billfold.

One minute please. Ricardo, he looked up and shouted at the door. The officer who had led him there opened the door and stuck his head in.

Quítale las esposas, por favor, the captain said.

The officer stepped forward and took a ring of keys from his pocket and fitted one into the lock on the cuffs and popped them open and removed them from his wrists.

Muchas gracias, he said to the officer and rubbed his wrists with relief.

You must remove your hat, the captain said.

He took it off and reached over and laid it on the table.

The captain then said something to the officer and made a wavy movement with his hands. The officer pantomimed what he wanted next and Jo Shelby put his hands on top of his head and stood stockstill as the man's hands began under his arms and moved downward. He slapped roughly along his sides, around his chest, patted the thin cigarette pack in his pocket then moved on, over his belt, around his waist, lower, pausing there, feeling out the objects through the material of his front pockets, then he raised up and said something to the captain. The captain ordered Jo Shelby to empty his pockets and he fished out the Barlow pocketknife from one and the cigarette lighter from the other and laid them on the desk beside the cap. The officer continued. Patted his billfold but did not ask him to take it out. Pressed around his crotch with his thumbs, raised his pants legs, peered into the boots and probed his hand around his ankles then slapped his legs, like he might a small child's whose shoes he'd just tied.

The captain looked at the officer and made a gesture with the back of his hand and the officer went away and closed the door behind him.

Hand me you billfold, please, the captain said.

He pulled the wallet from his hip pocket and handed it slowly to him. You speak pretty good English for a Mexican, he said to the captain.

The officer raised his brows and lowered his eyes before he spoke, his mouth grim from beneath the mustache. Yes, señor. It is necessary. Many gringos come here, he said as he pulled the contents from the billfold and fanned them on the tabletop.

Gringos?

Gringos. You are gringo. That is our word for Americans who come to Mexico to make trouble.

But I'm not here to make no trouble. I'm just trying to find my family.

You family?

Yessir. My family.

Then what for you want to smuggle this gun into our country? For why? He picked the gun up from behind the desk and laid it on top along with the items from his billfold.

He thought. I wadn't trying to smuggle it. It's old, real old. It won't even shoot.

The captain picked up the gun and examined it. He flipped open the cylinder and checked it and looked through the barrel then snapped the cylinder back in and spun it. He gripped the stock and pulled the hammer back with his thumb and pulled the trigger, dry firing the gun. The gun okay, he said.

No sir, you don't understand. It's gotta have powder in it first and the powder has to be packed down with a rod and it don't even have a rod much less no powder. That gun couldn't hurt nobody.

But, señor, it is a gun. It is against the law to smuggle guns into Mexico. It is forbidden, you understand. You have papers showing you claimed the gun.

Claimed?

At customs. When you enter Mexico?

It's there on my visa.

The captain sifted through the papers and money on the desk and pulled out the pink slip and unfolded it and spread it with his hands and studied it a moment.

Yes, this is visa, but do you have papers showing you claimed the gun?

He remembered the paper, the one where he checked N O in all the blanks.

No sir, he said. Didn't know I was sposed to. The woman never gave it back to me.

This is very serious, señor. Very. Smuggling gun into Mexico. He pulled out the driver's license and held it close to his eyes.

Where are you from?

Rome, Mississippi, he said, hoping the man didn't check the expiration date.

How much you weigh?

A hunderd and sixty pounds.

You height?

Five foot eleven.

What is you date of birth?

December seventh nineteen hunderd and thirty.

He put the license back into the side compartment of the billfold from where he had pulled it and gathered the other papers and pesos with his thick hands and stuffed them in the money slip and laid it aside.

For why you want to smuggle gun into Mexico?

But I wadn't—

Señor, he said, knitting his brows and leveling his eyes at him, you have no proof. There are witnesses. Many witnesses who saw the gun at the bus station. Where were you going?

Mexico City. Like I said, I'm trying to find my family.

The captain's face went sympathetic for a moment. You family, he said. So, tell me how it is you try to find you family in this country.

He told him the story. With folded hands and an emotionless face the captain listened. When he finished the captain pushed his billfold across the table toward him and for a moment he felt relief. The captain pulled some papers from a drawer and began writing on them.

He remained standing, watching.

The captain wrote. He finished one page and started on another.

Jo Shelby waited, shifted from one foot to the other. The captain finished writing and called for the officer again. The officer entered quickly, as though he had been standing just outside the door waiting, and the captain said something to him in Spanish and gave him the papers and the officer unhooked the handcuffs from his belt and motioned for Jo Shelby's wrists.

Does this mean I'm gonna be locked up? he said.

Señor, smuggling guns into Mexico is most serious business. You family is one thing. Smuggling guns quite another. I am very sorry but we cannot release you until you hearing.

But I told you—

Señor, he said, raising his voice and rapping the table loudly with his knuckles. We need you co-op-eration. You no co-op-erate, you no go free. You understand?

But I am cooperating. How much more can I cooperate?

There are ways. You can think about it.

What about the knife and my knapsack?

We keep all you things for you.

The gun?

The gun, he said, rocking his hand back and forth, as though he were weighing the thought there. The gun I do not know. The gun is different matter.

Aw, come on. That was my great-great-granddaddy's gun. It don't mean nothin to you.

I am very sorry, señor. But I do only my job.

But don't I git no lawyer.

There is no lawyer for gun smuggling. Like I said, very serious matter. If you wish you call your American embassy. Maybe they get lawyer for you. But I think it very expensive. You cooperate, maybe not cost as much.

But—

No more, señor, he wagged his finger in front of his face. We let you think. Maybe there be no hearing.

He reached over and picked up his billfold from the desk with his cuffed hands. No one helped, even offered. The officer led him away through a steel back door and he was told to get into the bed of a small Chevy pickup with another guard whom he had not seen. The motor turned over and the truck lurched forward and the jail they were leaving quickly vanished from sight when they turned a corner and he wondered what other jail they could put him in. He asked the guard across from him but he shook his head and mouthed that he spoke no English.

The truck rattled on over the washed-out cobbled streets, passing scenes he had seen before. Children with dirty faces standing in open doorways. Vendors pushing carts. Street corners where there were stalls of colorful vegetables and fruits stacked neatly beneath home-made tarpaulins. Larger open air markets where hawkers flashed their wares to passersby and called out in voices of urgency, as though their next meal was at stake. Trash and garbage along the curbs. School-children in blue-and-white outfits making their way home from school along the sidewalks, in the streets, mindless of the refuse, as though they'd learned to live with it, learned that was life.

The truck came to a stop and he heard a commotion up front and leaned his head around the cab to see. They were stopped at a red light and a child no more than ten was holding a pail and squeegee in one hand trying to wash the windshield with the other. The officer was waving him away. But the boy persisted and the officer paid him nothing and drove on. Everybody out trying to make a peso, and where he was from they'd be lining up at the welfare office for handouts.

The truck continued on, making its way along quieter, sleepy streets. He checked his watch, about the only thing he had left not taken from him. It was almost four o'clock. He wondered if he'd ever see the gun again not to mention the knapsack with all his belongings, the pictures, letters. The remarks of Edgardo and Athen haunted him. Perhaps they were right. He thought about the kid trying to wash the windshield and everyone else in this place trying to make their lives work surrounded by so much that wasn't. A person can get into trouble trying to do right for only so long, then something good's got to happen to him.

They pulled up to a large whitewashed building. From what he could see it was a large two-story structure. A chain-link fence threaded with loops of barb wire ringed the roof. Spotlights on tall slender poles periscoped high above the fence. The guard next to him jumped over the side and the officer who had been driving came around and let down the tailgate. He was ordered out. They walked to the front of the building which looked like no jail he had ever seen. A walkway lined with cedar shrubs led up to a broad yellow entrance the size of a garage door. Above it was a panel of bars painted yellow to match the door and above that, in large black letters, CENTRO DE READAPTACION SOCIAL. If it took that much to spell jail it must be either worse or better and by the looks of things so far he cast his bet with the latter.

He was led up the concrete ramp, between the green cedar shrubs. The guard stayed beside him and the officer walked on ahead, a thin roll of papers in his hand. A smaller door of the same color was set within the larger garage-size door and two men wearing dark green fatigues leaned slouchily beside it, one on each side, smoking. The officer stopped and spoke to them. With the hand holding the papers he pointed back to Jo Shelby. They were still talking when he arrived with the guard.

One of the men opened the door and spread his hand for him to enter and he did. He stood in a large bare foyer distinguished only by Mexican flags hanging from the ceiling and a wall of bars opposite him through which he saw a small square courtyard of similar size wherein grass grew and where concrete benches surrounded a single statue in the center, some saint by the way his hands were folded. It looked like something you might expect to see on the grounds of a church or a hospital, but not a prison. He stood between the guard and the officer and they all three stood in silence and waited.

A man entered from a door on the left and stood before them. He was of large compact build with a mustache that drooped over the edges of his mouth and he wore a white Western-style hat that appeared to be new. From his left jeans pocket hung a white medallion on a short gold chain. He looked like someone dressed up for a Saturday night dance. Nothing about him suggested warden or assistant warden, not even prison guard, but when he spoke the officer and guard gave him all the deference expected by authority. They conversed for a few minutes and the officer unrolled the papers and gave them to him. He took his time looking over them, moving his head up and down, making short grunting sounds to himself. They spoke again, a lengthy conversation, gesturing back and forth to Jo Shelby. Finally, the officer took out his keys and unhooked the handcuffs. For a brief moment he thought that they had decided he was not worth it. Then the man in the white hat shook the hands of the officer and the guard and they departed through the door behind them and he nodded toward the room from which he had come and motioned for Jo Shelby to follow him. He closed the door behind them.

The room was empty except for a large wooden desk with a wooden swivel chair and two metal folding chairs. The walls were bare but clean and smelled of new paint. A single barred window afforded a view of the street outside and the shops lining it, a bar among them. The sign over the door said Bar Botilla. People were sitting and drinking at sidewalk tables. Right across the street from a prison, he thought, now don't that beat all. The man motioned for him to sit and he sat, his knees spread apart, his hands dangling between them. The man went behind the desk and settled into the swivel chair.

So, señor Ferguson. I believe that you name. The papers, they say you smuggle gun.

Jo Shelby just looked at him, confused.

You have no-thing to say?

Yessir. I got plenty to say. But nobody believes it.

It is of no matter. You are here, and I am the comandante of this prison, and you must be here until—

Until I cooperate, that it?

The comandante raised his eyebrows and smoothed his mustache in a repetitive meticulous fashion with a forefinger and looked down at the papers. He stood up and paced along the wall behind the desk.

Jo Shelby sat.

The comandante paced, rubbing his chin with one hand, fiddling with a pencil with the other. Then he stopped and turned. Please forgive, señor, but my English no so good. So I do best I can explain to you. You understand?

Jo Shelby nodded.

This place here good prison. New. Very new prison. People all over Mexico know of this prison. Many good things about this prison. But Mexican prison not good place for you, not good place for gringos. Much trouble. Much hurt. It not good you to stay in Mexican prison long. He paused and paced a few steps, bumping a pencil meditatively over his Adam's apple, then turned and spoke again. The papers, he pointed to them on the table, they say you have meeting, ah . . .

He rolled his hands and waved the pencil as if to orchestrate the right word . . .

They say you have—

Hearing, Jo Shelby said, helping him out.

Sí. Hearing. And this hearing much time, long time before this hearing.

So what you're telling me is I'm gonna be in here awhile and if I cooperate I could get out sooner.

The comandante just stared at him, shifting his eyes left and right, his brain working to comprehend what he'd just heard. Sí, señor. But that you decision.

Jo Shelby thought a moment, his toes flexing over the pad of bills in his boot. How much do I need to cooperate? he said.

As I say, señor, that is you decision.

He thought again. I can cooperate a little, he said. I ain't got much to cooperate with.

The comandante shrugged his shoulders, his face.

So you're not gonna tell me.

Señor, it is no my decision.

But you could help me.

Possible. Is possible I can help.

The comandante sat down and they sat looking at each other, flies and gnats interrupting the space between them. Jo Shelby remembered something about Mexican standoffs and decided whoever came up with the phrase got it damn right.

They sat. The voices of children playing outside in the street. Cell doors clanging somewhere inside. A horn honking in the distance.

I ain't got much money.

The comandante shifted in his chair and shrugged again, with the same nonchalance he had before, then relaxed his shoulders and leaned forward and folded his hands on the desktop, his fingers interlaced in a tight grip. The gun, señor. It special gun, no?

Yeah. Special to me. It was my great-great granddaddy's. But that's all. It don't even shoot.

I see, señor, but it is very old special gun.

He saw where the man was going and felt the anger boil inside of him. No way in hell he was giving him the gun. He'd rot in a Mexican prison before he did that. That would be like spitting on the cross or digging up your dead. No damn way and he struggled to keep his head on and his hands between his legs and his butt in his chair.

It's a gun. A piece of worthless shit. But it's special to me, you understand?

A taunting grin creased the comandante's face. Sí, señor. I understand. But I think it is you who do not understand. You think. We let you think. He pushed himself up from the desk. Now, you go to you cell, but first a few things.

Yes?

You follow me please.

They entered again the vacant foyer and the comandante whistled to open the steel-barred gate that led into the courtyard. The gate clanged shut behind them. He saw yet another set of bars straight ahead and through them a colonnaded walkway of square pillars painted yellow and white and beyond that men loitering about in a shadowy area where the roof of the structure took up once again.

The comandante touched his shoulder and motioned for him to follow and they went through another door to the left and entered a room the size of the one they had left. There was nothing in the room, not even folding chairs, and he figured quickly the room served only one purpose and braced himself for the beating he had heard was the initiation rite into Mexican jails. A guard beat him once at Parchman, for talking back though all he'd said was Naw when the man said, ain't it a pretty day. Handcuffed him to an overhead rack and tore up his back with a lash until he passed out and he awoke in his bunk with a pain that stayed with him for days and had to sleep on his stomach long after the pain had gone. The only way to beat a beating was to not cry out because that was like caffeine to the one doing the beating, seemed to stir them up into a killing mood.

The comandante whistled again. No one came and he stepped out into the sunlit area and called and moments later a guard came puffing into the room, looking back over his shoulder, pointing, offering up to the comandante what appeared to be a litany of excuses for his tardiness. The comandante looked directly into the shorter, thinner man's eyes and spoke in the harsh tones of reprimand then altered his tone and pointed at Jo Shelby and began enumerating on his fingers the apparent instructions to be given, not once but twice, as if the guard was a nitwit who had become a guard by some other means than his intelligence.

I leave you now, the comandante said. But this man he take care of you, take you to you cell, give you instruction. He speak English. You have questions he no can answer, he come to me. He tipped the big white hat set squarely on his head and went away and the new guard commenced strutting around him, quick rooster-like steps, his eyes moving up and down him like he was something to be sold or bought at an auction. He was thin and lean but his arms were long enough to be whips and Jo Shelby turned with him, keeping his back to the walls, his eyes locked into his.

Take off, the guard said, and pointed to his shirt.

He unbuttoned his shirt, slowly, and pulled his arms out of the sleeves, keeping his eyes on the man as he did. He dropped his shirt on the floor then reached up and took off his cap, to save the man the trouble asking him and dropped it on top of his shirt. He could only hope the man would not see the lash scars across his back.

Take down you pants.

What?

You pants. The guard gestured with his own buckle. Take down.

The man had nothing in his hands so maybe someone else would come in to do the job, he thought and unhooked his buckle and un-snapped his jeans and pushed them down to his knees.

Todo, the guard said, and pointed at the underwear.

You gotta be kidding.

Todo, the guard repeated, louder, angrily.

Aw right a damn minute, and he pushed his briefs down and felt like something on display for a pervert.

The guard scanned his body briefly then told him to put his clothes back on which he hastily accomplished, the cap, too, keeping his eyes vigilant.

The guard moved quickly behind him, Jo Shelby turning with him.

Stop, the guard said. No turn.

He stopped dead still.

The guard began at his knees with his hands and frisked his legs and moved his hands down into his boots and whisked them around his shins then stood up. Jo Shelby thought he had it all bassackwards but it wasn't the first time he'd seen Mexicans do something in reverse order.

Okay. In moment we go to you cell. But first I tell you some things.

He listened attentively as the guard told him of the morning and evening listas, that they took place in the prison yard before breakfast and at six o'clock, that to be absent for these meant certain punishment but the nature of the punishment was not made known. That bed checks were at ten o'clock at night which amounted to another lista and even worse punishment if not obeyed. His knapsack, clothes and other items would be returned, but nothing considered harmful or dangerous. No mention was made of the gun. He could smoke in the prison yard but could not in his cell and would not be allowed to keep his lighter. He had already figured as much and knew he wouldn't get his razor or his pocketknife but knew also the resourcefulness within prisons and raised no objections. He thought about asking about the gun then thought again. Prison gossip was worse than that of a small town and the less said the better. For all he knew he'd run up against gunrunners and some of the people they ran them against and he'd end up caught in the middle, sliced up like bacon and left to fry in the hot Mexican sun with guards looking on. The guard asked if he had any questions. He had none, and he was told once more to follow.

A guard on the other side opened the last barred gate and they passed through on a concrete walkway along the colonnade and he saw off to the right the large dirt prison yard surrounded by high walls. There were guard towers at the corners connected by a continuation of the same chainlink fence and barbed wire he had seen from the parking lot. A basketball hoop stood at one end of the quadrangle but he saw nothing else of recreational value, except the emptiness of the yard, which was provided for grown men to invent their own depravity of fun and play.

They reached the end of the walkway where the aroma of cooked food came from nowhere then entered a small rectangular area of no particular purpose and a few steps further were under the overhang where he had seen the men earlier in the shadows. They stood about in small groups, talking and smoking, eating tamales and tacos, fingering chopped food into their mouths where it spilled from the ends of floppy tortillas and drinking soda from bottles emblazoned with logos he knew. Grapette and Sun Spot and Coca-Cola. Men brown and weathered, with dirty gravel-looking teeth, dirty mouths, dirty clothes, dirty feet. Few of them wore shoes. The men were only briefly interrupted by his presence, so comfortable they seemed in their pastime, their solidarity, as though he were just a small pebble dropped into their quiet waters. But he felt the anonymous stares on him, the muted curiosity, and studied them in the furtive ways he'd learned at Parchman.

There was a small stall to his left where a man, a trusty he supposed, sold toilet articles, cigarettes, matches, candy bars, cold drinks, and just about everything a person might buy in a small country store. Across the stall to his right was a counter, men leaning against it, eating and drinking. Behind it smoke rose from griddles and he saw two men wearing aprons working a short-order kitchen. He stopped to assess it all then bent his head forward to gain the guard's ear.

You can buy stuff in here?

Sí. Small store for you needs. Café. You no like what prison cook, you buy here. Snacks.

Well I'll be damned.

Cómo?

Nothing. Just had a friend once in a Mexican prison. He never mentioned no store or café.

The guard motioned him forward.

They entered a large circular room that was empty save for a concrete stairway that spiraled upward from its center. Doorways with numbers above them ringed the room, all of them closed except one whose double doors were open wide. Through it he saw men busily at work, hammering, cartwheeling woodframes in the air with their hands, some holding what looked to be paintbrushes.

What're they doing in there? he said to the guard.

This men, they work. What you call, fac-to-ry?

Factory? Yeah? What're they making?

For pictures, he said and drew a square in the air with his hands. Picture frames.

Sí. The picture frames.

Where do they git the pictures?

They make. He mimicked drawing motions. They make here, in the prison.

This prison very famous in Mexico. Many men here work. This only one factory, he pointed at the open door through which industry hummed, but in this prison there are others. Very different, no?

You can say that again.

Cómo?

Nothing. Just an expression.

The guard crooked his finger over his shoulder. You come. I show you you bed. He crossed the large rotund room. Jo Shelby followed.

They came to a metal door two removed from the door that led to the small factory and the guard opened the door and Jo Shelby saw bunkbeds, one right after the other, two rows separated by a narrow aisle, extending down a long arm of the complex that seemed to have no end. Over the footboards hung towels and shirts and pants and other assorted laundry draped to form two solid walls that made the bunks discernible only by the shapes the dishevelment of rags gave to them.

The guard motioned and Jo Shelby followed, down the gauntlet of beds, for it seemed a place packed for trouble, trouble that could come at you in a flash and no one would see, even with the lights on. They walked on, their heels clicking over the concrete floor, passing men asleep, men awake on their backs staring at the ceiling or the bunk above them or a sweetheart or wife they could touch only with the inward vision of their eyes. He knew. They were the ones that would come at him first, not the ones making the picture frames. There were men sitting with only space enough for their knees, so crammed were the beds against one another. He thought of the camps at Parchman and the barrack-like conditions within them, six units in a building and twenty-nine men in a unit, single cots far enough apart to put a footlocker between them and play five-card stud and blackjack, dominos, roll dice. Here if you farted the man next to you would think it was his. All about was the smell of spent tobacco and un-washed feet, of sweat and urine passed on through clothes and bedli-nen. It recycled in their breathing, curdled nauseously in the stale air, bore down upon him like some malignant cloud about to shed its load.

They were near the end of the long room when the guard stopped and pointed.

Here, señor. You bed.

It was a bottom bunk, a thin mattress covered with what he could not tell for all the dirty towels and clothes and magazines, newspapers, ashes and empty cigarette packs laying on top of it, cast there by bod-ies above or on either side or all together simply because it was empty and the first elbow room they'd gotten in no telling when and God help the next son of a bitch who came along and took it and made em take it all back. It was like that. He knew that, too. An extra cot next to yours was a lower forty suddenly tacked onto your spread. It was an extra room on the house for the wife to store everything she'd been bitching about for the forty years you'd been married. In prison it was prime real estate and in this one it was even higher and he was going to pay. He knew that, too. What he didn't know was how he was going to protect himself. Not to keep from dying, though many preferred that to living, even concocted their own deaths. But to keep from wishing he'd die because of the pain and torture they knew where and how to inflict, those so steeped and learned in that lore of the caged. His whole body seemed to be mind, those thoughts circulating through it as he looked down and around and saw the miniscule space to which his life had been suddenly reduced.

I go now. You have questions, no?

Yeah. I got one.

Sí?

When am I gonna git my knapsack?

You what? I no understand.

Knapsack. Satchel. Bag. Whatever the hell you call it.

Bag. I understand. It will come. They bring from the other station. Maybe tomorrow. Mañana.

Mañana.

Sí, señor. Mañana.

Mañana. He whispered the word under his breath, like a sigh he fought back, because he didn't believe he'd ever see the knapsack again or any of its contents. Just like the gun. And the money he was going to have to give to them to get out, or use to buy back his gun which he'd have to sell to get out. Either way he was going to be broke, in a land where he spoke almost none of the language, which meant sooner or later he'd be right back where he was.

So, you no more have questions, I go now, the guard said and walked away, his thin carriage and lanky arms nicking pieces of the articles hanging from the footboards, the passageway between the corridor of beds being that narrow.

He surveyed the bed once more. He bent down and began sorting the wadded items. He heard snoring toward the entrance, but nothing else. In front of a door at the opposite end of the room a large floor fan blew, its off-kilter blade ticking against something. The only light came from narrow barred windows near the ceiling.

He did not see the man lying on the bottom bunk next to him. Nor did he feel his eyes on him. He picked out a few towels that smelled of mildew and damp rot and looked to hang them over the footboard, but it was full. The headboard was as well. So he folded them and stacked them at the foot of the bed. He blew ashes off some underwear and held them at arms length with his fingertips, as though they might be alive, and laid them on top of the towels. He shuffled the magazines into neat stacks and placed them on the floor beneath the bunk and did the same with the newspapers. He thought of everything he could do to be polite and courteous, knowing none of it would be enough. He'd just raided somebody's claim and driven his own stake into it. The mattress was wrapped in coarse material a grade shy of burlap. There were no sheets. No pillow. He sat and buried his head in his hands, his knees pushing up against the bunk across from him. A slow ache pushed past his throat and turned warm and spread through his face and his eyes were ready to release it when a voice behind him spoke.

It is always like this the first day, it said.

He turned and looked. A man was lying on the bottom bunk behind him, his head propped up on a pillow, hands folded over a book that was splayed over his chest, wire-frame glasses low across his nose.

Naw it ain't neither. Cause I had a first day before, Jo Shelby said, then wished he hadn't. Informants. Planted to pick up leaks like that and feed them back to the guards who paid for them, then got paid by those over them and so the money chain went, intertwined on the prison grapevine, all of it gnarled together in a thickness that defied unraveling, so long had it been in its formation.

So you have been in prison before, the man said.

Jo Shelby leaned his head under the upper bunk to get a better look. He was a large-faced older man, early sixties perhaps. Hair graying around the temples. A few wisps across his forehead but otherwise bald. His body took up most of the bed.

Maybe, he said. What's it to you?

Allow me to introduce myself, the man said, swinging his legs over the side and planting his feet on the floor. José Ramón García.

He extended a hand and Jo Shelby leaned in further under his bunk and shook it.

But you can just call me Ramón.

Pleased to meet you. Mine's Jo Shelby. Jo Shelby Ferguson.

And you go by both names, Jo Shelby?

Yessir.

No need to say yessir. There are no formalities here. Pecking order, yes. But formalities, no.

Yessir.

Ah. You will learn. You are from the north, the States, no?

Yeah. I'm from America. But not the north, he said ironically.

That is much better. And let me guess. Your accent. Your two names. You are from somewhere in the south.

You got it. Mississippi.

Ah. Miss-is-sip-pi, he said, articulating the word with great precision. Yes, I know the place.

You been there?

No. Not there. He laid the book aside and propped his elbows on his knees, steepled his hands under his chin and leaned in closer. But I have been to Texas, and to New Orleans.

Your English is very good. Kinda caught me off guard. Better'n anybody else's I've heard down here.

I learned English in the university, the same one where I taught, in Monterrey, at the Universidad de Nuevo León.

You a teacher?

Yes. A professor. Or I was. He rolled his eyes wistfully. But then I was put here.

Jo Shelby swung his legs over the bed and placed his feet on the floor so their knees almost interlocked, their eyes inches apart. You were put here just for teaching? he said.

Something like that you might say. Mexico is not a democracy like your country. Whoever is president has much power. Anyone speaks against him, they feel his power. So in my classes, I teach political science, I make statements about your country, your democracy, how good it is for your people and how Mexico should be like that and—

And they locked you up for that.

It was not just that. It is very complicated, so I try to make it simple for you. He placed a finger to his lips and whispered. It goes back a number of years. There was a time in my country when five percent of the people owned ninety-five percent of the land, not unlike your south before your Civil War.

Jo Shelby listened without emotion, without movement.

My family has always been for the poorer people, the peasants. To give them land from the large haciendas so they can make their living, so they can feed Mexico, so Mexico does not have to get its corn from the United States and other countries. In 1946 my family did not support Alemán, Miguel Alemán, who ran for president. Instead we supported Ezequiel Padilla who we knew would follow the great work of Cárdenas who was true to the ideals of the revolution. There was still much land in private hands and we wanted to see more of it in ejidos, plots of land given to the people to farm, something like your share-croppers though not exactly the same. When Alemán is elected we change and decide to support him. I think, many of us think, he will be different. He will change Mexico. But it never happens. He becomes like the rest, Díaz and Calles and the Spaniards before them. Dictators. Corrupted by power. Alemán, yes, but the men around him, they become very corrupt. Corruption is so bad in my government, my people think if a man becomes a politician, he must be a thief. But we must talk no more of this. He looked around and slid his eyes back and forth. Too many ears, he continued in a low whisper. And you, you have the misfortune to be here for what reason?

Jo Shelby told him his story and the man listened with great interest, with steady unwavering eyes, sad dark eyes. When he finished the man removed his glasses and pendulumed them between his knees, watched them as though they were a clock ticking, then looked up and spoke.

You know, you are very lucky you did not get further and were not arrested in Saltillo or Matehuala or San Luis Potosí. There the prisons are very bad. But even here, this is very sad, this situation. His eyes were grave and glistened and for a moment Jo Shelby thought he saw the formation of tears along his lower lids.

Not any sadder than yours, he said.

Ah, mine. He forced a wrinkled smile, his face aglow from the yellowish light filtering down from the high windows. Mine is a matter of time. I only have to wait. But you, my friend. His face went serious again. You cannot afford to wait.

You're beginning to sound like that captain that put me here.

It is true. Americans die if they stay too long in Mexican prisons. Mexicans, well, Mexicans just outlive it.

That ain't what I heard. Some of em get knifed and cut up and get killed in here just like Americans do in American prisons.

What you say is true. That does happen. But I speak generally, you know. Mexican prisons are much like Mexico. Very corrupt. You pay the right price, you go free. He snapped his finger. That simple. Most

Mexicans are very poor. They can pay nothing. They can only wait. They can only hope.

How much you gotta pay?

That I cannot answer. They may want the gun you speak about. They may want pesos, American dollars. Who is to say.

I ain't givin up the gun. If its still even around. That captain may have already taken off with it.

But, Jo Shelby, he cannot. The gun is evidence. Without the evidence they can have no hearing. No, the gun, I think it is going nowhere.

Well they ain't gittin it.

I understand.

I'll give em some money.

You wait. We can talk later. I have some connections. He leaned in closer. Some of my students are in here, he whispered and grinned.

Some of em are prisoners?

Some. He winked. I can say no more.

Jo Shelby thought. And you're still in here?

Shuuu. We must be careful. Sometimes it is best a man be where he is. I cannot explain now.

Jo Shelby removed his cap and scratched his head and placed the cap at the head of the bed.

We can talk later, in the yard, after evening lista, away from hungry ears. He cast his eyes about the large room where the only sounds were those of a snore rattling, the steady clicking of the fan and a radio playing faintly. But for now you must know other things, he said.

Ramón went over some of the instructions covered previously by the guard, the listas, that the horn would blow and punctuality was of most importance. He pointed at the door behind the fan and told him it led to the toilets and showers, that the showers were crude and often did not work and the hot water ran out quickly so he needed to be early in line if he wanted a hot shower. There were rows of washbasins outside along the east side of the yard where one so inclined could wash his own clothes, and a line to hang them on though most brought them inside because of theft. The dining room was along the western wall of the complex and was entered from the yard and meals were served after roll call in the morning and at two o'clock in the afternoon.

What about supper? Jo Shelby said.

You Americans, Ramón smiled. You eat and eat, he said. He patted his stomach. Perhaps myself excluded, but how many fat Mexicans you see so far? Women, yes. But men? Do not answer. I know your answer. Maybe a few. But not many. We eat only two meals. Supper, as you call it, is a snack for us. The men you saw in our little cantina, they were eating supper, those with a few pesos to buy it. There is a snack served in the dining hall, at eight o'clock. There is no horn to tell you. You just go.

Any women in here?

No. They are in another prison south of here. Why do you ask this question?

Don't know. Just thought it might be nice if there were. Mexican women are somethin else, the ones I've seen anyway.

You like? He grinned.

Ain't seen a ugly one yet. Even the fat ones are purdy.

Ramón slapped his knee and laughed. You will see them on Sundays, he said, the day of visitation, but only at a distance, unless one comes to see you.

Not a chance.

You have someone special, a novia?

You might call it that. But she'd never come down here.

You could write to her. We have mail.

Naw. Nice thought. But I wouldnt want her to know the mess I've gotten myself into. Say, Ramón. That it, Ramón?

Sí.

Anybody ever escaped from here?

Do not think of it. No one has yet. Some have tried. They were foolish. But this is a new prison. They will keep testing it. Someday maybe, somebody. But for you, it would be very foolish.

But why's it here in town and not out in the middle of nowhere?

Because this prison is one for rehabilitation, like the sign on the front says. The people put here, how do you say it, they are the less criminal. Killers? Robbers? Yes, some. But most of us here are not the bad criminals. You saw the men at work, no?

Yes.

Once they stole with their hands. Now they learn how to use them to make crafts. These crafts are sold all over northern Mexico. Some maybe across the border. The money goes into a special account so when the men are released, they leave with some money.

I could do that. I work good with my hands. And they ain't never stolen.

Ah, but Jo Shelby, you are special case. Please excuse this thought, but Americans are no good for Mexico. By that I mean they come awhile then are gone. They bring nothing with them and they take. Oh, they leave dollars, but most Mexicans never see these dollars. So gringos are outcasts, pariahs in Mexican prisons. They take up a space, he palmed his hand at the bunk on which Jo Shelby sat, and they take food and drink, and give nothing back, except, of course, the payoff money they give to the guards and others above them. But nothing trickles down to the prisoners here or the people beyond these walls. So you see, gringos are set apart. It is like an unwritten rule among prisoners. All gringos are fair game, as you Americans say. Guards and officials look the other way. That is why, Jo Shelby, you need to leave here quickly. Gun or no gun, if you wish to live to see your family, he concluded, the grim eyes again leveling out beneath wiry eyebrows from which shot wild aberrant strands.

Gringo. I heard it before today. What does it mean?

The meaning goes far back some years, some say to the war your country fought with my country. In your history books it is called the Mexican-American War. In ours the American Invasion or the time your country robbed us of one half of our country. He gave a twisted smile. Others say the word originated when your General Pershing came here with his army to chase Villa, Pancho Villa. You know the name?

Yeah. Saw a picture show about him once.

Pershing's men wore uniforms of green color. Mexicans learned to say, *Green go home, green go home,* and so you have the word gringo.

They talked awhile longer, about the prison, their countries, the differences between the two. The bars on the windows above them were cast on the opposite wall which had taken on an orange tint from the dying sun. Moments later a horn sounded, one long blast, and after it bells from the town, the cathedral tower he guessed, long deep gongs, and then they fell silent and only their echo carried in the thick air.

That is the first one, Ramón said. We must go. Five minutes and the second one will sound. We cannot be late.

Jo Shelby reached for his cap to put it on.

I would not wear your cap, señor. It looks too American. Draws more attention than you need.

He left the cap and followed his new friend, down the long billeted corridor and through the large circular room where men were scrambling down the spiral stairway, through the cantina that was empty and into the dusty quadrangle that was filling rapidly and abuzz with the collected mumblings of the summoned.

Ramón told him to follow him and they joined a group in a far corner of the compound, beneath one of the towers. He learned the lista was done by cells and that each cell was comprised of one hundred men. A guard with a clipboard stood before each group and as their names were called the men answered. Ramón explained how they used to do it, with one guard standing on a raised platform behind the basketball hoop, which took a considerable period of time, then a prisoner, a man from Sierra León, called out that they take the roll by groups to save time and he was immediately struck down by a guard and taken away and not seen for a week. That same week they began the lista by groups, Ramón continued in a low whisper. The director stood on the platform and made the announcement, as though the idea was his own. We Mexicans are sometimes slow, he smiled wryly.

The calling of the names continued and Jo Shelby listened for his but it never came. The guard standing before their group finished and turned and walked away.

He never called my name.

Do not worry, Ramón said. You are just arrived. It may be days before your name is called, he said and smiled again.

They found a spot against the western wall where they could be alone and sat upon the hard ground, their backs against the wall, their arms wrapped around their knees. The sun cast a long shadow over the yard and the small groupings of men that followed their dispersement. A few shot basketball, passing it around in random fashion, making outlandish shots, clowning. Others smoked and talked, looked in his direction from time to time, sizing him up he knew, deciding who would go first.

You are the only Anglo here, Ramón said.

What?

Anglo. American. One has not been here in some time so they are wondering what is your crime. Of course, they would wonder anyway, but the fact you are American draws more attention.

But I didn't commit no crime.

And I believe you. But these men, they do not have this knowledge. So it is a game they play among themselves. Is he a killer? A horsethief? Cattlethief? Pistolero? Maybe he kidnap a señorita and try to take her across the border. Or he is a gangster smuggling drugs. They speculate, maybe even bet pesos. You are famous now. He looked at him and grinned. But they will learn. The gossip here goes very fast.

That's what I'm afraid of. By the time it gets around they'll git it all wrong and I'll be a gunrunner smuggling guns to some band of outlaws.

Do not despair so, Jo Shelby. That may be good for you, if they think you are a man of such important means.

Yeah. And the guards'll think I'm rolling in dough and want a bank to git me out. No thank you. I'll take the poor old horsethief.

But that would be much worse. Stealing a horse in Mexico extremely bad. Smuggling guns is much better. That way you are more one of them. It could save your life.

He thought. They both sat and looked out over the yard where the dust kicked up by the traffic of men blew upward from the shadows and into the last rays of sunlight assaulting the western wall and floated there in a bronze haze until the light was no more and they were again a part of the shadow whence they came. Higher up on the opposite wall, the silhouette of a guard paced the catwalk above them. Somewhere in the streets a dog barked.

You want a smoke? Jo Shelby said.

No, señor. I do not smoke. You smoke if you wish.

Jo Shelby pulled the crumpled pack of Camels from his top shirt pocket and fingered out his last cigarette then realized he had no lighter.

You got a light?

No, but one moment. Señor, tiene un cerillo? he shouted at a man not far from them who was smoking. The man was leaning on the wall with his back to them. He turned and regarded them with brief circumspection then walked slowly over and held out a book of matches between fingers stained by years of tar and nicotine and Jo Shelby took it and tore off a match and struck it and lit his cigarette in cupped hands and returned the matches in like fashion to the man who received them with the same reserve as he had offered them.

Muchas gracias, Jo Shelby said.

De nada, the man said and turned and walked back to his leaning post on the wall.

You speak some Spanish, Ramón said.

Naw. Just a few words, and he told him about his Venezuelan friend on the boat and the handful of expressions he'd picked up from him.

You were going to Mexico, all the way to Cuernavaca, to look for your family and you do not know Spanish?

Yep. Reckon so. He squinted as he sucked on the cigarette, as though a sudden pain might have hit him, and blew a long stream of smoke.

Ramón's brow creased in astonishment and he shook his head from side to side. Señor Jo Shelby, you are either a very brave man or a very foolish one. There is trouble enough for one traveling alone in this country, but to do it and not speak the language, that is asking for more than trouble. Here in Matamoros the people speak some English, because we are near the border. But the further south you travel, the fewer there will be who speak your language, except maybe when you get to Mexico.

The city you mean.

Sí, señor. It is the city of which I speak.

Just makin sure. He slapped at his ear where a mosquito whined.

You must let me teach you. He raised his back from the wall and scooted around so he was facing more directly his prospective student and leaned over and tapped him on the knee.

This would be very good for me, to teach you, he said, his face animated, a light for the first time in his black eyes. His teeth within the smile were perfectly aligned and flashed brightly in the shadows and reflected the difference between him and the others surrounding them of more obscure and desperate origins.

Jo Shelby looked at him, blew another stream of smoke into the air, contemplated it as if it carried his thoughts.

Yep. Reckon you're right. A feller ain't gonna git very far down here not knowing Spanish.

That is good. Then we have a deal. I am the professor once more, and you, my friend, are my student.

All right.

No, sí. You must speak in Spanish, as much as you can.

Okay. Sí.

Bueno, which means good. And we have here before us our chalkboard. He pointed at the ground. And the chalk. He picked up a small twig and displayed it in the air between them.

But something don't seem right.

Yes. And what would that be?

I oughtta pay you something.

Ah, but señor Jo Shelby. You do pay me. You pay for my time . . . with your time. He slapped his thigh and laughed and Jo Shelby felt a touch of humor, a chuckle, working its way around his mouth, drawing the muscles out in a grin.

Guess you got me there, he said.

For a while the older man of one language instructed the younger man of another. Ramón drew in the thin dust with his twig and erased with his hand and drew again and Jo Shelby listened when he was told to listen and repeated when told to repeat, and so the beginnings of new words and sounds went until the scribblings in the dust were no longer legible in the developing dark and they just talked.

You still ain't told me yet how you got here, Jo Shelby said. There ain't nobody around now.

This is true, Ramón said. But there is not much left to tell. My father was a banker in Monterrey. His bank controlled many investments, much land. He was willing for the government to buy this land to return it to the peasants. Others in the government were very much against this idea but my father rode with Villa at one time and his heart was with the revolution. Even though Calles, or Carranza, there is still some dispute, had Villa killed, my father's heart was still with the revolution, with the people. My father was a brave man. He accused these other men of their corruption, exposed them for all of Mexico to see and one day, walking across the Zaragoza Plaza, right in front of the cathedral, men drive by in a car. They stop. They pull out their guns. They shoot him. There in front of everybody. And they drive off and were never found. They were never brought to justice, he said as his exasperated hands came down out of the air where they had acted out the story and rested calmly on his knees and his voice choked and trailed off.

The hooded spotlights overhead had been turned on but Jo Shelby could not see his face in the recessed dark of the wall where they had been since the lista. He only guessed that the almost tears he had seen early had finally sprung and the sadness he could only know through another's words was finding its way to the surface one more time.

There was quiet awhile, then Ramón continued. My family, my brothers and sisters, uncles, we become marked people. Again, not so much by Alemán, but by the greedy politicians around him, who opposed my father and his principles. So when I taught that all of this is wrong and that the government should confiscate these lands, like Díaz had done, even those of the Catholic Church, for the Catholic Church was perhaps the richest, and I am a Catholic, and give these lands to the people, they come and take me. Not in front of my students but in the dark as I am arriving home and charge me with insurrection and they give money to the judges to say it must be so and I am sentenced and that, my friend, is how I come to be here. Not here at first. At first I was in a prison in Monterrey. Then they brought me here, to this new prison.

There was silence again. The tamped conversations of men at the cantina carried in the night air across the yard and they could hear the rumblings of passing traffic in the streets beyond the walls. Fragments of talk between the guards drifted down. Jo Shelby could not see the man's eyes but he felt them, tired and resigned, along with the voice that had grown weak with the burden of the story it was telling. He thought how to respond to a story so sad but nothing came to mind. Maybe there was nothing left to say. They'd said it all. Almost all.

How long you been here?

Since 1948. Six years, Ramón said.

That's a long time. That's how long I was in. And I didn't do nothing. You didn't neither.

Yes, but six years, it is not long. It is but a schoolchild waiting to grow. I think I will be out soon. My family's lawyers are working on it. That is best. Why should I stoop and do as they do? If I use my influence, my family's money, I only become one of them. We have a new president since 1952, Adolfo Ruiz Cortines, and he is for more honesty in government and is working hard. Just this year women can vote. But it takes time. Every thing in Mexico takes time. The Mexican and your Negro may have something in common. They have learned to wait. I do not worry.

Silence again.

They sat, their minds oblivious to the profundity of the last words, along with the countless others who were equally unaware of the revolutions building once again in their respective countries.

Listen, Ramón said. He looked left and right then at the guards above them. It is best we stay here no longer. It is too quiet. Everyone has left and the guards may get suspicious, that we are sitting here out of the lights.

They arose and walked over to the sheltered area around the cantina, where many men were gathered, men with eyes aslant, lowered lids. He bought a couple of packs of Camels and matches and a bottle of Coca-Cola and paid the man behind the thin warped plyboard counter with one of the twenty-peso bills. He received his change and turned and walked over to the open air grill and ordered three tacos, attempting some of the Spanish he'd learned.

Ramón looked on, then stepped forward and ordered a couple of sopes and they stood and ate and drank and said little to one another among the hubbub of talk around them.

His bed was as he had left it. Nothing had been reclaimed, even among the folded towels and clothes at the foot. There was a man on the bed above him and one on the other side that had not been there before. He spoke a howdy to each but they did not speak back, did not even acknowledge his speaking. The roll call in the barracks took place at ten o'clock as he had been told and his name was still not called. The high-hanging ceiling bulbs were turned out but single lights at each end of the long room remained on and his eyes grew quickly accustomed to the new dark, as they had so many times before. He had no linen but the room was warm with heat generated from all that was caged and pent up. He removed his boots, careful to leave the bills in place and reached at the foot of the bed for a handful of folded towels which would make do for a pillow. He placed them under his head. The odor was not as bad as before and he assumed his nose was getting about as good as his eyes at adjusting.

He lay with his hands folded over his chest, like an acolyte awaiting summons from on high, and tried to think amid the babble of voices that would drone on until the men grew tired of fearing the sleep they fought and the dreams that waited for them. He thought of Parchman and how he'd thought he'd never miss the place and how he was in a place where there would be no weekly letters. No homemade cookies and cakes and pies from the women's club at the church. No small wrapped presents they brought at Christmas. No hoe in his hand to take away the boredom. No reason to feel tired at night and the simple pride of a hard day's work for he would spend his days in the dusty yard with the restless others who, for whatever reason, did not qualify for rehabilitation and work in one of the factory rooms.

He closed his eyes and tried to see Athen. The stuck-out lips and puffed-up cheeks whenever he beat her in checkers or horseshoes. A mischievous grin peering down through the branches of a pecan tree after she had dropped a raw egg on him. The near-stricken look when her mother called and she was where she was not supposed to be and begged his help. A solemn sideview stolen of her while praying in church. Standing beside her while she cried over her pet dog dead at their feet, wanting to put his arm around her but afraid to. A face bright-eyed and smiling after a long afternoon horseback ride, her hair pulled back in a ponytail, ringlets wet with sweat across her forehead, the last time he saw her before he was taken away. He thought of her as he had seen her only days before, it seemed, the grown woman she had become, the kiss, what it meant, wondering if he was crazy to even think the thoughts he was thinking, that she might be in love with him. He thought of his parents and where they would be if they were still alive, and where he would be, and from the lidded dark played out the fantasy what-ifs until his mind grew tired from the long day and the dark received him.

The next morning he was beaten before he could even get out of bed and again in the john, by hands and faces he never saw, alien voices that said only a few words, as matter-of-fact as if they were conducting business. When he came to he was in a stall. His arm was around the base of a commode and he lay in misdirected urine and tasted blood and looked down and saw it on his shirt. He pulled himself up and the nausea hit him and he threw up. Then the nausea went the other way and he pulled himself up and settled his butt onto the rim of the cold seatless basin and his insides exploded. He heard his name called and he answered back and it was Ramón who told him the horn had sounded and he had not much time to get into the yard so he wiped himself quickly with what paper he could find scattered about and pulled up his pants and headed out of the stall.

This is bad, Ramón said, but we need to hurry. Your lip is bleeding.

Yeah. Feel like I'm bleedin all over.

But let us go. Quickly. Wipe your mouth. The men are like sharks. They see blood and they want more.

He wasn't sure where his mouth was bleeding but he wiped it with his hand and continued as they headed out of the cell, running, and into the sunny yard.

This time his name was called and when the lista was over he followed Ramón through a single door at the back wall not far from the basketball hoop and they entered a large hall wherein were arranged in parallel order long wooden tables and benches. Along one wall was a cafeteria-like line of steaming food behind which stood men wearing waist-aprons and holding long serving spoons.

I don't feel like eating nothin, he leaned over and whispered to Ramón.

But you must, Ramón whispered back. The men will think you weak if you do not, and if you do not, you will surely become weak.

He followed Ramón and they went through the line, gathering their metal trays and tin plates and cups and crude flatware spoons, taking what was dished out to them. Tortillas and frijoles and jalapeño peppers. A cup of black coffee, the consistency of which looked questionable. That was all. They walked to a table at the back of the hall where few were sitting and took their seats across from one another at the end of the table where they were alone.

Ain't you kind of singling yourself out, being here with me, Jo Shelby leaned over and whispered.

Perhaps, Ramón said. But I have been here a long time. These men know me. I am not involved in their struggles, their rival gangs. I think it may help you, if you are seen with me. Give you some status. He smiled and winked.

Well if it is, it's sure as hell slow in coming, Jo Shelby said and spooned up a helping of frijoles and placed them on a tortilla and rolled it and forced a bite and felt the pain again from the cut in his mouth. The welcomin committee must be new too, he said.

Lunch and the evening snack will be much different, Ramón said, raising his cup and blowing wrinkles across it before taking a sip. Today is Sunday. Domingo. Another word for you. You are a full-time student now.

I ain't sure what I'm learnin.

As I say, today is Sunday, the day of visitation. The families of the men come and bring food and gifts and items of need. There will not be many men in the dining hall, except here, he made an airy flourish with his spoon, at breakfast, desayuno. Say the word.

Des-a-yu-no.

Bueno. Muy bien. This morning I will be in one of the shops, making picture frames. But not in the afternoon. Then I am free. We work in shifts. This is to give more chances to work for the men. So, class this afternoon.

Guess I spend the morning with my back to the wall, pretendin it ain't the Alamo and I might just live?

The comment brought a tight smile from the older man, the kind that might be not-smile if you covered half of it with your hand. You are funny, señor, Ramón said. But the real truth of what you say is not funny. There is no place for you without danger. He leaned his head out over his tray. Maybe the yard *is* best for you. The guards do not care. He paused to take in a bite of frijoles he'd scraped up with the end of a rolled tortilla and continued speaking with fragments crumbling from the edges of his mouth. But at least in the yard you have a chance. Not inside. He waved his spoon before his face. Inside it is much more dangerous. Muy peligroso.

They ate.

I think I just met Montezuma or whatever the hell his name is, Jo Shelby said.

Just now?

Naw. Back yonder. In the john. The man on the boat. The one from Venezuela . . . ?

Sí.

He told me not to drink any water or anything cooked in water off the streets, even in some of the restaurants. I figure I already saved your Mexican friends in here some trouble. I might not even make it to the yard. Feels like I got a fever all over.

Ah, I know what you mean. This is true what your friend says about the water and food. But here, of course, there is no choice. You will have these problems for a while. That is why you need to make yourself eat. It will take time for your body to adjust.

Yeah. Back to time again. He took a sip of coffee that tasted like swamp water. Like it's become my middle name or something. Jo Time Shelby. Got kinda of a ring to it.

In Mexico our philosophy of time is very simple, Ramón said. For us, time is of little importance. Only two things start on time in Mexico: bullfights and mass. Everything else we just push behind us, like the swimmer, and look ahead to tomorrow, mañana. Even death for us has no conclusion. It is just a state of being, with its own mañana. He looked up over his food and grinned. You will hear that word many times in Mexico, mañana.

I already have. And no problema. Mañana and no problema. A man might could hang his hat on that.

They ate on amid the clamor of the hundreds around them and when they finished took their utensils to a receiving window near the doorway and exited into the yard.

He began the morning standing with his back to the southwest corner with the thinking that at least half of him was protected and the other half could keep a watch and it was Sunday and half of them were with family and wives and kids which meant he had half a fighting chance. But that wisdom lasted maybe a few minutes and he found himself rolled and beaten and kicked from one end of the yard to the other like he was a human football on a field with no goals and no referees and no way of keeping score unless it was who got in the most licks without killing him because if he died the game would be over which meant the fun, too. He'd shit twice in his pants and peed too many times to count and at times couldn't tell which was which. All that saved him was the horn at lunch which was obeyed as though it were the bell at a prizefight and after the lista he stumbled to his cell and the john to clean out his underpants and put them back on damp and dirty. He looked into a small cracked mirror that hung crooked over one of the corroded sinks and examined his face. It was lopsided and swollen as a pumpkin grown irregular by contrary elements. There were flecks of red along the blubbery blue and purple of his lips where blood had clotted and an upper tooth atilt. He splashed water on his face and let the pain rise and fall of its own. He went back to the bunk and collapsed and noticed the towels and dirty clothes had been taken away but not the rest of the trash with them. Ramón came in and complained about what had happened to him and offered words of comfort but they seemed a long way off where his ears had been pummeled by fists dirtier than the ground on which he rolled.

I think my nose is broke, he said, moving it back and forth with his fingers, feeling the slippage and pop of bone and cartilage along the ridge.

It does not look good, Ramón said. But you have survived.

So much for sittin with you.

I am sorry, Jo Shelby, that this terrible thing has happened to you. But it may be the beginning. Un momento. He left and returned with a wad of toilet paper. Here, take this, he said.

A little bit late for that. I done shit till I cain't shit no more.

No, señor. Make little balls with it and put it up into your nose, Ramón said and tore off a piece and rolled it in his hands and gave it to him. It will help your nose absorb the blows. Then he showed him how to layer his gums and lips with rolled padding from the paper.

Your face is already swollen, he said, so it will look no different.

Ramón reached for a towel hanging from the end of his bed and told him to take off his pants and roll it around the inside of his groin and bunch it around his privates, and Jo Shelby did so obediently but with much consternation.

I will be with you this afternoon in the yard but I am afraid it will be of no help, Ramón said. These men are bored and they will amuse themselves until they tire. I have spoken to someone, but they say it is of no use. They can do nothing.

Jo Shelby shook his head he understood and they went into the yard and he defended himself as best he could. He fought with his back to the wall and his back on the ground and his back spinning with nothing to support it and kicked and gouged and clawed but when it was all over and the six o'clock horn had sounded, and the cathedral bells afterward, he was a crumpled heap in the dust with no one around him until he felt a hand under one armpit and his body rising and looked up and saw Ramón's somber face.

Ramón shouldered him to one of the washbasins along the eastern wall. He almost crashed into the plywood shelving and realized his left eye was closed shut and he'd lost his depth perception. With a nurse's touch Ramón removed the soaked tissues from his nose and mouth and washed his face with cold water and he felt pain in different places as the water touched new cuts and it seemed there was no place on his body that was not in pain. When he opened his mouth it hurt back in the hinges and he was afraid he'd broken his jaw. There was the taste of new blood from the last blows that were thrown when an uppercut came from nowhere out of the sun glare and his teeth clapped down on his tongue which was right before he fell the last time, not long before Ramón picked him up.

Ramón half dragged him to his bunk as there was no strength in his legs and when he tried to move his arms discovered there was none there either, all of it drained from him by the beatings without and the hemorrhaging of his insides which had left his throat and anus raw as sandpaper. The fact he'd had nothing to eat came as an

afterthought. Ramón went to the cantina and bought him some frijoles and mashed them up and mixed them with water in a tin cup to
a soup-like consistency, propped the towels behind his head and
spoon-fed him until the pain of swallowing became too much and he
had to lie back and view the coiled springs of the upper bunk with the
only eye still open.

Sometime before bedcheck a guard came to his bunk. He stood
over him for a moment and said something brief in Spanish then
threw some bed linen at the foot of his bunk and set his knapsack on
the floor beside him and left. Jo Shelby asked Ramón to open the
knapsack and check the contents and Ramón did so and called out to
him the objects one by one as he removed them and laid them on the
side of the bed. A pair of blue jeans. A white shirt. Underwear, two
pairs. Pair of white socks . . .

Jo Shelby ticked them off in his mind as they were called out, waiting for what wasn't said than what was . . .

A watch, Ramón continued, fishing out the pocketwatch by its
chain then pulled out a small bottle. I do not know this but it looks
like medicine maybe, he said.

Damnation, Jo Shelby said. Pain shot along the sides of his jaw
with the excited word and he dropped his volume back to the tem-
pered level where it had been. Them's aspirin. Almost forgot about
them.

Ramón shook a few out in his hand and lifted it cupped and tilted
before his patient's mouth so they rolled in and Jo Shelby let them dis-
solve in his mouth and felt the burn as the amalgamated spittle
worked its way down his throat.

Go on, he said.

Some Band-Aids. A small box. But they will help. You packed for
trouble, Jo Shelby, no?

Naw. Somebody else did.

Then they packed for trouble. They must know you very well.

Don't wanna talk about it. Talkin hurts. Go on.

Toothpaste. A bar of soap. That is about all, Ramón said.

He pushed his hand deeper and rummaged further.

No wait.

He pulled out the pictures and the letters with them.

There are some pictures and old papers, letters maybe. Yes, they are letters. Very old letters.

Thank God, Jo Shelby breathed.

They are important to you.

Important ain't the word.

I think that is all but it feels like something else but the bag is empty.

Check the side pocket.

Ramón found it and pulled out the last item.

And a map. It is of Mexico. He held it up to the light where he could see it better. A very good map.

You sure that's all.

Sí. There is nothing else.

Shit.

There is a problem?

The knife. They took my granddaddy's Barlow knife.

But now you have some clean clothes, and linen. We can get you washed and dressed, your bed made. It will make you feel much better.

Hell, naw.

You do not want to feel better?

And give em somethin clean to beat on. And somethin clean to waller me in. Not a chance. I'll just keep what I got on thank you.

By midafternoon of the next day there were only skirmishes and he sensed the worst was over. His sleeves hung in strips from his shoulder and his jeans pockets were all ripped and hanging open like shredded tongues. His boots were scuffed but otherwise the only piece of clothing still in one piece. He retired to a corner and let himself down easy and hoped he was upwind and wouldn't have to smell himself. After a while Ramón came and sat beside him.

You reckon it's bout to stop?

I do not know, Ramón said. For now, you have outlasted them.

Outlasted hell. I feel like hammered shit.

But you were not knifed. You are still alive. It may give you some respect.

That like bein seen sittin around with you?

No, señor. Ramón grinned. They are not the same. This is something you have of your own, he said then recast his face in one of serious thought. But do not think it is enough. Do not turn your back. You have been once in prison. In your country. Among your people. In Mexican prison you must always keep the eyes in the back of your head. Always.

He said nothing back and tried to light a cigarette but couldn't hold it between his fingers and it dropped into the dirt between his legs. Ramón reached over and picked it up gingerly, blew off the dust and lit it for him and placed it in the side of his mouth where he held it loosely between lips so puffed up he could see them across the bridge of his nose with his right eye.

He bought some frijoles that evening and mashed them with a spoon and washed them down with a Sun Spot orange and took some more aspirin and went to bed with the concussions of recent days pounding in his ears and thoughts of prisons and how they were as different as one town might be from another, one country from another, and the things about them that never changed, like the human race. There was no shame in the pen where he had been and there was none here. There was honor, which was their confinement, and pride, their trades. Thievery. Murder. Prostitution. Smuggling. They were the best in their field and had graduated into the academy where they would learn more, perfect their craft, and disdain any and all who were different from them, which included him. He would know in time whether or not he passed the test. He thought, too, that they were boasting of their triumphs over him, of who hit him where and kicked him where and how he looked rolling and sommersaulting under their assault, the victory their violence had brought them and he followed these thoughts and thought it was really no different from town to town and country to country in a world that cannot see its own perversions in its wider circle of men. The last thought turned back on him and he saw on its reverse side the goodness of people throughout the world, families taking care of their own, and his mind held to it for as long as it could.

The next morning was Wednesday but he thought it should've been Sunday, the day a man once rose from the dead. He showered and dressed in clean clothes and went to the small tienda and bought some more Band-Aids and aftershave because of its alcohol content and the healing effect he figured it would have on his cuts, burning those sons of bitches away. Ramón gave him some Vaseline for the more serious wounds and he used it as well in the deep clefts of his buttocks where the pain burned like a hemp rope pulling back and forth every time he took a step. The diarrhea continued and seemed none the better despite Ramón's optimism to the contrary.

That day a pump was broken in Ramón's shop which gave him the morning off and Jo Shelby's lessons resumed under the shade of the eastern wall and continued after the midday meal in the shade of the western wall.

Men would walk around them and stop and look on with innocent stares, listen and mumble to themselves, then walk away. A few would stop and hunker down as though they were joining the class, their heads bobbing as though they caught the gist of the lesson, then push themselves up on their knees and move on.

The days seemed to melt one into the other without any clear demarcations of time except the sounding of the prison horns and the cathedral bells. The celebration the waiter had told him about had come and gone but bursts of revelry could still be heard in the street beyond the walls. There had been no celebration within, beside the fact that he was still alive. His watch had been stolen in one of the fights and he didn't miss it for two days. Six years he didn't wear one and for six years never knew the time and was glad not to. Didn't even keep a calendar, as so many others did, marking off the slow passage of days, protracting the pain. So when he thought he saw it on the wiry wrist of another nothing of revenge or anger welled within him but instead a feeling of pity for one poor Mexican who was toting around some extra time and he decided that justice had probably been done and left well enough alone.

He was learning enough of the new language to engage conversation with others, which he did timidly at first, cautiously, then proceeded more boldly and confidently until he found himself slowly drawn into that world of barter and exchange which every prison has if you speak the right language, verbal or otherwise. Someone wanted cigarettes, another matches. A man pointed at his cap which he now wore like one might the Flying Cross or the Purple Heart and gestured he'd give twenty pesos for it and he had to go running to Ramón to ask how to say, it ain't for sale. A man whose face was a blur of memory, maybe one of the ones who'd beaten him, saw him buy a can of tomato soup at the prison tienda and immediately came up and offered a handful of loose chewing gum sticks and cigarettes for it and he politely turned him down, as he had all the others, and for the same reason. They had nothing he needed or wanted. What he wanted was at a higher tier in the tangled politics of the walled village, removed from the struggle of status and position he was just beginning to break into, and he guessed he'd have to work up to it and hope for a little luck, and maybe some help from Ramón, though that was looking more and more remote and the messages he was getting from him more and more confusing. Twice he'd asked him for help in getting information about the gun and how he could get it back and Ramón's response each time led into the same circular argument.

You must first get your freedom, then you try and get the gun back. They may see it is of no use and give it back. Maybe it is no problem for them.

So I give em enough money and they let me out.

Sí, this is true.

But how much? You ain't told me how much.

That I do not know. What is enough for one man is not enough for another. One comandante's needs is not that of another's.

Okay. Fifty American dollars.

That might be enough. It might not.

So then I have to give em the gun.

Again, my friend, it is difficult to say. Perhaps so. Perhaps not. But in this case, maybe it is so.

But you just said it was no problem. Now you say I give em the gun and the fifty dollars and I git out then I don't have nothin and I'm back to square one.

But you have your freedom.

But I ain't givin up the gun.

Jo Shelby, my friend. There was a look of exasperation in his eyes, the lines in his broad face threads of tributaries drawn downward toward his chin. You have told me about this gun. It is a sentimental thing from your family's past. Your life is not sentimental, it is reality. Your life is one thing. An object of sentiment quite something else.

Naw now. May have started out like that. But I done invested a chunk of my life in that gun. It's like a part of my family. We done gone beyond what you call sentimental.

I understand this thing you tell me, Jo Shelby. You are a man filled with much passion, to find this family of which you speak.

It aint a this, it's mine, he said.

I am sorry. It is surely as you say. And your passion is one greatly to be admired. My family, it also is very important, and of great value, to me. Family is very important to my people. Without strong families there would be no Mexico. But a man must separate his family of the past and their history, from the family he has now, or the one he plans in the future. This is a big problem with my country. Many of my people are too attached to the old things, sentimental relics, ideas, the old ways of the past. They cling to them, as though they expect their salvation to come from them. But our salvations, Jo Shelby, he leaned in closer to him, his eyes flaring like fires rekindled, our salvations are always ahead of us. They are never behind us. Do you understand these things of which I speak?

Images and thoughts of home crossed his mind as the man spoke. Confederate flags waving at ballgames and crowds standing and roaring whenever the band struck up Dixie. His granddaddy telling him to never vote Republican because that meant voting for a scalawag or a carbetbagger, either of which was the worst kind of Yankee. A picture on the wall of the barbershop in Drew of an old Confederate soldier, sword drawn in one hand and the Confederate flag held aloft in the other and the words beneath FORGET, HELL.

I think I do. Go on.

This passion you have, my friend, if it is for relics of old, it will surely die, and become as lifeless as the relics themselves. There comes a time a man must let go of his past, and the sentiments of his past, and become a man of vision, ah, a romantic, that is the word. Do you know the word?

Kind of. I know what romance is.

Yes, but that of which I speak is more than romance, because so much of romance is sentimental, it hopes things will never change. But the true romantic is a man of vision, he is a man always looking for things to come, hoping against hope for things always to change. The sentimental man, he is a man imprisoned, buried in the nostalgia of his past. It is a good thing, this passion that you have, but you must decide which family it is you seek, and what you will have to discard to find it. One final thing. He raised a finger slowly into the air and held it steady. You are my friend and you do not have to do what I say. But I pray for you, that you think on these things.

I understand, he said and paused a long moment. Guess that's what's pullin at me, what you been talkin about, sentiment and all. Just some things a man caint give up easy, not right away anyhow. Maybe I will some day, but I just caint see lettin the gun go. It'd mean they won.

Very well, my friend. Maybe you will think more on it. But for now you are in the square one again, as you call it, entre la espada y la pared.

His granddaddy would've said it made the rock and the hard place look like a Sunday school picnic but he said no more at that time.

He broached the subject again one afternoon, in the middle of a lesson.

You are not listening to what I say, Jo Shelby. If you speak less of the gun and more of the money, I think you have more of a chance to get your freedom . . . and the gun.

That don't make a damn bit of sense.

You give the gun too much power. You give to it too much importance. They say to themselves, these officials, Why does this man want this gun so? Maybe it is something of great value. They do not think as you.

He patted his hand over his heart.

They do not know this feeling which it is you have.

Jo Shelby listened. And thought. Nodded his head he understood and Ramón continued with the new lesson of the day.

In the days that followed he stayed to himself in the yard during the morning hours, and calculated, moved the combinations around in his mind, the ones that might work and the ones that were sure not to. He watched who went in and out of the barred gate that led to the patio which led to the front offices. He needed to get to the comandante. Maybe he is a man hard-pressed. Maybe he has a son or daughter about to go off to some Mexican college. Or maybe the universal joint in his truck fell off and he needs another one. He had yet to touch the money in his boot, which at last count was about a hundred and eighty-five dollars, and was still living off the sixty pesos he'd had in his billfold and cigarettes which bartered better than money.

Then one afternoon.

I got a hunderd dollars, he said.

Ramón gave no reaction and bent over and with his hand smoothed the dust where he'd etched some new phrases with his stick then looked up and placed a finger over his lips. That is much money, he said. Muchos pesos para un mexicano.

Sí?

Sí. Es verdad, he whispered.

So, it's enough.

Ramón thought. He stroked his lower lip with his thumb and forefinger. It is possible, he said, still whispering, looking around to see who might hear. But you must be very careful. The situation, it is very delicate. You must bargain. You must let *them* think. That is best. You go too fast, they think you are desperate. If once they think you are desperate, you are lost.

So what the hell do I do? Just sit here and wait for them to come knocking on my door? You said I didn't need to stay here long.

All of this is true. You are in a most difficult position. You need to find your way out before they charge you. Once they charge you it becomes even more difficult, almost impossible. But you cannot move too quickly. I will see what I can do. Give me some time.

Mañana, huh?

He smiled. Sí. Mañana. Then regarded him gravely. Tal vez muchos mañanas.

More than several tomorrows went by. Three weeks. Almost a month. Neither of them spoke of the matter. Jo Shelby ate his meals in the dining hall to conserve his money and practiced what he was learning from Ramón on the few friends he had made. A teenager named Jesús from Monclova, in for stealing a car. A young dark complected Indian from somewhere down south who'd killed a man for raping his wife only to have the wife disappear on his hearing day. Two cousins named Paredes who'd tried to rob a café and shot and killed the owner when he pulled a gun on them. All of them told him what he had been told before. That he needed to get out before he was formally charged, but he said nothing to them of his plan.

He was ready to make his move when a hand shook him one night and another went clap over his mouth and he rose up with a drone of snoring in his ears, his eyes peering directly into Ramón's.

Do not speak, Ramón whispered in his ear. I have some news.

He raised up his head and Ramón pushed it back down.

The comandante will see you. I am taking away my hand but you must not speak. Comprendes?

He nodded he did and the hand was taken away.

In a whisper thin as the air it traveled Ramón told him he had spoken with someone he knew, whose family was from Monterrey, someone he could trust, a guard. This guard worked directly under the comandante, was something of an attendant who was also over the guards and assistants in the front sector of the prison. He would let Jo Shelby in to see the comandante, but he must have a reason. If this guard just opened the gate and let him through, others throughout the prison, who watch the gate like hawks, would become suspicious and cause great problems.

This is a most fragile world here, Ramón said. One little ripple causes a great wave. Ramón's mouth was almost touching his lobe and his breath blew hot down the ear channel when he spoke. You must become sick. Maybe you do something to make yourself sick, but you need to be sick where others can see it.

He put his hand behind Ramón's head and pulled it onto his chest and put his mouth to his ear and breathed, Can I talk now? and released his head.

They were close enough to be lovers in a place where homosexuality seethed and was treated as a sin deadlier than any crime. Their lips were inches apart and their arms in half embrace.

Yes, but very low, and in English, Ramón said. The words in here carry, especially at night.

I ain't been sick a day in my life cept being beat near to death.

I understand. But I have a plan. He put his mouth once more to Jo Shelby's ear and articulated what he should do and what he should expect and Jo Shelby gave slight nods with each step of the unfolding strategy and when Ramón had finished he leaned back and Jo Shelby pulled his head back to his chest again.

When does this happen?

Mañana. After the morning meal.

Does the comandante know?

He is aware of the meeting.

He know why?

Only that you wish to speak with him. That is all. But he is not ignorant. One more word.

Yeah?

I would say nothing of the gun. Remember what I said to you. Now, we must speak no more. He gave a grandfatherly pat twice on Jo Shelby's chest and returned to his bed.

Jo Shelby turned over to face the opposite direction and saw in the bed across from him, through the half-darkness of the half-lit barracks, the curled shape of the man he knew only as Carlos, his head only feet away, his eyes wide open with the raptness of a night creature.

It rained that night and fine beads of moisture drifted down from the open barred windows high above and brought with them fresh smells from the world outside and memories of other rains on other days, the way a fine steady rain will do. He thought about his mother's apple pie and could see her in the kitchen bent over pulling it out of the oven and slicing it up and sliding it from a spatula onto a blueplate china saucer and putting it in front of him, and the steam curling from it. He could see his father clear as day hitching up the mules to the middlebuster and the tobacco-stained grin as he hoisted him up in the air and placed him on the back of one, hear the coarse gee and haw of his voice as he steered them down the rows. He thought, too, about Athen, the hours spent climbing pecan trees, wrestling in cotton rows, passing notes in church, riding horses, the trails they'd ridden into sunsets and away from them, arriving home in the dark, the light of the moon leading the way. He remembered how she looked the last time he saw her, the filled-out body and madeup face, the deeper voice. And again the kiss. He closed his eyes and imagined it touching him again, the soft-wet of her mouth covering his, only remaining longer, and longer, while the rain drummed softly.

The ground was soft and his boots sucked in the mud as he walked from the dining hall to the sallyport that led to the courtyard. The sky was overcast and the air heavy with the smell of the threat of more rain. It was too early for sweat to break but his clothes stuck to him as if he'd come in from hoeing the fields. There were men loitering around the yard and he headed toward a spot where he would be in clear view of all. Midway he stopped and grabbed his sides and doubled up and fell to the ground. He didn't look up but heard shouts and the muted padding of footsteps across the congealed dirt. Someone leaned over and said something in Spanish and he groaned and the voice hollered at others nearby. Soon he was ringed with anonymous feet and boots and voices, probably the same that had kicked and cursed him from one end of the yard to the other, and regarded the contradiction with silent wonder. A guard came and bent over but did not touch him.

Estás bien?

No. Estoy enfermo.

De qué?

Mi estómago.

The guard reached down and cupped a hand under his armpit and he let out a groan as he was pulled up, his knees still half-buckled under him, his head bent downward, sagging like he'd seen outlaws shot in the Saturday picture shows.

Venga, the guard said and tugged on him and angled them both in the direction of the porticoed walkway.

He felt the weighted stares of the encircled men and could see only the ground and the corral their legs made around him then the legs swung open and let them through.

Médico! the guard shouted at another guard standing at the gate who quickly unbolted the lock and let them pass through then bolted it behind him. The two guards exchanged comments, an apparent discussion about rank and privilege and who got to take a prisoner out of the compound and all the while Jo Shelby hung onto the shoulder of the first guard wondering how much longer his knees could hold out half-bent. Then the guards concluded their discussion and the one keeping the gate won and Jo Shelby was exchanged and the other returned to the yard slamming the bolt through the gate as he left.

The new guard said nothing. They went through the first barred area that he had finally decided was a buffer against breaks, then the gated courtyard and he found himself standing in the large open room that was the foyer through which he'd come more than a month earlier. The guard sat him in a metal folding chair against a wall across from the comandante's office and told him to wait, then walked down a side hallway.

There were two women huddled together in the room across from him, peasant types, their heads bound in assorted rags, oversized men's shoes on their feet with the toes cut out. One had been crying, and the other, an older woman, was comforting her. From what he could gather from the fragments of Spanish he caught, the one crying had come on behalf of her husband and been denied a conference with the comandante. She clutched a small leather bag that might have held their life savings. Jo Shelby observed the scene a moment, its tragic poverty, futility. He rubbed his toe against the edges of the bills in his boot, toyed with the idea, then heard footsteps coming back up the hallway.

The guard reentered the foyer and told him to stand and he did. The guard leaned over and whispered the comandante would see him and motioned him to follow. They walked to the door marked CO-MANDANTE in large block letters and the guard knocked once.

Permítale entrar! a voice from behind the door said.

It was as Ramón had said it would be. Everything prearranged. No questions as to why there was a knock on the door or who was there to see him. Permítale entrar. That was all. That was the quiet power at work where more was understood in silence.

The guard opened the door for him and he entered and the door was closed behind him.

The comandante was sitting behind his desk studying some papers. He was not wearing his hat. The room was as before. Through the barred window Jo Shelby could see children kicking a ball back and forth in the cobbled street. He waited a moment then walked to the empty chair in front of the desk.

Con permiso, he said.

Sí, siéntate, the comandante said and looked up and smiled. So, you learn some Spanish while you here.

Sí. Un poco.

Bueno. Entonces vamos a hablar en español.

Well, I ain't got a degree in it or nothin.

The comandante coughed a dry chuckle into his fist. As you wish, señor. We speak in English. So . . .

He stood and brought his hands together in a loud clap.

. . . you come here today for a reason, no?

Yessir.

And this reason is for the mordida, no? He turned and began pacing toward a side wall.

Mordida?

Sí. It is like a, shall we say, like a tax.

Nobody said nothin bout no tax.

The comandante stopped. From his sideways profile he cut his eyes severely back at Jo Shelby in a manner that carried harsh enlightenment.

All right. The tax. Yessir.

The mordida. The comandante said, with emphasis, as if calling the practice by another name gave it legitimacy and clapped his hands once again and continued his studied pacing.

No one spoke.

Jo Shelby remembered what Ramón had said. He sat.

The comandante paced, his heels clicking across the concrete floor.

The children played in the street, their voices carilloning through the window bars.

Finally Jo Shelby realized there must be a set script for this sort of thing and the ball was in his court.

I got fifty dollars, he said. Six hundred pesos.

The comandante stopped and turned and faced him. For a moment he said nothing, just stared at him through dark and glassy eyes that seemed fired from deep below, a drug focus born of some violent potion. Then he leaned forward and planted his fists on the desk, his eyes sucked back up under his brow like they might be loading up.

Señor, that is money to piss with.

Jo Shelby thought of the woman outside clutching the leather bag. That's all I got.

The comandante rapped the desk once with his fist. No señor. This is not the truth. I am doing to make this easy for you. I need you help. Do not make difficult. You have more.

No sir. That's all I got.

You have no one in you family, no relatives?

I don't know.

You do not know?

No sir. My family's all dead, like I told the captain at the other station. That's why I'm in Mexico, tryin to find if any of em are left.

The comandante did a slow pirouette with his index finger pistoled under his chin then pulled out the chair and sat down.

This very confusing, señor. You say you family dead but maybe no dead.

Some of em may have come down here long ago.

I see. He rubbed his hands in a meditative fashion. So. No much money. No family. You have muchos problemas. He scooted back the chair and stood again.

More silence. More pacing and waiting.

Then the comandante stopped and turned and tilted his body forward from the waist like a bow, his hands akimbo on his hips.

But you have this gun, señor.

Jo Shelby read his eyes that darted back and forth in his head like trapped minnows in murky pools and the uncertain intent behind them.

You can have the goddamned gun.

Cómo?

The gun. You can have it. It ain't worth nothin. Won't even shoot.

But it worth something before, when you come here.

Well I changed my mind. But I want my knife back.

Knife?

Yeah. The Barlow knife.

This knife. How much it worth to you?

A whole damn lot.

More than fifty dollars?

Yeah. Almost.

Tell you what I do, amigo. You give to me the fifty dollars and the gun . . .

He paced a few steps and turned back.

. . . and the knife and I think we have the mordida we need.

Jo Shelby pushed the chair back and stood up.

Where you go, amigo? We are no finished.

Yep. We finished.

So. We have deal?

No. We no have deal.

Señor, this is not wise what you do. I make you good offer for you freedom and you are like arrogant gringo and spit on it.

Ain't nobody spittin on nothin, señor comandante. I just ain't leavin without my knife.

The comandante rounded the desk and stood in front of him, his breath washing over his face like a hot sick wind. You are funny man, you know. First it is the gun. And now it is the knife.

You got it bassackwards, amigo. I was confused when I came here. Then I got the livin sense beat into me by your inmates in there and ain't no way in hell I wanna be turned loose in Mexico with a gun that don't work but I damn sure am gonna have a knife that does if that's all I got left. Now how's that for confused? Comprende?

The comandante tilted his head back and looked down his nose, black hairy holes dilating with consternation. So, that is you decision.

That's it.

You make big mistake, señor. Guardia! he called and clapped his hands with a sultanic flourish.

The guard who had delivered him opened the door and entered the room.

Lléveselo! the comandante said angrily with a backwards flip of his hand and the guard seized Jo Shelby by the arm and hustled him from the room. The two women were still sitting in the waiting area, eyeing him roughed away as they might a helpless animal led to slaughter, as though they knew, too, what was also beginning to take shape in his mind.

His earlier conjectures about the room where he had been frisked and made to undress were quickly coming true to form. Another guard joined them and he was ordered to remove his shirt and drop his pants to his knees. He knew they would see the old scars but they had probably seen so many it would not matter. While one looked on and the other swung the whip he was lashed until the pain blended with the new pain from each stripping and it all ran together so that all he felt was one long continuous fire burning out of control across his back. With the same perfunctory casualness as he was commanded to undress he was told to put on his shirt and pull up his pants and was led through the series of gates and into the yard where he was turned loose, no longer an object of curiosity by the men who had no doubt heard the echo of lashes across the quadrangle and had already spread his tale among themselves. But his cries they did not hear. For he felt certain he would be called back if he did not cry out. And he had not.

He sat on his bunk while Ramón washed his back with a damp rag and the pain seethed with each stroke over the vein-bared derma. He asked and Jo Shelby told him what was said and what happened and the older man muttered consolations and reinforcement as he continued to pat his back with the rag.

You wait. He will meet with you again, Ramón said.

What makes you so all fired sure?

Because, señor, you said he was angry, no?

Yep. Could see it in his eyes.

The anger you saw in his eyes. That was not anger. That was greed. It was the comandante who blinked first, señor. Not you.

I need to buy me a knife. Know where one's for sale?

No. You do not need a knife.

You see the way the men looked at me when I come out of there, the way somebody looks at you by not looking at you. It don't look good. I can smell a knifin.

I do not read the yard the same as you, my friend. The men have seen this kind of thing before. To them it is nothing. Some may be a little confused. You go in sick, you come out beaten, but that is all.

Maybe. But Carlos, our next door neighbor over there, he nodded at the empty bunk, don't read like that.

Sí. What about Carlos?

He was wide awake last night when we was talking. He heard us. Bet on it.

Poor Carlos, Ramón said. He is a man to be pitied. It has not been a good day for him. His wife and mother came to make a mordida and the comandante refused to see them. He has been most depressed. I fear if he hurts anybody it will be himself. Besides, if he heard he heard nothing. He speaks no English.

Ramón took a towel and daubed his back dry and began spreading Vaseline with his fingers. Jo Shelby arched upward at the first stroke.

This will be very painful, Ramón said, but it will keep out infection. Here, take this.

He handed him a towel.

What do I do with that?

Aprieta los dientes y aguántate.

Jo Shelby took the towel and shoved a wad in his mouth and bit down but figured talking was better and he put the towel aside.

How the hell did you arrange this?

Shuuu. We cannot talk about this in here, Ramón said looking over his shoulder and around the room.

There ain't nobody in here now.

There is not a place where no one is not in a prison. You must remember that. One can never tell. He leaned in behind his ear and whispered. The guard who let you in, the one at the gate?

Yeah?

He is one of my former students. I told you about him earlier.

He's the son of a bitch who beat me.

The beating was not intended.

What the hell was intended? You told me not to push.

This is true. I thought there would be talk. Some bargaining. Hopefully a settlement. There is always the risk of a beating. Juan had to do what he was told to do. What did you do to anger the comandante so?

Not much. Just a shade this side of a dog-cussin. I figure I confused the shit out of him.

You are lucky a beating is all you got and not torture. In Mexico the torture, believe me, is worse than death. They will do almost anything to get a man to confess. Put electric shocks on his testicles. Cover his head with a bag of ammonia. Force carbonated water with chili pepper into his nose. Anything. They have no morals, some of these officials. They do not care. They are underpaid and the only way many of them can take care of their families is by the mordida. I have seen the police take students from their cars, right on our campus in Monterrey, for no reason. The students return hours later with their faces and heads bloody and swollen. The police took them to the barrios where no one would recognize them and beat them until they paid a mordida of only a few dollars. It is a bad situation. And getting worse I am afraid.

You ever tortured?

Once. Relax. This one is very bad.

Ouch.

That was the worst one.

What'd they do?

They put my head in a latrine and held it under until I could breathe no more.

You confess?

No, he chuckled. They thought they had drowned me and became afraid, because I was a sensitive political prisoner. After that they left me alone. There. That is all. He wiped his hands on a towel. How do you feel?

Like death takin a shit.

He laughed softly. You Americans and your imagination. You stay in and rest. I will bring you food.

Jo Shelby turned around on the bed.

No shirt, Ramón said, holding up a finger of admonishment. The wounds must breathe.

This air might kill em.

You have not lost your sense of humor, Jo Shelby. That is good, he smiled.

That may be all I got left fore this is over, if that.

I think not, señor. You are what we call in Mexico sobreviviente.
Somethin bout livin.
Por poco correcto. Survivor.

A WEEK WENT BY and nothing. No word from the comandante.
No signal from any quarter. No murmur along the prison grapevine.
The sun was tracking lower over the walls and the shadows laying flatter it seemed and spreading out farther across the compound. The
daytime heat had lost some of its heaviness and the night gained a cool
edge. The squared sky seemed a softer blue and the early and late colors in the clouds that traversed it brighter and lighter. Back home the
leaves were turning and falling and the black-eyed Susans were full-bloom along the roadsides and the dark fields dappled with late cotton
hanging from its black stems. Women were getting out winter clothes
and putting up summer's, raking their yards and picking turnip greens
and kale and cabbage from what was left of their summer gardens.
Men were gathering in the cafés in the early mornings and plowing
under harvested acreage, weather allowing, and when the weather didn't allow gathering in the cafés and drinking coffee and smoking and
talking about hunting and football. On weekends everybody that was
anybody was dressing up and going to one of the ballgames at State or
Ole Miss and the folks that were nobody were busying themselves in
their yards watching them drive by and it had been that way for as
long as he could remember and he was sure it still was and would be
when he got back. If he ever did.

Scabs had barnacled over the wounds that would be permanent
scars and he could wear a shirt without pain, but he still had to sleep
facing down, his nose captive to all that was sour and rancid of the men
before him, seeping upward through the thin mattress. The lessons
with Ramón continued in their school-like ritual and he played checkers a few times with a new friend, a man named Felipe from Santa
Teresa. He strolled one day through one of the shops and saw a set of
washers and bought them for a few cigarettes and dug holes in the yard

and introduced a new game and gained a handful of new friends. Each in his own way, and when the time was right, told him he should bargain for a mordida as if they'd heard nothing of his first attempt.

Carlos he watched with greater scrutiny, watched him watching him. For a month and a half side by side they had lived, their beds, their homes, inches apart. Undressed and gone to bed and risen and dressed side by side and even peed in the same urinal trough side by side and once stood side by side in the mess line and the entirety of the time Carlos had been mute, grumbling and grunting and lowering his eyes when Jo Shelby spoke to him, trying to make right whatever was wrong of which he had not the faintest notion. He spoke of it to Ramón but Ramón said Carlos was still depressed and a man whose mind had become the mouth of a scavenger turned inward to forage on the scraps his life had left behind.

Don't nothin about it look like it's turned inside, Jo Shelby said. Looks ever bit like it's turned outside and only got one thing in mind. He knows somethin. He saw his wife and mama last Sunday.

So, what if he does have some knowledge? Maybe he is resentful. Perhaps a little jealous. Maybe still mad because you took the bed and he had to readjust his life. But he is a mouse. You know his crime?

Naw.

He was arrested for having sex with a child. Men of this kind, they are not liked here by anyone. They are pariahs.

Yeah. I know. It was the same where I was.

So then, you must relax. No hay problema.

I cain't help it. He gives me the creeps.

Creeps?

Willies.

Creeps? Willies? I do not know these words.

Let's just say I wish I had eyes in the back of my head when he's around. Even when he's not around. Like you said. There ain't no time in prison when somebody's not around.

Eyes in the back of your head. Sí. But for Carlos. I do not think so. But you feel as you wish.

ANOTHER WEEK PASSED and it was Sunday. He could tell because the cathedral bells rang earlier and longer in the morning and the noise of street traffic was louder. Families and loved ones coming to visit which meant a quieter day in the yard.

Ramón was already up and gone and was nowhere to be seen or heard at the morning lista. Jo Shelby scanned the yard thinking he might have already checked in with the guard and was simply mingling among one of the other cell groups. That failing he waited inside the door of the dining hall and checked the men off as they went through the serving line but Ramón was not among them. He went through the line and got his serving of frijoles and tortillas and scrambled eggs and cup of coffee and went to a table in the back of the hall where no one was sitting and tried to eat, looking all the while at the door, thinking every scenario possible. The hall was only half full which was the norm for visitor's day and he finally concluded Ramón must have had early visitors and obtained permission to miss the lista which was not impossible, but near to impossible. He took his tray of half-eaten food to the disposal window and shoved it through and passed through the hall doorway into the yard to watch the comings and goings of men through the courtyard gate where they met loved ones who brought food and newspapers, cigarettes and other commodities of prison luxury and what money they could spare from their meager budgets. It was almost like Sundays at Parchman except there you couldn't see the men hunching their women up and down a concrete wall with the statue of some saint several feet away. There the men were allowed to see their wives in one of several conjugal houses, clapboard buildings set apart from the main camps where small rooms contained only a single-sheeted bed and chair and enough space for letting out their love but never enough time to catch up to it as one man put it who described the closet-sized chambers to him and what went on within the thin walls and how listening to what the others were saying and screaming was almost as entertaining as the tricks his woman did for him.

He was musing upon those thoughts when he saw Ramón pass

through the gate he'd been watching and head in his direction with what seemed a deliberate slowness in his pace. He was halfway across the yard then turned and walked toward the south wall.

Jo Shelby smoked and watched.

Ramón stopped at the basketball hoop and spoke to a couple of the younger ringleaders gathered there, then ambled toward the southwest corner and engaged conversation with one of the other older prisoners, a former professor like himself, whose distinction likewise was that of counselor and advisor to many of the prisoners.

Jo Shelby kept watching.

The two men spoke for a few minutes. They nodded and gestured with their hands and nodded some more. Then Ramón walked a few feet and sat, his back against the wall, his knees propped up, his face upturned absorbing the early morning warmth of the sun. He maintained that meditative posture for a half an hour, never moving a muscle, as though his eyes had locked onto some beatific vision, then suddenly pushed himself up and cut a diagonal path across the quadrangle toward the cantina. Jo Shelby was on his right about thirty paces away and it appeared he would walk past him with no acknowledgment then he turned suddenly, as if by some inward secret command and headed straight for him and sat down.

What in the unholy shit is goin on? Jo Shelby said. First you don't show up for the lista, then you don't show up for breakfast, then you come out of that front gate like—

Do not speak, Ramón said. He was leaning with his back to the wall so they were not facing each other but the tone of his words carried the same directness.

Jo Shelby took a final drag on his cigarette and flipped the spent butt into the yard.

Minutes passed. Nothing was said.

There is something I must tell you, Ramón finally said, in a low voice, but we must talk as though we are speaking of the weather.

Jo Shelby looked straight ahead. This weather here we're talkin about seems like it's bout to change, he said.

This is true, Ramón said, himself looking across the yard, showing no emotion. There is a change in the weather, he said.

I suppose you're gonna tell me what the hell it is so I can git out of its way.

The comandante wants to see you.

Silence again. Only the muted cacophony of scattered chatter throughout the compound. Vehicles coming and going, crunching gravel in the parking lot outside.

So the big boy's had a change of heart, Jo Shelby said.

It is all very simple, but I can say no more.

They were talking like two men watching something in the distance trying to figure out what it was they were watching.

So I just walk right up there to the gate in front of God and everbody and tell señor guard standing there I want to see the comandante? That it?

Sí.

You gotta be kidding.

No. The comandante said it would be most natural, that you are to say you have family waiting and give your family's name and the guard will take you to the front, to his office.

Idn't that guard standing up there now the same one that beat me within a inch of my life the last time?

Sí. This is true. But I think you have no fear this time.

How can you be so sure?

I cannot. Nothing is ever sure. But, believe me, I think you have nothing to fear.

How the hell did you pull this?

That I cannot tell you. I must go now. Just do as I said, but give it a little time. He pushed himself up and hand-brushed the dust from his pants and walked away toward the cantina and disappeared among the crowd of men congregated there.

Jo Shelby did as he said and smoked a cigarette and waited and smoked a second cigarette and decided enough time had passed and got up and ground the butt under his boot heel and made his move.

Sunday was a day of general distraction and he wondered why the comandante hadn't thought of Sunday before then decided he probably didn't think much, just went with the pressure of the moment. He approached the guard, his eyes on the ground, as though he were looking for something he might have lost there in the dust the day before. He spoke to the guard in Spanish and told him he had family waiting for him and the guard asked the name of the family and he told him Ferguson. The guard looked at him with cold black eyes then unbolted the gate and slid it open and allowed him to pass through and slid it back with a loud clang. He followed the guard across the stone walkway through another set of gates and the courtyard and into the foyer where a large crowd of people milled, families awaiting their turn.

The guard knocked on the comandante's door and the comandante opened it and told Jo Shelby to enter. The guard closed the door behind them and they were alone once more. The comandante walked over and stood behind his desk and the same chair was in front of it as before but Jo Shelby stood where he was.

So. You have had some time to think about you situation.

Jo Shelby said nothing but nodded that he had.

Please, sit, the comandante said and motioned toward the chair.

Jo Shelby walked toward the chair and stood beside it but did not sit. No sir. I'm still thinkin and I can think better standin, he said.

Very well. As you wish. He began pacing again. So what is you offer for the mordida?

Jo Shelby walked toward the barred window and looked out at the traffic passing, people sitting around tables at the bar across the street, then turned around. A hunderd dollars, he said.

The comandante stopped pacing and turned. His brows were knitted, forehead pushed down over them, a face contemplative, ruminating. It is good you have time, this time to think. He rubbed his hands together. And the knife?

Nope. No knife. A hunderd dollars. That's it.

The gun?

No gun.

But the gun, you say it is no important to you.

Yep. That's right. But I figure it and the knife's worth twenty dollars at the most.

The comandante rubbed his chin and balanced it in his hand a moment, the simple arithmetic running through his head. But you know, señor Shelby—

Jo Shelby. Jo Shelby Ferguson.

Sí. Señor Ferguson. This gun and this knife, I can keep them. You no control these things. He ticked his finger before his eyes like a metronome.

Yeah. And you can beat the shit out of me again and find my money and control that too.

Cómo?

Forgit it.

You think we criminals here in Mexico. We no criminals. This is business deal. You give, I give. Everybody happy. You understand.

Jo Shelby nodded and wanted to remove his shirt and show him the scars that crisscrossed his back like the etchings on a chopping block. A hunderd dollars, he said. I give, you give. I walk away happy. You go out and buy your esposa something bonito.

The comandante smiled. You Americans are tough customers as you say, no?

No. Ain't nothin tough about it. We just want a fair deal and I've just made you one. I ain't no gun smuggler and you know it. If I was a gun smuggler I'd a had a satchel full of em that could fire and I wouldnt've brought em straight through customs like an idjit or walked through no bus station in Matamoros but I'd've snuck across the border and already been halfway to Mexico City before you or any of your men could say shit a brick. Yessir. I been thinking. Question is, have you?

The comandante's eyes widened and he looked like some dazed mule suddenly struck by a two-by-four and he stood leaning forward in that frozen stupefied demeanor while the words he'd just heard completed their circuitry through his brain then he sat down and took a deep breath.

Tell you what, Jo Shelby said, not giving him a chance to crank his thinking up again. I'll give you a hunderd and twenty-five dollars which is more than the knife and gun put together are worth, and that's all I got. Todos. Final.

The comandante thought.

Jo Shelby turned and walked back to the window. He had calculated the comandante needed money more than things, that the gun and knife might bring him twenty or thirty dollars in Matamoros but not much more and the longer he stayed in prison the lower his money supply would drop and the closer it got to his hearing date, if there even was one, and he banked on the man behind him being at least half smart enough to put all that together and realize that the best deal for him was on the table.

Señor, the comandante said.

Jo Shelby turned around.

I accept you offer.

The remainder of the morning he did not see Ramón who seemed to have vanished again. He skipped the midday meal and bought some tacos and a Coca-Cola at the cantina and carried his food along with his map and letters to the southwest corner where there was shade and sat and ate and smoked and read once more the letters and spread the map and studied again its intricate enormity. Midway in the afternoon Ramón appeared, approaching him from the direction of the front gate.

What've you been up to this time? Jo Shelby said.

It is of no importance. What did the comandante say?

Like you don't already know.

Perhaps. Perhaps not. His face was averted toward the sky and a faint smirk passed over his lips then they straightened out serious again.

We made a deal. I'm gittin out. After the evening lista, but I gotta wait till then.

Ramón gave a single solemn nod, then smiled. Congratulations, he said.

I ain't so sure who there're for. Me or the comandante or somebody else.

And the mordida?

A hunderd bucks plus twenty-five.

Qué bueno! And you get your gun.

Maybe. I don't trust him.

I think if he wants the money you get your gun. And when does this take place?

Like I said, after the evening lista. He said I'm to go to the guard and the guard would let me through. That simple.

But it will be almost dark. Morning would be better. Night in Mexico belongs to the thieves and robbers and the police and there is not much difference between them.

Mornin. Night. Makes no never mind to me. I just wanna git out of this stinkin hole.

They talked a while longer. Ramón reviewed the map with him and gave advice about the country beyond and what he might expect and that he was crazy to hitchhike because of all the bandidos and cut-throats on the road. Jo Shelby reminded him of all the bandidos and cutthroats he'd been living with for almost two months and that what-ever was out there had to be an improvement. Besides, he would've used up almost three-fourths of the money he had and he needed to save. Ramón countered that his life was worth at least a twelve dollar bus ticket to Mexico and that he would be there in fifteen hours but Jo Shelby had already made up his mind and wouldn't hear it.

The shadows were touching the base of the eastern wall which meant the horn would blow in another hour and they would call the evening lista and after that he would pass through the gate and into the world beyond. He thought of what he had to do and excused him-self from Ramón and told him he would see him at the lista and after-wards they could meet and say their farewells and Ramón smiled and nodded in agreement.

The cell barrack was quieter than usual and he saw and heard no one as he walked through the narrow aisle of beds. He replaced the letters and map in the knapsack where it hung from the bunk post and sat and looked around once more to see if anyone was looking. He pulled off his right boot and pulled out the money and separated the pesos from the dollars and counted out a hundred twenty-five in dollars, then what was left which was less than sixty dollars, about twenty of that in pesos. He slipped the pesos into his billfold and replaced the remaining dollars in the boot and pulled it back on. He created three separate stacks with the bills on the bunk then folded them and put one in each side pocket of his jeans and the third in his top shirt pocket and buttoned it down.

He walked to the toilet at the end of the room. The door was open and the only sound he heard was that of water running through a john bowl where a stopper plug was hung up. He stepped up to the urinal which was a tin-sheathed trough bracketed to the wall and planted his feet. He was in that frozen attitude when the door closed behind him. He glanced over his left shoulder and saw no one. A stream of urine hit the metal trough and filled the small room with a dull musical whine. Above it he heard a slight slap, like a shoed foot on wet concrete and he looked back over his right shoulder and caught the blur of a crouched figure halfway between him and the back wall and with a stream of urine still at full force turned completely around and saw Carlos creeping toward him, his arms outstretched, a crude short-bladed knife in his right hand.

Alto, Jo Shelby shouted, hoping it would stop the little Mexican long enough for him to get his pants up but it had no effect and Carlos lunged forward and made a swipe with the knife and Jo Shelby jumped back and fell into the trough so his knees were hooked over the rim, his feet dangling in mid-air. There came a loud thudding noise, measured, like someone beating on the door then he realized it was his heart hammering in his ears. He grappled around for something to pull himself out with but the only thing of any substance his hands could feel was the mesh bottom of the urinal and before he could push himself out Carlos was coming straight at him. There was nothing to do but wait and when the thin wiry body was astraddle his and the dark brown screwed up face and mop of black hair practically in his eyes, the hand holding the knife drawn back, Jo Shelby, without aiming and with all the instincts of a trapped animal, sent the tip of his right boot upward into his attacker's crotch and watched as his eyes ballooned into their sockets and his mouth ovaled to make way for a chilling cry and the bony frame crumpled and fell on him and their combined weight wrenched the trough from its wall clamps, sending it clanging loudly on the concrete floor. Jo Shelby grabbed his attacker by the shoulders and pushed him aside then rolled out of the collapsed trough in the opposite direction and scrabbled to his feet. The door was straight ahead of him and Carlos was to his right, doubled up and laying partially in the trough, holding his crotch with one hand, the other fisted around the knife. Jo Shelby headed for the door, all the while trying to get his pants back up, his buckle and belt end flapping around his waist. Carlos rolled out of the trough and rolled once more and came upright on his knees as a weighted doll will do when tumbled. He was between Jo Shelby and the door. His legs were curled behind him, one hand clasped his genitals, and his face held a silent scream like some stone gargoyle fallen from its pediment. The knife was in his right hand thrust outward with a radial swath that cut off any access to the door. Jo Shelby watched first the glazed-over eyes that checked him then timed the back and forth sweeps of the blade that flashed dull silver in the scant light from the overhead windows then saw the beveled edges where it had been filed on both sides. Carlos was groaning and his upper lip was curled above his deteriorated teeth and he was breathing spittle that foamed and oozed from the sides of his mouth like a sick dog. Jo Shelby could hear his breathing, smell it, quick choppy gasps that reeked of tobacco and regurgitated food. He was sweeping the knife back and forth in the air and scooting forward on his knees, his eyes nervous and vigilant that he keep himself between his intended victim and the door. For a few seconds they shadow fought. Jo Shelby feinted one way, then another, the knife matching each move. His pants were up but not zipped or buttoned, the belt ends still loose. Carlos made another lunge. He sidestepped and swung a boot at the knife and missed. Carlos scooted backwards then released his hand from his groin and raised himself slowly to his feet, the knife straight-armed in front of him, licking the air. Jo Shelby thought but all he could think was he was going to die in a prison shithouse. Carlos was half-crouched and moving like a wounded ape and Jo Shelby saw all the anger a person could accumulate in a lifetime, drawn up from every extremity and nook and cranny of his body and packed in behind eyes where it smoldered like rarefied wild combustibles just before ignition. Carlos jumped forward and made another sweep with the knife. Jo Shelby sucked in away from the blade but heard his shirt rip. He jumped back and quickly assayed the damage. His shirt was torn from one side to the other but there was no sign of blood. Carlos stopped and planted his feet, the knife steady in his hands, no longer sweeping the air like a scythe but a dagger leveled straight ahead. Jo Shelby jumped backwards again and when he did the loose belt buckle hit his hand. With his right hand he grabbed the buckle and in a single movement cleared the belt from its loops with a slapping sound that echoed off the walls and reversed his hold on the belt so he was holding the tongue and began swinging the buckle-end over his head. Carlos stepped back, his eyes ablaze with surprise. Jo Shelby stepped forward, the revolving buckle whirring and whopping the air like a crippled fan blade. Carlos stepped back again. Jo Shelby crouched and lowered the path of the buckle so it was on a plane level with the Mexican's startled face and pressed his advantage. They were closer to the door which was a few feet behind Carlos. The obvious became evident and Jo Shelby began coiling the belt around his hand, taking up the slack before the buckle hit the side wall. Carlos must have seen it, too, and a twisted smile crossed his face and he took a few steps backwards toward the corner next to the door and waited. The belt tether was now half of what it was. The buckle swung faster on the shorter leash but it's range was cut in half. Jo Shelby moved in closer.

They were at a standoff. Carlos crouched into the corner feinting with the knife. Jo Shelby moved in front of him swinging the buckle inches before his face. Both of them timing. Guessing. Praying. Jo Shelby for someone to open the door so Carlos would be pinned into the corner in which case he could rush through to safety. Carlos for his enemy to move too close and the buckle hit the wall. They had been looking into each other's eyes, reading them, but the only message forthcoming was that one of them was going to die and one was going to live. It seemed they would stand there until the men came in from the lista when Carlos made a sudden move and threw out his left arm and caught the leather strap then dove forward with the knife. Jo Shelby sidestepped the plunge but the knife had already crossed his right shoulder and he felt the sharp pain. He spun around. His back was to the wall and he could no longer swing the belt. Carlos was in front of him. Jo Shelby's hand was wet and sticky where it gripped the belt and the pain further up in his shoulder was a dull ache but he still had movement and strength and he swung the buckle at the knife in an attempt to dislodge it and missed and Carlos took advantage of the opening and made a sweep across his mid-section and nicked his stomach. He knew he had been cut but did not know how bad and was afraid to look. There was less than a yard between them. A lost second was life or death. Jo Shelby slid along the wall toward the door making wild swats at the knife with the buckle. Carlos moved with him each time jerking the knife half-a-second ahead of the buckle then he took a half-step closer and pulled the knife back so his elbow was half-cocked for a forward thrust. This time Jo Shelby saw it coming and timed his move. Carlos lurched and he jumped aside and the Mexican's momentum carried him slamming into the wall. The knife popped loose and went clattering across the wet floor toward the collapsed urinal. Both men stood and looked at each other, then the knife, then back at each other again and their eyes telegraphed the same message. If his assailant went for the knife he was out the door and Carlos knew it too and for a moment neither moved. He was the taller and bigger of the two and even with his right arm wounded he knew the advantage was his and he swung his weapon one more time at the Mexican's face but Carlos leaned back and the buckle hit lower and Jo Shelby saw the sudden arterial stream spurt from his neck. Carlos seemed unaware of the damage and charged. His head caught Jo Shelby just below the rib cage and sent him backwards against the wall and they fell to the floor. At first Carlos was on top, flailing away with his fists, completely unaware a small river of blood was pouring from his neck. Jo Shelby was losing strength fast in his right arm and threw a hook with his left fist that caught Carlos on the ear, at the same time thrusting his left leg and hip upward and they rolled and he was on top. Carlos's white shirt was blooming with blood and Jo Shelby's hands were covered with it and it was splattering up into the air each time he landed a hit. They rolled back and forth in a growing pool of blood, gouging and scratching and clawing and swapping blows like two drunks in an alley fight until Carlos lay on his back, breathless, the blood running steady from his neck. He raised his head and whispered something. Jo Shelby couldn't make it out but the man's eyes were quiet and resigned and his arms flat and limp on the floor.

You had enough or you want more? Jo Shelby breathed, then repeated it in Spanish.

Carlos said nothing. His eyes blinked slowly. They were sad dark eyes and in them Jo Shelby saw the quietude of defeat and humiliation and the disappearing of a life that once was probably good but too poor to pay a bribe and the good people left behind to deal with the sorrow when he didn't come home for supper one night. A wife working hard to keep a hovel of a home that somebody else owned and children running wild in the streets because there was no daddy to play with them. A people much like his who'd only wanted the simple and good things in life but had the misfortune of being born in a place where they were luxuries and not the simple necessities they ought to be. A man happening along at the wrong place at the wrong time.

Jo Shelby quickly removed his shirt and ripped along the tear line from where the knife had made its cut and took a strip of cloth. Using his hand and teeth he made a tourniquet around his own arm to stop the bleeding there. He checked his stomach and saw only a surface cut with little bleeding. With the remainder of the shredded shirt he wiped the blood from Carlos's neck and saw the cut was not as bad as it looked. A small puncture which must have been made by the buckle prong when it hit his neck. He pressed the cloth against the wound and reached over and placed Carlos's hand over it and told him in Spanish to keep it there until he got back then he ran to his bunk to get a towel. When he returned Carlos had moved, in an effort to reach the knife it seemed for his arm was extended in that direction. Jo Shelby walked over and picked up the knife and rinsed it in the lavatory and put it in his hippocket. The horn sounded for the lista and he only had five minutes. He wet the towel in the lavatory and washed around his own wounds then did the same for Carlos and picked him up by his armpits and wrestled him over his left shoulder as if he was a sack of feed and carried him to his bunk. There he laid him in the quiet of the large room with the late light streaming down from the overhead windows and the eyes of the little dark man opening and closing slowly and running wet with tears.

Don't know why you did what you did little buddy but you ain't gonna die, Jo Shelby muttered under his breath. He looked in his knapsack and located the Band-Aids in the bottom. He took two of them and tore off the wrappers and the protective guards and crisscrossed them over the wound to slow the seepage of blood then he placed a damp towel against the wound and took Carlos's hand once more and placed it on the towel and applied pressure and Carlos all the time watching him with eyes of helpless fright.

No moverse, Jo Shelby leaned down and spoke to him softly, Guardar cama, and repeated again for him not to move, not to leave the bed.

Carlos gave a slight nod of his head but said nothing.

Jo Shelby did not know how much time he had left but knew it was very little and draining fast. He had one spare pair of jeans and quickly dispensed with the ones he was wearing and changed to the other. His arm had stopped bleeding. He put on a clean shirt and quickly stuffed his knapsack with what belongings he would need. He put on his cap and was about to rush away but stopped. He leaned once more over Carlos.

Be still. Do not move. I will tell Ramón. He will take care of you. I'm sorry. Lo siento.

He made quick strides across the yard to his cell group and arrived as the second horn sounded. He looked for Ramón as the names were being called out and saw him along the back wall and motioned him aside. He told him of the incident and the renewed urgency for him to leave immediately less he be detained further. Ramón listened with concern and patted his arm with assurance then placed a piece of paper in his hand.

This is my family's address in Monterrey, he said. They will take care of you. Please go there and tell them I will be out shortly.

When did you find that out?

That is of no importance now. You may learn later.

Jo Shelby put the paper in his pocket and heard his name called and answered.

Just take care of Carlos for me. It is not a deep wound but I think I hit an artery. He's lost a lot of blood.

I will see to it.

And if they ask what happened—

Do not worry. These things happen. The officials here care very little about them.

The lista ended and they shook hands and Jo Shelby headed for the gate. He looked back one last time to wave to Ramón but Ramón was hurrying toward the barrack cells.

The comandante was waiting for him and his belongings were on the table, including the gun and the knife. Very little was said. Jo Shelby took the money from his pockets and laid the three folded stacks on the table.

It's all there. A hunderd and twenty-five dollars.

The comandante nodded and raked up the bills and counted them. Jo Shelby could feel his heart beating fast in rhythm with the counting and expected a guard to enter at any minute and halt the transaction. The comandante finished and nodded toward the items on the desk and Jo Shelby picked them up and put them in his knapsack.

Buenas tardes, the comandante said. Y buena suerte! and he extended a hand and Jo Shelby shook it.

You go now, the comandante said. You go back to you own country and you own people. He made a backwards gesture of sendoff with his hand.

Jo Shelby turned and walked from the room. A guard awaited him outside the door and escorted him to the sallygate and opened it and he walked through it into a calm dusk that was settling over the city and onto a quiet street which led he knew not where.

FOUR

THE SUN HAD NOT YET SET and the western sky was
bloodred, the rooftops beneath it silhouetted in myriad
stairstep shapes. The street ran both ways and he had no
idea where he was in the city but knew Monterrey was to the west and
began running in that direction. There was little traffic in the street, a
few people strolling the sidewalk, couples holding hands and mothers
with children underfoot. Dogs jumped from hidden alleyways and off
porches and barked at him, snapped at his heels, but he paid them little mind and kept running.

He ran several blocks and stopped to get his breath and check his
bearings and ran again. He looked for street signs but he was in an old
part of town and there were none. He slowed his pace, began walking
briskly and came to a bar where a few men sat outside on the step
smoking. He greeted them in Spanish and they holaed back. He asked
the direction to Monterrey and one pointed up the street in the direction he had been running. The man spoke too rapidly for him to fol-

low every word but he caught ruta and Rio Bravo and Reynosa and the general picture that the prison where he had been for over two months was on the western edge of the town and he was not far from a major highway. He thanked the men and continued on his way.

Night fell fast, filling up the streets and alleyways first. A quarter-moon was cocked back on its rim and an evening star beamed not far from its horns. Together they looked like the ensign of a flag unfurled across the firmament. He ran along unlit streets where the buildings grew smaller and smaller and the shops became fewer until there were none and what dwellings he passed were matchbox shacks alit with single bulbs through the wide cracks of which he saw people gathered and heard the sounds of eating and drinking, of laughter, of family.

He ran on. Shops began to appear once more and with them cafés and bars where the lonely and romantic were beginning their rendezvous and he knew he had passed through the worst of the barrio though those who lived there might say it was the best, for they knew no difference, had known no other. Up ahead a line of streetlights burned above low tiled roofs and he heard the sounds of heavy traffic, people leaving the city, he hoped.

The street junctured the highway diagonally and continued on the other side, an intersection quartered with fruit and vegetable stands and makeshift stalls in front of which were rows of ceramics and brass pots and radios, hubcaps and used tires and other assorted wares, some of them displayed on blankets atop carhoods of vehicles that looked to be as traded and shopworn as the goods themselves.

He stopped at a stall where a man was selling coconuts. They were spread out in tiers on odd-shaped slabs of plywood laid across saw-horses and covered with tarpaulin strung between four unpeeled poles. The man asked if he wanted to buy a cup of coconut milk. He declined politely and asked the man which way to Monterrey.

Derecho, the man said, pointing at the highway, Reynosa entonces Monterrey.

Qué distancia?

Doscientos cincuenta kilómetros, más o menos, the man said, tilting his open hand back and forth in the air.

He had learned some metrics conversion in the prison and by studying his map knew that a kilometer was little more than a half a mile and did the breakdown in his head and put Monterrey at about a hundred and fifty miles away. About. That was not hitchhiking miles. He knew the road went due west through Rio Bravo to Reynosa then turned southwest to Monterrey which meant stops and stops meant waiting and if he didn't catch a ride soon he could end up stranded on some deserted stretch of Mexican highway lacking only a sign that said beat me and rob me.

Adiós, amigo, he waved to the man as he headed back toward the road.

Adiós, que te vaya bien, the man said, waving back.

Jo Shelby waved back, shouting he hoped all went well with him, too.

He stood for a long time, his arm outstretched, thumb cocked in the air. No one stopped, even slowed. His arm grew tired and he walked further down the outbound thoroughfare thinking a new spot might change his luck. The road was wide and lined with single- and two-story tiendas and other establishments, some with balconies and grilled railings. He passed a flower shop and lumberyard and a small factory that made loading pallets. Most were closed or closing. He passed a couple of street vendors pushing their carts homeward and people riding bicycles, some old enough to be his granddaddy. Open were the cafés and bars, their brightly painted colors visible in the furthermost reaches of light. Sounds of music and laughter and the tinkling of glasses and kitchenware came from them and smoke curled from beneath their corrugated eaves as if from something simmering for a long time on a stove turned down low. He walked until the streetlights were no more and the road darkened and the land before him lay flat and anonymous and lifeless except for a few lights shining nearby and those further in its endless void.

He stopped and thought about what he should do, continue on

and hope for a ride or find a resting place for the night or walk back into the city where the police might be roaming the streets looking for him. He thought about Carlos and his condition and how Ramón was making out with him and the story he had told to the officials.

He had lost track of time and the only timepiece he had was the pocketwatch in his knapsack. He decided he was better off in the dark unknown than where there were lights and people and he went on for a couple of hours, walking along the graveled edge of the highway, passing wayside tiendas closed for the night. Diminutive shacks and half-shacks and lean-tos, some disqualifed even as that. Excuses for dwellings, wired and patched together with the flotsam and jetsam people leave in a desert, or have had stolen from them there. Where whole families probably lived and ate and bathed and slept and all of that in the square footage his mama had used for an outhouse.

He had long since ceased extending his thumb in the passing lights that did not slow, wary of fools that would pick up another that late at night. In near lightless desert. In land where nothing grew from all he could tell. Lights from passing vehicles scoped the dark before him, their reflections riding the wires overhead, streaks of silver flying across the land then dying, like meteorites he had seen on Friday nights sleeping under the stars in his backyard. City glows bulged along the horizon ahead but they looked far away, too far for a person to try to reach walking.

He stopped at an abandoned jacal made of cardboard and scrub oak sticks and discarded car parts. It might have been used at one time to sell produce for there was the smell of rotting vegetation about the place. He made a sweep with his foot across the floor and found it level and settled onto the ground along the backside and used his knapsack for a pillow and thought about what all he had done and where all he had been until he could think no more.

Day was breaking when he awoke, the sun not yet up, the sky flooded with color over the monochrome land. He walked a short distance and a man in a flatbed truck hauling gravel picked him up and took him to Reynosa. He ate a breakfast of coffee and frijoles in a small café on the western outskirts of the town. He stopped at a tienda and bought a small flashlight and some batteries and some Hostess cupcakes he was surprised to find on the shelf. He used a restroom at a gas station and sponge-bathed with discarded paper towels he found on the floor and brushed his teeth and shaved and changed into the only extra pair of clothes he had and placed the ones he'd been wearing in the knapsack to be washed later, in Monterrey he hoped.

He caught a ride with a trucker who deposited him in a small town whose city limits sign said China. He stood beside the sign with his thumb hooked out wishing he could write and tell his mama that he was way ahead of her, that he'd gone more than halfway to China. But she knew. She was watching. He'd done her proud.

An elderly man driving a pickup laden with vegetables and fruit picked him up. He was friendly and toothless and seemed eager for company and the way his sombrero dwarfed his head reminded him of the old man who took him to Rome. Knee something was his name. Bonee. He was thankful for the Bonees in this world.

They exchanged pleasantries and agreed the weather was good and that Mexico and the United States were great countries. They were both going to Monterrey. There was very little else worthy of conversation. They rode across a flattened ash-colored land of arroyos and gulches and ponds the color of rivers he'd left behind in Mississippi, pools miraculously unaffected by the relentless heat and sun-blaze that seemed to have parched all else in range of its power. As far as his eye traveled all that grew was mesquite and scrub oak and tall cactus that looked like the still-living lopped off tops of coconut trees and scattered among all that a white-flowering shrub that gave the effect of a random scattering of snow over the otherwise bleak terrain. They crossed a stretch of grassland where fan-shaped trees sprouted, their boughs lowering near the tops of the high grass. He asked the man the name of the tree but the man could not understand and kept saying arbol and Jo Shelby dropped it. They passed charred timbers where there had been homes and occasional livestock foraging along the fencerows and young children carrying bundles of wood on their backs and women carrying pails of water and men riding burros and all of them moving in a barren and chalky land where there seemed to be no points of origin or destination.

They had been traveling not yet an hour and his eyes grew tired. He turned his head to rest it when something in the distance snagged his vision, something so new and different and strange he thought it might have been a dream or a mirage or some trick reflection off the windows. They rose from the land like humped behemoths from a time long removed, long bluish masses tiered beneath shelvings of gray and bluish clouds so intertwined were they in their own distant chemistry he could not tell at times where one left off and the other began. His vision held constant on them for miles and he hoped they'd draw near for he'd never before seen a mountain. He asked the driver their names and the man said they were the sierras and that they were the single most beautiful thing in his country and the symbol of its strength, that he could sell his produce in Reynosa or Matamoros but that Monterrey was the meeting place of the cordilleras and the most beautiful spot in the whole world and that it mattered not at all whether he sold anything because for him just to go there was like going to where God reaches down from the heaven and touches the earth and blesses all who are there to receive it. Jo Shelby told him of places in the United States that were as beautiful and the man asked him to name one. Jo Shelby thought a moment. Longer. Then finally said he guessed there wasn't one as good as that after all and they laughed.

Whatever else flashed by in the country they traversed he did not see for he could watch nothing else but the mountains that drew nearer and nearer. He scrutinized them as they tumbled down the sky toward the road, observed their shifting moods, their changing color—hazy blue to ambiguous dark, to browns and greens and grays rising up to meet him in the folds of the foothills. So focused was he, so drawn into their presence, he did not see the city when the truck crested a rise.

Monterrey! Monterrey! Sierra de La Silla! the driver called out.

Jo Shelby scooted to the edge of his seat for a better view. A sprawling city washed white in the light of the sun, dark mountains hovering around it and one of unusual design towering over all the others. As perfect a saddle as ever was crafted, perched on a long bareback mountain high above the inhabited valley below, a saddle on which a man could ride forever, he thought, up the ragged sky and through the cloudy draws as the words of a song went his father had taught him. He bet his great-great-great grandfather and those who rode with him saw it like that too, a cloud-capped saddle ready to ride, and they would ride it in their dreams for years to come as he would in his and the little Mexican driving the truck and anyone else who had seen it as they had, the place where God touched the earth and sculpted the idea.

The road into Monterrey followed a wide riverbed where only a stream fingered through its rocky, boulder-strewn width and from there the city fanned out on either side across the valley floor and up the slopes of the mountains. He asked the driver the name of the river and the driver said it was the Rio Santa Catarina but that it was only a river when it rained and if it rained hard and long it was a beast. They passed a foundry and what appeared to be steel mills and other large factories where smokestacks spewed dark columns into the air and lesser industries whose parking lots were filled with new model cars and trucks of all kinds.

Mucha industria, the driver said, nodding left then right.

Sí. Eso es bueno, Jo Shelby said.

The little man peered straight ahead over the steering wheel and lifted a nonchalant hand in the air. In solemn tones he said it was too soon to know if the industries were good for the country, that more money was going to the rich and little to the workers.

Jo Shelby knew all about the rich getting richer and the poor getting poorer. There was more money in the Mississippi Delta than in the entire state, maybe even in the Union, and if somebody was waiting on more money to make life better for everybody they might just better go to the end of the line. And if they were waiting on factories so people could have decent jobs they might as well start a new line. No planter was going to give up land that had been in his family for a hundred years and crops growing there at least that long. Land was as sacred as his mother's grave. Mexico had one leg up on where he came from.

The highway merged into a tree-lined boulevard where the traffic was bumper to bumper and in that congestion they moved slowly along. There were high-rises on both sides and tall office buildings and hotels with neon lights still on from the night that said *no vacancy* and in the bajada beneath them a cluttering of board hovels and the portable stalls of the campesinos eking out a meager survival in the shadows of commerce and extravagance.

They made a right turn and crossed a bridge and entered what appeared to be the city's busy center. Modern office buildings and hotels, restaurants and curio shops lined wide streets, some arcaded against the sun's heat and glare, all of them alive with color. The sidewalks were crowded with the slow movement of people of rank and standing, milling and peering into shop windows filled with the latest fashions and appliances and technology.

They passed a large square and the driver pointed and called out its name. Plaza Zaragoza. Jo Shelby leaned his head partially out the open window to get a better view of the place Ramón's father had been gunned down. Handsome government buildings stood solidly alongside a cathedral and its bell tower and beyond that he could see the mountain peak shaped like a saddle and the cragged Sierras to which it belonged. He drew his head back into the cab and remarked once more to the driver on its beauty and the driver nodded in quiet agreement.

In one section of the city through which they passed musicians strolled playing and singing. Carriages of ancient design drawn by aging and rattle-boned horses rolled sleepily along and for a moment he thought he might have passed some boundary of time.

The driver turned and they entered a grid of narrow cobbled streets and finally stopped at a small plaza ringed with vendor stalls that looked much like the town squares he had known any given Saturday.

He asked the man if he could help and the man said he needed none, that he had no tables or canopies like the others, only his truck. Jo Shelby told him he had sold vegetables from his father's truck where he was from and the man flashed a gummy smile but said nothing. He asked him if he knew Monterrey very well and the man said just a little, that he came only to be among others like him, to be near the mountains and go to the cathedral. Jo Shelby pulled the small piece of paper from his jeans pocket and opened it and showed it to the man and asked if he knew the address. The man held the paper close to his eyes and looked about, then back at the paper and finally said he had no knowledge of the street but that someone else around the plaza might be of more help. Jo Shelby thanked him and shook his hand and as he did saw in his face a look of kindness that seemed not to change from face to face in the others he had encountered along the way, faces of hope and honor and resolve and hard work. He held the man's hand longer than he should have, and looked at him, so he would never forget the kind face. He knew nothing else about the man, not even his name.

Others around the small plaza were as friendly and as generous with their time but none knew the street or the part of town in which he might find it. By the position of the sun he guessed it was mid-morning. He bought a Coke and a taco from a vendor and a newspaper and sat on a wooden bench beneath a laurel tree and took his time enjoying his snack and a smoke and gleaning what news he could from the paper. He noted with surprise the date, November 8, for he thought he was much further along in time. The headlines were about happenings in Monterrey and Mexico City of which he knew little. On an inside page there was some news about the United States, something about the general election and the Democrats regaining control of the Senate and House and something about a man named McCarthy and all the people he was accusing of being communists. The back page was filled with sports news, most of it about Mexico. He was about to close the paper and lay it aside when he glanced a heading atop a small column tucked into the right bottom corner.

E.U. FUTBAL. He lifted the paper and pulled it close to his eyes and tracked them down the file of scores and there it was. Ole Miss 51, Memphis State 0. The feeling at first was good, as though a piece of home had come to him and he had reached out and touched it. Then it began to sink in, like an innertube he rode once in the creek when it punctured. He knew it wouldn't take him home. He decided to stick with Mexican news.

Some small barefooted children with dirty faces came up to him and held out their hands for money. The hands were tiny and the fingers curled up, as though already holding on to what had not been given. He rummaged in his pocket and pulled out a few pesos and gave one to each. They thanked him and smiled and ran away. He was comfortable in the warmth and cool breeze and wanted to remain but the address he had was a small place in a large city. He threw his trash in a bin at a corner of the plaza and was about to cross the street when he saw a stylishly dressed señorita coming his way. He waited until she reached the corner then approached her. She was glad to help and looked at the address and said she had no knowledge of the place but that he should get a taxi and be taken there. He thanked her for the suggestion and crossed the street and flagged a taxi. He gave the driver the slip of paper and opened the door and got in.

The driver said he did not know the place but that he could find it. He was short and his head barely cleared the top of the steering wheel but his high-stacked black hair made up for any deficit of stature, or seemed so designed. He pulled a map from the dash and opened it, scanned it quickly, then refolded it and placed it back on the dash. He leaned forward and placed both hands on the wheel, put his foot on the clutch and downshifted then stepped on the gas and the car bolted forward.

The driver hung over the wheel like a crazed rag-topped demon holding a runaway steer by the horns, so sharp and jarring were the turns he made. The car bounced and fairly sailed through the narrow streets and crossed blind intersections and ran red lights whether or not cars were within crashing distance, all this urban terrain negotiated with one hand on the horn. If he had a brain he'd honk it, Jo Shelby thought, and watched between his fingers as the trumpeting phaeton skimmed the sides of buses and cars and swerved within inches of people walking and people on bicycles and children playing and dogs whose fate it was for their noses to have taken them that day so close to their last slavering breath, leaving in its wake a hysteria of squalling tires and blaring horns and profanity and barking dogs and no telling how many near heart attacks and spasms of panic thrown back on the curbs and sidewalks.

He had been fully and duly warned by others. The dangers that could befall him in Mexico. Bandidos and desperadoes and malcontents. Of all manner of corruption and greed and deceit. Montezuma's revenge. Venereal disease. But somewhere in the earnest and protective passing of information no one had bothered to tell him about Mexican cab drivers.

The car barreled out of the old barrio and onto a wide boulevard, its tailpipe scraping the pavement, its carriage bouncing on the worn shocks. Jo Shelby had sunk low into the backseat and saw only the rooftops of cars streaming from right to left across their path and he scooted even lower and covered his eyes with his hands and pressed his feet against the floor to brace himself. Tires squealed and horns beeped and he felt the side to side veer and sway of the death car he was riding, for he was certain not even God could save him this time. He was going to die on a Mexican street, without even time enough to mourn his own passing. There would be twisted metal and powdered glass and scattered hubcaps and wheelrims and fenders. Bodies. Blood spilled everywhere and people screaming and no one to claim or recognize his body and all he could think of, the thoughts whipping through his head like a film speeded up, was where he would be buried and who would attend his funeral and who back home, if any, would know when it was all over and done with.

Suddenly all was quiet and smooth. He lowered his hands from his face. Slowly. He looked out, first left then right. On either side the swift indifferent flow of traffic, as though nothing had happened, as though there had been no death call suddenly canceled. He glanced ahead at the driver who was still humped over the wheel, peacefully drumming his fingers on its rim to music played low on the radio. He whispered a prayer to God that if he was ever fool enough to get into another Mexican taxi he would skip all the preliminaries and commit his life then and there on the spot and go straight to preaching. He wasn't sure if it worked exactly that way but it might keep him alive while he was in Mexico.

The boulevard went for some distance then the driver turned sharply and they entered a narrow street and another barrio and he noticed they were climbing and, looking back, he saw the city falling away behind them. He asked the driver if they were heading in the right direction. The driver nodded.

They drove on, the scenery changing from block to block. Ramón had described his house and there were none of that description where they were and Jo Shelby spoke to the driver once more and asked if he might not be mistaken but the driver shook his head back and forth and never looked back. He slowed and downshifted and made a left turn that carried them along the side of the mountain for a few hundred yards where there was nothing but trees and tall grass then cut back to the right onto a street that climbed steeply then plateaued and suddenly everything was different.

The street was wide and clean and lined with small trees planted in holes created for them along the sidewalk. The homes were fashionable and a few had garages and small front yards. The driver slowed as he crossed the intersections, checking the street signs. He turned on Esteban, and began calling out the numbers to himself as he moved slowly down the file of homes.

Doscientos . . . Doscientos dos . . . Doscientos cuatro. He slowed almost to a stop. Doscientos seis. He stopped. Aqui estamos, he said.

And still alive and in one piece, Jo Shelby, thought prayerfully.

Number 206 was clearly indicated in white paint above a black wrought-iron archway from which spiraled bright red bougainvilleas. He studied the house. It was a small two-storied structure tidily tucked in among others of similar design. A stone walkway led from the arched entranceway to a barred door and around the door were an assortment of ferns and hibiscus staggered in clay pots of varying sizes. The small yard was covered with a dark green ivy that had been neatly manicured along the edges and from its center grew a small tulip tree. The garage door was closed and no lights shone in the house and there was a vacant look about it.

Vente dos pesos, the driver said.

Jo Shelby opened the door and got out. He gave the man a twenty peso bill and two peso coins, then reluctantly added a five peso coin for the tip, for getting him there alive. The driver thanked him and gave him back the paper with the address scrawled on it and screeched off. Jo Shelby watched as he sped away and disappeared over the lip of the plateau, a bat returning to his nook in hell, he thought, then recalled the Mexican character he'd seen on the Saturday picture show cartoons, Speedy something or other, and figured the man who'd created him had once ridden in a Mexican taxi.

The wrought-iron gate creaked open to his touch and he walked to the front door which was covered by an outer frame of steel bars and rang the doorbell. He waited. No one came to the door and he punched the button again. He listened for footsteps but heard none. He cupped his hands around his eyes and peered through a side window panel. Inside the place was dark and still and appeared lifeless. He could see furniture in a large room and a dining table to the left across from it and straight ahead through a rear window, a small patio area where there was a table and chairs around it, hanging plants over them. But he saw no movement and he rang the bell again and listened as it ding-donged loudly from inside. He walked back toward the street and turned around and looked for a passage to the rear of the house but the homes on the street were flush against one another and there was none. He looked inside again and saw cut flowers in a vase on a small table in the foyer. They looked too fresh for someone to have gone off and left them. He glanced from habit at his wrist then laid his knapsack by the door and stepped out into the street to check the sun's position. It was straight up. From the shelf of mountain on which the street was laid he could see the vast stretches of the sprawling city in the valley below and the mountains girding it and those that lay far away in a blue haze along the horizon, white thunderclouds columning over them as though it were smoke belched upward by a terrible fire and the sun's light playing over the land between the clouds and the passing colors it brought to life.

He walked back to the house and sat on the stoop of the small recessed porch and shook out a cigarette and lit it and smoked and thought what he should do next, glad that he had eaten a snack earlier. He examined again the paper and the address and doubted there could be another like it, even in a city as large. He sat and smoked and thought. He got up again and looked into the house and sat again. Ramón had said his wife would be at home and maybe one of his daughters. They were probably shopping, he thought. Gone to the grocery store or the bank. The post office maybe. He looked around. The porch was wide enough for him to stretch out. He was tired from the day's travel and still wrung out from the cab ride. He placed his knapsack against the brick wall and leaned back against it, extending his legs parallel to the threshold of the door so he could see both the street and inside the house through the window panel of the door. Breezes blew down from the mountain and stirred the bougainvilleas and small birds rattled the polished leaves of the tulip tree and he could hear the distant hum of traffic far below in the interludes but otherwise all was as quiet as a Sunday afternoon.

He tilted his head to one side and was letting his eyelids fold down when he thought he saw something move in the house, or the shadow of a movement, he wasn't sure. He steadied his vision through the window panel and kept it focused there for a long time and saw nothing else but he was sure he'd seen something move. Maybe it was just a house pet moving across the floor or a cloud shadow passing over the patio in the back. He gave it no more thought and resumed his napping posture and welcomed the darkness that came when his eyes closed and the renewed thoughts it brought with it. He hoped he would dream and that Athen would come and sit beside him and he would tell her of all he'd been through and survived and what lay ahead and that she would listen without interruption and look at him as one might a hero returned from a war far from home. Then they would talk of a life together and a home on land they owned outright and children that would play on grounds that would be there. Someday. He thought that if he thought these thoughts enough he would surely dream them and if he dreamed them enough they would come true and the breezes and birds moved through the bougainvillea and tulip tree limbs and he fell asleep but no dreams came to him in that timeless dark.

He awoke to a muffled noise that sounded like something shutting, a door perhaps. It could not have come from the street for no cars had arrived there and none were leaving. He glanced inside the house and saw nothing. He cocked his ear and listened and heard nothing. He looked around. By the lay of the shadow from the tulip tree he guessed he'd slept two or three hours. He got up and stepped back to the street and looked both ways and saw nothing but a few parked cars that were there when he had arrived. The air seemed cooler and the valley below him was dark with the mountains' shadows and he realized he'd slept longer than he'd first thought. He was hungry but the nearest place to buy something to eat was a good hike to the vendor back down the mountain and he had probably moved on. He walked back to the porch and was about to sit down when he heard another noise that came unmistakably this time from inside the house. He stood in front of the door and pressed an ear against it and heard nothing then slowly rolled his head around the molding and scanned with one eye the dark interior and saw the silhouette of a woman pass slowly across the rear window and disappear into the shadows of a side room. He held his breath and pondered the meaning of what was happening. Someone at home but not answering the door. She was alone and thought he was a burglar. He was some intruder of evil intent. A bill collector perhaps. He ran through the list of possibilities in his mind. The mail was slow in Mexico and Ramón would not have had time to notify her of his coming but he had written to her about him.

That much he knew for sure and on that certainty knocked loudly on the wood siding around the iron-barred security door and called out her name. He heard footfalls but they were faint and getting fainter and he rapped a second time, louder, and shouted her name again and identified himself and waited. The sound of footsteps returned and grew louder and the latch on the front door clicked and opened partially and through the bars of the security door he saw the small oval face of an elderly woman peering through the crack in the door, timid and inquiring blue eyes moving up and down him.

Sí? she said.

Perdone, señora, pero me llamo Jo Shelby Ferguson, un amigo del señor García, de la prisión.

Her eyes widened and an instinctive wave of expression crossed her face, one of joy blended with caution.

Pase, she said. Pronto. She hurriedly reached out and unbolted the barred security door and pushed it slightly open and motioned quickly with her hand. He reached down and grabbed his knapsack and slipped through the two doors she held only partially open and turned when he was inside and watched as she closed and locked them behind him with equal meticulous haste.

She turned around and he removed his cap and introduced himself again and stated once more that he was a friend of her husband's and was there at his request to inform her of his good health and good spirits. She showed no emotion as she listened and when he was finished told him that her name was Rosario and that she was happy for him that he was out of prison and sad that her husband was not there to greet him with her. Her speech was articulate and dignified and she spoke a halting unrefined English, of someone who had learned the language not by any formal training as her husband but absorbed what she knew by listening to others. He told her he already knew her name, that her husband was his best friend in the prison and had told him many good things about her. She smiled and bowed slightly at the remark.

She was a short woman with flawless white hair pulled back tightly in a small bun and she wore a dark full-length dress that covered her feet and a white lace blouse that buttoned all the way up her neck. Her skin was light-colored but darker around the eyes as if most of her aging had taken place there, the way the network of wrinkles spread outward across her face. She apologized to him for not responding to his earlier rings but she was alone, she explained, and afraid it might have been another investigator sent by the government.

She ushered him into a small sunken den, a tidy room filled with bamboo and wicker furniture and gestured for him to sit on the sofa and he did. She settled into a pose of dignity in a large fanshaped wicker chair across from him, her back erect, hands folded on her knees, chin slightly cocked. He thought teacher first, then his mother just before Bible reading time, then his mother before any occasion that demanded attention.

He sat and listened.

In a voice that was low but of gentle strength and resonating a deep long-suffering the señora went on to describe the harassment she had endured while her husband was in prison. She spoke gravely of sudden intrusions in the night and the herding of her and her family, her son and daughter living with them at the time, to the central police station and of ruthless interrogations that lasted hours and the unexpected loss of electricity and frequent stops and searches of their car and the mordidas they had to pay each time and the constant threats to their lives if they did not leave the country and Jo Shelby sat on the edge of the couch and moved not a muscle except to nod he understood and when she had finished said he hoped it would end soon for her.

They write, she continued. They tell us they . . .

She struggled for the word.

Release . . . Is that the word?

Yes ma'am.

They write and say they release him, she said, her face uplifted, her dark blue eyes excited but floating on the despair he perceived he saw beneath them. Many times they write, the officials in Mexico. They say yes, he can go. So I go to get my Ramón, to bring him home. Then they say no, there is problem. Many times this happen. So I not go to the prison to get him. I not go yesterday. Jorge, our son, he go.

He was supposed to be out yesterday?

Sí. Yesterday. All people say this. The comandante say it. The governor of our province. Even the presidente. She reached over and lifted a single white sheet from the coffee table and handed it to him. He took it and glanced over the brief letter, noting the seal pressed upon the page at the bottom and above it the florid signature which he could not read but the name typed below it identified the author. Adolfo Ruiz Cortines. Presidente de México.

Everything bueno our attorney say. Then this thing it happen.

What thing happened? he said.

Jorge he come home. He say some man he is much hurt, almost die and Ramón he help him and the comandante think he, Ramón, hurt him. He think Ramón maybe fight this man and hurt him. But Ramón old man. Much respected in the prison. He not hurt anyone. I do not understand. It is much difficult.

In the developing gloom of the room he sat and listened with great sadness, clutching his hat between his knees. He looked upon her placid face and into the tiny eyes sunken within it, eyes that held firm as though they were anchors holding the face together and the reason it could look so still and unaffected and he tried to think of something to say but could not. A clock down a hallway whirred and struck five times. He turned his head away from her. Through the large patio window wisps of pink clouds passed slowly beneath a bruised sky and over the tops of tall trees further up the hill behind the house within the old brick wall surrounding the courtyard dusk birds darted in and out of the ropes of vines looping between the portico columns. For a few moments nothing was said, the two of them counterposed, cameos framed against the orange light that rolled down from the mountain and splashed onto the courtyard outside, both reflecting the meditations of the other until he could no longer hold down the heavy guilt pushing upward against his throat.

Ma'am. I'm the reason your husband ain't out.

Cómo? she said.

He told her again in the best Spanish he could string together and she sat and received the news in that same transfixion of outward calm and lackluster of expression, with the same undisturbed eyes that he guessed were immune to disturbance because they had known and beheld it all. When he finished she inclined her head slightly and when it came back up her face was serene and a slight smile passed her lips and she told him he did only what any man would have done, what her Ramón would have done and that all was probably just as well, that it was a good thing the poor man lived because it would be only one more good thing Ramón had done in the prison.

He thanked her for her kind words and continued and told her the story of what had occurred, of the man Carlos, of the fight and what had happened afterward and Ramón's instruction that he leave as quickly as possible and that he did so but with no knowledge that her husband was to be released on the same day. He spoke in quiet tones and she listened, implacable and expressionless, as though it were a story she had heard many times over but not bored with the retelling and when he finished she smiled kindly and confirmed what he had already glimpsed in her eyes.

I believe these words that you tell me. I knew already some of it. Ramón, he tell my son. But there is more you do not know.

What?

It is of no importance and cannot be spoken. Ramón much like you. He say this in his letters. He want to help you. That is Ramón. He want to help everybody. That maybe why he in the prison. He wanted for you to—

She looked away for the first time, toward the window.

He arranged for me to git out, didn't he?

She looked back at him. This I cannot say, she said. I only say he will soon be free. With my heart . . .

She patted her hand over her chest.

With my heart I believe this to be true. You help him. He help you. That is as it should be. Now, no more, she said and brought her hands together in a soft delicate clap of closure and looked upon him with equal forthrightness.

There was the fragile silence again and the growing dark taking over the house, like a dark cloud invading, and he could barely see her face and she his but he discerned the truth that moved in that fullness of thought, as though he could reach out and touch it, and he knew there had been a package deal and he was but a small part of a larger game being played out in a country in which he was a stranger and of which he knew so little.

She showed him a room where he could spend the night and said that it was Jorge's room before he married and moved to another barrio across the city. It was small with a single bed and a chair and nightstand. A small bookcase filled end on end with books. A chest of drawers. Posters of Mexico hung on the walls and there was a map of the United States where she said her son dreamed of living and working some day.

Tejas, she said, and walked to the map and placed her finger on the large letters that spelled out the name of the state. He want to live in Tejas. Many Mexicans want this, to live in Tejas. Life much better there.

This doesn't bother you, that your son wants to live in another country, he said.

No. It is no problem. It is only a name. Tejas. Before Tejas, México. Siempre México. Todo esto es México, and with a finger she traced the borders of California and Arizona and New México, then of Texas, and moved the finger southward across the Rio Grande and contoured all of México and repeated what she had said. Todo esto es México.

It was yours and we took it from you. That's what you're trying to tell me.

Sí. Claro.

Lo siento, he said.

It is no sorry for you. No sorry for me. Así es la vida.

He didn't quite see it that way, that God would will the taking of one's land and home by another but did not challenge the force of a wisdom that came at him so directly, with such quiet conviction.

That evening she prepared a light meal and they sat in candlelight across from one another in the small dining room. He ate heartily of the tamales and rice pozole and avocado salad placed before him and sipped sparingly the dark wine from a glass with a size and shape he had seen but never before held. She wore a white rebozo draped around her shoulders and with her white hair and grand manner he imagined himself among royalty in exile, of how his great-grand-mother might have felt dining with the Empress Carlota.

Once again he told his story, as he had so many times, and she listened with great interest. When he finished she leaned away from the table and steepled her hands prayerfully beneath her chin and told him his search would be very difficult, that she was from the state of Morelos, from a place called Cuautla, not far from Cuernavaca, and that she had never heard of a Hacienda Michopa but that this was not unusual for the haciendas had changed hands many times over the years, that the dictator Díaz had given many away to foreign investors who had reshaped the land and the haciendas on the land and given many of them new names and that the process had almost repeated itself some fifty years later when Cárdenas broke them up and redistributed them. A hundred years was a long time and that much could happen. He told her he understood all of this and had given it much thought but that if his family had lasted through the generations as long as it had in America then why could not the same be true of families in Mexico. Through the flickering candle flame she smiled and congratulated his logic but said the reasoning he presented was not without problems. Then she leaned across the table so her breath rocked the flame and he saw its twisting image duplicated in her eyes and heard her tell of the intricate puzzle that was Mexico. Of bloods mixing and names changing and male lines disappearing. That his apellido of Ferguson may long have vanished from any records now kept. Then she leaned back once more and assumed a pose of instinctive motherly rectitude and joined the chorus of others who had admonished against hitchhiking in their country and advised he should take a bus to Mexico City and inquire there.

She left the table and returned with a sheet of paper and pencil and scribbled out the names and addresses of some who could be of help as well as the name of the central library which she said might have information. She went on to tell him he could best learn of this Hacienda Michopa in Cuernavaca, at the library and museums there, that those were places easy to find for they were all clustered together in the center of the city around the cathedral. He thanked her and folded the paper and placed it into his shirtpocket.

She got up again and returned from the kitchen with a small cut glass decanter and two globe-shaped glasses. She set one in front of him and poured from the decanter, tilting the glass at an angle with her other hand so the dark liquid slid down the side and pooled into the bottom and its golden-brown quality swirled there in the candle-glow like some distilled rarefied residue and the strong vapors arising from it an incense that filled his nose with a sweet burn that begged to be breathed again. She moved to the other side of the table and did likewise with her glass and held it up in the flickering light and they saluded one another. She said it was very infrequent she had guests and for special occasions reserved her best brandy. She offered him a cigar to go with it but he politely declined and smoked a cigarette instead and watched as she lit a long slender cigar and they moved to the den and passed the remainder of the evening smoking and talking like two long lost relatives suddenly reunited.

She spoke of her family and pointed to their pictures that hung on the walls around them. Her son and two daughters, and their separate trials in the wake of their father's arrest. Jorge's admission to the University de Nuevo León had been withdrawn twice and the fees increased but each time he had been reinstated and eventually completed his degree in engineering and had a good job with an American steel company. Clarisa, the oldest daughter, had married a wealthy financier and lived in Monclova. They had two children ages four and seven. A boy and a girl. Carmen, the youngest, had chosen to remain in Mexico City where the family had first lived, and worked as a secretary with a fabric firm. Her picture was larger than the others and hung alone on a wall adorned by nothing else, understandably so for her loveliness crowded the room. He remarked of her beauty and the señora smiled at his compliment and said her daughter had had many offers to become a model but had decided against it because of the demands the career required and the compromises as well, if he knew what she meant, that she had been schooled in a Catholic convent and raised with morals of purity and was a good Christian girl. He nodded he understood and continued to take in the exquisite features of the girl's face and the silent power its presence spread throughout the room. Her long black hair, high-colored cheeks, full-lipped wide mouth, prominent nose and dark eyes and eyelashes seemed to project, as if in relief, from the canvas.

I give to you her address also on the paper, the señora said. She will help you.

He pulled the paper from his shirtpocket and laid it on the table and the señora pointed to it and he nodded and placed the paper back in his pocket.

He opened his knapsack and removed the pictures of his family and spread them on the coffee table for her to see and pointed and told her the names of each and their separate histories as they had been passed on to him. She lifted them one by one and held them in the dim light and said Qué bueno! of each as she placed them back on the table. He pulled out the letters and read them to her, making interpretations as best he could. She took the letters from him and examined them with great circumspection and commented on their durability to have been written so long ago then handed them back to him and he refolded them and placed them back in the knapsack. He recapitulated his family's plight and the land they had lost but that all he wanted was to find what family he had left.

She asked him what he hoped to find, if by chance and the grace of God he was able to locate his blood-kin on the Mexican side of his family, and he looked at her dumbfounded and said he did not understand her question, that he would have found his family, which was why he had come in the first place.

Yes, I know this thing you tell me, she said. But I think, señor Ferguson, family in your country mean one thing. In Mexico it mean something different.

He told her how he had been raised and what his parents had taught him, that God came first and family second in the arrangement of things important in life and everything else came afterwards, that without those two nothing else would be important or worth having because one would not know love and if one did not know love then he was cut off from salvation, which meant he would go to hell. He went on to say that it was a man's duty to have a family, that it was God's will, that it was in the Holy Bible, and that that was what he had been taught all of his life.

When he had finished, she tilted her head against the back of the chair and took a long puff on her cigar and blew a white cloud of smoke upward toward the ceiling where it evaporated among the dark rafters and told him he was different from most Americans she had known and very wise for one so young. She told him that he would make a good Mexican because, in Mexico, blood and passion were the history and the glue that held everything together, that if the family fell apart the country would disintegrate with it. In a serious and thoughtful air she told him she was sorry for what had happened to his family and to his family's land and agreed with him that without God and family, land was nothing because it had no passion, only the passion the people gave to it. Without the people and their families, the land was an unfeeling desert with no love and no heart. She congratulated him on his courage to find his heart in tracing the lives of others but added that there was never the total retracing of another's life, much less the journey, only approximations and chance stumblings onto their path and the offshoots of their path. One must eventually make their own way and find their own place and their own family, she said with that calmness with which she said everything. Then they lifted their glasses and drank to Mexico and to family and he wondered if Ramón, too, were not mysteriously present, whispering into his wife's ear, for so much of what he had heard, he had heard before and the words followed him long into the evening and on into sleep.

The next morning she prepared him a breakfast of chilaquiles and eggs and freshly squeezed papaya and black coffee with molasses and cinnamon she called café de olla and drove him to the bus station near the center of the city. It was old but in better shape than the one he'd seen in Matamoros and less crowded. At seven in the morning it was a near deserted place. A few patrons sat on benches and chatted. A taxi dropped off a well-dressed man carrying a briefcase. But little else stirred within the large colorless room. The señora watched as a sleepy clerk handed him a second class ticket, for which he doled out forty-five pesos, about seven American dollars. The clerk told him the trip would take about twelve hours, but maybe longer depending on un-scheduled stops. The buses looked the same as those he'd seen every-where along the way. Brightly colored rattletrap renditions of old school buses with baggage railings around the top. They were all parked in rows, in staggered slots, large signs of destination on the front of each, as though to compensate for their small size.

She hugged him before he boarded and kissed him on each cheek and wished that God would go with him and he said likewise to her. She told him once again he should contact Carmen in Mexico City, that she would surely help him, but it was a reminder he did not need and he watched her as she walked away, turning once at the depot's doorway to wave at him, then disappearing into the cold emptiness of the building. He continued to say silent good-byes to her with the heavy sadness he might never see her again, someone who reminded him so much of his mother, of her kindness and nurturance, her strength, then he stepped up into the bus and took a front seat, where he could see the land his forebears had seen a century before.

The bus was old and smelled as though it had not been cleaned in several trips. Scraps of tissue and chewing gum wrappers and pop bot-tles and newspapers several days old lay scattered throughout. The seats, loosely bolted to the floor, gently moved with the idling of the engine.

There were only a few other passengers. A mother and two small children. A man of uncertain means, though by his shabby and un-kempt appearance, Jo Shelby guessed he was one of the many unemployed going to the big city to find work, possibly leaving his family behind. An elderly couple huddled together on the backseat, hoping no one else would join them, he thought. A young boy put on by his parents. They stood outside by his window until the bus backed from its slot and pulled off. They waved but the boy never looked back.

The morning sun glistened on the dew dampened rooftops and cobblestones as the bus trundled and rick-racked through the narrow streets and onto the main thoroughfare that ran beside the dry rocky bed of the Rio Catarina and eventually into the countryside where the sun-capped edges of the mountains rose steeply on both sides like gleaming gray teeth and the valley floor as far as he could see was scrubby and gravelly and the only vegetation sagebrush and some wiry bushes and rising occasionally above them the prickly and tortured shapes of the yuccas. But the near-voided terrain seemed not to matter to him and he felt it must not either for the people living there along the way in their straw jacales and cardboard huts for the mountains drew all attention unto themselves and left none to be indulged else-where, as though there was nowhere else to look but up. He recalled a psalm he had had to memorize once in vacation Bible school—*I will lift up mine eyes unto the hills, from whence cometh my help? My help cometh from the Lord who made heaven and earth.* The truth it carried had taken many years to reach him and he wondered if the children in this desert wasteland had to memorize it as well. If not, they should, he thought.

For miles it was like that. The bottom of the sky spilling light. The slate-colored mountains on either side, the Sierra Madre Oriental, mother of the East. The road was flat and straight along the feature-less desert valley between them, like a silver vein threading the land.

They passed early model cars of American make and big trucks and small trucks. Trucks carrying chemicals and produce, poultry and live-stock, all of them moving along at a steady pace. No one in a hurry. The rhythm of mañana. Except for an old Ford pickup that passed them.

There were people sitting in the bed and a red canvas, its ends come undone from the tailgate, flapping wildly about them. They were smiling and laughing and passing a bottle between them and for a moment he wished he had hitchhiked and was among them. Then again he reconsidered the señora's wisdom, all that she had said about the land and its heritage, its passion, but especially the part about the retracing of another's life or their journey, that one must find his own way, his own place. He understood why Ramón had loved her and none other and why he had chosen his place in the prison until the time was right, and Jo Shelby reflected upon the man who was responsible for his freedom and hoped that Ramón would be drinking brandy and smoking a cigar with his espousa before the sun descended once more.

The valley through which they traveled fanned out into a broader plain. The mountains seemed to come and go, one chain receding, another beginning, no end to them, stretching fold upon fold, crumpling all the way to the horizon that carried their wrinkled imprint across the southern sky. He reflected on his grandmother's letters and her description of the land, and of General Shelby and his men and their families and how they must have stopped many times to take in the unfolding rawness and awful beauty but also to question why they should have left a place as grand and comfortable as Monterrey. It had at least some color. Here there was only the drab and lifeless replica of a land, ashen and gray, rock broken from the crumbling mountains that looked old and scarred, a place that looked so unvisited, as though it was meant to have been, and would be for years to come.

The ride south ran over roads washboarded and loud, teeth-jarring. Wind whipped in along the side windows and circulated roughly throughout the cabin but the cooling effect it had was welcome. A baby cried randomly in the back, its mother singing something in Spanish to it each time. He tried to make out the words but could not. A man behind him kept spitting out the window and he felt the occasional spray on the back of his neck. He rubbed it a time or two and looked back but the man never got the hint and he wasn't going to start trouble on a Mexican bus where he was the only gringo. There were frequent stops, sometimes every fifteen minutes. More people were getting on than getting off and the overall effect was an accumulation of body odor and heat that not even the rush of wind could sweep away.

They rode the high northern plateau and dipped into valleys and crested passes that afforded vistas of the cordilleras far to the south, layered in lazy hazes and trailing off in shades of blue until they were the color of the distant hanging clouds and no longer distinguishable from the vapors gathered there. In the cloud-shade the mountains looked greener and there were more signs of life upon their uneven slopes and every valley had its own shape and around every curve the scenes changed. There were lush fields of yellow sunflowers and corn and farmers harvesting and bulls and cows grazing in the shade of green pastures then rocky desert spotted with maguey and yucca then valleys of orchids and vineyards stretching from valley wall to valley wall then another steep grade and another gap and back to desert again and so it went, the land resolving into a mixed patchwork of feast and famine, of rich and poor, and never did it change.

They passed signs along the way pointing to towns but none were in sight, only random shacks pieced together with tin and plywood and cardboard, wood slats and old beverage signs wired together, garage doors and wooden warehouse pallets for walls and rusted bed-springs for fences, anything a man and wife could find to make a home. The signs bore the names of some place or some person of importance—El Castillo, Santa Teresa, La Providencia, San Rafael, La Trinidad—as if the names themselves carried the hope of the peasants whose fate it was to have been born there. He thought of towns in the Delta named Midnight and Black Coffee and Panther Burn and his wonder was rekindled as to how they were named or even had names at all. At a few of the signs people stood and waved and the driver stopped for them and they got on, some with baggage and some holding cartons of fruit. There was one old woman with chickens slung over her shoulder, their feet tied together, ready for a market somewhere down the road. Some boarded with nothing but the clothes they wore which looked as though they had never been washed since the day they were bought. He speculated about the people who lived there and how life could go on in places so remote and so isolated, so abandoned. Washed out adobe buildings that had once been homes or restaurants or cantinas. So much that was untended. Wild horses grazing along the shoulders of the highway and wild burrows and occasional herds of goats with no one watching over them. The deception of it all. The faraway mountains grand and smooth and green, but up close aproning out into thin chalky soil pimpled with yellowtufts of grass and cactus and sagebrush, nothing it seemed with which man or beast could survive, but somehow they did. And the reminders of death and tragedy all along they way. Little handmade wooden chapels, some balanced on top of rocks, some set back in small indentures in the bluffs, put there presumably because a loved one was killed there, or died en route to somewhere else. Sometimes there was only a crude cross made of poles lashed or nailed together and hanging from it, a single tire, from the death car in which someone rode and died, he guessed. For many years to come, he'd recall the images and what they evoked of the land. The best of suffering and of endurance and of resolve and of patience and of honor. And he would call upon these representations in the mind many times the remainder of his years, and dream of families being born and dying and being born again, and they would remind him of the timeless river he once rode and how it kept on rolling and the part he would play in passing his life along to others.

They crossed into the state of San Luis Potosí. Uniformed soldiers with automatic rifles slung over their shoulders and carbines packed on their hips waved the bus to a halt. He thought immediately of the gun in his knapsack and asked the driver what the soldiers wanted and the driver told him it was a routine checkpoint, not to worry. Slowly, he pulled his knapsack up from the floor where he had held it between his feet and put it under the driver's gear on the seat beside him.

Two of the soldiers swaggered aboard the bus and walked toward the back, turning their heads left and right as they went, examining the passengers and how they looked and what they might be carrying.

They spoke to no one and made their way slowly back toward the front and stopped at the front seat beside Jo Shelby.

Pasaporte, one soldier said to him and motioned for him to stand.

He stood and fumbled in his backpocket for his billfold, all the time recalling what Ramón had said about jails further south of the border, particularly San Luis Potosí. He tried to calm his hands and fished out his visa and handed it to the soldier. The soldier took it and handed it to the other soldier who scrutinized it with great care then handed it back to the first soldier who did likewise as though something might have been missed.

Maletas? the first soldier said.

Jo Shelby looked first at the driver who looked away then back at the soldier. No. No maletas. Todo, he said and lifted his arms to add emphasis to the fact he carried only himself and his clothes.

The soldier returned his visa to him and told him to sit down then said something to the driver. Both of them stepped down from the bus and looked back. One said, Pasa! and motioned forward with his hand and the driver cranked the bus and they rattled on. Jo Shelby wished he had something strong to settle his nerves and dispel the numbness in his hands and feet.

Around noon they stopped in San Luis Potosí. He bought some tamales and a beer. They were off again. He dozed off and napped, awakening briefly at stops along the way, some of them with names he remembered from the letters. Hidalgo and Querétaro and San Juan del Rio.

Past Querétaro the land seemed to open. Ranches and orchards and broad fields of crops, all under cover of slow clouds. The bus was constantly gaining altitude and the villages were becoming more frequent and the land greener with vegetation of all types as though at last the pockets of desert were behind them. The sun was no longer visible and its last rays shattered upward from behind the beveled mountains burning the clouds pink and orange and mauve and above them a lavender domed sky moved through its shades of early dark. A disappointment fell upon him. He would not see The Sleeping Lady and the Popocatépetl volcano as General Shelby and his men had first glimpsed it and as his great-grandmother had written so grandly of her first view. He would not enter the city as they had entered it and see it as they saw it, with the morning sun glittering off the tops of its buildings, striking color along its wide boulevards, bringing life to its masses. He would enter it around midnight and see it under the cloak of night and the only glitter would be the neon signs of the cantinas and bars and hotels and he began to think about where he would spend the night and how much it might cost. He recalculated once more his finances and wondered how far some forty odd dollars would go in Mexico City before he could get to Cuernavaca and how far they would go from there.

The city was more alive than he imagined it would be at midnight. Storefronts were lit up. Buses roared by. Sparse traffic moved freely along the four lane boulevards and there were still people strolling along the sidewalks and couples sitting on benches along the alamedas and in the lighted plazas. Restaurants and bars were abuzz with patrons and music, an electric thrill about it all.

The depot was on a major boulevard and busier than he had expected, but not crowded. He found an unoccupied bench in the cavernous building that echoed with the sounds of loudspeakers squawking out arrivals and departures and hurried feet and the nasal calls of the vendors hawking food and last minute souvenirs. He sat and gathered his thoughts. A large clock on the wall over the sally-gates to the buses said half-past twelve. He should have been sleepy but the naps along the way had helped and the energy of the city was working on him. He headed into the night.

Outside the air was thin and cool. He walked to a newspaper stand and inquired of the vendor which way to the centro and the vendor told him he was on Lázaro Cárdenas Avenue, that if he would follow it straight he would come to the Paseo de la Reforma and there would begin the centro, but that it was a long way to walk and he might wish to take a bus. Jo Shelby told him he had come a long way from Monterrey, sitting all day on a bus and would welcome a long walk and the vendor laughed his understanding and wished him good luck.

He struck a slow stride down the much wider sidewalk, beside the wide street, and all he passed greeted him and he returned their greetings in the new language that was not his own and felt the confidence rise within him as he did. He came to intersections where several streets ran together and traffic circled islands covered with flowers and plants geometrically arranged and he watched with awe as the moving vehicles threaded their way into and out of the roundabouts without crashing or running over each other. He stuck to the outer curb of the sidewalk to better see the length and breadth of the street and the height of the buildings and stopped occasionally to gaze in the shop windows and at the well-heeled people there who gazed with him.

The Paseo de la Reforma was an even wider street and more brightly illuminated, its streetlights stretching in both directions as far as he could see, like tiny moonclusters strung through the trees. Along its broad median through the tapestry of leaves he saw floodlit statues and monuments and fountains and the colorful walls of buildings in the litup night crowding the scene with a beauty untouchable by sunlight, morning or otherwise. He was glad he had arrived when he did and stood for a while and let his eyes take in the gleaming liquid shapes, and he listened to the city and its sounds and the sounds were those of something great winding up and not down.

There was a small cantina on a corner not far from him and he went in and ordered a beer and tortillas wrapped around grilled chorizo and melted cheese. He found a table outside and ate for the first time since San Luis Potosí. A waiter came out to inquire if he needed anything else and he ordered another beer and smoked a cigarette and watched the late night strollers. The waiter returned and Jo Shelby asked if he knew of the street Avenido Toltecas and the waiter shook his head but held up a finger and said momentito and left. Jo Shelby waited. The waiter returned and had with him a large map of the city. Jo Shelby thanked him and opened the panels and spread the map on the table and began searching for the name of the street given to him by the señora.

The map was a maze filled with fine print and in the faint glimmer of light he had to hold his eyes close to it and in this manner moved his finger slowly from street line to street line but the name did not appear. A gentleman next to him joined in the search and together the two of them scoured the large plat like prospectors moving silt with their fingers. For several minutes they did this when the gentleman spoke loudly that he had found the street and Jo Shelby saw where the man's finger was anchored at a spot in the northwest quadrant of the city back in the direction from which he had just walked a few country miles. The man told him he should take a taxi and that thought went in and out of his mind like a bullbat's swoop at first dark and he told the man he'd rather walk and made a vague reference about a promise to God and preaching which the man did not understand. Jo Shelby thanked the man for his help and offered to buy him a beer but the man politely declined and said it was nothing and resumed his seat at his table.

He paid his bill and tucked the map into his knapsack, along with the other of the country, and walked the Paseo de la Reforma with its circular traffic islands of palm trees and desert cactus and statues and fountains blooming silver in the floodlights. Mixed in among its ancient buildings and sequestered plazas along the way, he passed smart-looking hotels and restaurants and business buildings and a few tall apartment houses.

He stumbled onto an alameda that was larger than any he had seen, wide well-lit paths crisscrossing in all directions. Behind a large monument topped by a statue, he bedded down for the night, curled up at the base of its massive pedestal, out of the path of passersby and potential thieves, his coat spread over him and his knapsack for a pillow with one arm strung through a shoulder strap and sleep came quickly upon him.

He awoke in the morning with birds caroling in the branches overhead and the crisp heady air moving fresh through his head and the smell of the nearby grass. He arose and shook down his clothes, brushed them off, and looked around. There were red calla lilies blooming from concrete flower boxes around the trees and everywhere, flowers of all colors, statuary of all dimensions, spread throughout the park, as pretty a place as where people bury their dead.

There was a fountain nearby and he walked over to it and cupped his hands and rinsed his face in its chilling waters. He looked around and saw no one nearby and no one looking and opened his knapsack. He took out his lather and razor and shaved with only the feel of his hand to guide him and was satisfied afterward with the smoothness of his face against his palm.

The street cleaners were busy at work with their long-handled brooms and the shopkeepers were washing the sidewalks in front of their shops and the vendors along the edges of the alameda were stoking their portable ovens and setting out their wares.

He ate in a small café, asking the waitress to just bring him something good. She brought him a dish that looked like pound cake with a fruity syrup spread over it that tasted like cornbread and hot dog relish.

He entered a small clothing store and bought a pair of corduroy pants and a white shirt that were on sale and some underwear and socks he desperately needed. The señora who waited on him allowed him to change in the back room and she gave him a paper shopping bag for his old clothes when he finished. On his way out of the store he eyed a wide-brimmed straw sombrero with a thin blue-corded band and took off his cap and tried it on, checking out his new look in a mirror. Ran his finger around the brim. Flipped it up then down. Shifted the hat so it sat slantwise on his head and imbued him with a touch of gallantry and went back and paid for it and returned to the street wearing it.

He was low on pesos and had two twenty-dollar bills left. He stepped down a side street and glanced around to make sure no one was looking, and took one out. The first bank he came to was closed and the sign above the large brass handles said it would not open until nine o'clock. He cupped his hands around his eyes and peered inside and a clock on a dark marble wall said half past eight. He took out the map and checked his bearings. Along the panels of the map were photographs of various monuments and points of interest. He looked at them and read the captions underneath. Plaza de la Constitución. Catedral. Palacio Nacional. Templo Mayor. Bellas Artes. Castillo de Chapultepec. He looked at the map again and pinpointed the Avenida Toltecas and checked the legend and guessed he was in for about a two-hour walk, at the most.

He considered what he might do to kill time, then decided to see the city where his great-grandparents lived for a short while. Walking where they walked. Sitting where they sat, maybe even in the lobby of the hotel where they stayed. What was its name? He reached down to pull out the two letters and quickly scanned them but the name of the hotel was not in either of them. It was a funny name and he decided it might come to him later or he might see a sign and remember. He folded the letters and put them in the sidepouch of the knapsack and took the old clothes out of the shopping bag and squeezed them into the main compartment. The knapsack bulged so the straps barely reached far enough to buckle. He didn't need anymore baggage than what he already had, he thought, as he dropped the shopping sack into a trash bin on the corner and checked the street sign overhead before walking east.

The sun struck the buildings as though it had been thrown against them and sparkled through the leafage overhead. A lot can change in a hundred years the señora had said and he wondered what had. The cityscape around him. What was there that hadn't been and what was still there that was and he tried to envision how the city would have looked then. The modern buildings weren't there nor was a skyscraper several blocks away that looked like pictures he had seen in his Weekly Reader of the Empire State Building. There was scaffolding and cranes all around it but it looked almost completed. The streets were still there but they were probably narrow and made of stones back then. Riding along them would have been finely dressed men on groomed horses and women in frilled carriages, just as his grandmother had described. Along the way there would have been hitching posts and he dropped them visually into the places he thought they might have been. The churches. Nobody tears down a church. Some of the trees in the parks looked old enough to be a hundred, but not many. The street vendors. They never die. The shops. They were there but they'd been torn down and rebuilt. The hotels he saw all looked too new, except one or two, their edges dark and rough with wear and age. One he had passed earlier stuck in his mind. The Hotel Cortez. It looked old enough to have been there two hundred years. Featureless buildings four and five stories tall, many of them looking old and faded, paint peeling across their edifices. They might have been there.

He came upon La Alameda where he'd spent the night. It looked more expansive in the sunlight but was as big as he had guessed, about two blocks wide and equally as long. There was a festive air about it in the sunlight, bright flowers spread throughout, palm trees. He passed the monument where he had slept and stopped and gazed at it in the full wash of sunlight, an imposing semicircular structure of white marble with white columns, two sculpted lions in the center supporting a massive pedestal gilded in gold and atop it the huge statue of a man with two angels hovering over him. He stopped and walked closer and read the inscription encased in a circle of corded goldplating:

AL

BENEMERITO

BENITO JUAREZ

LA PATRIA

The name revolved a while in his brain then clicked into place and he stood before it for a long time remembering all his grandmother had written about the Juaristas and the fall of Carlota and that that was the last she had written. He looked up at the face of the man, its stern, unforgiving countenance, the fixed gaze. And he had slept there, beneath him. He crossed the street.

The church he faced looked ancient and he checked a bronze plate beside the door and saw it was built in 1724. Street vendors had set up stalls along the sidewalk in front of it and he bought a banana at one and continued on, passing office buildings and hotels and old churches, one which had been converted to a museum and there he entered.

The foyer was dark and an older woman sat behind a desk off to his right. He removed his sombrero and approached her and inquired if there was a fee and she said there was not. He explained he was new to the city and had some questions and she told him to ask and she would answer as best she could. He spoke of a hotel a hundred years or so ago where Confederados from his country had come and stayed and that his great-great-great-grandfather and grandmother had stayed there and that he wanted to find it. He told her it was famous in those days and luxurious and one that only the rich could afford. She listened thoughtfully and when he finished told him there were many hotels that fit his description. She asked him to wait a moment. She returned holding a large book winged open in her hands, which she placed on the desk. She began running her finger down one page. He told her if she called out the name he would know it. She did not acknowledge his comment and continued looking over the pages, her gaze moving with her finger.

He waited.

She read the names of hotels in the centro. He recognized none. Gran Hotel Ciudad de México, Hotel de Cortés, Hotel de Juárez, Hotel San Carlos, Hotel Gillow, Hotel de Iturbide—

Alto, he said.

Hotel de Iturbide?

Sí.

No es más. Cerrado.

Cerrado?

She looked up at him, and pushed her glasses back into place. The building was still there, but the hotel closed in 1928.

Dónde está? he said.

It was not very far away. She walked with him to the doorway. She pointed back up the street and told him it was two blocks on the right, just past the Ritz. He bowed and thanked her and she smiled and wished him luck. He adjusted the sombrero on his head, pulling the brim down across the front, and walked in the direction she pointed.

Hotel de Iturbide. The name was right there on the brass plaque. It was a three-story building. The top story had two wide tower-like structures. The first floor balcony was framed by ornately carved pilasters that looked like they supported the towers and across the front were wide richly decorated window frames. Above the doorway two carved figures knelt on large scrolls and all across the facade was a meandering of patterns that were repeated on the jambs and window frames and all of it done with mastery and patience, he thought, as he pictured his forebears standing on the balcony looking out over the city on a bright sunny day, talking among themselves of the uncertainties ahead, awaiting word from the Emperor.

He stepped closer and looked through a window, at a large front sitting room where furniture of decades past, the velvet-covered chairs of which great-great-grandmother Caroline had written, was draped in white sheets. He moved to the opposite window and through its dim panes discolored with smudge and dust discerned the outlines of a bar and further back a long front desk and further still a large room that looked to be a dining area. It closed in 1928, he said to himself. And no one had done anything with it. It was just sitting there, like some ghost building haunted with memories of great feasts and stories told long into the night amidst clouds of cigar smoke and the clinking of glasses and the smells of bourbon and tequila and love affairs held secret forever within its walls and memories of homesick people awaiting the imperial signal for their lives to start anew.

He crossed the street to better see the whole building and found a quiet spot out of the way of passersby. He removed his knapsack and placed it on the concrete beneath him and eased down upon it so as not to dirty his new pants and leaned his back against an anonymous building. He remained there for a long time in that meditative attitude, his thoughts circulating with the specialness of the place, that his kin had really stayed there and stood on that balcony and walked and ridden along this street and strolled along La Alameda where he'd slept, and maybe even worshiped in the church where he had just been, even though they weren't Catholic. He guessed at their routines and tried to put his mind inside of theirs, his consciousness into theirs and see how that world looked through their eyes as they moved through it and his ruminations lifted him into a state of timelessness, as though maybe nothing had happened over a hundred years and he might just bump into them in the street and they would enter the hotel together and order drinks and talk about family. A tamalera came along crying out and shook him back into time. He remained a while longer, until he was satisfied he had paid his homage then pushed himself up and continued eastward toward the Zócalo.

The sky was pale, flawed by a sun that burned too brightly. So taken had he been with the city and its adornments he had taken little notice of the mountains that rose in the distance before him, snow-capped ridges shaped clearly above the skyline, one taller than the others, a plume of smoke rising from its cone and trailing laterally north, furring the tips of other peaks and he looked closely for there was an image in the configuration. A ridge of face, forehead and nose. Breasts. Hands, perhaps folded. Legs extending and feet slightly up-turned. A body reclining from north to south. The Sleeping Lady. It had to be. And Popocatépetl. As vividly as his grandmother had written of them. He stopped and let his eyes gather in the grand scene. The city may have gone through a thousand changes but the sight he looked upon had not and he was seeing them as his family had also seen them, and the hundred years that separated them seemed like nothing, if only for a moment. And he knew these mountains would be anchors for his vision in the days to come.

The sidewalks leading to the Zócalo were filled with peddlers, their wares spread out on bright colored blankets. Ceramics and mara-cas and souvenirs. Cheap costume jewelry and shoes and guitars, wood carvings. He stopped and looked but bought nothing. He strolled around the Plaza de la Constitución and stood in its center, counted the streets radiating from it and had the feeling he was stand-ing in the center of the country, on its heart. He surveyed the cathe-dral that rose from the ground as though it might once have been a pink granite mountain, carved down to what it was by many men working many years because no army of workers could have erected it from the ground up, not in a hundred years, not even if they were Egyptians and a pharaoh had decreed it. He stepped inside and and marveled at its massive towering columns tiered with statues all the way to the ceiling and arches and beams held in place by God only knew what, at its guilded altar that rose from floor to ceiling and glittered with the color of jewels and he beheld the breathtaking enormity of it all, as if there were neither light nor space fully enough to admire all that was in the place. Surely this was a place where God was.

He walked up Hidalgo past La Alameda and turned left onto Paseo de la Reforma and stopped in a bank and changed the twenty dollar bill in his billfold and counted out the pesos which amounted to about two hundred with a little extra change. He continued walking for over a mile it seemed until he came to a large park. The sign said Bosque de Chapultepec and another sign pointing to the right said Castillo de Chapultepec and he turned and saw the castle, crowning a hill at the east end of the park. He found an empty bench along one of the many walkways and sat down. The park was shaded by majestic cedars and lesser growth that shimmered with the moving shadows. He looked back at the castle and tried to remember all he could from the letters. Maximilian and the Empress Carlota had lived there. His grandmother had been invited there once for tea. He remembered that. She sat on a patio. They probably talked about the weather and the shops, and their families and their well-being, their children and grandchildren, their latest escapades, the ones that brought laughter. They probably did not talk of politics or their respective futures and his grandmother would not have mentioned her boredom at the hotel and its poor services and the Empress would not have mentioned her loneliness and her husband's unfaithfulness. They were strong women whose strength was reflected in what they did not say. His great-great-grandfather Cal went there with General J. O. Shelby and several others of the inner circle of Confederates. They probably went at night and sat in a large dark high-ceilinged room, in large leather chairs around a fireplace and in flickering firelight sipped bourbon and smoked cigars and spoke of conquests, of battles won and lost, and trading war secrets and boasting of what each could do for the other, disbanding in the late evening air with promises of hope that rode even higher on the liquor they had consumed.

He watched a Mexican family who were picnicking in front of him, how lost they seemed in themselves, how carefree. For a moment his thinking drifted to Athen and what she might be doing, if she might be thinking of him as well. Probably not. It was mid-week and she was in class or studying in the library. But she just might glance up through a window at the sky and wonder about him. She just might. And she would be proud of him if she knew how far he had come with so little.

Judging by the angle of the sun in the sky, Jo Shelby decided it was a couple of hours past noon. There was a vendor at a corner not far from him and he walked over and bought a couple of enchiladas and a Coca-Cola and returned to the bench to eat. The family was packing up their belongings. He slipped his knapsack back onto his back and left with them.

By following the city map, and walking what seemed miles, he found the Avenida Toltecas. It was not a long street. On both sides were freestanding cinder-block dwellings, small one story apartments they looked to be, and at the end where the street ended, a large villa that had seen better days. There was nothing comfortable-looking about the houses. They were small and built closely together, but they looked livable. A few had stucco on them and a few were painted, dif-ferent colors of pastels. Most were in disrepair. Windows broken. Screens torn and curling. Sagging rooflines. Rusted rebar projected upward from the corners of some. There was trash in yards and along the sidewalks. The address on the small piece of paper said 521. He found it at the end of the street. It was one of the worst of the lot.

The sun was angling down behind the mountains around him. He guessed he'd been walking for about two hours and estimated the time to be between four and five o'clock. She was probably at work but he approached the door that had been painted red, the only adornment about the place, and knocked anyway.

He looked around. There were two small screenless windows on either side of the door. A pane in one was broken. A thick bougainvillea vine rose from one corner of the house and spread out halfway in smaller vines across the top eaves but there were few blossoms on it. He noticed his breathing was quicker and coming in shorter puffs and decided it was the long walk plus the altitude. He sat down.

Just then an older woman stepped from a doorway in the adjacent hovel and walked to the street. She tossed a pan of water and was on her way in when he spoke to her.

Yes. She knew the señorita Carmen. Yes. She lived there. No. She did not know when she was coming home and abruptly reentered her house to let him know she had no time for his questions.

He sat on the raised step in front of the house and waited. Some children were playing across the street. He watched them. He felt the quiet, out-of-the way calmness of the place. Across the broad vista of the city he could see Popocatépetl, a thin wisp of smoke rising straight from its peak, as though it were some huge bell hanging by a gossamer thread from the sky. And not far from it, the Sleeping Lady, outstretched like a maiden awaiting burial. The sun was descending behind the mountains to his back, casting long shadows before him that crawled slowly over the city. He felt chilled and put on his coat. A parent's call broke the silence. The children lingered as if they didn't hear it, then the call came again, louder, and they scurried to one of the houses along the street. At the other end traffic passed, buses stopping occasionally at the corner to let people off and on.

He had almost dozed off, his head tilted back against the doorjamb, when he heard footsteps, the faint measured clicking of a woman's heels striking pavement and he looked down the street toward the bus stop. She was walking toward him and from a distance looked to be about the size of Athen. She wore a dark straight skirt and white blouse and moved with the slow glide of a lady at ease with herself. One hand rested on a shoulder-strap purse that swung slightly at her waist and the other carried a small shopping bag, one seeming to balance the other as she walked. She looked straight ahead and her face in the late afternoon light had an undisturbed bronze glow about it. She had not seen him and he waited until she was closer then he stood up and walked to the sidewalk and she saw him and stopped. She was yet twenty yards away, but even at that distance he could see with clarity the face he had seen hanging on the wall at the señora's and he thought there was truly none more beautiful, nor more improbable, for that place or any other. He removed his sombrero and called to her.

Señorita Carmen?

Sí.

Yo soy Jo Shelby Ferguson, una amigo de su padre.

She took a few steps closer, her eyes cautiously surveying him, and stopped.

Cómo obtuvo mi dirección?

Su madre en Monterrey, esta dio a mí.

She continued looking at him, regarding him with amazed curiosity.

Usted es norteamericano, no? she said.

Sí. De Mississippi.

Why do you come here, to my apartment? she said, her brow furrowed, drawing an edge to her eyes. Her full mouth cast down at the corners, weighted with cautious concern.

He should have known she spoke English and the familiar words brought some comfort to him and he told her briefly of his search and his visit with her mother and her willingness to give him her address, that she might be able to help him.

She remained standing where she was. She wore a single silver necklace. He looked down at her shoes. They were slightly frayed along the soles and there were fine cracks in the leather, but they were polished, well-cared for. She planted one foot in front and rested her hip on the other. And my father, how is it that you know him? she said.

That's a long story, but one I'd like to tell you, if you'd permit.

She stepped closer and extended her arm and he shook lightly the fine-boned hand outstretched to him and her composed mouth that had shown little expression curved into a smile revealing strong white teeth and her dark, almost oriental eyes, flashed with a soft sincerity and she invited him in.

She apologized for the condition of her dwelling as they crossed the threshold. The entire block had once been a villa but the city took it over and in its decline it was purchased by a Venezuelan oilman who converted it to apartments, that he had died and his widow had done nothing since other than collect the rent, she told him.

He stood in a small living area. The floor was made of large ungrooved planking, but polished and swept clean. There was an old couch with lumpy cushions, two armless upholstered chairs, a lowset coffee table, a shaded lamp. All of it looked borrowed, or handed down. A few pictures hung on the wall over the couch. He recognized two of the faces. The place had an old smell about it, but also the light fragrance of youth, odors of bread and floor polish and perfume. Everything neat and in its place.

It is not much, but it is sufficient, she said as she set her shopping bag on the small table and switched on the light. Please have a seat. One minute and I will be back, and she left through a door at the back that led into a small room that looked like a bedroom.

He sat in one of the chairs and placed his knapsack on the floor between his feet. He looked around. The kitchen was across from the living area. It, too, was small and consisted of a stove and an icebox, a sink and a short counter beside the sink. Cabinets above the counter and beneath it, but that was all. There was a wooden bowl on the counter containing fruit. Oranges and bananas, papaya. A glass jar holding various utensils. A hotplate and a coffeepot. Everything she needed, nothing more.

She came back with her hair combed and a fresh application of lipstick. She sat across from him, her legs crossed above the knee. She studied him shyly, with intelligent eyes. A pose not unlike her mother's, he thought. Everything prim and proper. Except the stockinged legs, their silky sheen in the lamp glow.

My mother, she is well?

He was still sitting, holding his hat between his legs. Yessum. She's quite some lady. He went on to tell her of her mother's hospitality and good cooking and the trip to the bus station.

That is my mother, a very generous woman, she said. And my father, he is not so well. He was supposed to be released from the prison but I hear, my brother, he sends bad news that it is not so. How is it that you know him?

He told her of his misfortune in Matamoros and his incarceration, how the friendship with his father came about and how he taught him Spanish and how he would not be there if it were not for him. She listened, nodding her head from time to time, but said nothing until he had finished.

And the gun, you still have it?

Yessum. It's here in my knapsack. Would you like to see it?

Yes. That is all right. But one moment please. She got up and closed the curtains on the two front windows, dusk leaking along their edges, and returned to her chair. He opened the bulging straps and removed his dirty clothes and a few other articles then lifted the holstered pistol into the dim light and she put her hand over her mouth and let out a sigh.

I need to put it back? he said.

No, no. Not there. She pointed to his knapsack. It is not good for you to keep it there, she said. This is not a good time for Americans in Mexico. Give it to me.

He handed the holster and gun to her, as if trust were not even a thought, and she took it and walked to the back room where she had gone earlier. She remained a few moments. Soft rustling sounds. Something being moved, maybe lifted and let down. She returned.

What'd you do with it? he said.

I put it in a safe place. Do not worry.

He wanted not to. Besides his granddaddy's Barlow knife, it was the only thing of real worth he had on him, sentimental or otherwise.

Would you like something to drink? Coffee? A beer? Maybe a glass of wine?

He thought a moment. What're you gonna drink?

A glass of wine perhaps?

All right. That'll be good.

She walked into the kitchen area. He watched her, the sauntering movement, delicate and refined. She opened the refrigerator and removed a tall bottle of red wine that was three-quarters full then opened an overhead cabinet and pulled down two tapered glasses that clinked musically in the stillness of the apartment. She walked back to the sitting area and set the glasses on the coffee table and poured wine into each and handed him one and took her seat and waited. Both sat holding their glasses looking at each other then he realized he was supposed to propose a toast.

To mañana and finding my family.

She repeated the toast in Spanish and leaned toward him, her eyes steady on his, and they clinked glasses and saluded each other and drank and he had the same feeling he had at the señora's, as though there was some solution to his life after all.

So, she said emphatically, her eyes telegraphing a simple directness, tell me more of why you are here, of the family you seek. She shifted to the edge of her chair and leaned toward him.

He told her the story, of his false arrest and incarceration in Mississippi and eventual release. Of the death of his parents and grandfather, the trunk and the letters, the hundred-year history behind the letters and the remnants of family he hoped were still thriving somewhere in Mexico. She listened intently and interrupted him only once, to replenish their glasses. He told her of his trip down the Mississippi River on the towboat and across the Gulf of Mexico by tanker, went into some detail about the gun incident and his bargaining with the comandante and his eventual release.

The gun, it is very important for you, no?

Yeah, you might say that.

It is worth much money?

It's worth more 'n money, he said. It was my great-great-grandfather's or his father's, I'm still not sure. It's been in my family bout as long as it's been a family. It's over a hunderd years old.

Madre mía. She let out a slight gasp and her eyes widened. Then it is most valuable.

To me it is. To somebody else maybe not.

And you gave the gun to me, she said accepting the compliment.

Yeah. Guess I did, didn't I. He smiled back.

But you are in Mexico, not the United States. In Mexico one would not take the time to become your friend then steal from you. In Mexico they just steal and run.

They both laughed.

In my country friendship is very important, she continued, her face serious again. You break bread with someone, or have a drink, she raised her glass symbolically, you become their friend.

That simple?

Es verdad. It is that simple.

Es verdad. Yo soy hombre muy suerte.

Your Spanish is very good. My father taught you well.

Thank you. Your father's one good teacher. So good my Spanish is probably better'n my English.

That is a very nice thing you say of my father.

Es verdad, he said.

And so it went for a while, the two of them talking and drinking wine, sharing their families' tragic histories, their own personal stories of struggle. She told him that she was sent to a convent in San Luis Potosí at an early age. It was all part of the Acción Católica, a movement decreed by Pope Pius XI that reached Mexico in 1929 when the Calles administration was enforcing the anticlerical laws of reform. He did not understand and she explained some of the history, that the Catholic Church in her country was at one time persecuted because they would not go along with government reforms, that it was during that period that her father changed his position, primarily because of what had happened to her, but for other reasons as well. She told of the structured life in the convent, its rigidity, that rules broken were severely punished. Once she could not leave her room for a week because she was late to prayers. Her room was a small cubicle with only a table and a bed and a religious picture on the wall.

It was like being in a prison, she said.

He nodded grimly.

She was marched to meals and to prayers and her father had to pay a fee for her to be treated in this manner, like an animal, she told him. The food was good and nourishing, but not plentiful and most nights she went to bed hungry. Her mother was in favor of the convent because it brought one up to be a "good Christian girl" but against her mother's protestations, her father took her out when he saw how frail and sickly she was becoming and arranged her admission to La Ciudad Universitaria, which was in Mexico City where he taught and where they lived. When her parents moved to Monterrey she dropped out of school and got a small job modeling in a department store and took night courses in stenography and bookkeeping and English. He said nothing about what her mother had said about the modeling career, for he could see how she would be much sought for and fought over, but he asked why she did not go with her parents to Monterrey, that it was a beautiful city.

She hesitated and took a sip of wine, swallowed slowly, glanced upward at the ceiling as if an answer hovered there.

It was a difficult decision for me. My family's history, it is much complicated. My grandfather, my father's father, was a powerful man, a banker here in Mexico.

Yes. I know.

Then my father told you.

A little.

Then you know he was murdered in Monterrey.

Yes.

My father was offered a less paying job at the Universidad de Nuevo Leon and he took it to take the family out of the political pressure that was building in the city. There were threats against our family, by people beneath Alemán but in his administration. But I could not go. How can one go to a city where their grandfather was murdered? This city is my home and I would not leave it or my friends again. There are some things that cannot be replaced. I am glad of my decision. My parents and brother and sister were more persecuted in Monterrey than they might have been here and my father is in prison because of it.

All of this he absorbed with rapt attention as she spoke and discerned a beauty beneath the outer beauty of the person, not unlike that of her mother, of independence and integrity and indomitable will, the fullness of womanhood, and his only desire for her was that of adoration and worship. He would have sat and listened to her all night and into the next day.

She drank the last of her wine and ask if he wanted more and he said he did not. There was an awkward silence and they sat looking at their empty glasses. A clock was ticking. He hadn't seen one.

Where is your hotel? she said.

Nowhere.

You do not have one?

That's right.

Where did you sleep last night?

In La Alameda.

In La Alameda? In the city?

Yep. On the ground behind a monument. I was tired. I slept okay.

With the gun in your bolsa you slept in La Alameda. Madre mía. She rolled her eyes in a gesture of concerned dismay. Tonight you stay here.

I don't want to be no trouble.

It is no trouble. It is more trouble if you do not. You can sleep there on the sofa. I have guests before. It is no trouble.

He thought about that, about having guests before and who they might have been. Surely she had a boyfriend. Somebody that good looking would have to have a boyfriend. But he wouldn't ask. He didn't want to know.

She collected the glasses and the empty bottle and returned from the kitchen and stood in front of him.

Tonight I will show you the city, my city.

I've done seen some of it, he said and she asked what he had seen and he told her the places he had been.

Ah, but you have not really seen *the* city. And at night it is magnifica.

I wouldn't argue that.

You stay here. I will change and we will go. If you need to use the bathroom it is the small door there just beside the kitchen, she said and left and entered the bedroom at the back.

She emerged from the bedroom wearing the same heels, a redpleated skirt, a simple white crew neck sweater and over that a black satin jacket with a red floral design of roses. Her long black hair was partially gathered in a bun revealing the fullness of her face.

He dropped the hat he had been spinning between his fingers and stood up. His mouth was open but no words would come out.

Yes? she said.

Nothin. I was just gonna say . . . nothin.

Nothing?

Well . . .

He looked down at his hat on the floor and back up at her.

You just look really purdy.

Muchas gracias, she said smiling and made a slight curtsy.

Guess I better leave my hat here.

No. Wear it. It looks good on you, makes you look masculino. But you will need your jacket.

The night sky was clear. Away from the city lights, the dark shapes of the mountains stood out against the lesser dark and rimmed the horizon so the bespangled vastness of the city below seemed collected in a huge bowl and the stars burning brightly overhead a rounded mirror of the glitter below. An upturned quarter-moon seemed to smile its approval.

She hooked a hand in the crook of his arm and they walked to the corner to catch a bus. He let her step ahead of him and she handed the driver two coins and they took a seat toward the back where there were fewer people. Through the window she pointed to special places and said their names and told him the reason for their importance. He listened without interruption and tried to remember all he could. The bus crossed the Paseo and turned south and they got off at the next stop.

Come, she said. I want to show you something.

What is it?

You will like it. It is called the Plaza de Garibaldi. Mariachi bands play there in the evenings, sometimes as many as a hundred, and there are many cafés and bars. The food is good and not expensive.

She grabbed his hand and held it and he followed. They strolled through the cobblestone plaza and listened to the bands. Men in black silver-buttoned costumes playing guitars and violins and trumpets and bass fiddles. Brown-skinned cupids of the night out to stir up a little romance, he thought. Her hand was still in his but she was leading the way. Occasionally she would shift it back to the bend of his arm and lean slightly inward against his shoulder and he could smell the clean aroma of her perfumed hair. She picked a restaurant for them, one where she had eaten before, and they sipped wine and ate in the soft light of a quiet corner and listened to a marachi band that serenaded from table to table. When it came to theirs the leader looked at him and asked if he had a request and he spoke the name of the only Spanish song he knew, Malagueña, but the song they played and sang was a tune he had never before heard. He fumbled in his pocket for a coin and tipped them when they finished.

That was good but I ain't never heard it before.

She laughed softly. There are many Malagueñas, she said. You Americans have probably heard only one. What you heard was Malagueña Salerosa. She went on to tell him that it was a girl's fondest wish for her boyfriend to contract with a mariachi band and take it to her balcony and sing a serenade. She said all of this to him in a bright-eyed manner but one that veiled any underlying hints he was supposed to take. He noticed the way other men in the restaurant were looking at her and his thoughts could hold back his curiosity no longer and he finally asked.

She did not respond to his question right away. She lifted her wine-glass and held it before her face in the lamplight and looked over it, an unhurried gaze viewing something a long way off, then took a thoughtful sip and set the glass down and wiped her mouth daintily with her napkin and placed it back in her lap. Then she folded her hands on the table and looked directly at him and told him that she had had a boyfriend, had been recently engaged, to a lawyer whose office was in the building next to the factory where she worked. He was much older, about fifteen years. He had been previously married and had two teenage children who lived with their mother. They had been dating for almost a year and engaged for about six months when she broke off the relationship. The tone of her voice was not that of sadness but of anger, one that was old, smoldering, he sensed. She did not say why she ended the engagement as she drifted in her discourse, purposively it almost seemed, but she spoke disparagingly of men of pretense and men who put on airs and men who made promises and broke them, that she might not survive a convent but she could survive being single. The message was clear. But he could read nothing else about her. Maybe she looked upon him as family, a brother replacing another moved away and married. Maybe friendship meant something different in Mexico than in America. Maybe it was the passion and everybody had it. He knew only that he had never been treated as such by another woman in his life. The sheer sincerity of it all, coming straight at him, with no in-between. With Delta girls, Athen included, there was always the in-between stuff, the teasing and the games and the guessing, never knowing where you stood. He'd always wondered about that, why they couldn't just come right out and tell you what they meant, why Athen waited until he was out of prison to tell him she cared the way she did. He decided to enjoy whatever it was with Carmen, and not try to figure out why she was so different.

She reached over and tapped a bright red fingernail on his arm where it lay upon the table and her finger remained a moment after the tap then she withdrew it but the tingle it sent through him lingered longer. And? she said with a questioning smile.

Me?

Yes. You have no novia?

I did. Once. A long time ago.

And what happened to her? Ah! Do not tell me. You went to the prison and she married someone else.

Not exactly.

Her parents would not permit it.

Close.

Then forgive me. I do not know. Tell me.

With reluctance he began telling her about Athen, how they had grown up together on the plantation and that his father worked for her father, on land that had once belonged to his family. He had intended to say very little but once he started, it seemed he could not stop, an energy inside of him pushed the words along. He described the house she lived in and the one he lived in, the two different worlds in which their parents moved and the simple common world he shared with her, one filled with riding horses and bicycles, picking dewberries and cotton, fishing and swimming. He ended with how the relationship grew and where it stopped, and the different worlds into which they went.

She listened and looked upon him with dark eyes that searched and penetrated and when he was through placed a hand on his arm and patted it.

By the way you speak of her, I think she must still be very special to you. Even if you may not be her novio, she is still your novia.

You Mexican ladies are somethin else.

How do you mean?

I mean, you don't beat around the bush.

Beat around the bush? I do not understand this meaning.

Let's just say you tell it like it is and that ain't somethin I've had a whole lot of, leastways from my so-called novia. There was an edge to his voice that surprised him, an anger, too, that was equally surprising. He guessed it had been there but gone unnoticed because he'd never talked about it, never had anybody that seemed willing to listen. It was an anger that didn't feel right, didn't sit right inside of him.

Don't git me wrong now, he continued. She's purdy, like you. And sweet. He leaned back and thought. She's good at a lot of things. She can ride horses and climb trees with the best of em. She makes good grades in school, I think. She's a senior in college so she must to stay there that long. Now, she don't speak Spanish, just English and . . .

Jo Shelby, she said, speaking his name for the first time. Are you trying to convince me or yourself?

He stopped, turned his glass in his hands and looked at it, embarrassed at how much he had said. Sorry. Guess I was just running off at the mouth. I don't usually do that. This stuff here, he lifted his glass into the air, kicks it into gear.

She laughed and withdrew her hand and for a while nothing else was said, as though everything that had been said was too delicate to touch again.

There was music in the background, the soft clatter of plates and a low hum of voices around them.

He pulled the piece of paper her mother had given to him from his pocket and laid it on the table between them. He told her they were the names of places where he might find information about his family. She took the paper and held it close to her eyes. For a long time she held it there, longer than it took to read what was written on it. He noticed her eyes were no longer focused on the paper but staring beyond it, other thoughts moving in her mind. Then she turned and looked at him.

I can help you, she said.

But you gotta work.

It is no problem. I have vacation time.

But—

I will help. That is that. Fin, she said crossing and uncrossing her hands across the table in a gesticulation of finality.

De verdad, he said, and shrugged.

They laughed.

The sidewalks were filled with people. They strolled down the Paseo, passing distinguished facades, decorative doors and window frames, cornices, moldings, some of the buildings with a rusticated stone that suggested they had been there at least a hundred years. They looked in shopwindows and made comments about articles of merchandise. She telling him what was too expensive. He telling her anything was too expensive, that he needed nothing more than what he had and to find his family. She squeezed his arm.

They passed a library and the American embassy and she reminded him they were both on the list her mother had given to him, that her mother was wise to think of them. They crossed the street at the glorieta where the Monumento de la Independencia rose commandingly, the golden winged angel atop its tall column a sign of guardianship. She took him into the Zona Rosa, the "hip" area of town, she said, where the young and sophisticated lived and worked and partied, but that it was expensive. They listened to the music spilling into the streets and peeked in nightclubs where people were dancing. He asked but she did not want to go in. He bought her a single long-stemmed rose from a street vendor and told her it would go well with her jacket. Then he broke the stem off and asked her to stand still and in a pool of streetlight threaded it through her hair and under the barrette so the blossom lay slightly to the side of her head and she said Qué romántico teasingly and that no one had ever done that before and he said he hadn't either. They were walking along a street canopied by trees where the streetlight played through the leaves like specks of glass.

They stopped at a small sidewalk café and had coffee. He asked her about her job and what she did and did it pay enough. She told him she was a secretary for an American garment industry and that her job paid well because she was bilingual, that most secretaries make about only one thousand pesos a month, but she was making eighteen hundred which was about a hundred and sixty-five American dollars.

And that's all? he said with astonishment.

Yes.

And you can live on that?

It is not so difficult. My rent is one hundred fifty pesos a month and food is about two hundred pesos and thirty pesos for my electricity and heating gas. My Social Security payments are three percent of my salary. So, you see, I am really doing quite well. I am able to save almost one thousand pesos each month. Soon I will buy a car. She smiled.

You got me beat a long ways.

Others have it so much worse, she continued. The clerks in the stores only earn three hundred to six hundred pesos a month. And they have families to support. I am by myself. That is the reason why so many working girls live in a casa chica. But most Mexican girls are not like that, she said. Their mothers rule them and they come home immediately after work.

What's that?

What?

Casa whatever.

Casa chica?

Yeah. Chica means little girl, don't it?

She blushed. Casa chica is the nice term in Spanish. The vulgar term is casa de las putas. That is what you in America call, I believe, a whorehouse.

He looked away and asked if he could smoke a cigarette and she said she did not mind and he pulled out a Camel and thumped it once on the table and lit it. He asked her where he might get a job in Cuernavaca and she asked why he needed one and he told her he was about out of money and it might take him a long time to find his family. She offered to help him and he said it was out of the question, that he had been raised to take care of himself. She responded that she was no different and he said there was a difference and so their discussion went, escalating, their voices rising until people at other tables were looking at them and she held up her napkin in a sign of truce and said she had a better idea.

What's that?

The national pawnshop.

Pawnshop? You got pawnshops down here?

Yes. They are set up by the government to help people in need. There is one on the Zócalo, where you were today. People can get loans on anything. Sewing machines, bicycles, electric motors, even jewelry and fine furniture. I know. I helped with one when I was in the convent. Sometimes only the price of breakfast is asked. People are seldom refused and the interest is low.

But I ain't got nothing to pawn.

She raised a brow and drummed her fingers on the table.

Wait a minute, he said. You're not . . . naw now . . . you're not thinkin . . . naw. He crushed his cigarette in an ashtray.

You said it was valuable.

But only to me. It ain't valuable to nobody down here. Ain't nobody down here gonna be interested in a hunderd year old gun that won't even shoot.

If the gun will not shoot, then of what use is it to you? It is just something else more for you to carry.

You know somethin. He leaned in close to her. You're beginnin to sound just like your daddy. Like I told him, I kinda got attached to it. Might just need it for company. Me and that gun been through a lot. Your government tried to take it away from me onct and now you're asking me to give it back to em for safe keeping till I git back God only knows when. Ain't no way in hell I'm gonna do that. Anyway, I'm not even a Mexican citizen, all's I got is a visa and it's just supposed to be a tourist visa and as far as I know I'm already breaking the law again.

She leaned over and placed a hand on his arm again.

Jo Shelby. You are my friend, no?

Yeah.

You are my father's friend, no?

Yeah.

Mi casa es tu casa. What is ours is yours.

All right.

Then you give the gun to me, as a trust. I take the gun to the government pawnshop and request a loan. I bring the money to you. It is still your gun. It is your money. After you return from Cuernavaca I go back to the pawnshop and get the gun. It is no problem.

Only one problem.

Yes?

What're you gonna use to git the gun back with?

Whatever money you have left. It is no problem, believe me. If you need a job to pay it back, I can help you get a job, in the factory where I work. Or you can get your own job. It is little difference. First you must find your family and this way you can do it.

He thought. It didn't sound good but nothing else he could think of sounded better. She was right. He didn't need to be carrying the gun around and it would only stay at her place gathering dust.

One more thing, she said.

Yeah?

Everything that happens, there is a reason. There is a reason you still have the gun. It is God's will. Do you understand what I am saying?

Yeah. Let me sleep on it.

They took a bus back to her apartment and she made up the couch for him, brought in a clean sheet and tucked it around the cushions and added a pillow she said she did not need and a serape she brought down from the closet shelf. She told him goodnight and hoped he slept well and he remarked likewise to her and watched her leave and close the door to her bedroom. For a long time he watched the light under her door and when it went out he removed his clothes and pulled the serape over him. That night it rained and its rhythm drummed softly on the roof and he slept and dreamed of children playing in fields white as cotton and above them on fields as white were parents watching and the fields where the children played began to rise and joined the fields on which the parents stood watching and all of them rose together and disappeared.

She rose early, letting him sleep and when he awoke she had a small breakfast of fruit and cereal and coffee prepared. She wore an ankle-length orange skirt gathered high at the waist and a brown short-sleeved T-shirt with a scooped neck that revealed the cleavage of her breasts. Her hair was unpinned and curved around her face and around her neck was a gold and silver beaded choker with a large oval-shaped centerpiece of polished black onyx and smaller pendants hanging beneath it. On her feet she wore thin-soled sandals with gold-beaded straps that tied at the ankles. The clothes he had worn the day before and left in a pile on the floor by the couch lay in a chair, neatly folded. She told him she had washed his dirty clothes and they were drying on a line at the back of the apartment then she left the room so he could dress.

They ate breakfast and she went over the day's agenda, where they would go first, then second and so on, something about each place. She told him the same thing her mother had told him, that the Hacienda Michopa may no longer exist. He listened and ate. She told him how much she had enjoyed the evening and he told her no more than he did. She pointed to the rose in a glass jar at the center of the table but he had already noticed it. She asked about the gun and he told her he'd slept on it and thought about it and could not depart without it.

But you will have no money soon. How will you sleep? How will you eat? Her eyes pleaded with a soft despair. You must let me do this for you.

Naw. Much obliged. But I just cain't. The gun's kinda like . . . it's become kinda like another part of my body. I can git a job. Somethin'll turn up. It always has.

She flipped her hands in the air and shook her head at him in playful disgust and cleared the table. He helped her and dried the dishes as she washed them.

I will look like you today, she said and winked at the closet, pulling out a wide-brimmed sunbonnet made of straw with a yellow ribbon.

They took a bus back to the centro, both of them looking like a couple trying to look like a couple, with only one half doing the trying, he thought.

They went first to the American embassy. The receptionist was Mexican and friendly and listened attentively as he told her he was an American citizen and needed knowledge of his family. She told them to have a seat in the lobby and they waited amidst the extravagance a wealthy country could afford. It was an hour before a tall distinguished-looking Mexican came and asked them to follow him. He was middle-aged and wore a blue suit that fit too loosely and took them down a long polished corridor and into a small office where a window overlooked the Paseo.

She sat quietly as Jo Shelby told the man what he needed to know, of the plight of his grandparents three generations removed and presented him with the last letter his great-great-great-grandmother Caroline had written. The man read it with concentration then reshuffled the pages and read it again then handed the letter back to him, remarking as he did on its condition. Jo Shelby asked if he knew anything about the Hacienda Michopa and the man said he did not but that did not mean it did not exist. Carmen interrupted and inquired about records of American families or descendants of American families, that that was the real reason they were there. Did they possess in their archives any documents of Americans who had lived or owned property in Mexico? The man shook his head sorrowfully and said that such did not exist, at least not to his knowledge and not in the embassy. They had a list of American businesses in Mexico and records of individuals and families requesting assistance from the embassy but that trying to keep up with all of the Americans entering and leaving Mexico would be like trying to keep up with all the Mexicans who moved into the city every day. Thousands each month he said. He stated further that because Jo Shelby's relatives were Confederates and enemies of the American government, he doubted they would have contacted the American consulate, thus there would be no record of their name on any document.

Unless, the man said, raising a finger, unless there was a warrant for their arrest in this country, or your government wanted them arrested and extradited, then we might have something.

He wadn't wanted by nobody, Jo Shelby said, bristling. He wadn't runnin from nobody. He was just trying to find a home for his family. The emperor and his wife was their friends and they found a home for them and the revolutionaries came and burned it to the ground and

ran em off and they went to this Hacienda Michopa close to Cuernavaca and alls I wanna do is find whats left of em. Seems to me a hacienda wouldn't just up and leave the face of Mexico.

Carmen reached up and tugged at his coat for his voice was getting
louder.

But señor, the man said. With all respects, the Emperor Maximil-
lian may have been your family's friend but he was not a friend of the
U.S. government. I am afraid we cannot help you. All of this happened long ago and much has happened. Revolutions. Uprisings.
Earthquakes. Many records and documents have been rifled and destroyed or burned. I am sorry, señor, señorita.

Jo Shelby looked down at Carmen and motioned with his head to
leave and she rose. They turned to go and the man called them back.

I do have one suggestion for you, Mr. Ferguson. This Hacienda
Michopa, I would recommend you look for it. Much has happened to
the haciendas over the years but some have survived. Only a few, but if
you find it, I think you will come closer to finding something about
your family than looking for records. Finding records in Mexico is like
working in an archaeological excavation. You sift and sift and sift
through many layers of time and maybe, just maybe, you find what it is
you are looking for. With one exception. If any members of your family married Mexicans, those records might still be available to you.
Even if they were women. In Mexico the woman's name goes with her.
If they married in a Catholic church, the church might still have the
records. But I do not know. These are only recommendations.

Where would the records be? Carmen said.

At the civil registry. Here, I give you the address. He opened a
drawer and fumbled with some papers and withdrew one and read out
the address: Arcos de Belén y Dr. Andrade. It is not far from here.

Jo Shelby thanked him and they left on their own.

No offense, Carmen, but why've we only talked to Mexicans and
no Americans. I mean, after all, this is the American embassy, he said
to her as they were walking briskly down the paneled hallway.

It is common in most of the embassies, she said. They hire our people because of the unemployment we have, to help our economy.

Excuse me for saying so, but they're suppose to be helping Americans and they ain't helped me one damn bit.

But he did help you, she said. He told you where to look.

The civil registry was a few blocks away, an ordinary office building made of gray stone. The older man behind the main desk just beyond the foyer spoke no English and Carmen guided the conversation. Jo Shelby could tell by the way he was shaking his head it didn't sound good. But the man wrote something on a piece of paper and handed it to her and they turned and left.

What was all that about? Jo Shelby said as they passed through the double doors.

The man said they do not have marriage records there that go back that far. He said you would have to go to the civil registry in Cuernavaca which is the capitol of the state of Morelos. Each state has its own civil registry and many of their records go far back in time.

What'd he give you?

The address. She pulled it out and showed it to him. Salazar y Humbold the words said. Put it in a safe place, she said handing him the slip of paper. You will need it when you get to Cuernavaca.

He folded it and put it in his jeans pocket. What about the Hacienda Michopa? he said.

He said to go to some of the museums. They may have some knowledge of it.

The rest of the morning they spent in buildings, museums and libraries, and no one had heard of the Hacienda Michopa or anything that sounded like it. He took her to the Hotel de Iturbide and related its story and the connection with his family and they ate lunch at a sidewalk café down the street from the Ritz. The air was crisp and clean from the evening rain and the winds that came with it had carried away temporarily the smoky clouds from the industrial plants and he could see Popocatépetl and the Sleeping Lady more clearly than ever before.

I could just sit here all day and look at em, he looked at her and said.

You mean Popocatépetl and Ixtaccíhuatl.

I guess, one's the volcano and the other's The Sleeping Lady. Ain't they?

She smiled. Yes, but their names, they are from the Aztecs. Popocatépetl, which means "mountain that smokes" and the other is Ixtaccíhuatl. Ixta means white but I do not know the rest. There is a beautiful but sad story about them. Would you like to hear it?

I'm not one for sad stories but go ahead. He pulled out a cigarette and lit it and leaned back in his chair to listen, and to watch her as she talked, the way her mouth shaped the words and the smoothness with which the sounds came out. That was really what he wanted to hear.

Many, many centuries ago there were two Aztec lovers, from different families of nobility, she began. The families did not agree on their love for each other and in those days the families arranged the marriages. The man was sent off to war and the lady was told by her family that he was killed in the war. She was so distressed that she went to the mountain and laid down and let herself die. But the man was not killed in the war. And when he returned he went to the mountain to grieve over her and he let himself die. If you look carefully you can see her figure stretched out under the sky and beside her his figure leaning slightly toward her, contemplating her.

She had long finished the story and he had still said nothing, his eyes fixed upon the cream-coated peaks, the sun sending light to them and them alone, as though the mountains around them were undeserving of such attention.

You look unhappy. You did not like the story, she finally said.

Like I said, I'm not one for sad stories. But you told it good. Real good.

She feigned a pout and slapped playfully at his arm. He paid the bill and they left.

She told him there was one more place they could go, that surely would have some information, that it was the best library in all of Mexico. They walked back to the Paseo and caught a southbound bus that went for several blocks and stopped. They got off and took another bus that took them along Insurgentes, the main thoroughfare running through the heart of the city. The bus followed the long avenue some distance and they got off at the city limits. He found himself amidst a collection of modern buildings of unusual architectural style, all of them rising in contradiction from fields of solid gray and brownish-black rock. Off in the distance he could see the bowled shape of a stadium that looked big enough to seat the entire city.

Where are we? he said.

La Ciudad Universitaria. It is the new university, only recently built. As I told you, my father taught at the old one. It was really many buildings scattered throughout the city. By 1950, so many students were enrolled they had to build a new university, one of the better things Alemán did for my country. There, she said, pointing to a cluster of buildings. There is where we are going.

The library was decorated with stone mosaics in muted colors that were repeated in the windows that she told him were made of Puebla onyx, a stone native to their country. The building sat between two other buildings, one that rose in glass to skyscraper height and another low-roofed linear building with flat yellow walls and none of the three seemed to go together or have anything in common.

She negotiated their entry and must have done well he thought for they were led by a well-dressed female of some authority down a long tiled corridor and through an arched doorway where an overhead sign said REFERENCIA and into a large carpeted room covered by a bubble-shaped glass roof. The center of the room was filled with large polished tables that glistened in the overhead light. Extending on either side, shelving, row after row after row and he glanced up and saw a second story of more of the same. Aisle upon aisle of bookshelves encircling the entire room. Besides the library at his high school at Tutwiler he'd been in only one other in his whole life and the one in Drew would have fit in the foyer where they stood waiting to be told what to do next.

The lady told them to wait and she disappeared into a small office on the side and returned followed by a portly young man. He looked to be in his early twenties but the slight stoop of his carriage and thinning hair and granny-like wireframe glasses gave him the appearance of youth grown old, as though by intention under the weight of intellectual pursuit. His name was Albert, the woman said, and he was an American from Birmingham, Alabama completing his doctorate in Mexican history and working in the library as part of student–work exchange program. He would be their assistant for the afternoon.

Jo Shelby and Carmen introduced themselves and the purpose of their visit was made clear and Albert nodded and pointed them toward a vacant table and told them to wait. Shortly he returned with several volumes and explained these were books that could not leave the library but that they were free to examine them and he left to bring them more. Throughout the afternoon he kept them busy with theses and dissertations, government documents and newspapers, books and journals of every description. Most of the titles were in Spanish, some a paragraph long. A few were in French. A handful in English— *Evolution of Seward's Mexican Policy. Maximilian and Carlota of Mexico. Brazil, The Home for Southerners. The Land Systems of Mexico. An American in Maximilian's Mexico. Shelby's Expedition to Mexico.* That one Jo Shelby wanted to read but the time did not allow. He wrote the title on a piece of paper and put it in his pocket. Because of his limited Spanish scanning the texts was slow and tedious. For every selection he completed, Carmen completed five. For several hours they searched and found nothing.

Then Albert came with yet another volume and laid it before them and apologized that he had not brought it earlier.

You might find something here, he said.

What is it? said Jo Shelby.

Bound copies of *The Mexican Times,* he said. It was an English-language journal, actually a newspaper, that was published from September 1865 to June 1867 by a Mr. Henry Allen, a former governor of Louisiana. Maximilian subsidized it. Much of it will be unimportant to you, but there is considerable news about the Confederates. It listed new arrivals and even printed the names of persons for whom the Mexico City post office was holding mail, things like that.

It was in English, which was a relief. While Carmen looked on, Jo Shelby began poring over it, his eyes carefully scanning its faded and yellowed columns. He checked first the headlines and the smaller subtitles of columns, looking for anything pertaining to the Confederates, anything that held promise of a list of names. The first few pages were uneventful. An article about the justification of the flight to Mexico. Another containing warnings about returning home. One glorifying the Emperor and Carlota. A few about happenings back in the States. He turned a page. The headline was in large bold letters, just beneath the date line:

CONFEDERATE EMIGRES REGALED BY
THE EMPEROR AND EMPRESS

What's regaled mean? he looked up at her and said.

It is a banquet. The emperor and empress gave a banquet for them.

He bent his head back over the page and moved his finger quickly through a narrative that told of the decree just issued by the emperor granting land between Mexico City and Veracruz for the establishment of a colony for the American expatriates and that other decrees were soon to be issued for other colonies throughout Mexico. The article went on to tell of the emperor's good wishes for the Americans whom he considered his allies and of his desire for peaceful relations between them and all Mexicans. There were a few other statements of equal import, as if the emperor might have told the writer what to say, and then—

In attendance at the banquet which took place at the Chapultepec Palace were the following...

Jo Shelby looked back up at her. He'd a been there, he said. My great-granddaddy would've been there.

She smiled and patted his back and he began tracing his finger through the long list of names—

... William P. Hardeman, Judge Oran M. Roberts, William M. Anderson, John G. Lux Y. P. Oropesa, F. T. Mitchell, General J. O. Shelby—

Looka there, he said, his finger on the name.

Yes, I see.

I was named for him. He was a great Confederate general. That's who my granddaddy followed into Mexico. Can you believe it? He looked up at her, his mouth beaming, his eyes flashing like those of a child's on Christmas morning and she patted him gently, softly tapping in the truth that it really was so.

He looked back down and continued his silent reading of the list.

Colonel David S. Terry, Richard L. Maury, Major R. J. Lawrence, Colonel Calvin T. Ferguson, Captain Richard Taylor—

Wait, he said and moved his finger back. There it is.

She leaned in to take a closer look.

Colonel Calvin T. Ferguson. That's him. Hot damn. I cain't believe it. He was breathing fast and an excitement ran through him as though he might have reached out and touched a charged wire. He kept his finger on the name and continued gazing upon it, as though it were a vision of the man himself, kept rubbing his finger over it as though it possessed physical qualities that might reach out and touch him back. For a long time he just stood there in that transfixed meditative focus of a pilgrim having found, and touched, a long sought sacred relic possessing powers of redemption and salvation.

Her hand was still on his back and she leaned in closer and whispered.

Qué bueno! This is very special for you.

Yeah. Very, he said without looking up.

Now you know.

I knew already.

Yes. She paused. But now you *really* know. Es verdad.

He looked up and smiled.

Infused with renewed hope he completed his review of the

Mexican Times but there was no other mention of his great-great-great-grandfather. Albert continued to bring more volumes and journals and he and Carmen continued tirelessly the search but nothing else of any significance surfaced. Just the name Calvin T. Ferguson. No mention of the Hacienda Michopa. No shred of a clue that it had ever existed. And his thinking was driving him despairingly toward that conclusion, that there had never been such a place or that his grandmother had either misspelled the name or had been badly misinformed. Then suddenly Albert came running from a side aisle of stacks, his face beaming discovery.

He held the front of a journal up for them to see the title, *Diario del Archivo de la Historia de México*, then spread it before them and opened to an article entitled *Confederados de los Estados Unidos en México*. He flipped several pages to where his finger anchored a place and pointed to a passage and in the soft light streaming through the overhead glass, Carmen began reading it aloud, translating haltingly as she went—

With the fall of Carlota ... the Confederates were a broken and ... disoriented group . . . without a leader or a cause. Most left the country by way of the port at Veracruz ... Brazil and Venezuela were destinations for many . . . Some caught ships bound for Canada and Europe . . . and as far away as China . . . A handful remained in Mexico ... finding refuge ... wherever they could. One such popular place . . . that was being made ready for settlement . . . was the hacienda at Michopa ...

She looked up at Jo Shelby and smiled.

Go on, he said, not returning the smile.

... near Cuernavaca ... and others like it whose hacendados were sympathetic to their cause ... and their way of life.

She stopped.

Keep going, he said.

There is no more, she said. The rest is about Cuba and people who went there.

My grandmama wadn't wrong then, he said. It was there.

Yes, she said. So you know they were here, and the place did exist.

But it said the hacienda at Michopa, like it was a town, not the name of the hacienda. You got a town around here named Michopa, Jo Shelby said looking at Albert.

One minute. I'll get a map.

Albert returned with a large road map and laid it out on the table. They all searched. Michapa appeared as a small dot near the city of Taxco, a small town about fifty miles southwest of Cuernavaca.

That could've been it, Jo Shelby said.

Perhaps the hacienda was named Michopa because it was near Michapa, which is not unusual, Albert said. You can go there and find out.

I intend to.

Are you through? Albert said. It is almost five and I get off at five. I think this may be as close as you are going to get.

Yeah. We're through. I guess, Jo Shelby said. There ain't nothin else in there about the Hacienda Michopa?

No sir. I got this by checking the index in the back and if there were other references it would have noted them.

They helped Albert organize all of the materials scattered about on the large table. They thanked him and wished him well in his studies and he told Jo Shelby he hoped he found the hacienda, but not to get his hopes up, that much had happened to them over the years and it may have even been destroyed by Zapata or some other upstart revolutionary with an ax to grind.

They caught a bus back to the centro and bought snacks for themselves from a vendor at the alameda and sat on a bench that faced the Avenida Juárez, not far from the monument where he had spent the night, and watched the passing traffic and pedestrians and ate. The air was cooling down, a moist wind blowing down from the mountains with a hint of rain. He had not brought his jacket nor had she hers. He could see Popocatépetl and the Sleeping Lady, their snow-capped crowns pink in the sun's fading light and he recalled the story once more and felt he had known it longer than the mountains themselves. The globed lights along the street and in the park came on. The shadows of branches overhead moved on the sidewalk and the sound of birds flittering and jumping among them ceased. A few pigeons still strutted around, looking for a last bite before roosting in the eaves and ledges of the city. He thought of the next day, and that he would be leaving, and it weighed on his heart which was already strangely heavy with the place, and with her. He asked what they would do next and she suggested seeing an American movie.

In English? he said.

The actors speak in English but it is subtitled in Spanish.

Subtitled?

The lines are written across the bottom on the screen in Spanish. It is really quite a good way to learn Spanish, and English. My father took me often to see them.

They walked down the Paseo and found a cinema. High Noon was playing starring Gary Cooper and Grace Kelly. He bought their tickets and a box of popcorn and they entered the theater and waited until their eyes adjusted to the dark then found seats on an aisle toward the back. He remembered other picture shows, other times, on Friday nights or Saturday afternoons in Drew and Clarksdale. Once Mr. Pat took him and Athen on a Saturday while he attended to business in town. He remembered nothing of the movie but never forgot that she held his hand, that it was the first time she had touched him like that, and one of the last, for he saw her only a few times afterward. He thought of holding Carmen's hand then decided it was not a good idea. When the bad men came to the town and Gary Cooper was walking down the street she grabbed his arm and clung to it and did not release her hands until Grace Kelly held Gary Cooper and the man began singing Do not forsake me o my darlin.

He left the next morning before she arose. He wanted to leave it the way she had left it the night before. A kiss on his cheek and a hug his body felt all the way to his knees. He wrote her a note and left it on the kitchen table, next to the rose. He thanked her for all she had done and offered to do and that he wanted to see her again and hoped she would forgive him for asking for his gun back and slipping off like he

did, but he thought it best and did not want to be any more of a burden to her. He erased the last part and changed it to read: I can just say
good-bye better to folks at night than in the morning. He signed it,
Your friend, Jo Shelby Ferguson and added P.S. I think you are a wonderful person and I do want to see you again, very much.

   With the morning light barely breaking over the eastern cordilleras
he walked to the corner and caught the next bus going south toward
the centro. He told the driver he wanted to go to the highway that went
to Cuernavaca and the driver told him to get off at the Paseo and take
the Insurgentes bus as far as it would go and he would be on the highway to Cuernavaca. He did as the driver instructed and found himself
deposited on the outskirts of the city on a two-lane thoroughfare teeming with early-morning traffic. He stuck out his thumb and within
minutes was picked up by two women in a pickup truck that was fairly
crackling on its axles the engine was chugging so hard, oil pan vibrating
near the ground. The front fenderwell on the right side was missing
and part of the hood oxidized away like something gnawed at by tiny
teeth with a design. The oil-coated innards looked like they'd been
worked and reworked beyond torture and he wondered how the contraption ran at all. The one driving was middle-aged, the other much
younger, both of them dressed up like they were going out on the town
then it dawned on him that's where they'd been. He sat on the shotgun
side next to the younger girl. Both wore short skirts and low-cut
blouses that hung around their shoulders and spiked heels and the
makeup on their faces looked like it had been mauled in the night. The
wind whipping through the open windows did little to neutralize the
odor of alcohol and cheap perfume that filled the cab and he pondered
the difference between his current situation and sleeping with a skunk
all night and weighed the two options in his mind and the two women
tipped the scales. They giggled and laughed and chattered away thinking he could not understand but he made out they were arguing which
one was going to get him and finally he said something to them in
Spanish and they elbow punched one another and quieted.

   De dónde es usted? the one driving said.

   Estados Unidos. De Mississippi.

Ah. Mississippi, the younger one said. El rio largo.

No el rio. El estado de Mississippi.

Y donde va? they said.

A Cuernavaca.

Bueno, said the older one. Nosotros tambien.

Muy bueno, he said and smiled thankfully at them and they rode in silence.

For a while the sky was clear and without clouds then they penetrated a wall of gray mist and the sky disappeared completely from sight and all about them was fog and he realized they were riding a high ridge that had taken them into the clouds. The highway was wet where it had rained and the air was much cooler as the road tilted upward and they rode the incline for some distance. Tall pines rose on both sides of the road, their tops invisible in the slow-drifting mist and occasionally there were clumps of maguey. Then the road began a sharp descent, hugging the sides of the mountains as it snaked its way down. Huge rocks jutted outward almost in their path and he worried about the unsteady hand on the wheel and if the older woman could drive around them, whether she saw them or not. The road leveled out a ways then descended once more and suddenly they were below a ceiling of dark clouds where the sun had torn a hole and a fan of light burst through onto a vast valley with myriad shades of green fields and, rising from its floor, crater-shaped hills and above them mountains and ridges looming like the backs of great prehistoric animals asleep and he was above it all looking down and he had seen nothing more beautiful in all of Mexico or anywhere else.

Qué bonito! he said.

Sí, they said back and nodded at one another. They told him Cuernavaca was as pretty and began telling him the places he should see. He thanked them but said he was trying to find only one place, the Hacienda Michopa or a town named Michapa.

No sabemos, they said and shrugged their shoulders.

He told them it existed a long time ago and they both laughed and said they were much too young for such matters and the one sitting next to him winked, as if to telegraph a hidden message.

The highway began to level out on entabled land between the mountains and the familiar scenes that announce a city began to appear. Roadside cafés and tiendas and adobe dwellings with pole corrals that held cows and burros and occasionally ponies, people of all ages on bicycles, pulling carts, taking their wares to market. Advertisements in English on ruined walls: Bardahl. Pepsi-Cola. Coca-Cola. Esso. A Chevrolet dealership. Soon they were on a street worn down in places where the cobblestones showed through and a sign said Boulevard Emiliano Zapata. They passed buildings with clean looking glass fronts and double glass doors and bars across the doors and nice houses behind stone and chain-link fences and barred doors there as well and he thought of a city on guard against its own. The world was full of prisons, each in its own way.

He asked their destination and they said Jiutepec, a town just east of Cuernavaca. The one sitting next to him shifted her leg against his and rubbed it up and down and he could tell they were communicating with each other by sidelong glances. He asked if they were going through the centro and the one driving said they were going right through it and he asked to be let off there and she said she would and the one next to him moved her leg away.

The older woman brought the truck to a sputtering stop in front of a large gray stone building that by its appearance looked like a castle of old. Across the street was an alameda with pathways and iron benches with backs shaped like fans, colorful flowers and trees. They told him the building was once the Palacio de Cortez, one of the oldest buildings in Mexico, and the alameda across the street was the Plaza de Armas, the centro of the city.

He got out and kept a hand on the window frame and asked where he might find Americans in the city and they told him in the centro bars at night and the Bella Vista Hotel on the Plaza de los Tepetates which was run by an American lady. The young one said he might even see them there, that it was where some of their best customers went and they laughed and drove off, the old truck coughing and belching blue smoke, their two heads through the rear window bobbing with talk he knew was about him.

It was about midmorning and he had had nothing to eat. He strolled through the plaza. It was quiet. The clouds had cleared and the air was blue with sky. Only a few people were sitting on the benches. A few pigeons pecked around for breakfast.

He walked on and crossed a street and saw the name Salazar glazed into brick on the side of a building and he reached in his jeans pocket and pulled out the piece of paper the man at the civil registry in Mexico City had given to Carmen and opened it: Salazar y Humbold. He looked at the buildings around him and marked the place in his memory and continued down a side street where he ate a breakfast of orange juice and pan dulce at a café counter then returned to the alameda and rested on one of the wrought-iron benches and smoked a cigarette. He counted his money. Two hunded and forty pesos and the twenty still in his boot, still nearly about forty American dollars. He planned his strategy. The cigarette burned down to his fingers and he flipped the butt into the air and got up and walked back across the alameda to the street named Salazar and turned right and followed it down a sloping hill. He saw the barranca he had crossed earlier in the day in the truck and beyond Popocatépetl and The Sleeping Lady, puncturing the flawless blue horizon like white tents pitched by giants. On his left was a high wall of stone and atop it a market of colorful canvassed-covered stalls, row upon row, that stair-stepped the wall halfway down the hill then stopped and on the right following the natural downward grade were chic shops and cafés. At the bottom of the hill the street intersected with another that dead-ended into it. The sign said Humbold and he turned and looked around and the building was behind him. He climbed the steps and went inside.

Beyond the double-glass doors was a short foyer with wooden benches end-on-end against the walls and beyond an archway there was a long counter and then a large well-lit open room where people worked at desks arranged in orderly rows. Around the room, from the floor to the high ceiling, was tier upon tier of huge green volumes with leather spines like those he'd seen in the courthouse at Indianola when he went once with his father to check on the trust of probate of the old

colonel's estate, to see if there might have been a mistake or sly ma-
neuver somewhere along the passage of property from one owner to
the next, that the land was not great-granddaddy Cal's to lose and so
on. His father would wait for another election and another chancery
clerk before trying again, and again the answer was the same. He remained convinced that the old colonel was still alive in 1875, albeit in
Mexico, and that legally, technically, the land was still his, and no one
else's to throw away in a midnight crapshoot and that the courthouse
records would indicate as much if the people who managed them were
not so afraid of the planters who got them elected.

Those thoughts came to him as he stood there, his hat removed,
waiting.

A middle-aged lady saw him, rose from her desk and walked to the
counter to greet him. He asked if she spoke English and she said politely she did not. He introduced himself and abbreviated his story as
best he could and told her about his search. She listened with an expression of grave concern, nodding her head, as though she, too, had
had loved ones vanish over the generations of revolution and destruction and their whereabouts blown to the far corners of the country.
When he finished she motioned to a younger coworker to join them
and recapitulated the story told to her and the coworker listened with
equal interest and the contained excitement of something new and
unusual occurring in the otherwise monotonous tedium of recording
deaths and births and marriages and divorces. The older woman then
turned to Jo Shelby and told him about some records dating back to
that time, but that they were few because the records had been kept
over time in a number of different places, some burned and ravaged by
either Zapata or General González in their war against each other,
that Zapata often could not control his own men, many of whom were
former slaves on the sugar plantations who looted and burned without
respect of ownership. Jo Shelby told them the year his great-grandparents were in Mexico and of their journey to a hacienda near a place
called Michopa and inquired if they had ever heard of such and neither had. He asked for a sheet of paper and wrote upon it the family

names as they had been passed down to him, which was all he knew. Colonel Calvin Ferguson, wife Caroline Bouchillan. Children: Two sons, Taylor and Jonathan. A Daughter, Caroline. Both sons were married but he had no knowledge of the names of their wives or children and from all he could remember the daughter was unmarried at the time they entered Mexico. The older woman asked him if he had more information, names or dates or places, and he said he had told her all he knew.

Ay, Dios mío! she said and turned and looked at a clock on a back wall and he noted, too, the day had passed the halfway mark.

Tenemos mucho trabajo que hacer, the woman said to the young girl standing beside her and the girl smiled, as if to say thanks, that she welcomed much hard work as long as it was different from what she'd been doing.

They told Jo Shelby to have a seat in the foyer and wait. They would call him. He walked back into the dimly lit area and sat on a wooden bench worn smooth along its front edges, by others who probably came for the same reason, he thought, looking for a place in life to hold on. He placed his hat beside him and stretched out his legs and crossed them at the ankles and folded his hands across his stomach and waited. He thought about Mexicans in general and their friendliness and willingness to help and all of it without suspicion or circumspection of character and wondered of the prospects of a Mexican entering the courthouse in Indianola, Mississippi getting the same treatment and considered it quite dim, if at all, that they would be treated just like a nigger. And he thought about that, too, of how he had treated the members of that race in his own country and looked down upon them and considered them on a plane equal with farm animals because that was all he'd been taught and knew and the revelation sunk in and followed him into a dim horizon of reverie then sleep and a dream of finding home, wherever that might be.

He heard the sound of his name called and opened his eyes. The señora was motioning for him and he grabbed his hat and knapsack and quickly walked to the counter. She told him they had been most fortunate and had located some records of 1865 and examined them but found nothing resembling the name Ferguson. She spelled it aloud for him to make sure she had it right and he nodded she did. Her assistant looking attentively on she told him there was little hope of finding any information on the two sons because the liberal Juaristas were taking control of the country at that time and anyone allied with the emperor would not have registered their name with the government for fear of reprisals, possibly even execution and for that reason those lines were probably lost. He told her he had already been so informed by the official in Mexico City but was also told that the woman's name was continued if she married a Mexican. She told him he had been correctly informed and that they would continue their search but that his request was most unusual and one they did not often receive and there were many volumes with many names to examine and it would take a long time and for him to come back the following morning. He thanked them and expressed again how important their work was to him and in words of great care and concern they shared their understanding and he tipped his hat and thanked them once more and left.

He climbed the hill back to the centro and began walking. He walked up and down the hills of the city, exploring its network of twisting narrow streets and paseos, covered sidewalks streaming with people and peaceful plazas where yellow and red blossoms from tulip trees dappled the ground, and all of it had the smells of an old world very much alive. He looked in shopwindows at goods with American brand names as new as those he might see in Clarksdale or Memphis and passed buildings as ancient as the city itself and walked along hedges intertwined with crimson flowers and high mysterious walls where bougainvillea surged over the top and now and then a gate opening on a garden of hibiscus and oleander beneath the shade of a mango or tulip tree. He entered a small callejone that climbed gradually and he followed it to the top where it ended at the steps of a quaint whitewashed church of red-tiled roof that seemed to rise from nowhere amidst a clustered foliage of palm and magnolia trees. A small flag of Mexico hung over its arched doorway. A beggar sat on a step at its entrance and Jo Shelby dropped a peso in his hand and asked him the name of the church and the man said only one word. Tepetates. Jo Shelby retraced his steps back to the callejone's entrance and the plaza he had just skirted and surveyed the buildings surrounding it and the Hotel Bella Vista was where the two prostitutes who'd driven him to town had said it would be.

The building was massive and old but well kept and immaculately clean. He inquired of the desk clerk the cost of a night's stay and the clerk told him one hundred fifty pesos for a single. He thanked him and looked around. There was a restaurant that opened out into a large patio and bar along one wall. The place was half-full with Americans and Mexicans and he decided not to stay but to return later and left to sit on a bench in the plaza where he smoked a cigarette and thought, then resumed losing himself in the hills of streets for he had discovered that was how one really came to know a city and its people. In this random circuitous fashion he came upon the market he had seen from below on his way to the registro and made his way through its narrow arcaded streets and walkways and discovered a world set apart from all else he had seen. Scrawny brown-skinned men in unbuttoned shirts hawking in shrill voices and women with broad hips and wide feet and long hair sitting in slat-back chairs nearby watching with quiet eyes and the rich odors of coffee and baked bread and flowers commingling with those of raw meat and fish and human sweat. He saw whole hogs and hogheads, chickens and pigfeet hanging from hooks over meat counters and fish of every species laid out on makeshift tabletops drawing flies. There were huge bins of candies and breads and mushrooms and chiles, vegetables of all kinds, some the shapes of which he had never before seen and old women with blank stares sitting cross-legged on the pavement, mounds of different colored beans spread before them on old serapes, and he saw the prices and wondered how they ate even if they sold all they brought. All along the narrow winding aisles there were stalls filled with hats and shoes and watches, dresses and T-shirts hanging wherever there was a place to support a hook. One white-bearded vendor wearing a poncho had only a set of buckets filled with herbs and signs of cardboard in each bucket telling the ailment the herb could cure: kidney stones, urinary problems, epilepsy, high blood pressure, asthma, diarrhea, even one for a runny nose. Whatever need there was in this city, he thought, its satisfaction could be found here. And if one did not have a need, the market would surely invent one.

Further and further he descended into the congestion of barter and commerce and there seemed to be no end to it and the further he went the more crowded it became until he was having to push himself along. He began to feel the sidelong looks of the people, the dark eyes, calculating, and he felt a tug on his knapsack and turned and a small boy was trying to undo the straps. He remembered what Ramón had said about gringos on busy Mexican streets and he quickly slipped the knapsack from his shoulders and clutched it with both arms across his chest. A few steps further he felt something brush across his buttocks and he slapped away a hand trying to lift his billfold and he pulled it out and tucked it inside his shirt. He could feel his heart beating through the knapsack and felt his solitariness as he had in the prison yard just before the first blows fell and he wanted to run but there was no place to run and he saw no way out. People were pushing in on him from all sides and he was inching along using his elbows as levers. Sweat was running in streams from beneath his hat and into his eyes but he dared not mop it away lest he lose his grip on the knapsack and if someone grabbed it there was no way he could chase them. His eyes burned and blurred but he saw a hole of light up ahead and prayed it would be an opening and he kept pushing toward it and moments later found himself facing a street and a uniformed policewoman directing traffic. She threw up a white-gloved hand before a line of cars and blew her whistle and motioned for him to cross and he did so and tipped his hat to her but she gave no acknowledgment of his gesture and dropped her hand and blew the whistle once more and he heard the roar of the traffic behind him as he stepped up onto the curb.

He kept his knapsack close to his chest and secured his wallet inside his shirt along his waistline and continued on. He walked along Hidalgo and viewed the cathedral but did not go in. Outside its stone walls a woman was frying small round wafers on a homemade comal. They were no bigger than a half-dollar and looked like miniature pancakes. He asked her what they were and she told him corn gorditas and he bought a handful and ate them leaning against the wall. On the opposite corner from the cathedral was an expansive iron-fenced area and within it was a mansion of colonial design surrounded by beautiful gardens of hibiscus and bougainvillea and oleander with graveled pathways circulating beneath cedar and magnolia and mango trees. He asked the lady the significance of the place and she told him it was called the Jardin Borda and was a hotel but that once it was a palace. He asked her if it was the palace of the Emperor Maximilian and she shrugged and said she did not know, only that it was once a palace where the very rich lived and now it was a hotel that only the very rich could afford.

He continued his meandering through the town and found a small hotel on a side street off Avenida Morelos and negotiated a fee with the desk clerk, bringing him down from eighty pesos a night to sixty and paid him for two nights for he knew he would be there at least that long but asked if the room could be his for longer if he needed it and the clerk told him that would be no problem.

The building was old but quiet as a hospital and cool. The stone floors were patinaed with years of passing feet and there was a large yellow cat asleep at one end of the counter. The lobby was small with only a couch and two worn chairs and there was no restaurant as he had seen at the nicer establishments, no porter to take his baggage had he had any. The clerk handed him his key and he climbed the stairs to the second story and found his room.

It was small with high ceilings and decorative molding suggesting it had once been a place of luxury, perhaps an old colonial home. A thin cotton spread covered the bed and the linens looked clean and fresh and were folded back with an even crease and neatly arranged upon them was a set of clean white towels. A sashed window opened onto a narrow street below and was partially raised and he walked over to it and raised it higher to let in more breeze. He leaned out to check the view but all he saw was the street he had just left and the drab gray building fronts encroaching upon it. Below, people passed along the sidewalk and their aimless talk drifted upward and he caught fragments of their conversations. A lovers quarrel. A business deal gone bad. A small child begging his mother to return to the market for a candy. The world that never changed. At the corner an old vendress sat on a mat surrounded by ceramic pottery of many sizes and colors. A black rebozo was pulled over her head and her rattling voice was asking for help for her family. The scene was too much for him and he walked down the steps and through the small lobby and into the street and purchased a small cup from her, one that would fit in his knapsack, and paid her twice her asking and stopped at a nearby vendor and bought a beer and returned to his room. He rinsed the cup in the lavatory and emptied the beer into it and sat in a chair by the window and drank from his newly purchased chalice. Carmen had said she liked pottery and when he returned to Mexico City he would give it to her.

He put his hat on the bureau and pulled a chair to the window and smoked a cigarette and drank and looked across the rooftops of the city and listened to the street noises below and a great feeling of sadness came over him and a thought with it, that the loneliest a person could be was in a large city where no one knew him and he knew no one. Then he thought again, of something beyond lonely, of having no family and belonging to no one and no one belonging to him, unless it might be Athen, and God only knew if she felt the same kind of belonging.

The beer had made him drowsy and he stretched out on the bed and watched the slow-turning of the fan blades overhead and drifted off to sleep. When he awoke the room was dark. A cool breeze came steady through the window. He turned on an overhead light and laid his knapsack on the bed and opened it, took out the pistol and looked for a place to hide it. Putting it under the mattress was too simple and obvious. He eyed the nightstand which was a solid piece and had a scalloped base. He reached his hand beneath it and felt around and decided there was enough space and lifted it up and placed the holstered gun under it and let it back down. He removed two twenty peso bills from his wallet and slipped them under as well, and kept the rest on him.

He went into the bathroom and ran a tub of water and bathed and stayed awhile in the warm water, soaking up its comfort. He shaved and put on a clean shirt and pair of jeans that Carmen had washed and ironed for him. He brushed his teeth and combed his hair, put on his hat and raked the brim down across the front. He stopped and thought and looked around the room to see if he were forgetting anything. He removed his billfold from his hip pocket and took out the pesos he had left which were two twenties and a five and folded them and put them in his shirtpocket then slid the billfold under the nightstand with the gun and the forty pesos. He pulled the two letters from the knapsack and unbuttoned his shirt and slipped them inside and rebuttoned it and placed the knapsack under the bed and stopped and thought some more. He walked over and got his Barlow knife off the bureau and slipped it in his front jeans pocket and determined this time he was more prepared for the city and got his jacket and left.

The night air was cool. A dry wind blew down from the mountains and channeled through the streets. The old vendress was gone and where she had sat with her meager holdings two lovers stood leaning against the building kissing. It was not yet the weekend but the traffic along the street was heavy and the sidewalks filled with people. He walked down Morelos and turned on Hidalgo at the Jardín Borda and by that route returned to the Plaza de Armas to get his bearings. The area was full of people in colorful dress and the trees festooned with lights and the music of the mariachi bands came from every corner. Neon lights lit up the night. The scene vibrated with a carnival spirit.

He walked past the market but dared not enter it again and turned back west following landmarks he had remembered and at times making turns only by instinct. He stopped once and inquired and a father with two small sons told him the Plaza de los Tepetates was only two blocks away and pointed out the direction.

The Bella Vista was busy and noisy. The attractive señorita who greeted him at the archway of the restaurant told him all of the tables were occupied. He asked about those on the patio and she said those were taken as well. She could take his name and he could wait at the bar or in the lobby. He asked to see a menu and took one look at the prices and told her he would just stand at the bar, that he wasn't really hungry anyway. She smiled and extended an arm for him to pass through.

There were a number of Americans at the bar. Most were casually dressed but with a certain elegance, an air of importance. A few wore T-shirts and blue jeans with woven belts and leather sandals. On some of the T-shirts were the names of colleges. Southern Cal. Texas. One from Louisiana. None from Mississippi. He found an unoccupied stool at the bar and took a seat and ordered a beer. The bartender asked him what kind and he told him a Tecate. He felt regarded by the patrons around him as someone different, as if he had invaded a private club. He decided it was his sombrero for no one else wore one and he removed it but there was no where to place it so he put it back on. A young man next to him asked where he was from and he told him dryly Mississippi and there was no further conversation.

He drank his beer and ordered another. He asked the Mexican bartender where he might find the owner of the hotel, that he understood she was American. The bartender pointed toward the entrance and said he must ask there. He left his drink in place to hold his seat and walked back through the patio and restaurant. The woman told him to ask at the front desk. The clerk told him that the Señora King was on her terrace dining. He told the clerk that he was an American looking for lost relatives and would he convey that information to the señora and ask if she would kindly help him at a time convenient to her. The clerk nodded and stuck his head in a back room and called for a replacement and left. He was gone several minutes and returned down a side stairway and told Jo Shelby she would receive him.

No quiero molestarla si está comiendo.

The clerk said it was no problem that she had finished her meal. Jo Shelby asked him to wait a moment and he returned to the bar and retrieved his hat and beer and followed the clerk back up the stairs and down a corridor and through a suite of rooms of extravagant polished furnishings of walnut and oak. There were porcelain figures and vases and a walled bookcase filled with old volumes and along an opposite wall, oil paintings of bright colors depicting various scenes of Mexico. There was an old armoire, its doors open, refashioned with shelving to hold sets of fine china and crystal and beside it a sideboard of similar vintage and on top of it framed family photographs arranged in a row. In a single room by itself a grand piano with sheets of music on its stand.

The terrace was well lit and was reached through French doors around which were gathered lace curtains. At the corners were huge clay pots holding laurel and palm trees and surrounding them and along its iron spiked railing were smaller pots of hibiscus and jacaranda and oleander and down a wall tumbled vines of bougainvillea. He removed his hat as he followed the clerk onto the slate tiles.

The lady was seated at a wrought-iron table. A pair of glasses hung from a cord around her neck. Her brownish-gray hair was tied back in a bun and she was smoking a cigarette. She was a broad-shouldered stout-looking woman who might have passed for a man without her gown-like dress and makeup. She laid her cigarette in an ashtray and rose to meet him. She said her name, Blanche King, and extended her hand and he walked forward and shook it and said his name. She thanked the clerk and dismissed him and told Jo Shelby to take a seat at the table with her and asked if he wanted something to drink.

Nome, I already got one, he said, lifting his beer for her to see. But I wouldn't mind smoking a cigarette with you.

Please do. An American brand?

Yessum. Camels.

So, how can I be of help to you, Mr. Ferguson?

He told her why he was in Mexico and some of the details of his history, no more than was necessary. She listened and smoked thoughtfully. He told her of his visit to the registro and the fragile hopes he held of finding information there and of the hacienda that seemed to have disappeared.

Michopa, she said. There is a Michapa, a small town between here and Taxco, but I have heard of no hacienda by that name, and I have been here a long time, was here when Madero took control of the government from Díaz. That was in 1911.

She rose and asked him to follow and took him to the rim of the terrace and pointed to the flagpole below at the entrance of the hotel and showed him the exact spot President Madero stood when she raised the British flag and defied the Zapatistas to advance a single step.

I was a young woman then and it was not a good time for foreigners to be in Mexico, she said. But we stayed on despite the turmoil and made a go of it. My husband died several years ago and I decided to stay. This hotel is the only home I've ever known, and the Americans and Mexicans here my only friends, you might say my only family. I dare say not a single American ever traveling through Cuernavaca has not been through here for one reason or another. Some famous ones too, she emphasized and rolled off the names of movie stars and politicians, a psychologist named Fromm. He'd never heard of most of them.

They walked back to the table and sat down.

Ever met anyone by the name of Ferguson? he said

Ferguson. Ferguson, she said, mumbling the name over to herself. No, I can't say that I have. It is not a name that stands out in my memory. I usually sit in the portal downstairs and greet people as they arrive, have been doing that for about forty years, too. My ears are better than my eyes and I will remember a name before I do a face. But Ferguson. The name does not come to me. Of course, that does not mean they never came here. I just cannot recall. Perhaps it is my age. I'm eighty-one you know.

Nome, I didn't know. You don't look that old.

She smiled and blew jets of smoke through her nose. You are kind. And you are from where in the South?

Mississippi.

Ah yes, you told me that. You see. One's mind . . . Oh well, enough of that, and she lifted her cup and took a sip.

He smiled shyly and drained his beer.

She got up and walked to the railing and leaned over and called to one of the porters below and another beer was promptly delivered along with a glass of sherry. They sat and drank and talked into the evening. She told him about her family and how she came to live in Mexico, that her father had investments and bought the hotel in 1905 and died the following year and her mother two years later leaving her and her husband the responsibility of its continuance. She had two daughters both of whom left Mexico some time in the thirties and went to the States.

Life here was not good for young people growing up and my husband and I agreed it was best, she said. I have seen them only a few times, on trips back home to Texas. They will not come here. They think I am stubborn to stay in this backwards country but I really have no where else to go and it is where my parents died. Their graves are not far from here, in the cemetery of chapel San Jose Tlaltenango. The country is backwards in many ways but the hearts of its people are in the right place and they are good and hard-working and loyal. I could do worse staying and no better anywhere else.

He told her he understood and felt he could do no worse either in trying to find what was left of his family, and of those who begged him not to go for many of the same reasons. He told her of his experiences along the way and she leaned in closer to the table, the terrace lights reflecting in her eyes. He spoke of Ramón García and his wife in Monterrey and daughter in Mexico City and the help they had extended to him and that he would not be in Cuernavaca if it were not for them, probably he'd still be in prison in Matamoros. He paused and awaited a response for her mouth had been open several minutes as if words of importance were gathered there awaiting an opportunity to be spoken. He continued waiting and her mouth was still agape and he unbuttoned his shirt and slipped out the two letters and unfolded them and handed them to her. She reached for her glasses and guided the temples into place and held the sheets of paper away from her, focusing her eyes on them.

He drank his beer as she read and looked out over the city, its colorful neon and silver and amber streetlights skirting out to the edges of the muted dark where no lights shined, where the peaks of Popocatépetl and The Sleeping Lady rose dim and chalky against the purple sky, and he thought of all the people among the lights between him and the great dark beyond and that out there somewhere was someone that belonged to him and he was transfixed in that reverie of hope when she removed her glasses and put the letters on the table and spoke.

Mr. Ferguson?

Yessum. You can call me Jo Shelby.

Then Jo Shelby. I have sat here for many years, and I have heard many stories over those years, most of them tales, but I can truly say I have never heard one so compelling or touching as yours. I am not sure what I can do. I know many people, many Americans, descendants of expatriates who came to Cuernavaca before the turn of the century, and they may have some knowledge of your family. As you have probably already learned, much has happened to the haciendas over the years. There are a number of them in the state of Morelos but only a few that still exist from the times you mention. The hacienda of which your great-grandmother writes may have been one near Michapa and somehow the name was misspelled. That is not uncommon in translations from Spanish to English.

Yessum. That's what the man at the library in Mexico City told me.

Where are you staying?

Hotel Mercado. I think that's how it's pronounced. It's not very big.

Yes. I know the place. It is on Lerdo de Tejada, off Avenue Morelos.

Yessum.

If I learn of something, I will get a message to you.

Yessum. I'm much obliged.

Now you must excuse me. I must go and mingle with my guests on the patio.

I wouldn't mind kindly having another beer there myself.

He followed her back through the suite of rooms and down the steps as they parted at the patio doorway and she wished him good luck and he tipped the brim of his hat and thanked her again. He found a vacant seat toward the end of the bar and ordered another beer. He was feeling good about his visit with the kind lady and the beer was kicking in some of its own good feelings. He was hungry and ordered a plate of tamales and ate them and decided to move on.

The streets were more crowded than before. The people seemed dressed as if for a holiday, their colorful casualness blending with the lights and sounds of the city. Mariachi bands strolled the sidewalks and music blared from the open doors of bars. He stopped in one that was filled with people his age and ordered yet another beer and talked in Spanish with a couple who said they were students at one of the city's language schools. He asked if they had ever heard of the Hacienda Michopa and they had not but encouraged him to ask others and he decided he would do just that. He went from bar to bar and stopped at small sidewalk cafés, the beer he had drunk erasing any regards for decorum until he was finally run out of one establishment by the owner. Fragments and glimmers of conversations, scenes and remembrances of his past skimmed along the edges of his thought then dissolved and he crossed a line of vague reality where focus became a struggle and the name Michopa came out Mochapi and Moorchaspa and Machalpi and people brushed his tottering and stammering away with backhanded waves and looks of scorn and he realized he was drunk but no longer cared because the whole world was drunk and swam around him in waves of confused light and color and sound. Where he tried to step the pavement moved and the people and things he tried to swerve around he bumped into and there was nothing to guide his thinking except the narrow streets that rivered before him and walls of dark buildings that swayed as though they might tumble.

When he awoke he was facedown on wet cobblestones that smelled of vomit and his face and head throbbed with pain and there was pain in his back and along his legs. He heard short raspy sounds that seemed to be right in his ear and raised his head and saw street

cleaners sweeping around him. A policeman kicked him in the buttocks and told him to vamos and remained standing over him until he
pushed himself up and steadied himself against a wall. The policeman
walked away and he rubbed his eyes to clear his vision and moved his
jaw around to see if it was broken. He remembered shadows and scuf-
fling of feet and falling and hard blows to his face and stomach and
along his legs, but nothing else. He looked around and saw he was
standing just inside an alleyway. He stepped away from the wall and
onto the sidewalk and sunlight exploded through the corridor of
buildings and he turned his head and pain rolled around like a huge
ball ricocheting off the insides of his skull. He grabbed his head with
both hands and realized his hat was gone. He looked around and saw
it on the ground a few yards inside the callejone and it looked to be in
better shape than anything else he could see or feel. He stumbled over
and bent down and picked it up and the ball in his head rolled again,
harder. He ran his fingers into his shirtpocket and his money was
gone. He felt in his jeans pocket and his granddaddy's Barlow was
missing as well. He padded his hand over his shirt and felt the crin-
kling of the letters around his waist and breathed relief that at least
they had not been taken.

   He stopped at a small café that had just opened and asked the
owner for a cup of black coffee but said he had no money. Seeing the
shape he was in, the man asked if he wanted a shot of tequila in the
coffee and Jo Shelby nodded and told him that might help. He drank
the coffee and tequila which tasted like something siphoned from a
polluted well and waited for a shock of revival. He had only been
drunk once in his life, at a high school prom when his date left with
another classmate. He remembered the aftermath and the concoction
his father had stirred together and made him drink, black coffee and
molasses and bourbon and something gritty his father later told him
was gunpowder. He vowed he would never again drink as much again
but understood why some can be driven to do something so foolish
and mindless if there was nothing else around to hold their world together or make them feel it was held together, if only for a night, and

how they might string the nights and the days out so they all ran together, just to keep the pain at bay.

By asking people along the street he made his way back to his hotel and collapsed on the bed and slept. He had no idea of the time when he awoke. He looked out the window and along the street and the thin shadows of the building walls indicated it was near noon. He went into the bathroom and looked at himself in the mirror. His face was cut and scratched and his right eye was dark and swollen and looked like a bad oyster. He dampened a wash rag and dabbed at the cuts, washed away the dried blood. The wet coolness brought some relief and he balled up the rag and held it to his eye for a while. He turned on the faucets of the tub and began running water, regulating it and testing it with his hand until it was just the right warmth. Slowly and with pain he removed his clothes that were torn and soiled and managed to halfway wash himself in the tub. He put back on the clothes of the day before and reached under the nightstand and pulled out the two twenty peso notes and folded them and tucked them into his jeans pocket and and made sure the gun and wallet were still as he had left them and put on his hat, raking the brim so it cut low across his face, and left.

When he crossed the threshold the two women from the day before saw him coming, rose from behind their desks and came forward, their faces animated. Then he stepped up to the long counter under the bright lights and they saw his face. They ducked down and glanced up at his eye beneath the brim of the hat and their expressions turned suddenly grave and their hands to a nervous roll and they questioned him about his misfortune. He told them he'd been beaten and robbed. They asked about his injuries and how much and what was taken and he told them all that was hurt was his pride and that the thieves, for he was sure there was more than one, took less than forty pesos. He spared telling them of his granddaddy's Barlow knife and the years of memories and stories it held and the price, in pesos or in dollars, no one could ever have paid for it. They said that what they had to tell him would surely make him feel better and forget his losses.

The older woman directed him to the end of the counter away

from others. She told him to wait and left. The young woman kept staring at his eye and asked if he had seen a doctor and he said he had not, that a doctor couldn't help where he hurt. She tilted her head to one side and gave him a bemused look and he pretended not to notice and looked away at pictures of Mexican heroes along a back wall. The older woman returned, cradling in her arms a large volume of uncertain condition, its spine torn away from the bindings. She lowered the big book gently onto the countertop and opened it with great care to a place marked by a piece of lined writing paper then rotated it sideways for him to view it with her. He took off his hat and laid it aside and bent over and tilted his head allowing his uninjured eye a closer angle. The ledger sheets were yellowed with age and its dim lines written upon in brown ink that was barely legible in places but he saw immediately a blurred inscription on the second line of the left-hand page. He sawed a finger across his swollen eye and blinked several times and moved his face in as close as a watchmaker and for a moment it were as though all time had collapsed into a single moment as unreal as the self-awareness of one's first and last heartbeats and he heard not a sound around him nor felt any movement at all in the world and he froze in that transfixed state of disbelief begging belief, allowing time to readjust to the new ordering of his life.

The name was written in a florid cursive style with overlappings among the letters but the shape brought forth from the interconnecting string of characters was unmistakable and he whispered the name to himself.

Carolina Suzanna Ferguson.

Sí. Lea todo, the older woman said, inserting her finger beneath the line and moving it across the fragile page and he followed it and read aloud the entire inscription. Carolina Suzanna Ferguson c. Fernando Alfonso Cruz Linares, 6 de Julio, 1867, Estado de Morelos, Ciudad de Cuernavaca.

He stopped to let it sink in then read it again silently.

Qué significa? he said.

Casados, the younger girl said. Matrimonio.

En Cuernavaca.

Sí, they both said.

Dónde?

No sé, the older woman answered. Imposible saber. Catedral. Iglesia. No sé. Tenemos sólo los nombres y la fecha y la ciudad.

He could see that was all the information they had, names and dates, but thought there might be more. He looked at the date again. She was probably in her twenties at the time she married. He ran some figures through his head. If she'd lived to be seventy she'd have been alive almost twenty years into the next century and only some few odd years from when he was born. He glanced again at the name of her espoused, Fernando Alfonso Cruz Linares. He spoke the name aloud, to see if it sounded as important as it looked on paper, and it did, the rich accented syllables evoking privilege and wealth, one who was landed.

Cuándo murió? he said.

They told him they had no records of deaths and that because of the instability of the governments that came and went in those times their records of births were very few. He asked about any children she might have had and the older woman made a single clap with her hands and her eyes opened wide the way his mother's would when she'd forgotten a cake in the oven.

Elena, otro volumen por favor, she said pointing to another book on a nearby desk.

With a flourish of excitement the young girl quickly retrieved the tome that was equal in size to the first and in similar condition and laid it on the counter ledge. The señora opened it to a marked page where the title across the top said NACIMIENTOS DE 1868 and ran her finger down a column and stopped beside a name and he read with equal astonishment the name and the date beside it: Carlita Cruz Ferguson, 10 Noviembre 1868.

La hija es mi parienta.

Qué bueno! they both said, smiling.

Well I'll be damn.

Cómo? the señora said.

No es nada. Es una espresión americana.

Hay más, the señora said and directed her assistant again to another volume that was brought and aligned with the others and opened. The señora smoothed the pages with her palms and ran a veined hand down the left-side column, the tips of her fingers stopping on a line she had marked with a lightly penciled arrow and before she could read to him he reached out and placed a trembling finger beneath the lined inscription and moved it across the faded page and with a voice as tremulous whispered to himself.

Carlita Cruz Ferguson c. Gabriel Raúl Navarro López, 11 de septiembre de 1886, Estado de Morelos, Ciudad de Jiutepec.

He stopped, his finger still unsteady on the last word.

Dónde está Jiutepec?

Un pueblo cerca de Cuernavaca, the younger woman said. A unos cuantos kilómetros de aqui.

Did that mean they lived in this town he asked and they told him probably but not necessarily, that people often married in places special to them or their families but regardless of where they lived the marriage was always recorded in the town or city where it took place. The señora told him she had two more records for him to see but he held up his hand and asked her to wait, that he needed time to think and the two women stepped back and folded their hands at their waists in an attitude of near servitude. The books lay before him in the order they were presented and he bent low over them again and traced his finger beneath the names in the sequence of their lineage and read them quietly to himself once more, sorting out who was who and who was whose and how in all of the entanglement of deaths and marriages and births they all somehow connected to him and were they grandparents or aunts or cousins or what. He stood back from them and ran his hands through his hair and thought. If Carolina was Foster's sister then that made her the aunt of any of his children and the great-aunt of their children and he followed that logic down the family tree and came to the conclusion she was his great-great-aunt. Then that would make her daughter, Carlita Cruz Ferguson, his great-aunt along that limb of the tree and if she had any children they would be aunts and uncles. Or were they cousins several times removed? He processed the succession of families and offspring again, rethinking the lineage over and over until his mind grew dizzy and confused with the puzzlement of it all and finally decided that what they were was of no importance, it was the who that was, that the bloodline was there and he had found it and that was all that really mattered and he motioned to the two women who were still standing erect as butlers that he was ready to continue.

The señora brought forth another volume, emphasizing the difficulty she had had in finding it as she heaved it up from behind the counter and muscled it with her flabby arms onto the worn surface. She opened it alongside the others, which by then were taking up considerable space and drawing the attention of others, and pointed to the recording of one Carlita Cruz de Navarro, born 5 de Mayo, 1888 and barely giving him time to absorb that, wrestled up another and opened it and pointed to the recording of her marriage to Gilberto Moncada Alvarez in 1908 in Jiutepec, and said there was no more, that she and her assistant had gone as far as they could go and done all they could do and she stood back and beamed a smile of self-congratulations.

He was in a daze, the implication of the last discovery washing over him like some revelation suddenly sprung forth from the heavens, a pilgrim's welcome light flung from darkness and as blinding in its brightness as the dark had been in its darkness. He blinked his eyes and pinched their noseward corners with his fingers to stopper the tears forming there before they hit and faded more of the pages that lay before him like gates of a new life thrown open. He said nothing but raised a finger, a gesture for them to allow him a moment, and he reached for his hat and put it on and walked back through the foyer and through the large double doors and into the sunlight and sat on a sidestep to the building's entrance and covered his face with his hands and wept.

When he returned the counter was cleared. The books had been returned to their vaults the señora told him, but presented him with a sheet of paper on which she had written all of the important facts he had requested. He apologized for having to leave but she told him she understood, that in all the years she had worked in the registro, which was longer than he was old, no one had shown greater interest in finding their family. You must be part Mexican, she said and smiled.

Pain radiating along his jaw he returned the smile and thanked her and told her he had just a few more questions. He asked the married name of the last Carlita, for he could not remember all the names, and the señora pointed to the paper she had handed him, to the name Carlita Navarro de Moncada. He asked if she and her husband had had any children and if so their names and she told him she had already thought of that and looked, but that in all probability the children would have been born between the years 1905 and 1915 and those records were either missing or never recorded. Those were years of the revolution, she explained, and there was much movement among the families as well as chaos in the government not to mention the destruction Zapata and Gonzáles brought upon the land and the cities, that she was most fortunate to obtain the records she did because they had been stored in steel vaults. He told her he had done some figuring and that this last Carlita, who would be an aunt or a cousin, he wasn't sure which, on the Mexican side of the family and born the same year as his grandfather on his American side, would be sixty-six years old and probably still alive, given the general longevity of his family, and were there any other records that might identify her whereabouts. She shook her head sadly and said she knew of none, that she had considered checking the records of deeds and land transactions but that it was a hopeless puzzle because of the disarray of such records and the fragmentation of land over the years. He asked if she knew of a small town named Michapa and she put a finger to her cheek and thought then asked him to excuse her a moment. She walked toward the back of the large room and engaged in serious conversation with another lady seated at a desk. They talked a long time, like he had learned Mexicans do even with simple questions, then returned and told him one of her associates had lived at Taxco and said indeed there was a small village nearby named Michapa. He told them about the map he had seen in the library in Mexico City and asked how far Taxco might be from Cuernavaca and she said about seventy kilometers. He thanked her and asked if he owed her anything and she told him he owed her nothing, that she was paid by the government, that he had already made her happy in finding his family. He told her he hadn't found them yet but was closer than he had ever been and might be and that he would remember her kindness as long as he lived and asked her to convey the same to the señorita who helped and she smiled graciously and he touched a finger to his hat brim and left.

The lobby of the Bella Vista was quiet when he entered. The dining room was dark and empty and only a few people sat at tables in the outside patio. The receptionist told him Mrs. King was not in, that she had left for a day trip to Mexico City.

He walked back to his hotel and asked the clerk there if he had any messages and the clerk told him there were none. He walked upstairs to his room and found the writing materials he needed in the top drawer of the nightstand along with a *Biblia Sacra* and a gold inscription on the red front cover that said *Donada por Los Gideons*. He placed the lamp on the floor and moved the small table so it was astraddle his knees and began writing.

Dear Athen,

Please forgive me for not writing sooner, but a lot of things have happened and I just hadn't had the time. I made it to Mexico and right now I'm in a city called Cuernavaca. It is old and very beautiful and not far from Mexico City. You'd love it and I've thought many times how much I wished you were here. Today I learned the name of relatives in Mexico and one who is probably still alive. It is Carlita Navarro de Moncada. Some ladies at the place where they keep records helped me. They were really nice. I also found out about my great-great-aunt and the name of her daughter, my great-aunt, then my aunt. I can't believe it.

I don't know much else except about some property close to a town not far from here. I am very low on money but I got this far low on money and figure I can make it all right. If you have been praying for me I thank you because somebody's been looking after me. I just wanted you to know all of this just in case for some reason or another something happened to me. I've been through a lot but I can't go into all of that now. I will write you again, real soon I hope, when I know more. I miss you very much and hope you are doing all right.

He thought for a while about how to sign the letter and finally wrote Love, Jo Shelby.

He pulled out another sheet and scribbled off a short letter to Carmen, telling her he had found the names of relatives but no more than that and confessed he should have let her pawn the gun for him, that he had maybe two more days of money left. He folded the letters and put them in envelopes and bought stamps from the clerk downstairs and the clerk said he would mail the letters for him. He asked the clerk how long it would be before the letters arrived at their addresses and the clerk said he did not know but that the mail in Mexico was very slow. He told him the one addressed to Mexico City might take a week or less but the one to the United States, a month. Jo Shelby thanked him and returned to his room and laid down and thought and drifted off into a long deep slumber filled with dreams of yesteryears and a land of plantations and mansions and cotton blooming in the fields and families going to church on Sundays.

He awoke to the idle chatter of street cleaners and vendors and the rumbling of their cartwheels along the cobbled street. A soreness ached throughout his body but he pushed himself out of bed and washed his face and dressed and checked himself in the mirror and saw the swelling of his eye had gone down some but it was still like a plum.

The hotel was quiet as sleep and his bootheels clicked loudly down the tile steps and across the stone floor of the lobby. There was no one behind the desk but the cat was asleep in its self-appointed spot and its tail feathered upward when he dropped the key in the return box.

He walked to a bus station on Morelos just north of the Jardín Borda and the lady at the ticket window told him there was no bus to Michapa but that he could purchase a ticket to Taxco and catch a bus there to Michapa. He asked how long it took to get to Taxco and how much the ticket cost and she told him the trip took two hours and the fare was ten pesos. He asked if there was another shorter route. She told him there were other routes but the route through Taxco was the quickest. He turned away from the window and thought a moment then turned back and gave her ten pesos. She took the money and spooled off a ticket from a roll and gave it to him and told him the next bus left in half an hour.

At a small café inside the station he ate some eggs and drank coffee. Through the windows he could see the Jardín Borda not a block away and rising from its thick green foliage the rooftop of the palace that had once been Maximilian's, the emperor who chose to die with his men rather than flee safely to his homeland and his family and he wondered why some men would die for themselves and not live for their wives and children, and which was the most honorable and which created the least pain for all concerned and no answer came to him and his mind would not give the thought rest. He would think of it often in years to come.

The call for the bus came over the speaker and the clock on the terminal wall said seven o'clock. He boarded with only a few people and took a front seat again to better view the countryside. The sky was overcast with curtains of dark gray clouds thinning to lighter gray as the eyes stretched so the cordilleras along the southern horizon were barely visible in the leftover mists that glowed orange and yellow and amber where the dawn-burst shone through and touched them. The road wound through folds of mountains green with pine and laurel and occasional points of color where hibiscus and jacaranda grew wild.

At midmorning the bus arrived at Taxco, a village of clean antiquity laid out on craggy and uneven terrain. The largest and tallest building was a twin-towered cathedralesque church around which little square white red-roofed houses one atop the other climbed the surrounding hills and all of it appeared to him as he first glimpsed it from a distance like something assembled from a catalog model set.

The next bus to Michapa left midafternoon. He looked around. There wasn't much he could do in the meantime. Lounge around the town's colorful plaza from which radiated silver shops and cafés in every direction. Watch the tourists, many of whom were American. Shop. Eat. Drink. He counted his money. Thirty pesos and the twenty dollar bill still in his boot. He asked the ticket attendant the direction to Michapa and the attendant kindly drew him a map on the back of an old route schedule.

By way of his thumb and one type of conveyance after another he arrived at Michapa by noon. The place was a small pueblo set among the hills. There was nothing about it that invited one to remain longer than the time it took to pass through. A rider of old would ride on, he thought. He passed up some vendors selling ears of steamed corn and cacahuates and natillas and bought a Coca-Cola and some cheese and crackers and balogne at an abarrotes and sat on a bench in the small plaza that was ringed with laurel trees and ate the only meal he might have all day. The air was dry and warm and sunlight came and went along the street, the clouds overhead a shutter, opening and closing over it.

He did not know where to begin but saw a small adobe church with a single bell tower and entered it and inquired of an old priest who was cleaning the chancel if he knew of a Hacienda Michopa or Michapa, that it might be spelled either way. The priest said there were a few haciendas not far from the town but none by that name. He told the priest that it was a hacienda of many years ago and might have changed names and the priest said that was very possible but that he had been the priest of the parish for over forty years and had never heard of a hacienda by that name. Jo Shelby said the time of which he spoke was much more than forty years then told the priest of his quest and the history surrounding it and the priest raised his brows and folded his hands prayerfully and invited him to stay and tell him more.

They sat sideways on a front pew. On the walls were faded frescoes and between them hand-carved sconces of unusual design. The sanctuary smelled of the earth and dust and the only light came from a portal window over the doorway and candleflames that burned on the altar. Jo Shelby talked and the old priest listened. In the hollowness of the building he could hear his own words as though they came from far away and when he was finished they seemed to linger in the cloistered air. The priest told him he had long been a student of Mexican history and that much of what he had said was true, that confederados did come to his country and there were several colonies but that none were successful and he had never heard of one near Michapa or Michopa, regardless of how it was spelled. Jo Shelby asked if there were records in the church that might help him in locating his family and the priest told him the church was partially destroyed in 1910 when General González overran the town chasing Zapata and the current records dated back to 1912. Jo Shelby asked if it were really true that he had been the priest of the church for over forty years that he was a Methodist and where he came from preachers stayed no longer than five or six at the most. The priest smiled and said it was indeed true, that he had had opportunities to go to other parishes but had chosen to stay and grow old with the children he had baptized, and their children's children, that leaving them would have been like leaving his own family, of which he had none because he was a priest. Jo Shelby pulled a piece of paper from his shirtpocket and unfolded it and handed it to him.

Qué es eso? the priest said, taking the paper with a trembling hand.

Es un papel del registero civil de Cuernavaca. Información sobre mi familia.

The priest held the paper close to his eyes and it shook in his hands as though buffeted by a steady breeze. He scrolled the fluttering paper slowly upward between his fingers and when he had finished laid it on the pew between them.

Quiénes son sus parientes? he said.

Jo Shelby leaned over and pointed one by one to the names of his relatives. Carolina Ferguson de Cruz. Carlita Cruz Ferguson. And toward the bottom of the page, Carlita Navarro de Moncada.

Son mis tías, he said.

Aja, the priest said and looked at the paper closely again and told him the names were not known to him, but there was one that looked familiar.

Cuál?

Este, the priest said and held the paper up into the refracted light from the portal window and pointed to the name of Fernando Alfonso Cruz Linares.

Cómo lo conoce?

He told him he never really knew the man because he was very old when he became the priest of the parish and died a few years after he arrived but that he was very wealthy and owned many hectares of land and was very well known and respected throughout the area.

Era miembro de su iglesia?

The priest shook his head and said he was not a parish member because he lived too far away and Jo Shelby asked how far and the priest said closer to Cuernavaca, west of Jiutepec, but that sections of the land he owned were near Michapa. He said he actually only saw him once, when he attended a baptism at his church for the child of one of his hacendados.

Entonce, usted ve a mí tia, Jo Shelby said and pointed at the name of Carolina Ferguson Cruz.

The priest said it was possible he saw her but that it was a long time ago and he saw many people at baptisms as well as weddings and funerals.

Cuál es el nombre de la hacienda? Jo Shelby said.

Yo no me acuerdo. Eso fue hace mucho tiempo.

Jo Shelby asked him to try and remember the name and the priest looked upon the cross that hung in the grainy light of the apse and placed his fingers on his forehead as though he were marking the spot for the almighty to send him the name and closed his eyes and began rocking back and forth, whispering to himself in a language that was neither English nor Spanish and there was no other sound except the scattered laughter of children in the distance. Then he stopped rocking and opened his eyes and turned to Jo Shelby.

La Hacienda Tierra del Puente, he said, his old eyes blinking in the dim light, and went on to say he was uncertain but that that was the only name that would come to him, that his memory was like the morning vapors that evaporate in the sun's light, that the mind of one growing old was like that, fading in the radiance of the world to come where no mind was needed and he was smiling when he said it and tilted his head toward the altar and crossed himself with his hand.

Jo Shelby moved to the edge of the pew and leaned into him and asked if the hacienda still existed and the priest said it did not and repeated to him the same history of the country's land and the haciendas that had shepherded it over the centuries and that only few existed from that time but none the names of which he knew. Jo Shelby asked him about the haciendas he had said earlier were nearby, the ones that would be in the vicinity of land once owned by Fernando Alfonso Cruz Linares, and how he might find them and the priest told him to take the road that went northeast from the town and ask others along the way and they would tell him.

He picked up the sheet of paper from where it lay on the wooden pew and refolded it and pushed it back in his shirtpocket. He thanked the priest and told him how helpful he had been.

No se si sea de mucho valor, he said.

Jo Shelby told him to the contrary, that what he had told him was of great value, muy importante, and rose with the priest and shook his feeble hand that was marbled with veins and spotted flesh and told him once more of his gratitude and how merely shaking the hand of one who had seen his great-great-aunt had brought him more happiness than he had known in a long time and the old priest nodded his head and said he hoped that God went with him.

Midway up the aisle he reached into his pocket and pulled out a five peso coin and dropped it in the alms box and turned as he did and waved to the priest and stepped into the afternoon sunlight.

He walked along eroded and potholed streets, passing mud brick houses that were crumbling along the edges. In the doorways sat old men in sockless huaraches and women in homemade cotton dresses and rebozos regarding him with speculative eyes. An occasional cur sallied out and barked and snapped and kept barking until he had passed. The sun bore down with its dry heat and he seemed to see everything through a film of dust and he thought of the movie he'd seen in Mexico City with Carmen and recalled the song and the words and the refrain played over and over in his mind. But his thoughts were of Athen and the last time he saw her, and he asked himself would he forsake someone who had not forsaken him, and the question played on long after the refrain had faded.

The road north out of the town was unpaved and wound its way up through the tanned hills dotted with greenery like the switchbacks of a muddy stream in its infancy and behind it the blue high sierras rose like the mother of all beginnings. He walked several miles, past decomposing adobe chozas and crude jacales made of poles and brush with brush roofs beneath which people with ruined but optimistic faces sold vegetables and fruit and souvenirs of pottery and beads and silver.

Dónde esta la hacienda Tierra del Puente? he would stop and ask and they would arise and come from their doorways or shaded stalls and stand with him in the glare and shrug and say they knew of no hacienda by that name. Then he would ask for the hacienda nearby and with great elaboration and gesticulation of hands they would give him directions and wish that God went with him and in that manner and with rides by locals in vehicles of uncertain age and condition he located three haciendas and made inquiries at each and no one had heard of la hacienda Tierra del Puente.

Except one old administrador at a ranch north of Miacatlán who told him the hacienda which he sought did in fact exist at one time but was now owned by the government and being made into a place of recreation for the people. Jo Shelby showed him the paper from the registro and pointed to the name of his great-great-aunt and those of her progeny and asked if he had ever heard of them and he shook his head that he had not, then his eyes widened, and like the priest, he pointed to the name at the top and said it was the same as that of the man who was once the hacendado of la hacienda Tierra del Puente and spoke on at great lengths and with much reverence of don Fernando, as he addressed him, so that by the time he had completed his monologue the figure of the man loomed legendary and almost mythical, like some Zorroesque chevalier whose spirit still lived on in the chequered memory of the land and its people.

They were standing at the arched gateway of the hacienda where the administrador was supervising some masonry work on the exterior wall and he left to speak to the workers then returned. Jo Shelby asked the aged manager if he knew where the hacendado died and the whereabouts of his family and the administrador told him only that he knew he died in Cuernavaca where he had lived and he knew that because he had read it in the newspaper. Jo Shelby asked if his family still lived in Cuernavaca and he said he had no knowledge of his family but to give him a moment and let him think. He leaned against the whitewashed archway column and stroked his white goatee and looked out over the land as though divining some secret knowledge from it.

Jo Shelby waited.

Several moments passed.

The old man kept rubbing his goatee and looking at the land.

Jo Shelby removed his knapsack from his back and set it on the ground and continued to wait.

Finally the administrador turned to him and said there was some history that might be useful to him and was he interested.

Sí, Jo Shelby said, and leaned in closer to hear.

The administrador asked him if he knew the name Porfirio Díaz and Jo Shelby told him only that he had heard the name, that he was a dictator, but nothing other of significance that he could remember. The administrador confirmed that Díaz was a dictator, but one who loved his country and tried to do all he could to help his country and its people. He went on to tell him that despite Díaz's good intentions he allowed most of the land in Mexico to be purchased by only the rich and that after the turn of the century most of the land was owned by a few thousand large owners and that don Fernando was one of them. When Francisco Madero launched the revolution in 1910 there was much conflict and bloodshed and in the south Zapata called for splitting up the huge estates of the landowners and he and his rebellious peasants with their battle-cry "Tierra y Libertad" destroyed many haciendas in the surrounding area. He told him that those haciendas not destroyed by Zapata and his rebels were affected in other ways, that the year after the revolution began, Díaz was forced to retire and many hacendados who had been allied with him either lost their land or were forced to sell it to the government at a loss. It was during this time that don Fernando died, the administrador said, but what happened to his land or his family he was uncertain. Of one thing, however he was certain, and this was the information that might be helpful. Don Fernando was very wise and an astute businessman and he divided the Tierra del Puente into several haciendas just before the revolution broke. He said he knew of this because his father who was the administrador before him worked at one time at one of the other haciendas.

Dónde está la hacienda? Jo Shelby said.

No sé exactamente, he said, but went on to say he thought it was near Cuernavaca, to the southeast of Jiutepec, but that that was all he knew.

By that time the day was well along, the sierras beginning their claim once more on the sun. He thanked the administrador and walked back to the main road and continued on. The dying light slatted through the louvered clouds coloring sky and land alike the blood of the ancients and the burn behind the dark and dimensionless mountains reddened so it appeared the great ball would rise again instead of set and he saw it like that as the road curved back toward the darkening east.

He had no map but knew he could not be far from Cuernavaca. In the small village of El Rodeo he stopped at a café and drank a beer and ate several tacos. He asked the waitress if there was a hotel in town and she said there was none that the pueblo was very small but that there was one at Alpuyeca about ten kilometers away. He asked her how far he was from Cuernavaca and she told him about thirty kilometers. He paid his bill of five pesos and left.

The road climbed the hills and followed the valleys. It had been paved since Miacatlán but it bore little traffic. One man in a pickup stopped but he was turning off a shortways to go to Cuentepec. Jo Shelby touched the brim of his hat and thanked him anyway but waved him on. Dusk had come and gone and the night accomplished. The dark canopy overhead glittered with stars and a bowl of quarter-moon tipped slightly over the sierras banked against the sky and down their soundless purple escarpment scattered lights of homes and campfires flickering in the night haze and the mountain breezes blew around him and he stopped and pulled his coat from the knapsack and put it on. He counted his money in his head and figured he had more than enough for bus fare should one come by but none did. His feet were sore and his legs ached and blisters were forming along his shoulders from the jostling movement of the knapsack across them but he walked on without complaint or any seepage of self-pity because the wires he'd been tripping over in his head suddenly came together and he knew where he needed to go next and with that discovery his heart floated and he wished it could sail for he could not get there fast enough.

He did not know the time when he entered Apuyeca but he knew he'd been walking several hours, taking rests from time to time. There were a few bars and cantinas open and two gas stations on either side of the main highway, a number of tractor-trailer trucks parked around them. He stopped at one of the bars, a rectilinear concrete-block building with neon runners across the front eaves and a Tecate neon

logo blinking feebly in one of the windows. He entered a single room
blue with smoke and loud with blaring music from a radio that sat on
one end of the bar. There were only a few people inside, mostly men
still in their work clothes. A couple of señoritas in their late teens,
overdressed for the place. They seemed to belong to no one.

He stepped up to the bar and placed his knapsack at his feet, for
he'd been carrying it in his hands, and ordered a beer. The camarero
pulled one from an icebox and opened it and handed it to him drip-
ping wet and told him the cost was four pesos. He gave him a five peso
coin and the camarero flipped a peso coin back onto the counter where
it spun and swiveled flat. Jo Shelby placed a finger on it and pushed it
back and the camarero thanked him. He took a few swallows of the
beer and looked around. He counted seven men in two groups, four in
one and three in the other, and the two girls at a table by themselves
between them and whatever entertainment of talk or flirtation had
been going on seemed to have ceased. They were all turned sideways
in their slatback chairs eyeing him and whispering among themselves.
He turned back to the bar and studied them through the long warped
mirror on the barwall around which were tiered bottles of liquor on
wood shelving and the wavy distortions of their images made even
more ominous the feelings he'd had than when he was looking at them
straight on.

A dónde va? the camarero said.

A Cuernavaca, Jo Shelby said, loud enough over the radio for the
others to hear, to let them know he was just passing through and not
there to cause trouble.

Y de dónde viene?

Taxco, he said, as loudly.

En este día?

Sí.

En coche?

No.

Autobús?

No.

Entonces, cómo?

He drank from his beer and checked the group behind him in the mirror and they were silent and listening, watching, their heads half-turned and lowered like a pack of wild animals bonded to the same feral notions, their eyes set in that attitude.

He finally answered the camarero and told him he had hitchhiked. The camerero raised a brow. The clotted group behind him turned their heads slowly and looked at one another and mumbled among themselves, satisfied he was one more crazed lost gringo trying to find himself a little silver in the hills, he thought as he lit a cigarette and tried nonchalantly to blend in.

He asked the camerero where the bus terminal was and the camerero told him next door at the gas station but that the next bus would not be until in the morning. He asked if there was a hotel and the answer he got was the same. The gas station. There were beds for rent on the second floor but most were usually taken by the truckers who stopped to rest on their north and south routes.

He was down to his last swallows and noticed three of the men rise and push back their chairs and amble slowly across the room and exit the door. The others talked quietly on but kept throwing glances at him. He asked the camerero what kind of town he was in and the camerero said it was a quiet place of mostly peons like himself and farmers and pregnant women and a few whores and nodded in the direction of the two girls. He asked if the gas station stayed open all night and the barman said it did but so did the bars if there were still people who wanted to drink. The thought occurred to him then that he might have stumbled into a casa de las putas and the bartender was the pimp and the girls might even be his daughters.

He thought again about the three men who left and their looks back at him as they crossed the threshold on their way out. He didn't want any trouble but trouble was what he saw. Through the open doorway he could see the graveled apron to the road and it received some surplus light from the gas station next door, enough to stop a deed of darkness he hoped because as soon as he finished his last swallow he was making for the door and taking a sharp left and hauling hinie. He had about a swallow left in the bottle. He slipped his boot toe through one of the shoulderstraps of the knapsack and raised the pack up to where he could grip it with his hand then drank the last of the beer and headed for the door, stopping at the threshold to look both ways. There was no one on either side. He didn't know what he would have done if there had been. He turned left and fast-walked next door to the gas station where there were lights and an attendant and presumed safety.

The attendant was a boy about the age of the girls next door. Jo Shelby asked him if he had any beds and he said he did not that they were all taken by the drivers of the trucks and he pointed at a row of rigs parked along a side lot. He asked when the next bus left for Cuernavaca and the young mozo told him it left Taxco at six and arrived at seven o'clock, más o menos. A cheap plastic bubble-covered Coca-Cola clock on the wall said twelve thirty. Beneath it there was a space on the floor between a counter and a neatly stacked pyramid of Bardahl oil cans, enough for a person to stretch out and sleep. He pointed to it and asked the mozo if he could sleep there and the mozo told him he could but that it would cost fifteen pesos. He asked what the price was for a bed upstairs and the mozo said twenty-five pesos.

Sólo tengo trece, Jo Shelby said, and dug in his pockets and pulled out two five and three single peso coins for proof.

The mozo wiped his hands on a rag looped through his belt and looked closely at the coins he held outstretched in the palm of his hand.

Eso es todo? he said.

Sí. Todo. De veras.

Entonces cómo vas a comprar tu boleto por el autobus?

Jo Shelby just stood and looked at him and thought. Not about the money but that the mozo was smarter than he looked and that maybe he should just turn this whole venture over to him and stay and run the station. He told him that was all the Mexican money he had, that he had some American money but was saving it to buy his ticket and didn't think the mozo could change American currency. The mozo asked how much American money and he told him twenty dollars then the mozo said he didn't believe him so Jo Shelby pulled off his boot and reached in and tweezered out the twenty dollar bill with his fingers and held it up for him to see. The mozo went to his cash register and pulled a key from his pocket that was tied to his belt loop and opened the register drawer. He counted some money, running his fingers from one tiny bin to the next, then closed the drawer and locked it and put the key back in his pocket. Through all of this Jo Shelby was watching through the front plateglass window and saw the hulks of the three hombres leaning against a truck cab in the shadows off to the left of the building.

No tengo cambio, the boy said.

They stood looking at one another. A car pulled in and the boy left to go attend it.

Jo Shelby stood in the station house and waited. The three men sat outside and waited. If he had to, he'd give the mozo the twenty dollars and that would still leave him enough to buy his ticket.

The boy returned and shook his head and said he couldn't sleep on the floor unless he had fifteen pesos. Jo Shelby pulled out his pack of Camels which had about five or six left in it and laid it on the counter beside the register then told him of his journey from Taxco and that he had walked the distance from El Rodeo and just arrived and was very tired and would throw in the American cigarettes with the thirteen pesos.

Ay, Dios mío! the mozo said and threw up his oil-grimed hands and told him he could sleep inside for the thirteen pesos and could keep the cigarettes but he must leave when the bus came and Jo Shelby told him he'd be out so fast he'd think his ass was on fire.

Cómo? the mozo said.

No es nada. Americana expresión, and grinned when he said it and the mozo grinned back as though they had shared some private joke.

He put his knapsack against the counter and turned it so the hardness of the gun was on the bottom next to the floor and laid his hat on the floor in front of him and stretched out, curling his legs slightly so as not to kick a bottom can of the Bardahl display and send oil cans rolling helter-skelter in every direction and get him turned out into the hostile night where certain trouble awaited.

The single bulb in the ceiling of the small station house flickered as though it might blow any second. The mozo sat outside in a chair, waiting for God only knew what. Another sucker to pay him five times the worth of a concrete floor for a bed, he thought. An occasional truck or car droned by. He could hear music from the radio next door. He thought about the two girls, how pretty and innocent they looked, how tempting. His lids grew heavy under the monotonous blinking of the light, fluttered with the last of his energy running across them and closed then bolted wide open when the thought somehow slipped between the closing gates of sleep and pinged his brain. Would the bus driver be able to change his twenty? The question, and probable answer, haunted him into the sleep which eventually claimed him. Not because of the physical exertion which should have knocked him out when his head hit the knapsack but because of the thinking he got tired of fighting.

He felt a foot kicking his boot bottoms. It was the mozo telling him the bus had arrived. He arose and gathered his knapsack and hat and thanked the mozo and walked to the bus. He told the driver he was going to Cuernavaca and the driver told him the fare was six pesos. He handed the driver the twenty dollar bill and the driver eyed it with a grimace and said he had no change for that amount. Jo Shelby told him that was all he had and the driver took it and told him he would get change for him when they arrived in Cuernavaca.

The trip took about an hour, the bus traveling back over the same road he'd taken coming down the day before and arriving at the same station in Cuernavaca he'd left. The driver told him to wait at the parking slot and he would return with his change. He sat on one of the benches aligned in front of the slots where other buses were parked, some idling about to leave, people scrambling on. He waited five minutes, then ten and the driver did not return. Instead a new freshly uniformed driver stepped up to the bus and asked him if he were a passenger for the trip to Mexico City and Jo Shelby told him he was waiting for his change from the last driver and asked if he had given it to him. The new driver shrugged and said he knew nothing about any change. Jo Shelby ran quickly into the station and scanned the small waiting area. The ticket windows. The small cambio office which was dark and appeared closed. The driver was no where to be seen. He went to one of the ticket booths and explained the situation to the clerk behind the window and the man told him there was little he could do, that the drivers were responsible for their fares and he may have gone into the café or down the street to one of the shops to get change because the cambio booth was closed and did not open until nine o'clock. Jo Shelby asked why there was a new driver and the clerk told him they exchanged drivers in Cuernavaca that the driver had come all the way from Puerto Escondido and regulations would permit him to drive only so many hours without relief and the bus he was driving would continue on to Monterrey. He thanked the clerk and hurried to the café but saw no one resembling the driver then he ran into the street and saw no one there as well. He went back into the terminal and sat on a bench where he had a good view of the entrance and the sallygate to the buses and he waited, and watched. After thirty minutes the reality of what had happened sank in and he left the terminal and entered the Avenida Morelos and began walking.

The desk clerk told him Mrs. King was having breakfast but he would notify her that she had a guest. He sat in one of the cushioned wicker lobby chairs and waited. He conjured ways of making money, if only a few pesos to cover food, for he'd learned that a person could sleep anywhere if they'd just let their body take over. He could mop and sweep and wash dishes. He could pump gas and change oil and wipe windshields and recalled the young street boys in Matamoros and others like them he'd seen all along the way. Anybody could make a peso in Mexico if they wanted to bad enough. He even thought of cooking. He'd watched the cocineros at the prison enough to know how to make tortillas and fry diced meat and vegetables and put them together in the various assortments. They all seemed roughly the same to him, just different shapes and names.

A quarter of an hour passed and his mind was still moving through the checklist of jobs when Mrs. King emerged at the bottom of the stairs. She was wearing a light robe, cloth bedslippers and still had on her pants pajamas. She greeted him warmly in a low early morning voice and told him not to mind her dress that after all this hotel was her home and she owned it and everyone else was a guest, however be it a paying one she said and rolled an ironic eye, as if the statement had been meant to evoke humor which in his mind she'd already accomplished by where she was and the way she was dressed but he smiled at what she said. They went through the dining room which was crowded with people eating breakfast, people who cast strange glances at them as they paraded through. She waving her cigarette ceremoniously in the air, her robe billowing around tables and her slippers slapping the stone flooring, and he following along behind her, as though he might be a wayward grandson about to get a dog cussing for being out all night honky-tonking. He looked that bad. She pulled back a louvered screen that partitioned the open terrace from the dining area and motioned him through.

We have to shut this in the morning to keep everybody corralled in one place, she said. Helps the waiters serve breakfast faster rather than having to trot all over the place.

He shook his head that he understood.

He followed her to a table at the edge of the terrace, along an untrimmed hedge of hibiscus over which they could see the city and beyond it the saddle ridges of the eastern sierras scalloping the horizon and the peaks of Popocatépetl and the Sleeping Lady. She asked if he wanted some coffee and he said he did and she walked back to the partition and called out to a waiter and returned, the slippers smacking the brick tiling.

He told her he had some good news and some bad and she said she wanted to hear the good first. He handed her the piece of paper the señora at the registro had given to him and she leaned over and tilted her half-smoked cigarette into an ashtray and received the paper with her free hand. She put on her glasses and looked at it and immediately recognized the name and said of course she knew don Fernando, that he and his wife came frequently to the Bella Vista, his wife more than he because it was a popular gathering place for Americans.

That she you're talkin bout is my great-great-aunt, he said.

The woman's mouth fell open. Why didn't you tell me this before?

I didn't know it before. When I learned it I came back to tell you and you were gone to Mexico City. He went on to tell of his trip to Taxco and the encounters along the way and the additional knowledge he'd gained about la hacienda Tierra del Puente and that he was told don Fernando had divided it before the revolution and she was nodding her head up and down and confirmed she knew of these things but only secondhand, that her customers never discussed their personal and private dealings and she never asked. She was about to rise and point to the flagpole again and tell what she'd done to the Zapatistas and he politely reminded her she'd already told him.

A waiter came and set a white porcelain pot of coffee on the table and matching cups and saucers and left. She poured a cup for each of them and asked if he'd had breakfast and he told her he had not but that he wasn't hungry that the coffee would do just fine. He was more interested in talking and asked her if she knew where in Cuernavaca don Fernando and his great-great-aunt had lived.

I cannot tell you where they lived exactly, she said, drawing on her cigarette, except that it was in a very fashionable part of town along the barranca where a number of former generals lived. Cuernavaca was a very popular retirement area, still is. Don Fernando was quite wealthy and like most of the hacendados at that time did not live on his hacienda but hired others to run it for him. The city has changed much since then and some of the larger villas that were there along the barranca, and in other parts of the city as well, are now hotels, like the Bella Vista, or private clubs. I was much younger then but it all comes back to me now as we talk about it. Your great aunt . . . didn't you say great aunt?

Great-great-aunt.

That's right. Well, your great-great-aunt was a most lovely and gracious lady, quite beautiful. She and don Fernando would come here for dinner, sit right here on this very patio. They'd have a drink or two, sometimes eat out here. I remember because I was often the maitre d'and seated them. I saw her more times than I saw him because, as I told you, many Americans came here and she longed to see them and talk to them and learn about what was happening back home in the States.

She was talking uninterruptedly and noticed his vision was off-center and looking past her, his eyes tearing in the corners.

Did I say something wrong?

Nome. He cleared his throat. You're sayin everthing right. Keep goin.

She went on to tell him that Carolina preceded don Fernando several years in death and that she only saw him a few times afterward, always on the patio, by himself, as though he came there to commune with her spirit, that he would order two glasses of wine and regardless of how many he drank afterward one of the first two he never touched. She told him she knew very little of the family but thought they had three sons, maybe two, besides the daughter Carlita whom she only saw once and of the dispersion of family she knew nothing except what she had already told him, that she, too, had heard don Fernando had divided the hacienda and left the largest tract to the eldest and parceled out the rest to the other children. He asked if she knew where they were buried and she said she did not but probably in the family cemetery on one of the haciendas.

You know anything about these haciendas, where they're at? he said, interrupting her.

No. Nothing at all.

He told her what the administrador had told him about the haciendas southwest of Jiutepec.

All of that is quite possible, she said. There are haciendas south of Jiutepec. Those were turbulent times and much was going on. When don Fernando died I lost all contact with his family. I am sorry, but there is very little more I can tell you. You said you had some bad news.

He told her about his trip to Taxco and the return leg to Alpuyeca and the ordeal at the gas station and of the three hombres and the bus driver taking the last of his money.

You poor dear. Her brows furrowed and she leaned toward him, her elbows on the table, her face drawn with concern. So, you're broke.

Yessum. I need a job. I've worked on a farm and done some gardening. I've been a deckhand on a river barge and on a tanker. There's lots of things I can do.

She leaned back and sipped on her coffee, looked contemplatively into it before she spoke. Unfortunately, I cannot give you a job. I gave an American a job once and the government almost shut me down. You see, it is the law. I can hire only Mexicans. Their unemployment rate here is so high it almost has to be that way. There are a few Americans in Cuernavaca with jobs but they are with large companies or with the universities and schools and through agreements worked out with the Mexican government they are allowed to work in the country. However, she lifted a finger in the air, even though I cannot give you a job, I can certainly give you a place to stay, at least for a few days. She was looking at him sympathetically.

Nome. Much obliged. But I cain't take no handout.

She frowned and regarded him sternly. Mr. Ferguson!

Jo Shelby kindly ma'am.

Mr. Jo Shelby, I'll have you know that I do not give handouts, but I am gracious and I do offer gifts from time to time to people whom I like and respect and if you cannot accept a gift from someone then how in God's good name do you expect to get to heaven? What're you going to do, stand there at the pearly gates and tell Saint Peter what you just told me, that you can't accept a handout?

He looked down and rubbed his chin then raised his eyes timidly. She was leaning back even further, her arms crossed, her eyes dark, hard looking.

Guess I never thought about it like that.

Well, think about it, she said crisply, talking to him like his mother would. Also think about what you have that might be of some worth. Are you carrying anything of value that you could pawn? Mexican pawnshops will take just about anything. Watches. Rings. Anything of leather. Pocketknives.

He rolled his thumbs and looked out over the city. He thought about Carmen and wondered why he hadn't given her the gun, then again why he'd kept it. He looked down at the knapsack on the brick tiling beside his chair then back at the her.

Yessum.

What you got?

I got a gun.

Well, what kind of gun is it?

He told her about the gun and how he came by it and some of what he thought was its history, then the more recent history of Matamoros and how it landed him in prison. She listened and when he was through she leaned forward again, hunching her broad shoulders around her neck so he could see the wrinkled cleavage and sagging white mounds of breasts that in their day must have been something to behold.

It sounds to me like you've been bit by it about like the Philistines were by the ark of the covenant. Might be time to find a new home for that firearm.

He told her it was more than a firearm, that besides the letters and some pictures he had with him and a few other items he left back in Mississippi it was all he had that belonged to his great-great grand-father and that parting with it would be like breaking a commandment of the Bible.

She asked if he had the gun with him and he didn't remind her he'd just told her but nodded he did and she asked to see it. He pulled his knapsack up onto the table and opened the flaps and reached in and brought out the holstered pistol and she took it in her hands and un-snapped the holder strap and removed the gun as though she had done it a thousand times and turned it over in her hands, studying its design and craftsmanship.

It's a Navy Colt, he said. Made sometime around eighteen hunderd and fifty.

I'll say. It's in good shape.

Yessum.

Somebody took care of it.

Yessum.

Well if it's that old its valuable and you could get a good price for it in one of the antique shops here, enough money to carry you through. As you've probably found out, American money goes a long way in Mexico. Why do you think my father came here and why do you think I stayed? There's no way I could live like this back in the States.

Maybe somebody else could give me a job, at a café or bar or something, washing dishes maybe.

Perhaps, but it is not likely. The penalties are high. Do you have a visa, a tourist visa?

Yessum.

Let me see it.

He pulled out his billfold and took out the contents and shuffled through them and handed her the pink slip. She took it and looked it over closely then handed it back to him.

It's outdated. Did you know that?

No ma'am. I didn't know it had a date on it. Never looked to see.

It's dated September fourteenth. They're only good for sixty days. Today's November fifteenth. Based on my calculations, you're one day over. Anyone considering you for a job, regardless of how menial, would ask to look at your visa. In fact, if the police checked you they could put you back in jail unless you paid the—

Mordida.

Yes. You know about the mordida, the bite, as they call it.

That's how I got out of the jail in Matamoros.

The Mexican police, mordilones as the people call them, thrive on it. And with no money you could stay in jail here a long time, or a short time depending how long you could survive.

I know. I been told it. And I've lived it.

Your best bet is to hock the gun or sell it, as much as it means to you. Maybe you could buy it back later. There is a reason for everything and your grandfather or any of his fathers would be proud of you and would want you to use it if it meant finding your family.

Yessum, I done heard that before, he said and reached for the pot and poured himself another cup. He blew across the top and took a sip and thought. He was going to say something but she spoke first.

Tell you what, young man. You take the rest of the day and get the best deal you can for the gun then come back here. I've got some hedges that need trimming, as you can well see, and some plants that need to be repotted and you can do that for me and spend the night in a small room we seldom use because it doesn't have a private bath and I'll consider us even and you can be on your way in the morning.

He drank his coffee and thought a long time then told her he'd accept her offer, but that he was going to think about hocking or selling the gun a while longer, which he did after she left him, sat on the terrace a long time thinking about it, watched the sun till it was well over the Sleeping Lady thinking about it.

The pawnshops were sleazy looking and would offer him almost nothing for the gun, because it would no longer fire, they said. He found a couple of antique shops along Hidalgo between the Jardín Borda and the Plaza de Armas and the clerks there were more interested because of its age but seemed to know little of its mechanics and place in history. Six hundred pesos was the most they would offer and he had to bargain them up from five hundred fifty to get there and he wasn't selling the gun for fifty dollars. A dealer off the Plaza offered him six hundred and fifty pesos, but he kept looking. By noon he'd found no offer worthy of the value of the gun. He was tired and hungry and out of cigarettes and the thought of prisons and how they came to be crossed his mind, that some people got so down and out they couldn't lose. Steal and be fed by what they stole or steal and get caught and be fed in prison. Either way they survived.

He worked his way from the centro out, trodding the narrow tilting streets, inquiring in shops of every trade, whether they collected and sold antiques or not, for often they could tell him of those in the city who did. A block from the registro on Guttenberg he came across an old gunsmith who took great interest in the revolver and spoke with knowledge and in some detail of its history but offered him only seven hundred pesos. Jo Shelby bartered with him and finally the man said seven hundred fifty pesos and Jo Shelby said he'd take it but asked first a favor and the man was receptive and asked what the favor might be. Would the man hold the gun for a month for him to return and buy it back for eight hundred pesos and if he wasn't back within a month then the man could do whatever he chose with it?

The man scratched his head and thought a moment. Another customer walked into the store cradling a rifle in his arms, like a person might take a sick child into a clinic.

Un momento, the man said to the customer then turned to Jo Shelby.

Pero, por qué?

Jo Shelby explained it was a long story but that the revolver had been in his family for many, many years and had a lot of sentimental value for him and asked if the man had understood his Spanish.

Sí. Yo lo entiende.

Jo Shelby could see the man's muscles ripple along his temples as if that was where the tempest of thought was brewing. They both stood, their eyes shifting from the revolver to each other. The other customer was waiting, still clutching his gun as if it might cry if not given attention soon and the gunsmith held up a hand and told him just a moment more.

He looked back at Jo Shelby and said he agreed and counted out seven hundred fifty pesos and laid the sheaves of currency on the counter then took the pencil from behind his ear and scribbled something on a yellow sheet of paper and gave it to Jo Shelby and told him he might need it for customs. Jo Shelby took the paper and said nothing to the man about his entry into the country, that he had never declared the gun. He asked one final favor of the man, that he might just hold the gun a moment longer and the man assented and went to help the other customer.

Jo Shelby took the pistol and turned it over in his hands then ran his fingers over the brass encased handle and down the shiny black barrel and spun the cylinder one time, as a gesture of good luck, then called to the gunsmith and told him he was sorry but that he could not part with the gun and put it back into the holster and into the knapsack and laid the money back onto the counter along with the piece of paper and turned and left without looking back.

There were still several hours left in the afternoon. He walked around the city, looking for opportunities to make a few pesos. A café owner listened to his story and felt sorry for him and let him wash some dishes and sweep out his back and empty garbage and gave him seven pesos. He bought a burrito and a Coke from a vendor and ate them as he walked and he stopped and with the last of his money bought a cheap cigar and a pack of Lucky Strikes.

Mrs. King had her plants all lined out on the patio for him to repot along with a bucket of soil and a gardening trowel and some hedge-clippers. He didn't tell her he hadn't sold the gun and went to work immediately and accomplished the job before sundown and she remarked how well he had done and led him to a small room at the end of the second floor, down the hall from her suite. There was a single bed and a dresser and small closet. The only light was an overhead bare bulb. A curtainless window afforded him the same view she had from her terrace, only smaller. She showed him the toilet and bath adjacent to it which she said might need cleaning because it had not been used in some time. He took a bath and shaved and brushed his teeth and changed clothes. He lay down on the bed to take a short nap and contemplate the morrow and where it would take him and there was a knock on the door. He got up and opened it and the desk clerk told him he was invited to dine with Mrs. King on the patio terrace, that she would meet him there in half an hour. Afraid he might fall asleep and not awaken he stood at the window and smoked a cigarette.

He had no idea of the time but the snowcapped peaks in the east glowed pink in the tentative dusk and across the city and barranca and the volcanic plain beyond a tide of mountain shadow swept slowly over the land until that was all there was, the shadowed darkness of the quiet land, and he turned and left.

She wore a blue dress with a white rebozo draped around her shoulders and the blend of her face with the colors in the half-circle of lamplight lifted the youth that still remained within her to the surface of her features and her voice was almost that of a young girl's with most of her life ahead of her. They sat at a table pushed away from the others, for privacy from "the Friday night crowd" as she described the lively bunch gathering. From a ceramic carafe with floral designs they drank red wine she said came from vineyards not far away and smoked their cigarettes and ate steak and baked potatoes and English peas and sliced homegrown tomatoes. He told her it was the first such food he'd had in over six years. She inquired of that past and he told her, related the history of his incarceration and why he thought he might have been framed, or was at least so quickly handed over by the owner of the plantation that had once been his family's, and how for six years he toiled in the fields under the hot Delta sun and was not even allowed to attend the burial of his parents and grandfather not ten miles away because he'd disagreed with a guard about the weather. She listened passively and without interrupting and, when he had finished, dabbed at her eyes with the corner of her napkin.

They finished eating and she asked if he'd ever had brandy and he told her about the evening with señora García and how it was very much like the one with her. She called the waiter over and ordered two brandies and he asked if she minded if he smoked a cigar he'd bought that afternoon and she said not unless she could smoke one, too, and smiled and waved a hand to the waiter, pointing to his cigar as she did, and the waiter brought her a long cigarrillo. Between the smoking and sips from the brandy snifters there were intervals of silence he filled with images of his Aunt Carolina and don Fernando, sitting perhaps where they sat, next to hibiscus vines perhaps as old, talking about kids and grandkids and work on the haciendas and the next family vacation and occasionally soft words of love and romance in a land the likes of which such passions never burned out. Perhaps they did that, he said to himself.

The waiter brought no bill and he said he'd need to work a little extra in the morning for the meal and she told him it would be taken care of when he cleaned the bathroom which she knew he would before he left in the morning and she winked and smiled and raised her glass in a final salud then asked him how much he got for the gun.

HE ROSE WITH the first chorus of roosters and while the sky was still dark. He cleaned the bath with cleaning rags and disinfectant he'd found in a hallway closet. The desk clerk had just assumed his position when he walked down the stairs and he asked him for a piece of paper and pencil and the clerk provided them. He sat on a chair in the lobby and using a dog-eared Time magazine for support scrawled out a note of thanks and handed it to the clerk along with the pencil and asked him to see that the lady of the house received it and the clerk nodded he would and slipped it in a pigeonhole behind him.

Sabado the day of market and the streets were already abuzz. Pickups loaded with produce. Women carrying bundles balanced on their heads and rebozos tied around their necks and hanging full down their backs with serapes and camisas and T-shirts, pottery and brass cookery. A small boy with colorful parrots, ribbed cages swinging in each hand, the cages bumping the uneven cobbles occasionally. Jo Shelby watched him. He was without any adult escort. He stumbled once and the swinging cages seemed to steady him and propel him forward and he kept on walking with his little adult strides and little adult vision of where he was going.

He walked to the Plaza de Armas and asked an old man carrying a basket of bamboo whistles the way to Jiutepec and the man told him to go to the Avenida Emiliano Zapata and stay on it and it would take him to the town.

The eastern sky was a blush of orange and Popocatépetl black against it, a cloud of smoke rising from its peak and streaming north-ward over the Sleeping Lady, as though a silent message were being sent to awaken her. Traffic was light on the street and he walked a long way before it became a road and a lone driver picked him up and car-ried him into Jiutepec.

The town lay in a valley between the foothills of higher mountains and what he first saw of it amounted to a string of low-roofed tiendas and cafés and storefronts along both sides of the main thoroughfare, many of them still unopen, their corrugated cortinas pulled down and bolted. Between them and the road's edge there were no sidewalks or driveways, only potholes of collected rainwater turned muddy and rut-ted rails of dirt and gravel where vehicles had circled in and out. He saw no plaza or cathedral. No alamedas with trees of whitewashed trunks or pathways with benches on which people could sit and sip cups of coffee and browse the morning paper and watch the early movement of pedestrians and traffic. He recalled Westerns he'd seen at the picture show and decided all the place needed were a few false storefronts and a saloon or two and hitching rails in front and horses and buggies tied to them and he'd be fifty more years back in time from the fifty he'd already subtracted.

He was let out at a government-owned Pemex gas station. On one side of it was a tire store and on the other a Cocina Economica where a few men sat around tables drinking coffee. Several doors down from it was a nightclub, its neon light still flickering, the last letter com-pletely gone so it said El Habit.

He walked over to the café where the men were sitting drinking coffee and stopped and asked a group at one table the location of the centro. They looked at one another and laughed and told him he was standing on it. He asked if they knew of a Hacienda Tierra del Punta and this time they did not laugh but rolled sudden quizzical looks over their steaming cups. He told them he had come many miles and was trying to find an aunt whom he had never seen and that her name was Carlita Navarro de Moncada and she was believed to be living on the hacienda.

De dónde viene? one said.

De Mississippi.

De Mississippi? De Estados Unidos?

Sí.

Ahí, exclaimed a couple and they looked at him with earnest and turned to one another and began mumbling loudly among themselves, pointing in different directions. This went on for some while as he expected it would and finally the one who had spoken first told him there was a hacienda by that name, or used to be, that he was unsure if it still existed but that if it did it was through the valley beyond La Joya.

He asked the location of this La Joya and the man told him not far, two, three kilometers at the most, that it was a very small pueblo, much smaller than Jiutepec. He thanked them and went inside and asked for a cup of water. The man behind the counter asked if he did not want a cup of coffee, that he had some of the best coffee in all of Jiutepec and Jo Shelby told him he had no money. The man shrugged and gave him a cup anyway and waved him on. He came back out and sat at an empty table several removed from everyone else and sipped on the coffee and smoked a cigarette. The men turned and looked at him from time to time, glances of disbelief, wonderment. The air was cool and moist and the village lay still in the gray early morning shadows of the mountains, the small valley echoing with the crowing of roosters and dogs barking, the two seeming to vie for control of the new day not yet fully dawned. On the hillside across from him streetlights still shone and one by one yellow squares of light began blinking on in houses that seemed stacked one on top of the other all the way to the top of the ridge.

He finished his cigarette and coffee and began walking along the street south. He walked a mile or so, the scenery unvarying. Tiendas and gasolineras. Nightclubs and bars. Occasionally houses with porches and verandas around which grew hibiscus and amarilla and fig-cactus. A dentista and farmacia. A florista. No city limits sign. No demarcation indicating he was leaving one town and entering another.

He stopped at a cocina overlaid with gas pumps and Coca-Cola signs and smells of cooked food and asked how much further to La Joya.

The man behind the counter told him he was in La Joya and made a wide sweep of his hand that all about him was La Joya. He asked the man if he knew of a Hacienda Tierra del Puente and the man said he did not, that he had not lived long in the village but that there were some haciendas, or what was left of them, further down the road.

The day was still in the forenoon and the traffic heavy on the road. He had walked about a mile and passed the last remnants of town and commerce and the road snaked through low hills devoid of any habitation and he felt a cool wind channeling the grassy slopes. He continued walking, for several miles it seemed, when he made a final turn in the wandering canyon and before him opened up a broad green volcanic plain bordered by folds of hills where mists still gathered in the hollows untouched by the sun. There were small farms of terraced land, some climbing the slopes and in places cattle grazed within fenced pastures. He saw men plowing with oxen and a man on a tractor.

There were several junctures where single lane roads veered left and right, but no sign of any haciendas. A small boy on a bicycle came by and he stopped him and asked. The boy twisted around on the seat of the bike and pointed down the road and said the entrance to the hacienda was about two kilometers back. He asked the boy if there was a sign and the boy said he'd never seen a sign but that there were two rock piles on either side of the road that led to the hacienda. He asked how far the hacienda was from the highway and the boy said he did not know, that he had never been, but that it was a long way, maybe three, five kilometers. He thanked the boy and the boy wished him good luck and pedaled off.

Another half hour and he came to the two rock piles as the boy had said he would. Between them lay a rough stone-paved road overgrown with weeds and from either side extended the remains of what had once been a fence. Blackened posts irregularly spaced, the remainder of the file fallen or leaning with the groundrot that would soon claim them, most still raveled with the barbed wire that had once connected them. And from there to the valley wall of foothills he saw nothing growing but briar and bramble brush and cactus and wildflowers and only the faint tracks of tires and slightly flattened grass in the road bed to suggest it had been traveled at all.

He walked along the shoulder of the single-lane road to avoid the ankle-twisting stones on it, rearranged from earlier years of smoothness by rain and washout and groundshift. Small birds flitted back and forth in the sidebrush ahead of him and an occasional lizard whispered away into the dry grass. His legs brushed against wild lantana and buttercups and sunflowers and beneath their foliage and as far as his eyes could track in the undergrowth, traces of furrows where the land had once been plowed, had once been planted. He passed jacales of mud and sticks around which naked children played and grownups sat on crates and watched with vacant stares. He wondered why they were there and how they lived at all. Further down the rocky road he passed two small children no older than five or six with bundles of sticks strapped to their backs and he spoke to them but they could barely turn and speak, their heads bowed down by the burden they carried.

There were mountains in front of him and mountains behind him, rising up out of the north and trailing off to the south beneath thin layers of clouds, two ragged shorelines upon which foamed a common sea. He thought of what he would say and how he would say it, rehearsed the lines in his mind and the more he did the more nothing seemed to fit so he took to whistling instead and when he grew tired of whistling he sang songs his parents and grandparents had taught him, some his grandparents had said their parents taught them, they were that old in music time.

> *An old cowhand went ridin out one dark and dreary day*
> *Upon a ridge he rested as he went along his way.*
> *When all at once a mighty herd of red-eyed cows he saw,*
> *A ridin through a ragged sky, and up a cloudy draw.*
> *Yeepee ai ayyy. Yeepee ai oh–ooo.*
> *The ghost riders in the sky.*

He sang others. Oh my darlin Clementine and She'll be comin' 'round the mountain and Oh Suzanna and Jimmy Crack corn and I don't care. And when those ran out he turned to hymns. Come to the church in the wildwood and down by the riverside and swing low sweet chariot. Rock of ages and I am pressing on the upward way and Let the lower lights keep burning and I am coming home. And remembering no more of those he broke out with Dixie and was into the second refrain when the road came to the rim of a rise and the land swept outward from it and he saw the heavy stone walls cornered by watchtowers and the arched entranceway and the red-tiled roof of a mansion rising above them and for the first time fields green with crops that looked to be sugarcane and in some sections rows of maguey cactus alternating with the cane and it all lay before him too good to be true, like some mirage or dream wished or thought into being that when he blinked his eyes it would be gone, but he did and it was not.

The road sloped gradually downward and he approached the old estate slowly. Parts of the walls had crumbled and the arched gate was in ill-repair, pink adobe brick showing through where the whitewashed plaster had chipped and flaked away and the watchtowers had missing shingles between their small roof beams and were absent any sentinel to announce his coming. He'd expected someone to have seen him, to have been there to greet him as had been the case with the other haciendas he'd visited. But no one came forth. Through the archway he could see the main house but not its full breadth and height and when he stepped through the gate it loomed before him more like a fortress than a mansion. It was brown adobe stucco in the style of the land with a long front porch of pillars and heavy arches curtained by flowering vines and a second floor balcony of equal design and on either side of the house unkept gardens that had gone to seed. From a single fountain in the center of the clay courtyard dirty children and women with babies slung in rebozos were carrying water in metal pails. A few glanced in his direction but paid him no mind.

He took a few more steps into the compound and looked around. To his left and right along the inner walls were adobe huts roofed with discarded pieces of corrugated tin or shingles held down by stones and concrete blocks and he guessed the workers lived there. He kept looking for someone of authority but all he saw were the women and children collecting and carrying water to the huts.

He walked toward the fountain to get a drink and a voice shouted at him.

Hombre!

He turned and saw a tall lanky man, darkened almost black, walking toward him. He wore a white Western-style hat like the comandante at the prison in Matamoros had worn and the brim was pulled down low shading his eyes. His thumbs were hooked in his belt and he swaggered in the exaggerated style of one who has less authority than that invested in him.

Qué es lo que quiere?

Busco a alguien.

Who is this person you wish to find?

He was surprised the man spoke English and had to stop a minute to think what to say next.

I'm looking for a señora Carlita Navarro de Moncada. I been told she lives here.

Yes. And this information, who tell you?

Nobody in particular. I just heard she lived on this hacienda.

The man grimaced and took several steps and stopped so he was between Jo Shelby and the fountain. He looked down and moved the toe of his boot in the dirt as if to draw a line then stood erect with his legs spread and his arms akimbo, like a security guard. And your reason for wanting to see the señora? the man said.

My name's Jo Shelby Ferguson and I'm from America and—

So what business is it you have with the señora? he clipped. One eye was brighter than the other as though all of his scrutiny funneled into it.

He could see there was no use trying to reason with the man so he reached in his shirtpocket and pulled out the piece of paper. Just give this to her and tell her my name is Ferguson, he said.

The man took the paper and unfolded it and thumbed the rim of his hat so it cocked back on his head and held the wrinkled sheet at arms length and ran his eyes up and down it. It is nothing but names, he said. What will she know of a paper with just names?

I'd be much obliged if you'd just give it to her. I done come a long way and I ain't here to cause no trouble. When she sees them names she'll understand.

The man shrugged his shoulders and cocked his hips.

I do not know, señor. The señora, she is not well. You are a stranger. How do I know you do not want more from her?

You don't, he said, growing weary with the resistance. All I wanna do is just talk to her. Comprende?

The man narrowed his eyes and looked at him gravely. Señor. I understand, maybe better than you. I will do this thing you ask but I do not promise the señora will see you. And if she will not see you, then that is that and you must go back down the road the way you came and no regreso. Comprende?

Yessir. I just think she's all the family I got left and I done come—

Sí, sí. I understand. You have made a long journey and I, Ricardo, the administrador of the hacienda, I will tell her. Está bien?

Sí. Bien.

So, we understand one another, no?

All right.

You wait here, at the fountain, the administrador said and turned and clomped toward the big house, puffs of dust under his bootheels reporting loudly on the stone porch, silenced when the big wooden door slammed shut behind him.

He unloaded his knapsack from his shoulders and set it on the ground and sat sideways on the rim of the fountain and waited. He removed his hat and washed his face and rinsed his mouth in the water that tasted like iron but did not drink of it and spat it out onto the the ground where it cratered the dust. He addressed the ladies filling their buckets at the fountain's spigot and they spoke kindly back but didn't look at him. Nor did the children who pressed their faces into their mothers' long dresses and kept them hidden until some distance from the fountain. He thought of the places he'd been, from Matamoros to Monterrey to Mexico City to Jiutepec, and nowhere had he encountered such strange and secretive behavior. There was no laughter about the place. No music. At a barn in the distance he saw some men unloading freshly cut sugarcane from a cart. There was no conversation among them, no bantering back and forth as even prisoners in chains will do. He thought of how far he'd come and what all he'd been through and knew, just knew, if there was a God he would smile upon him and he could finish what he started out to do. She would recognize the names. Once she saw what was on the paper she'd know why he was there. She'd sat on that porch in the dusks and evenings and listened to the stories just as he had where he'd grown up and she would see the names and remember the tales and legends spun through the generations that went with them and she'd tell the man to invite him in.

The late afternoon sun was warming him in the confidence of those thoughts and the children were peek-a-booing at him from between the huts when the door of the house creaked open and the bootsteps clapped loud again on the porch and he put his hat back on and stood up to receive what word the administrador brought to him.

The man walked within a few feet and stopped and held out the sheet of paper. I am very sorry, señor. But the señora is not feeling well and said to tell you she could not see you.

Jo Shelby reached out and took the paper from him. Did she even look at it?

Sí, yes. She look.

She didn't say anything?

She look at it, señor. That was you request.

But when she looked at it she didn't say what she saw?

The man folded his arms across his chest and tilted his head at an arrogant angle. Señor, do not make difficult this meeting between us. This hacienda here is private place. You come to it and no one know you come. You give to me this paper and I give it to the señora and she look at it and say nothing and give it back and say she is too ill to see you and that is that and now you must go.

Jo Shelby bent over to pick up the knapsack but kept his eye on the man standing over him and when he raised up the man took a step closer and leveled a forefinger at the gate.

I'm much obliged and sorry for any trouble, he said and slipped his knapsack through his arms and onto his shoulders.

It is no trouble, señor. Trouble only if you do not leave, he said, his eyes tightening into hard little points.

All right. I'm going.

The children were still peeking around the corners of the huts and he waved at them as he crossed the yard toward the gate and their heads disappeared. He stopped at the gate and turned and looked back, to see if there might be a figure or the shadow of a figure watching from one of the sashed windows but there was none. He made a final sweep of the grounds with his eyes, noting the situation of the barn and what appeared to be a workshop on its near side and some farm equipment laid out on its far side and further down the likes of a large storeroom or silo where the men were passing the stalks of cane from the cart and next to them a pole corral where several horses were prancing around and he calculated the distance of the corral and the outbuildings from the wall and the configuration relative to the house then he turned back around. He walked on up the road and looked back once more and the administrador was standing beneath the arch watching, to make sure. He kept walking until he crested the low escarpment where he'd first glimpsed the place and continued on until he knew he was out of sight and he stopped. You just been lied to by somebody worse off than a habitual criminal who does it for a living, he mumbled to himself. The son of a bitch didn't even show her the paper if he even talked to her at all.

There was nothing between him and the main road but the jacales and the beggared people inhabiting them. It was late afternoon and the valley was growing dark in the shadowed coolness of the mountains and a soft breeze blew down out of the low hills. He was tired and thirsty but tried not to think of either and whatever hunger he'd had he'd lost. He looked around for any sign of human life, anyone that might be watching, and all he saw as far as he could see was the waist-high infestation of weeds and wild shrubbery and flowers he'd seen coming in, their tops bending with the wind. He left the stone road and walked through the thick growth, his eyes vigilant on the ground for snakes and vermin. Grasshoppers sprung into the air ahead of him and the sound of his clothes against the brush was loud in his ears and he stopped every now and then and cocked his ears for other sounds but there were none, not even the hum of traffic or dogs barking and he thought to himself that was good and he continued on. He went about a hundred yards and stopped and with his boots trampled out an area long and wide enough for a person to lay down and settled into his matted den and thought.

He opened the knapsack and reached in and took out the holstered revolver and popped the holster snap and slipped the gun from its leather scabbard and held it. Weighed it back and forth in his hands. Let his right hand grip the heel of the handle, get the feel of it. Then laid it in the grass at his side. *Everything that happens, there is a reason.* She got that damn right he thought to himself. It might not can shoot but don't nobody else know that. He put the empty holster back into the knapsack and placed the knapsack where he could rest his head upon it and he stretched out. The tall weeds and brush around him whirred and clicked with life of another world, one far removed to sound so near. Smells of woodsmoke from the jacales floated down and a kite skated the wind across the patch of blue overhead, hovered, then swooped downward with its killy killy killy cry and he knew a rodent or rabbit had made a mistake and would never make it home. He lay there a long time, his thoughts drifting with the shoaling clouds, their colors changing in the refracted rays of the sun's descent. He thought of where he was and how far he'd come and of his chances and what he had to lose and what he had to gain and weighed both sides of the equation and decided there were times in a man's life where simple arithmetic broke down and nothing was more than something but there was no book that ever taught that. He lay a long time watching the changes in the sky until it lay crimson over him, the color of boiled skin and as fragile, he thought, with only the fading light of the sun holding it together and he drifted off to sleep.

When he awoke all was dark about him. Overhead the great milky way trailed the heavens like a gauzy band of smoke, the stars within it hot white sparks carried upward as though from some celestial inferno, and a quarter-moon low in the east tilted over the sierras. By its angle in the sky the evening was not yet late which was good. As old a woman as she, she'd still be awake.

He stuck the gun into the top of his jeans and the long barrel ran cold across his stomach. He pushed it in so it rested snugly with the handle hanging over his belt then slipped the knapsack into place on his back and retraced his steps back to the old road. He stopped and looked both ways and saw nothing but the polished stones gleaming softly in the quarter-moonshine. He turned right and moved slowly along the eroded shoulder. He walked where he had walked before. He stopped now and then to monitor the sound and he heard nothing but his own breathing and the wind through the wild brush and the lonely hooting of an owl far off. He came to where the land rose slightly then bowled outward and he could see the lights of the hacienda below and the shadows of its walls and thin ribbons of smoke rising from the workers' huts and lighted windows across the balcony of the mansion's second story. From the dark outlines he reconstructed what he'd recalled from his earlier reconnaissance of the place then put his feet in careful motion, one after the other, creeping half-crouched along the low wall of brush so his head was beneath the lowest growth, so he blended with the shadows.

He drew near the wall and heard guitar music and someone singing.

A man's voice straining at a high pitch. It came from one of the huts across the wall. The strumming and singing were irregular and not always simultaneous, as though the man was learning a new song or relearning an old one, and he moved along the outer edge of the wall, stopping when the music stopped and starting when voice or instrument or both together took up again. By this method he reached the end of the wall where it cornered and ran south and he followed it another hundred feet where he could see the outline of the barn's roof against the sky and he stopped. There was a scalloped gap head-high on the wall where it had crumbled and a mound of mudbrick rubble at its base sloping up to it. The man had stopped playing and singing but he could hear voices. He placed a boot on the mound and tested its firmness. It seemed secure enough and he pushed himself up and planted his other boot and loose pebbles and matter scattered loudly underfoot and he stopped. He held his breath and waited. His arms were outstretched, palms pressed against the wall, his body hugging it so close he could feel the hammering of his heart against it. He heard nothing different from what he'd heard before and breathed again and took another step up, this time onto a solid slab of mortar and brick that had broken away in one piece. The top of the wall was just above him and he took one more step up the heap of ruined debris to a point high enough where he could look over.

The barn was on his right and the shed to his left. He could see three of the workers' huts but the wood shed blocked his view of the rest. If he went any farther down the wall he'd be farther away from the huts but closer to the horses and spook them for sure. Straight ahead of him between the barn and the work shed was a short corridor about six feet wide and through it he could see what appeared to be a patio and behind it wide windowed doors that entered the mansion from the side. There were lights on behind the doors but no signs of movement. He looked back at the huts. Before one of them sat two women and a man in cane chairs, silhouettes against the dim light from the doorway and he could not make out their features. A guitar lay across the man's knee and he was conversing with the women who were laughing at what he'd said.

He stayed still and watched.

The three people continued sitting and talking.

He kept vigilant, waiting.

Then the man leaned the guitar against the wall of the hut behind him and stood up and he stepped into the doorway and in the rectangle of light Jo Shelby recognized the thin gangly appearance of the man who'd run him off. He had not prayed in a long time but he whispered a prayer to God and thanked him.

The administrador remained inside the small domicile and it seemed he would not come back out and with his mind telling him to go. Jo Shelby put his hands on the decaying rim of the wall and pulled himself up and let himself down quietly on the other side and moved quickly so he stood with his back pressed against the back wall of the barn. The night air carried the rich odors of hay and manure. The rear portal of the barn was on his left several feet and he thought through what he should do next. He placed his right hand on the heel of the gun and pulled it out. He bent down and with his left felt around on the ground for a rock. There was nothing on the ground but dried manure. He moved several paces left and right and found more of the same. He got down on his knees and crawled back to the wall and located what felt to be half of an adobe brick and gripped it securely in his hand and crawled back to the barn wall. He whispered another prayer and took a deep breath and heaved the brick into the air and onto the tin roof of the shed and the brick hit the metallic sheathing like a loud shot and rumbled off the other side and the effect in the otherwise soundless night was that of thunder come from nowhere.

He sidled down the wall of the barn to the portal and waited. He did not move but stood as though he were a fixture to the wall that supported him. He was breathing deep and fast and his heart was beating like a runaway tom-tom and he tried slowing his breathing to calm it.

He listened.

Footsteps across the grounds. Heavy clomping. By their sound, only one person. They stopped and by the sound of where they ceased the person was in front of the shed. The beam of a flashlight bounced left and right along the wall then went away and the footsteps began again and he heard them coming through the gap between the shed and the barn and saw the jerking beam of light that preceded them and he slipped around the corner of the barn portal, holding the gun with both hands close to his chest, and the footsteps and light kept coming and turned and entered the barn portal and in the heartbeat of a moment he stepped into the glare of light and raised the revolver and leveled the barrel at the face of the administrador.

Stop right there, he said and the administrador took a step back and froze with his arms slung out from his sides and his face screwed up like a man already shot from behind about to fall facedown.

What is this? he said, his eyes stretched out of their sockets. His arms still transfixed so the flashlight beam was pointed at the ground, as though light were bleeding from the hand that held it.

This here's a Navy Colt 36 caliber and if you don't do what I tell you to do it's just liable to go off and take your head across that wall yonder behind you.

The administrador let his arms fall to his sides but angled the light back up into Jo Shelby's face.

Turn off that damn flashlight and git them arms back up, Jo Shelby said and the light went out and the administrador's arms went into the air.

Now drop the flashlight.

The flashlight hit the ground with a soft thud. This is bad mistake you make, señor, the administrador said.

No sir. Only bad mistake's gonna be if you don't walk in front of me to that house like me and you's old buddies and tell the señora you got a friend you want her to meet. Comprende?

The administrador nodded.

Now git in front of me and bring them hands down slowly and walk to the front of the barn.

Why you do this thing?

I done told you onct and I ain't gonna tell you again. Now move.

He stepped back and the administrador passed in front of him and he fell in behind and they walked slowly through the darkened cavity of the building, passing stalls of hay. They reached the front portal and

Jo Shelby told him to stop.

Where you want me to go? the administrador said.

You can go to them wide doors there on the side or the one on the front. I don't give a shit. Just git the señora.

But you are just one man, señor. There are many in the houses. He pointed to the huts along the wall. You kill me you have to kill them.

I got six shots. It don't make no never mind to me. Six of you and one of me. You ever take rithmetic in school?

Sí.

Well use a little of it. Now walk slowly. You run and you're a dead man. You holler and you're a dead man. Comprende?

Sí, but you will not get away with this.

We'll just see about that. All I wanna do is meet with the señora and show her my paper that you never showed her and talk with her. That's all. Don't want to hurt nobody. But I will if I have to. I come a long way and if I go away emptyhanded I ain't goin alone. Now start walking, real slow like.

The administrador did not turn around and Jo Shelby tucked the gun back into his pantswaist and pulled his shirt out over it and they began walking. The two women were still sitting in front of the hovel but he saw no one else. They crossed the courtyard and were going in the direction of the side doors then the administrador turned and angled for the front of the big house. The fountain was to their left and Jo Shelby did not see the men until they were almost parallel the fountain then he saw the two seated shadows silhouetted on the lip of the basin. He knew the administrador saw them, too, but he said nothing for fear it would cause suspicion. The administrador said something to the men in a rapid Spanish he could not understand. The men did not speak back and did not move and he and the administrador kept walking. The fountain was behind them some thirty feet and he grew nervous and looked back and the men were gone. Slowly he moved his hand to his waist and gripped the handle of the gun and held it there. They were almost to the porch landing when he heard something behind him and before he could bring out the gun a force slammed against his legs and another across his back and he heard something go crack like it might have been his back and he went sprawling into the dirt. His arms were wrenched back behind him and the toe of a boot kicked the side of his face once, then again. The men were shouting among themselves and he could hear the administrador's high whiny voice telling one of them to get some rope. He was still struggling and the boot made another sweep and glanced off the side of his head and the administrador was yelling something at him in Spanish and amidst the rancor a voice called out from above.

Qué pasa? It was the voice of a woman, one cracked with age, but strong, deep.

He could not look up. Someone held his hands behind him and another kept his face pushed into the ground. He tasted dirt. He turned his head to spit and the boot toe came again, this time into his cheek and he thought he heard his jaw crack. He tasted blood.

It is nothing, señora, the administrador hollered. Just a gringo intruder. It is no problem.

He knew the boot was coming again but he turned his head anyway and yelled. I'm a Ferguson from America. I'm kin to—

The blow caught him in the mouth and he felt the sudden bolt of pain through the roof of his mouth and he spit out two teeth and hollered again. I'm kin to you.

Let him up, she said from somewhere above them. Do not kick him again, Ricardo.

But, señora, he is dangerous man, the administrador said. He had a gun.

The gun don't even shoot, he shouted. All I wanna do is talk to the señora. That's all.

Let him up, I said, the señora repeated, her voice almost shouting.

One of the men had gone for a rope and the one holding him down loosed his grip and he rolled over. He blinked his eyes to focus them and the lids hurt going up and down and what little light he could see was painful to look at. He pulled his lashes down with his fingers like his mother had taught him to do when he got something in them and released them and blinked again and some of the debris was gone.

The administrador was standing over him, his arms folded, legs spread. The other two men were behind him, one of them holding a noosed rope. He blinked again and looked up. In a second story window directly above him he saw her, a figure thin and diminutive against the yellow light, the contours of her body visible through the nightgown she wore, a knob-headed stick-person a child might draw she looked, a frail crucifix with her arms outstretched against the windowjambs.

What is your name?

Jo Shelby Ferguson.

Bring him inside, she said, then disappeared from the window.

He felt a hand under his armpit then another under the other and he was lifted up.

You will not get back the gun, señor, the administrador said, holding it out before him.

He wiped blood away from his mouth and spit and moved his tongue around and felt the gap where his front teeth had been. I might not git it now, but I'm gonna git it back.

We will see, señor.

Yeah. We gonna see all right. He looked around and located his hat and hit it against his leg, shook out the dust, then put it on.

He followed the administrador onto the porch and through the front door and into a marble-floored hall from which spiraled a carpeted staircase to a balustraded landing. The administrador motioned to the left and led him from the spacious zaguan into a large room cluttered with antiquity and pointed to a couch and told him to sit and he sat but not because anyone told him to. He was near collapse.

You wait here. The señora will come en un momentito, the administrador said curtly, then grinned and brandished the gun as a final torment and left. He heard his footsteps as they crossed the zaguan then the front door close and the footsteps fading until he could hear them no more.

He took off his hat and set it on the floor beside his feet and removed the knapsack and placed it beside the hat. He rubbed his eyes again, trying to help them adjust to the light. He looked around. The salon was filled with elegant pieces of furniture. A mahogany table with matching chairs. An old fan-backed rocker. A Spanish desk encrusted with a family crest in pure silver. There were crystal candelabras on carved chests and statuettes on ebony pedestals. Oriental rugs covered the floors and paintings of landscapes with misty trees hung on the walls. The accumulation of many lives passed on.

He heard the shuffling of slippers across the zaguan and looked up as she entered the room. She was short and light-skinned, thin-faced, her hair a dirty-gray pulled back in a bun. She wore a pink robe that looked oversized and hung loosely from her narrow frame and she carried a towel in one hand and a white enameled water basin in the other and she approached him like someone who had nursed and had known the habits of nursing for a long time.

We've got to get you cleaned up, she said, a gentle crankiness in the raspy voice, one that carried the accent of that world but the faint drawl of another. She sat on the couch beside him and set the basin on the coffee table before them and dipped the end of the towel into the basin of water. Now who did you say you were?

But before he could answer she had the wet end of the towel over his mouth, wiping around it and dabbing at the corners, her eyes focused with the intensity of a sculptor making finishing touches.

My name's Jo Shelby Ferguson, he said.

Here, you take the towel. I don't want to hurt you. Your mouth is bleeding. Your two front teeth are out. Did you know that?

Yessum.

Do you want some water? I'll get you a glass of water, and she pushed herself up and left.

He dipped the towel back into the basin and mopped his brow and the sides of his face. He rotated his jaw to see if it was broken. It hurt in the joints but seemed to be intact. He sopped the towel in the basin again and put a wad of it in his mouth and held it there and felt the cool along with the points of pain that stung where the wet touched them. He heard her coming again, the old feet shuffling with care, and he removed the towel from his mouth before she entered and it was a small mop of blood.

She sat beside him again and handed him a tall glass of water and he thanked her and sipped slightly at first then took several long swallows, the pain of the water passing over the cuts overcome by his thirst.

Are you hungry? You must be hungry. María can fix you something to eat. Do you want something to eat?

Yessum. That'd be mighty nice of you.

You wait here and tend to your cuts, she said, and she left again. She was gone a long while. He finished the glass of water and washed his hands with the unused end of the towel and leaned back and waited, continuing to let his eyes roam the room, guessing the history of its artifacts.

She returned and told him María was cooking him something to eat. He thanked her and she asked again who he was and he told her and reached down and unbuckled the knapsack and pulled out the two letters he'd been carrying, took them out of their envelopes and unfolded them and laid them on the couch between them. Then he reached into his shirtpocket and pulled out the piece of paper and unfolded it and held it in his hand. He reached down and picked up the letters and handed them to her.

Read the letters first then read this, he said, handing her the paper from the registro, and it'll explain why I'm here.

She took the letters, adjusting herself as if she were missing her bifocals, and read. He watched the pale hazel eyes move slowly down each page, watched them widen and the pupils grow larger and her mouth open and drop further open and the wrinkles spread out over the amazed face until she was finished and her hands and the papers in them collapsed in her lap.

Well I'll declare, she said. If that doesn't beat all.

The accent was there along with the idiom, the homegrown phraseology passed down through the generations, of his parents and

theirs and theirs before them and further back still and all of it voiced
once more, an echo blown down the canyon of years and he trembled
at its sound and smiled and she took out the towel and wiped his face,
brushed away the tears that came unhurried down his bruised cheeks.

She stopped and looked at him and smiled. I guess we are something like long lost cousins. Is that the phrase?

Yessum, something like that. You speak pretty good English.

My mother spoke only to me in English when I was growing up
and everyone else spoke Spanish. Therefore I learned to speak the two
languages. Bilingual. When I was older my mother told me it was the
way she had been raised.

I thought maybe you might be my aunt.

I may be. We can figure all that out later. In Mexico it does not
seem to matter, just so you are related. A cousin here counts as much
as a brother or a sister. The blood runs as thick out on the limb of the
family tree as it does along its trunk. I knew there was another side to
the family but so little was said of it. I knew my great-grandfather and
great-grandmother on my mother's side of the family were American,
that he had been an officer in the Confederate army and sought refuge
with his family in this country, somewhere south of Cuernavaca, and
that all ties were cut with his people back in the States for fear of
reprisals from his government who had recognized Juarez as the new
leader. On occasions my grandmother Carolina would speak of the
colonel, as she called him, and my great-grandmother Caroline and of
the family and the land they left behind but it was not often these
matters were mentioned. It seems they had resigned themselves to the
sad and terrible fact they had crossed into a new world and their lives
had begun anew and any mention of their other lives, their other
world, was a pain too heavy to bear.

I can tell you what I do know, she continued. They settled into a
hacienda near Michapa, as one of the letters mentions, a very small
village southwest of here. In fact they are buried there in the church-
yard. There were two sons and a daughter, Caroline, my grandmother,
who, early on I think, or maybe it was when she married, I am not

sure, took on the Spanish spelling of Carolina. The hacienda at Michapa bordered with La Hacienda Tierra del Puente and the colonel, following the custom of the time, contracted with Rodrigo Fernando Cruz Alfonso for the marriage of his daughter to the eldest son Fernando. I have little knowledge of the two sons except their names I believe were Taylor and Jonathan. Perhaps they stayed on the hacienda, which is no more. It is in ruins. What is left of it are only walls and empty doors and windows. Zapata destroyed it. And the rest you know from the geneology on that side of the family you somehow came by.

The registro civil in Cuernavaca. A couple of ladies there got it for me.

I see. Well, you are to be congratulated on your research. I do not know what more I can add.

Yessum, there is.

And what might that be?

What I want to know is how come your administrador never told you about me. I came this afternoon, gave him the paper to show you.

She leaned forward with enlarged eyes that seemed to pull her in that direction, fanning a hand across her breast as she did. Her brows were arched and the small round face that had been pale, the way his mother's would be before she went to bed, began taking on color. She began tapping a forefinger on her cheek and tapping a foot on the floor at the same time and he watched her and with the way all of her blood seemed to be collecting in her face decided it was an old person's way of counting to ten, to keep them from stroking out. She did that for a while. A clock somewhere in the room ticked. There was kitchen noise from further back in the house. Then she ceased the tapping with the finger and the foot and sat upright and folded her hands in her lap.

It is most unfortunate what happened to you, Jo Shelby. Is that it, the two names, Jo Shelby?

Yessum.

And I apologize for the way you were treated. I will deal with

Ricardo about that later. Of course, he must be punished. I do not
know how to explain his behavior in any way that would be brief. It is
a story that goes back many years and has as much to do with the history of my country as it does with my family.

Don't reckon I'm goin anywhere right soon. Least I don't think I
am.

No. You are fine here and no further harm will come to you. I will
tell you the story. As you know from the paper you gave to me, my
mother was Carlita Cruz Ferguson and her father was Fernando Alfonso Cruz Linares, the hacendado of La Hacienda Tierra del Puente.
Many years ago the hacienda was one of the largest in all of Mexico
and Fernando was a most powerful man. He and Díaz, the presidente
in those days, were friends. Then came the revolution. Villa in the
north and Zapata in the south and Carranza in between. Do you
know of these men?

Some of em.

Well, it was a time of great change. Most of the land in Mexico was
in the hands of people like my grandfather, very rich and powerful
men. The peons and peasants were wanting their share. My grandfather saw what was coming, that the great haciendas would be divested
and divided and most of the land given to the peasants. As I said, La
Hacienda Tierra del Puente at that time was very large. It stretched
from here south of Cuernavaca all the way to Miacatlán and he even
owned hectares of land south of there near Michapa. Before the revolution broke, he divided the hacienda and made of it three haciendas and
gave one to each of his children. Marcos, the eldest, got the southern-
most section which was the largest, Miguel the center and Carlita, my
mother, the northern sector which retained the original name. All of
this was quite unusual because land was usually not in the woman's
name, but in the man's, but my grandfather was a fair and judicious
man. Then came the revolution in 1910 and Zapata. He was an Indian
of very poor origins. As the story is told his father punished him severely, beat him at the orders of a hacendado and Zapata never forgot
and the haciendas that lay in his path reaped the destruction of his

rage, and two of those were my family's. For some reason he never came here and we were spared. This house is over a hundred years old. The Empress Carlota herself danced in these halls and Díaz was often here. He was an old man when the revolution came, in his eighties. There were popular uprisings all over the country. He was forced to retire and Madero took over and he was assassinated shortly after. Then there was civil war throughout the country. Through all of this my mother and her husband Gabriel were able to hold the hacienda together, but it was most difficult. For about twenty years the situation became more stable. Leaders became less enthusiastic about land reform and my parents and the hacienda were left alone. My mother, for whom I am named, died in 1930 and my father the next year. My brother, whose name was Juan, and my husband Gilberto and I took over the hacienda, then Juan was mysteriously killed. To this day no one knows who killed him or why and the murderers were never caught. Gilberto and I had three sons. Juan, Raúl and Fredrico. We lived on the hacienda. We were a happy family. Calles, a strong presidente who was dedicated to large industry and had many followers of wealth, declared land distribution a failure and it came to an end, but only temporarily. Then Gilberto died suddenly of a heart attack. The year was 1934. There was movement once more in the country for land reform. We paid little attention to it and I tried to manage the property as best I could. There was much fighting among my sons, jealousy about who was being treated fairly and those kinds of things one expects of smaller children. That was enough trouble. Then Cárdenas became presidente, a man who believed in laws. In 1937 he began using the constitution of 1917 which stated that the government had the right to divide public lands in the public interest. We, along with many other hacienda owners, were dispossessed of our lands. We were allowed to keep our homes and barns and farm equipment and each hacienda was allowed to keep at least two hundred and fifty hectáreas of land that we could choose ourselves. And what you have seen today of the place is what is left of the great Tierra del Puente. Are you following me?

Yes ma'am. Some of it I'd already learnt.

That I would expect of you. Now to Ricardo, my administrador. Ricardo was at first only a worker, but a very good worker. He was responsible and dependable, something I could not say of any of my sons. They had become very spoiled and perhaps their father and I shoulder much of the blame for their lack of industry and independence. They ate off fine china and we had servants. They slept between silk sheets. They never knew where their money came from. When the land was taken away and we were left with only the two hundred and fifty acres, they had to think. They became more dissatisfied with their lot in life and Fredrico and Raúl left. They live in other places and have families and are able to feed them and those are other stories. Juan stayed. But he was indolent and irresponsible and very jealous of Ricardo's successes with the crops and the workers and one day they fought, out there in the yard by the fountain. I thought they would kill each other and I had to get a gun and threaten to shoot them if they did not stop. Juan left that day and vowed he would never return and he has not. He has never forgiven me for not taking his side. I have seen him only twice, when I attended the baptisms of his two sons in Jiutepec and even then he would not speak. Ricardo must have thought you were sent by Juan, for what reasons I do not know. Perhaps a peace offering. Perhaps to get even with him. Juan blames Ricardo for where his life has taken him. He does nothing. He lives in a hovel. He does some carpentry work for an American mission in La Joya but I think that is all. It is enough to feed his family so at least he has learned to work.

She stopped. He waited to see if she would continue but she did not. He was not sure what to say. They sat in the silence of the large room, the house empty except for her and a maid and himself. Only the ticking of the clock and the light clatter of noise in the kitchen were heard.

Your food may be ready, she said. I will go and see. She got up to leave and he asked if there was one thing further she could do for him and she inquired what that might be and he told her about the gun and something of its heritage and how important it was to him and she assured him the matter would be quickly resolved.

She returned shortly and told him his meal was prepared. She pointed out a bathroom down the center hallway where he could wash up and he did so and looked at his face in the mirror and wondered if it would ever be normal again, with all it had been through. He returned to the salon where the señora was waiting for him.

He ate in a large dining room at a long table. A chandelier hung over the table but no lights on it burned. The only light came from two wall sconces on either side of the room that burned dimly. There was a large sideboard and upon it sat pieces of china, but other than it and the table and chairs there was no furniture. María was younger than he'd expected. She was short and plump and dark-skinned. She spoke to him in Spanish and he spoke back to her in that language and she smiled. Excepting her age and the soft texture of her voice, she moved about the room with a sense of command and the comfortable familiarity of one who belonged and in those ways she reminded him of Sissy. She placed before him a bowl of soup which contained rice and English peas. The señora explained to him it was called mole de olla, that it was a beef stew but María had removed the chunks of beef because of the condition of his mouth. He'd requested a beer and one was brought and he ladled the soup to his mouth with a large spoon and ate and swallowed slowly. The señora sat across from him and sipped a glass of wine. She told him there was much she wanted to learn from him and about him and how he came all the way from Mississippi to La Hacienda Tierra del Puente but that he must eat and not talk, that they had much time to talk later.

But you can talk.

Yes, she said. She held a small goblet in both hands and took a sip. He thought of señora García and another evening. There is more you want to know? she said.

Your sons. They all left. But you stayed with the land.

Yes. This is where I was born and this is where I will die. What will happen with the hacienda after that I cannot say. Maybe one of my sons will come back and take it over. Maybe that is one of Ricardo's worst fears for there was much dislike between him and my sons. But right now this is my hacienda. I have put much time and work, even labor, into it, denying myself what young people love. I have put my money here instead of buying extravagantly or traveling abroad, because I love the land, because I wish to do my duty by the people who live on the land and depend upon it. My people love me. We have become like family. We are working hard now to produce as much as we can. Sugarcane grows, as you saw coming in this afternoon, and between the rows maguey from which pulque is made. I can manage these men well, for most of them still believe they are better off than those on the ejidos. I make few changes. Here I can see things grow and for me that is life, not dealing with the politicians who continue to try and take my hacienda from me. But I, a woman, have saved and worked and denied myself for this land. It is mine, and they are taking it bit by bit. You saw when you came in, the fields gone to weeds and cactus.

Yes ma'am, he said, drawing another spoonful of soup to his mouth.

That is an example of why land reform failed. Those lands were once farmed productively and now they are a waste. The peasants do not know how to farm them. They do not have the tools. When we were stripped of our land and told we could keep our houses and machinery and implements my sons took up all the implements and told the peasants, now go and farm your land, see what good you can bring from it. After they left I tried to give the implements back but the peasants would not take them. There was too much resentment in their hearts to receive back what had been taken from them. So the land goes to waste, little by little, and I try to hold on.

María came and took the bowl and spoon when he had finished and brought him a custard and he ate it. The señora asked if he liked brandy and he told her he'd never had any until he'd come to Mexico but that he was developing a taste for it.

I offer it reluctantly because it may burn your mouth.

If it does, it'll burn it good.

They adjourned to the salon and María brought a cut glass decanter of brandy and two snifters and poured drinks for each of them, then she left for a while and returned holding what appeared to be a roll of bread wrapped in a towel to keep it warm and delivered it to the señora who placed it on a table beside her then she disappeared for the remainder of the evening.

The señora sat in the large fan-backed rocker, her feet barely touching the floor to make it rock and he sat in a cushioned wingback across from her and in the quiet shadows of the large room, surrounded by the relics of her history, he told her his. He told her about the plantation and its enormity before the War Between the States and she asked was it not called the Civil War and he told her that only Yankees called it that and she smiled and let him continue. He retrieved his knapsack where it still lay on the floor by the sofa and pulled out the sheaf of photographs that had curled and cracked with the jostlings and shocks of the journey and passed them to her one by one, telling her stories about each as she held them. She inquired about the son who remained behind to care for the plantation and he told her he had no pictures of him nor any of his family then told her what he had been told as to how the plantation had been lost and its passage through the generations and that his family had stayed with the land and been dutiful servants. He told her of his incarceration in the state penitentiary and the death of his parents and grandfather and how he was not allowed to attend their funeral and of his release and all that was left by his family in the trunk and his subsequent journey by car and towboat and tanker to Mexico and his incarceration in Matamoros and the friendships along the way. He tried to skip over portions, telling her that most of it was probably boring, but she wanted to hear everything and he left out not a detail and when he had finished they were on their second glass of brandy and she reached over and lifted the towel and what it held from the table and handed it to him and he pulled back the folds and the brass frame of the gun shone dimly in the meager light.

How'd you git it back so quick?

Ricardo is Maria's father. I told her to go to her father and get the gun or he would not have a job when the sun rose and, as you can see, the rest was no problem.

He bent down and raised the flap of the knapsack and pulled out the holster and rescabbarded the gun and snapped the holder strap and slipped the holstered gun back into the knapsack.

It's worth about a hunderd dollars, he said.

I would have thought it worth more than that.

They'd only give me sixty for it in Cuernavaca.

You tried to sell it?

Sell it. Pawn it. Thought I had to do somethin. I was broke. But when it got down to the lick log I couldn't do it. Somethin told me not to.

Lick log?

That's just a expression.

I see. Well, I'm glad you still have it. Are you still without money?

Yes ma'am. Ain't got a cent, or peso rather. Used it all up gettin here.

And where will you go next?

He thought. He took up his brandy snifter. Made little rotations with it in the air. Watched the dark liquid swirl. Don't rightly know, he said. I know I can farm. I can saddle and ride horses. I can put up fences and keep em mended and I can lay brick. Come to think of it there really ain't much I cain't do onct I put my mind to it.

And your home in Mississippi, you do not plan to return to it?

It ain't a home no more.

But it is where you were raised, just as I was here.

I guess so, but it ain't the same.

The girl you told me about, Alene—

Athen.

Yes, Athen. She is not waiting for you?

Maybe. Maybe not.

Do you love her?

He thought again, longer. Don't know. I met someone in Mexico City. Her name's Carmen. I told you about her.

Yes, the one who helped you.

Yeah. She's really purdy and nice. She would've probably done anything I asked her to do. I wanna see her again, but then . . .

Perhaps it is she you love.

I don't know. It's real confusin. When you come down to it, don't reckon I know what love is I've gone without it so long.

The señora rocked forward and stopped and leaned forward, her eyes narrowing, reaching.

But you miss one more than the other, no?

No'me. Yeah. Maybe. One kinda stays with me, like I never really left her, or she never left me, like I carry part of her around with me all the time, if that means somethin.

The señora smiled. Then that is the difference, Jo Shelby, that is the one you love, that is where your heart is, and where your heart is, there is your treasure, or so the Bible says, she said and resumed rocking.

There was silence awhile as he took in what she had said and recalled the favorite scripture of his mother and similar words spoken to him by Ramón and his wife. There was a difference between the two women in his life, not one he could think out in his head, set them up side by side and measure this for that and that for this, because he had known no others finer. But there was a difference, like if he could hold the feelings for each in his hands, one would be heavier than the other. He was letting those thoughts settle when she spoke again.

Whatever you decide to do, you may stay here on the hacienda as long as you wish. As you can see, this is a big house, too big for one old woman. You may have one of the bedrooms upstairs, one that belonged to one of my sons. You can work and I will pay you a fair wage. There is certainly plenty of work to be done.

She rose and motioned him to do likewise. He picked up his hat and knapsack and followed. They ascended the staircase in the zaguan and she took him down a hallway and opened a door and switched on an overhead light and he followed her in. There was a large bed with a coat of arms on the headboard and slender rods to hold a canopy but no canopy. Across from the bed was a shaving-stand with cut-glass knobs. The washstand was fitted with what remained of a set of china and some pieces of crude pottery. The rest of the room was filled out with a bentwood rocker and a straight chair, a chifferobe and a chest of drawers and a nightstand on which sat a globed lamp.

This was Juan's room, she said. It is as it was the day he left. As I told you, I change very little. Put your dirty clothes outside the door and María will wash them. The top drawer of the dresser is empty so you can use it. I will treat you like you are family, which you are. The bath is down the hall. I have my own, so you need not worry about privacy. You look tired so sleep as long as you wish. María will cook your breakfast when you arise. She is very loyal and steadfast, as are most of my workers. If you need anything, my room is down the hall on the left.

She said everything to him in a clipped matter-of-fact fashion, as one who had been conditioned by that kind of world, but the sincerity was there, in her eyes and the embrace she gave him, then she left and closed the door behind her.

He put his knapsack on the bed and opened the flaps and began emptying its contents. He pulled out first the gun, removed it once more from the holster and laid it on the white bedspread where its bronze plating looked brighter than ever, like gold, he thought, but far more precious. He took out his toiletries and clothes and the pocketwatch he'd forgotten to show to her, along with the picture inside of it, but he could do that in the morning. He had plenty of time. He heard rattling in the bottom of the satchel and looked in and saw what was left of the ceramic cup he'd purchased in Cuernavaca for Carmen, the crack he'd heard when one of the men slammed into his back, he guessed. It was in several pieces. One by one he brought them out into the light and laid them onto the bed to see if they could be glued back together. He deemed they could, that there really wasn't much broken that couldn't be fixed if a person really put his mind to it, then thought of his own life, the hell and torment he'd gone through and the strange solitude in which he found himself. He could feel it in the air, the walls, the foreign room with all its musty memories of somebody else who should've been there instead of him. A whole lot of good had befallen him in the span of a few hours but something wasn't right, something nagging inside, something he couldn't put his finger on. He should've been leapin for joy, runnin through the night shoutin the good news to any and everbody that'd listen. Maybe he was just tired. He'd been beatin and come within minutes of dangling from a rope and maybe he was just plumb tired and wore out, and that was all it was.

He had not noticed when he first entered the room that the double windows were doors that opened onto the front balcony of the house. He walked to the wall switch next to the door and turned off the overhead light then walked over and opened the doors and stepped out onto the wooden planking and into the cool night air.

The sky was clear and the moon, hidden by the gabled roof, was somewhere high overhead, having traveled far from the mountain rims where he'd glimpsed it earlier, and its light substantive as silverdust cast an ashen luminence across the land. There, shaping the horizon, were Popocatépetl and the Sleeping Lady, phosphorescent in the paler sky-dark. He stood and studied the scene, took in its vastness, and thought about why he had come and what he had found and what it all meant. What he had gained and what he hadn't, what he'd left behind and whether it was worth it all. He leaned over the balcony railing and listened to the wind and heard the murmur of the land, as once on the boat he had heard it from the river, and emerging from the chalky night, blowing across the purple plain, came the ghost voices of his ancestors, tempting, bending his ear, and he heard again the story of the land, of honor and glory lost and of dreams of honor and glory regained, of duty and loyalty and a South rising again, the old values in place once more, the old pride restored. And as he listened another voice came, as though blown from the mountains themselves it was that clear and true . . . *first decide which family it is you seek, and what you will have to discard to find it.* He thought further of what Ramón had said, about how a man must separate his family of the past and their history from his family of the future, about the man who hangs on to his past and the man of vision . . . *the true romantic . . . he is a man always looking for things to come, hoping against hope for things always to change* . . . He thought, too, about what señora Rosario had said about the land, that without people and their families it was an unfeeling desert with no heart, that that was what life was all about, finding one's heart. He thought about home and what one should be and where his might be, could be. The floating fragments of his thinking began to drift into place and hook together and he glanced once more at the distant mountainscape, feeling his hopes go out to its heights, and saw in it a story different than the one he had been told and whispered a word of thanks to God that it was so.

He could not sleep the night. He lay on the bed fully clothed, too exhausted to undress. Pain throbbed around his jaw and his head still hurt from the blows where he had been kicked. His tongue kept probing and massaging the empty space where his two front teeth had been. But there was something else keeping him awake, a strange feeling stirring the night air, for he had left the doors to the balcony open and occasionally he looked through them, his gaze traveling beyond the distant purple-faded mountains and a recurring vision kept coming to him. In the vision he saw a small house surrounded by rows of shrubs neatly trimmed and beds of flowers in full bloom, and Athen, yes it was Athen, standing on the porch, her cheeks full with color and stomach bulging beneath a long robe, waiting for a man walking in from nearby fields, his cap pushed back on his head, a smile breaking across his face.

It was not yet dawn, a faint blush of light outlining the mountains. He pushed himself up from the bed and pulled on his boots. He turned on the light and found a broken pencil and piece of paper in a drawer in the nightstand beside the bed. The note would be brief.

Dear Senora Moncado,

I don't know how you're gonna take this because I ain't much good at saying good-byes but this'll have to do.

You are a fine brave woman and have already helped me more than any words I know could say. I would like very much to stay and help you but there's something just not right about it all. I've got a home and it's not here but back where I came from and there's somebody still there waiting for me. You helped me see that, too. I'm much obliged for your kindness and hospitality. I will be back to see you someday. You can count on that.

Love,

Jo Shelby Ferguson

The air was cool as he slipped quietly through the arched gateway in the violet dawn and headed up the ruined road he felt he knew by heart. At the top of the ridge he stopped and looked back once more at La Hacienda Tierra del Puente and thought about its name, land of the bridge, and smiled. He had no money but there was a gun dealer in Cuernavaca that would buy his gun. He knew, too, the way home, and how to get there and that people along the way would help him. And that was enough.

Acknowledgments

I am indebted to many people for helping this book along, but a special thanks goes to the following:

The late Evans Harrington, professor-emeritus of English at the University of Mississippi, who taught me more about writing than I'll ever touch and whose guiding hand helped this book see the light of readers' eyes. Thanks, too, for the spark that fired the story, an anecdote told on a summer eve.

Sandi Perry Morris, my wife and a former English teacher, who read every draft and re-taught me much of the basics I had forgotten, and was the gentle critic I needed at times.

Sue Herner, my agent, and her associate, Sue Yuen, for their patient guidance and insightful editing, for steering my writing to the next level.

Beau Friedlander, publisher, editor and friend, diamond-cutter of sentences, who personalized every step of this seemingly endless process . . . and made it fun. Also to his wife, Melissa, and cannot leave out little Ella Beatrice, a calming force through it all.

Phyllis Harper, grand dame of north Mississippi writers, who never lost faith and kept the hope alive that it would happen. And to her sister and brother-in-law, Jean and Mike Talbert, for joining that same chorus.

Josefina Rayburn, my Spanish teacher, who made my bad Spanish good and kept my interpretation of Mexican history honest.

Brian Hargett of the Lee County Library, reference librarian *extraordinaire*, who responded to every request and kept coming up with resource after resource on General J. O. Shelby and Confederados in Mexico, not to mention the dates when the moon was full and when it wasn't.

Bill Sitgbauer, owner of Baxter Southern Towing, for allowing me to ride the Mississippi on one of his barges, and to the boat's crew for their camaraderie and abundance of river lore.

First United Methodist Church in Tupelo, Mississippi for the opportunity of mission trips to Mexico, from which the story drew much of its inspiration. And to all my LaJoya mission buddies who kept me on my toes and my thinking popping with ideas.

Edgar Rodriguez, true Mexican amigo who searched for, and found, the ruins of the lost Hacienda Michopa, and for proving to me that it really did exist, once upon a time in magnificent splendor. *Muchas gracias,* Edgar.

Edgardo, Mapi and Christina Paredes, for getting me into a Mexican prison, and the entire Paredes family for the unparalleled hospitality shown to me while in Monterrey.

The people of Mexico, whose noble and enduring spirit infuses this work.

And to these indispensable ones:

Betty Harrington, Martha Francis Allen, John Bryson, Rich and Roberta Abel, Francis Patterson, Bowen Burt, Bruce Smith, Shawn Prince, Peggy Webb, Larry Brown, Barry Hannah, Steve Yarbrough, Francis Sheffield, Vera Perry, Gloria Williamson, Beth and Henry Brevard, John Corlew, Joe Wilkins III, Gerald and Julie Walton, The Open Door Sunday School Class, Don Cruz and his family in LaJoya, Mark Denham and Mike Sahler.

The comandante of the Centro de Adaptacion Social Prison in Matamoros, The American Consulate in Mexico City, Civil Registry in Cuernavaca, Jerry Thompson (History Professor, Texas A & M) and Diana Tamex Walters (Promotion Director, Laredo Chamber of Commerce) and to all those whose names I missed. I'll catch you next time around.

Lastly, and most fondly, to my mother, Joan F. Morris, a strong and proud Ferguson, and my late father, William Edward Morris, good and unpretentious man, who *was* Jo Shelby Ferguson.